JORDIE

JORDIE

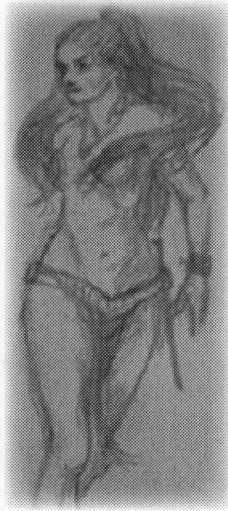

RIC SMIT

Rev. date: 10/07/2014

To order additional copies of this book, contact:
Xlibris LLC
1-800-455-039
www.Xlibris.com.au
Orders@Xlibris.com.au
520246

CONTENTS

PROLOGUE

STAFF SERGEANT HARRY Knott of the Water Police nervously observed the dim interior of the boardroom at HQ. He looked at the four WSA (World Security Agency) dignitaries seated behind the long table. Two of them regarded him over their reading glasses, of the other two one watched him through a set of slightly tinted glasses and the last one, either had not earned the right to wear glasses as a badge of rank or was still too young to need them. That thought nearly caused Harry to break out in a nervous giggle. Over to the left and away from the inquisition table sat the commissioner, Harry's boss. It was plain to see that the commissioner did not want to be there either. No-glasses kept looking at his watch and finally, after fifteen looks, Harry had been counting, he cleared his throat and proclaimed, "This hearing is to determine the truth about the alleged disappearances of the sailing vessels 'Sea Shell' and 'Stella Maris' and the associated rumour that governments are making so-called trouble-makers disappear by sending them into another Dimension."

He leaned back in his chair and looked expectantly at SSgt Knott. Harry's hands were sweaty and he promised himself that he was going to have some serious words with Wilson, the local journalist who started all this. When the silence became embarrassing, one of the other interrogators spoke up, "What can you tell us in relation to those matters?"

Harry looked at the commissioner for guidance but the latter looked as though his breakfast was repeating on him so there was no immediate assistance forthcoming from that quarter. In the end, Harry decided to go it alone and he answered the question with a question, "In the first place; who are you people and in the second place, what makes you think my reports are incomplete?"

The commissioner now stepped in, "Staff, the identities of those gentlemen must remain undisclosed as a matter of National Security. I can vouch for their bona fide and advice you to answer their questions to the best of your abilities."

After looking at his boss, Harry turned to the board of inquiry and said, "OK. I assume that WSA stands for World Security Agency. What do you want to know?"

No-glasses must have been the junior dignitary or he had drawn the short straw, or, he was just impetuous and wanted to do all the talking, "In October you submitted a report in which you stated that you had seen the sailing vessel 'Sea Shell' vanish in front of your eyes. The board would like you to repeat what you saw."

For a moment, Harry refreshed his memory and then spoke, "From memory it was the thirteenth of October when…"

"According to the report you submitted it was the fourteenth of October." Harry's face turned redder than his hair and he was about to explode but he controlled his temper to a certain extent but there was nothing friendly in his reply, "Look what is with the damned questions? You got the report in front of you so read it already!" No-glasses turned a shade of purple that darkened considerably when he heard one of the interrogators snicker.

"Would you please tell us what you remember?" One of the others asked and Harry nodded his head,

"Yes, well, on the FOURTEENTH of October we, that is Senior Constable Tomkins and myself, were in the process of looking for a stolen yacht when I saw the 'Sea Shell' in the distance..."

"How did you know that the vessel you saw was indeed the 'Sea Shell'?"

"You do like to spoil a good story!" Harry was silent for a moment then continued,

"The 'Sea Shell' is a converted lifeboat, thirty-six feet, or twelve meters, long and carries two masts and is gaff-rigged on both. I know the yacht well because it belongs to a friend of mine. His name is Morgan Turbot. Besides that, when we got closer senior constable Tomkins was able to read the name 'Sea Shell' on her bows. Next, as we came nearer a sudden fog came up that engulfed the vessel..."

"It says in your report that it was a local electrical disturbance. How did you come to that conclusion?"

"Within the fog, lightening could be seen flashing and both radar and radio on the launch went static".

"And you are sure that the yacht disappeared during this local electrical phenomenon?"

"Yes, before the radar went out we could see the yacht on the radar but when the radar came back on the blip was gone."

One of the other investigators now spoke up, "I noticed that a couple of times you spoke of this Morgan Turbot in the present tense. Was that a slip of the tongue or is he alive and if so, where is he?"

For long moments Harry studied their faces when next he spoke he did so in a very serious tone, "Three weeks ago I came in the possession of the Travel Journal of the 'Sea Shell'. The journal was up to date until the third of September. Morgan wrote it, I recognised his handwriting and he sent it to me as proof of life."

"So where is he?"

Harry looked at their expectant faces and slowly said, "This, no doubt, is where the conspiracy theories will come in. He is in another Dimension. As a matter of fact he calls it the Dimension of Wind, Wood, and Water."

The statement set off a flurry of activities among the four interrogators. No-glasses was babbling something about lies and innuendos, the two Reading-glasses were frantically shuffling through files marked with the red ' Top Secret' stamp, while Cool-shades snapped, "Produce that journal."

For a tense moment Harry glared then he snapped back, "Why?"

"A matter of national security."

"Well I cannot give you the journal because I do not have it any more."

That got their attention; all four stopped whatever they were doing and looked agog at Harry. No-glasses always the first cab of the rank asked, "Who's got it?"

Harry shrugged his shoulders and answered, "Morgan Turbot I presume."

Exasperated Cool-shades asked, "Please tell us,

"A. How you obtained that journal and,

"B. How you lost it?"

For a long time Harry studied the four men in front of him wondering what he could tell them but in the end, he decided to give them a shortened version of what he understood had happened. "A girl by the name of Serah brought the journal from the other Dimension into ours with the express instruction to deliver it to me…"

"What's her surname and where did she enter our world?"

No-glasses again. Harry frowned at him but continued, "Serah and her dinghy splashed down, or materialised, in Cleveland bay off Townsville. Her dinghy was stolen from her and in an attempt to get it back, she nearly drowned. The 'Stella Maris' rescued her just in time and eventually brought her here".

"The 'Stella Maris'. That is the yacht that disappeared as well?"

"Yes"

"Tell us about that."

"I can't I did not see it happen."

"So, how do you know that it did happen?"

"The owner saw it happen and he told me."

One of the Reading-glasses coughed and turned red. The others looked at him and one asked, "What's the matter?"

Reading-glasses muttered something that the others could not hear or understand so Cool-shades demanded of him, "What do you know about this?"

"Nothing, I was surprised that Kalahari van Straaten was not on board."

Cool-shades glared at the speaker and asked, "Who is Kalahari van Straaten?"

"The owner of the 'Stella Maris' and I assumed that he was on board."

"Why?"

"Because, he did not draw his pension for the last two months."

This time it was Harry's turn to be surprised. "How did you know Kal owns the 'Stella Maris'?"

"Aw come on you know as well as I do that van Straaten is a loose cannon and as such we have to keep an eye on him."

Cool-shades interrupted with, "Why is this van Straaten of interest?"

Reading-glasses looked at Harry in the hope that the latter would enlighten those present but Harry was too smart for that, he was not going to tell those that did not know, that he and Kal had been sent on an illegal 'hostile' action in a 'friendly' country and that both had been captured. Harry managed to get away but Kalahari van Straaten endured months of mental and physical torture that left him with a body and mind full of ugly scars and a deep-seated hate for anything political and all politicians. To top it off, the Army declared Kal totally incapacitated and therefore unemployable. When the spin-doctors then declared that the action never took place and that Kal therefore could not receive any special assistance or consideration Harry Knott also resigned from the Army. In the end, Reading-glasses turned to Cool-shades, "This is not the right place to discuss the matter, I will tell you more later on."

Cool-shades glared at his colleague but then turned to Harry, "How come this van Straaten was a witness to the vanishing of his own boat?"

Harry cleared his throat and addressed Cool-shades, "Kal was halfway through salvaging a yacht, the 'Lucy T', when a fog patch similar to the one I saw when 'Sea Shell' vanished, enshrouded the 'Stella Maris' with the girl Serah on board. He too reported seeing lightning within the fog. He also reported hearing a loud, tearing sound and seeing what looked like a tear in the sky through which a bright glare showed. The fog dissolved as quickly as it had formed and the 'Stella Maris' was gone."

"Just like that, hey?"

"Yes, just like that."

After some more file shuffling, Cool-shades addressed Harry again, "Do you know where van Straaten is now?"

Harry nodded his head and said, "I saw him go off into the Dimension."

"Can you give us the details?"

"Well, when Serah and the 'Stella Maris' went, Kal was left with the 'Lucy T' and Serah's dinghy. That night I got a message telling me of his predicament so the next day I went out to see him. I informed him that the owner of the 'Lucy T' had been locked up for drug smuggling and that I would have to hand the vessel over to the authorities."

"What was his reaction?"

"He couldn't care less and all he said was, 'There go my salvage rights.' He refused point blank to come back with me because he wanted to stay in the area where the transfer took place…"

No-glasses who had been quiet too long now interrupted, "You haven't told us anything about the journal yet."

After looking daggers at No-glasses, Harry continued, "Ten days after I collected the 'Lucy T' I had occasion to pass the place where I last saw Kal, so I called in. It was then that Kal gave me the journal. He found it in a watertight compartment in Serah's dinghy."

No-glasses just could not help himself, "He was still there…" Before he could go on—and he was intending to—Cool-shades glared at him and said, "Do you mind?"

Then he turned to Harry and said, "Please proceed".

With a nod of his head, Harry acknowledged the invitation and continued, "The journal described that when the 'Sea Shell' was inside the fog bank they could no longer see the water or the sky but they experienced the sensation of tremendous speed. There was total silence and a circular shaped patch of bright glow rose in the east and rapidly travelled to a point directly overhead. There it hung for a short time and then quickly sank back to just above the eastern horizon. The fog cleared in a matter of minutes and the bright patch proofed to be the sun."

One of the Reading-glasses now said, "I have a question. You said there was total silence?"

"I did not say that, the journal did. In it, Morgan describes how he dropped an object but could not hear it hit the deck. Apparently, Shelly, the girl with him, said something but although he could see her lips move he could not hear her."

Just then, a secretary walked into the boardroom and whispered in the commissioner's ear. She left the room and the commissioner stood up saying, "Gentlemen there has been a fatal accident on the wharf and I need Staff Sergeant Knott to attend to the matter. We'll have to reschedule this meeting for another day."

Harry was out of that door so quick he never even heard No-glasses complain.

The death was straightforward; a freezer box being loaded onto a trawler slipped out of its noose and fell on top of the deckhand. No one was to blame, it was the deckhand himself, who attached the lifting noose and who operated the winch. When the sling started to slip, he ran towards it as though trying to steady the box in the sling. His move was purely panic-driven reaction because a frail human could not stop the box, over two tons in weight.

It had been quite a day so far for Harry so he decided to have a relaxing ale before going home that evening. When he walked into his favourite watering hole, who did he see in deep but somewhat slurry conversation with Wilson—his not so popular journo—No-glasses from this morning. Harry growled, shook his head and walked to the bar where the bar tender had the 'usual' waiting for him before seating himself at 'his' table over in the corner of the bar room. Harry was on his second mouthful of beer when he saw No-glasses rise none too steady, Wilson too got up and together they headed in Harry's direction. Harry noticed No-glasses bump into some tables and chairs and as they came closer, he heard him say a few times, "So solly".

They finally made it to Harry's table and uninvited they sat down. Harry noted that Wilson was nowhere near as drunk as No-glasses. Unimpressed Harry waited for the others to open the conversation if there was going to be one. No-glasses, none too suave, leaned back and turned around to look at the bartender, at the same time he held up his right hand and snapped his fingers. When the bartender eventually decided to notice him, No-glasses circled his left hand over the table indicating it was his shout. While they were waiting, No-glasses asked, "You know Mr Wilson, here?"

"Yes I do."

"Oh good, that's going to make things so much easier."

Although not really interested, Harry grumbled, "What is going to be easier?"

Just then No-glasses stumbled upright and with his hand securely clapped over his mouth headed off at speed and in a reasonably straight line towards the bathrooms. With No-glasses presumably calling for Barf, Harry turned on Wilson, "Did you get the WSA on my back?"

After a slight delay, Wilson slowly nodded his head, "I might have."

Indignantly SSgt Knott snarled, "What do you mean, 'You might have'?"

Wilson held up a placating hand, "I asked a contact in the secret service what this WSA is all about. She went all-coy on me but would not tell me any more then what we already knew. Next, she became very interested in what you told me about the vanishing of the 'Stella Maris' that was all!"

Harry was still mulling things over when No-glasses came back. He looked rather pale and sloughed as he sat down. Before Harry or Wilson could say anything, No-glasses said, "My name is Ben Bellmore, BB for short, and, as you know, I am involved with the World Security Agency".

He took a sip of his rum-and-coke then continued morosely, "Originally, when I became involved with the organisation I believed that it was a good thing. Representatives of many free world security organisations secretly combined to carry out watchdog duties over each other's parent governments. All went well for a number of years but then politicians inserted themselves until we became a hit squad for the use by crooked politicians."

He looked at Harry and continued, "What happened to you and van Straaten is a good example…"

Wilson piped up, "I've been trying to find out for ages!"

Harry could not help but smile when he saw the frown of frustration crossing BB's face at the interruption. BB continued, "A consortium of British and European politicians with financial interests in a number of SE Asian countries found their interests under threat. The activities of terrorist and revolutionary agencies were eating into their profits. The WSA charged Australia, being the closest member to the trouble spot, with providing a team to infiltrate the country and to 'Bite off the head of the snake.' You and van Straaten were the lucky ones picked for the job. Within days after your insertion some wheeling, dealing and skulduggery reversed the fortunes of the main players who suddenly could see massive profits go up in smoke should you and van Straaten succeed."

"So, what happened?"

"They blew the whistle on you two."

"Who is 'they'?"

"Those members of the WSA that stood to lose their black money."

"Were any of them there this morning?"

"Hardly, those present are only lackeys. You won't see the big boys."

By this time Harry was shaking with rage if it had not been for a childhood friend, Harry grew up in that country, he, and Kal would have been dead. Even Wilson, usually so ready with annoying questions, decided it to be saver to let Harry handle things his way. Wilson, instead signalled the bartender for another round. By the time the round of drinks arrived, Harry was in better control of himself but still his voice grated when he asked of BB, "And why are you telling me all this?"

Harry gave the man his most interrogative stare and for the first time noticed that Bellmore was shaking and now stone cold sober. Something sure as hell was rattling his drainpipe. BB picked up his rum and coke and downed it in one gulp. He closed his eyes for a moment and grimaced. When he opened his eyes, he solemnly said, "After the meeting I overheard that the three of us are scheduled for a 'transfer'".

Before Harry could react, Wilson chirped, "So it is true, they do transport people into other dimensions!"

Harry gave him a hard stare and warned, "Before you get all misty eyed, have a thought at what this means; we will be *Wraiths*, solid flesh by night, gas by day". Next, he turned to Bellmore, "How do they do it?"

BB was miles away and asked absent-mindedly, "Do what?"

"Transfer people into the other dimension?"

BB waited while the waiter placed another round on their table, this time it was Harry's shout, but then said, "It is nothing new really. Until recently, transfers were a haphazard technique practised by witchdoctors, Shaman, and others that could create 'out-of-body' trances through hypnoses or drugs or both. Those that experienced them in a recognisable manner actually spent some time in another dimension before they came back to their bodies. The bodies of those whose mind did *not* make it back remain in suspended animation until gradually their system shuts down; their souls are long gone before their bodies die."

Harry looked pensive then said, "Didn't you say that this so called 'transfer' is used to get rid of people who could become an embarrassment?" BB nodded his head and said, "That is right."

After a few moments of silence Harry asked, "If that is so, won't their mindless bodies be an even greater stumbling block?"

Bellmore let out a disparaging chuckle, "How often are we told that such and so, a brilliant scientist, architect, political leader, yes even a feared antagonist, has been admitted to a mental institution? Do you think for one moment that if those sorts of people were still in control of their own mind that they would quietly succumb to a life in an asylum for the mentally challenged? They are the ones whose transfers were botched and whose bodies are like ships adrift without anybody at the helm."

Wilson now turned to Harry, "You told me that the 'Sea Shell' journal spoke of Wraiths, beings that are flesh and blood during the night but that don't exist during daylight hours. Would they be the ones that were transferred but whose transfer was botched and whose bodies did not make the jump?"

Harry thought for a moment but then shook his head, "No, that can't be right because that would mean that during the times the Wraith has a body, that body would have to be in two places at the same time, here in the core and there in the dimension, and that cannot be."

"Then how do you explain the fact that the Wraith is solid during the hours of darkness but becomes gas during the day?"

"How would I know? Perhaps the frequency of the Wraith's vibrations slows down enough during the normal hours of sleep, or darkness, for his body to solidify but during hours of daylight his vibrations speed up and his frequency, not being in sync with that of the dimension, makes him gaseous?"

"Hmm, but then what about those whose bodies are alive and locked up in asylums?"

"Oh! Look Wilson, I don't know! Perhaps they got lost in transit and their bodies were returned to sender?"

With a frown on his face Harry turned to Bellmore and asked, "I can understand why they want to get rid of me, I know too much about that business overseas, but what about you and Wilson?"

"Oh that is easy; Wilson has been asking the wrong people his questions and even though he might not realise it, he has hit the wrong nail on the head once too often. Me? I have made it too clear that I do not want anything to do with their illegal and/or shady deals. That makes them very uncomfortable so I have to go as well."

CHAPTER 1

THE TURTLE AND THE 'HARE'

IT WAS WITH a degree of sadness that Serah and Kal waved goodbye to Serah's sister Sianksey and her 'coreling' husband, Morgan. It had become a joke and a form of endearment amongst them. Both, Morgan and Kal and their sailing vessels, transferred from the Core into the Dimension of Wind, Wood, and Water. Morgan Turbot's 'Sea Shell' was in fact a 12 meters long lifeboat built in the Dimension that somehow finished up in the Core during the Second World War. At some time during the 1950s, the lifeboat was converted into a ketch with gaff rig on both masts.

The fact that the 'Sea Shell' originally came from the Dimension may have been the cause for her spontaneous transfer back into the Dimension.

Kal's case is different his sailing vessel was a home built junk he built himself. Due to financial restrictions the vessel, 'Stella Maris' was as basic as basic can be, it had no engine, or fancy winches, there was no electricity, fibreglass or synthetic rope on board and most of his cooking was done on an Indonesian charcoal grille set in a clay dish on deck.

Kal's connection with the Dimension came through Serah who had by accident been transferred into the Core. Kal was in the right place to prevent her from drowning and later rescued her when the people that stole her dinghy tried to end her life as well. When the Dimension retracted Serah from the Core it brought along the 'Stella Maris' but not Kal who was not on board at the time. His tie to the 'Stella Maris' was the thread along which he, and Serah's dinghy, were later pulled into the Dimension.

It became a joke that whenever something happened that was out of the ordinary the sisters would gang up and say that it was "the Corelinger's fault". It became a convenient moniker to express that a misunderstanding or anything indicating a lack of pre-knowledge was because one party was "Corelinger" and the other was "Dimenser"— "Dimensionist" is too much of a tongue twister.

Kees, a Dimenser who had befriended Morgan when the latter just arrived, travelled everywhere in his younger years. From comparing their knowledge of the world, Morgan concluded that both worlds exist in the same place and in the same time and that only a difference in frequencies could make this possible.

During the consumption of many jugs of the local rum, the pair came up with a theory that man's technical development is comparable with a tree. The trunk is called the Core. This core vibrates, like everything else, and the frequency of vibration affects man's brain thereby stimulating the invention of anything within that frequency range. The inventions continue until the vibrations at the tip of the core out-pace the frequencies that gave birth say to the technology of sail. Then what happens? The people that were in tune with the technology of sail both lament its passing and try to adapt to the new, higher, frequency, or, if they cannot adjust, slip into the Dimension where the vibration frequencies level out and development becomes lateral instead of vertical as it is in the core.

They theorised that each frequency band occupies a definite ring or band around the trunk of the Tree of Technological Advancement. Like all trees, the tree of technology grows taller as well as wider in girth. The band of the technology of, for instance, bronze or, later, sail, becomes too tight until finally it bursts outwards so creating a frequency disc that extends outwards and which creates a platform where only the frequencies of the corresponding technology are found. That lateral disc has the frequency range matching the technology that inspired it.[1]

People living in that dimension can expand the technology present laterally but not vertically. Their progress is measured in techniques such as growing selectively modified woods, like for instance Balon wood where the lightweight properties of balsa wood are married to the strength of silver ash hardwood, better sisal for better and stronger rope, and so forth. They do not have the interest or mental frequency (capacity) to, say, invent the process to make electricity or any of the inventions based on electricity. Anyway, they concluded that the final separation from the Core took place *before* the English exploration of the Pacific and before the industrial revolution reached the Southern Hemisphere.

Australia—*Antipodia* is what the locals call it—is not a nation as we know it. The Dutch found the place and looked after it for a bit. They did not hit on the idea of using it as a penal colony and the Caucasian minorities living there are mainly Dutch and from other European seafaring nations. Although the final separation of the Dimension from the Core took place in the early 18th century, there still were many great sailing vessels in use in the Core. What happened to them? A few became museum pieces while others became coal bunkers but many more just disappeared. Yes, they and their crews of dedicated sailors sailed into the Dimension of Wind, Wood, and Water.

---

[1] See Adjunct for representation of Core and Dimensions

Morgan Turbot, together with wife Sianksey, wanted to sail 'Sea Shell' across the top of Antipodia, then cross the North Indian Ocean, follow the coast of Africa South—*the Suez Canal does not exist in the Dimension*—come round The Cape of Good Hope and follow the sail route across the South Atlantic to Brazil and then onto Europe and England. Morgan told Kal that this entire dimensional thing would become real for him when he saw London in a pre-industrial mode. Kal, on the other hand, was interested in visiting some of the islands in the Pacific to see how they were different in the Dimension. The islands of particular interest to him were Tahiti, Hawaii and Easter Island.

About a month after Morgan and Sianksey set sail in 'Sea Shell', Kal and Serah set off across the Pacific in 'Stella Maris', the weather was good and they followed the coast South to where they could pick up the Westerlies. Kal did not go so far south that he would get into the 'Roaring Forties' but tried to stay on the edge. Even so, they encountered mountainous waves and shrieking winds but 'Stella Maris' took it all in her stride. On a number of occasions, a sudden gust of wind would send the mainsail scooting up the mast. The first time this happened Serah got the fright of her life and Kal had to explain to her that it was a very clever trick really. In the Chinese Junk rig the foot, or bottom, of the sail is not anchored. As a result, when a sudden gust hits the sail, the sail between the battens billows and drags the battens up so reducing the impact area of the sail. When the pressure of the wind gust reduces, the weight of the sail battens bring the sail back down.

Serah was impressed.

After a week of high seas and howling winds the bottom fell out of Hue's basket, the winds abated and the white creaming howlers lost their teeth and became heaving mountains of water that did no more than send 'Stella Maris' on a waddling sleigh ride. Even though the wind was no more, the air came straight from Antarctica causing Serah to huddle in a blanket in the cosy cabin. That night Kal did not have the heart to call her out for her watch on deck and left her to sleep. Over the years he had spent as a solo sailor, he learned to be aware of any change in the wind or movements of 'Stella Maris' while 'asleep at the wheel' so to speak. On this particular morning, just as he came fully alert, he saw a two masted topsail schooner away over the starboard bow. The vessel was on the same merry-go-round as 'Stella Maris' and at times she was not visible as one or the other of the ships was hidden in a trough while at other times she was clearly visible as they both rode a swell. Kal estimated that the schooner was about a mile away. What intrigued him was that even in the light wind conditions, the schooner only carried a stay sail. Her mainsail and her mizzen sail, nor any of her other foresails or top sails were set. The stay sail was not trimmed and the schooner should have been able to make much better time. He was still wondering about the schooner when 'Stella Maris' cabin hatch opened a crack and a shivering voice announced, "If you want your breakfast you'll have to come in. I'm not coming out there. Too cold!" Kal lashed the helm and climbed down into the warm cabin, 'Stella Maris' would have to look after herself for a while. He turned around and wrapped his arms around Serah who had her back to him. Somehow, her blanket finished up on the floor and her warm skin met Kal's cold skin, as a result, both shivered. Slowly Serah turned round and mumbled, "Gee you are cruel!" Regardless of her statement, she held him tight, breakfast would have to wait for a while, and the schooner was forgotten.

Later, with an inner glow not entirely due to breakfast, Kal came back on deck and was surprised to see the schooner limping along under her badly trimmed sail and no more than four hundred yards away over the starboard bow. Surprised, Kal realised that 'Stella Maris' was actually overtaking the schooner.

The wind was coming in over the starboard quarter and this meant that when 'Stella Maris' would overtake the schooner she would be downwind, or in the lee, of the schooner. Kal, being somewhat suspicious by nature, did not want to place himself in a position where the schooner could attack him by turning downwind and gaining speed. He steered 'Stella Maris' up until the wind was amidships on starboard. The altered course would take 'Stella Maris' behind the schooner's stern so she could then pass upwind of the larger ship.

As they came closer, Kal could not see anybody on deck and he wondered if the 'Vrouwe Irene' was a derelict ship but that did not seem right either because, except for the badly trimmed stay sail, everything appeared neat and tidy on deck. Kal decided to let sleeping dogs lie and slowly overtook the 'Vrouwe Irene'. By late afternoon the schooner was no more than a speck on the horizon astern of 'Stella Maris'.

When Kal took over the deck watch at four in the morning on the next day, Serah informed him that the schooner raced past about an hour earlier. Serah reported that the schooner had her top sails hoisted as well as her stay sail, jib, and flyer. The 'Vrouwe Irene' even showed navigation lights. Kal was intrigued but reasoned that the ship might be under-manned and that the crew had been too exhausted after the bad weather they had encountered to maintain a day crew. He did not think they would see the schooner again anytime soon.

The day was pleasant with a steady fifteen-knot wind blowing from the south west that allowed 'Stella Maris' to gambol along at six knots in an easterly direction. After completing their chores on deck and in the cabin, they both stretched out on the warm deck to enjoy the moment. The sky was a purplish blue with a few white tufts of clouds way down on the southern horizon; the azure sea undulated with a lazy swell, leftover from a storm somewhere to the west. The massive mountains of water were no threat, as there were no combers and only the occasional white-cap. Serah was exhilarated by the behaviour of 'Stella Maris', she laughed and Kal wanted to know what was funny. "I am laughing because 'Stella Maris' is having fun."

"How do you mean?"

"Look at her! When she is in the trough between two swells she hesitates, her sails are not really pulling, then when a swell comes up behind her she heaves a big sigh and rises until the full force of the wind hits her sails. Then she takes off trying to stay on top of the swell for as long as she can until she slides off the back and the whole game starts again."

As she threw her arms around Kal's neck she murmured, "This is living Kal, just the three of us; you, me, and 'Stella Maris'."

Little did she know!

CHAPTER 2

BETRAYAL

Sgt Harry Knott moaned and slowly opened his eyes; groggily he looked at the unfamiliar surroundings. He vaguely remembered the drinking session with BB—what was his name? Oh yes, Ben Benson? No, Ben Bellmore—that's it, Ben Bellmore from the WSA and Wilson with his conspiracy theories.

While he agonisingly gathered his thoughts, he noticed someone lying on his side with his back turned towards him. Slowly and still groggy his mind formed two questions, who was it and why was he naked? It was not until then that he realised he too was in the buff. As the light came on in his brain, he recognised Wilson as the other. Harry leaned over and shook Wilson's shoulder,

"Hey, wake up. What the hell is going on? Where are we?"

Wilson pulled himself into a sitting position and replied, "What, I'm an oracle now?"

Harry who was not happy at all remarked, "Answers like that will get you a fat lip!"

He did not really mean it because other surprises demanded his attention. "This is not a room at all; we are in the back of a truck like a removal van."

Wilson looked around and remarked, "You are right and I bet that it has WSA painted on the sides".

With a frown Harry asked, "What leads you to that conclusion, Sherlock?"

"Well, do you see BB around? And who did he work for?"

"What, you reckon he set us up?"

"Yes."

"Set us up for what?"

"How does a transfer to a faraway dimension sound."

"Hmm, you could be right, but why take our clobber?"

"Oh, that has something to do with the vibrations and frequencies. BB must have been preparing me for the transfer. He told me that a transfer is initiated by lowering the subject's vibrations and frequency. Apparently clothing has a negative effect on the vibrations or frequency, I forgot which."

Harry mulled over what he just heard plus what Kal had told him and the hints he found in the 'Sea Shell' journal, after a while he remarked, "How are they going to lower our rate of vibration? We vibrate at the same rate as the Core and, as far as I understand, the vibration of the Core is the frequency to which our brains are tuned".

Frustration sounded heavy in Wilson's voice when he said, "Oh, I don't know!"

A small loudspeaker near the ceiling came to life and a distorted voice said, "That is right, Wilson, you don't know. You ask too many stupid questions about things that are none of your business. While you, Staff sergeant Harry Knott, are too closely connected and show too much interest in the where about of Kalahari van Straaten."

Harry came to his feet and shouted, "Does that give you the right to destroy us?"

"Who said anything about killing you? It might happen but that is not our intention. We see it as that we are providing both of you with an opportunity of a lifetime. You Harry, have the chance of catching up with your friend, that wacko van Straaten, while you Wilson, can finally find out all there is to know about those assisted transfers."

There was a pregnant silence but then the voice continued,

"Harry, you are right, the truck you are in does resemble a furniture van but it does not have WSA painted on the side, like Wilson suggested. We thought it would be less conspicuous if we instead painted it with the slogan, 'You pack it. We stack it.' You know, a slogan just vulgar or smart-alecky enough to keep people from wanting to do business with us."

Wilson took up the baton, "So why a truck?"

The voice chuckled, "Our services are required in many places and by building the required apparatus into a truck we can quickly and cheaply attend to our needs".

Neither Harry nor Wilson was in the mood to listen to the distorted but smug voice any longer. They had their backs against the wall of the van and could feel a resonant vibration travel up and down the cargo bay as the truck's speed gradually increased. At one point the loudspeaker voice enquired, "Hello, are you there? Is there no more you want to know about your future?"

At first, Harry wanted to ignore the voice but then his curiosity got the better of him and he asked, "What is going to happen to us?"

The voice chuckled again and said, "It is happening already Harry my boy. Let me enlighten you; you may feel that as we speed up, the resonance in the truck's vibration is changing. Well, once we reach critical mass— oh I love saying that—but I mean of course, critical frequency, and our secret machine bounces off its modulated resonance; everything within the resulting energy field dissolves. We never knew what happened to those we zapped but, thanks to your friend and his 'Sea Shell' journal, we now know you become a Wraith, flesh and bone during the night but a whippoorwill during the day. So exciting, isn't it?"

Neither of the two men answered and a strange lassitude came over them. Harry who had been standing, slowly sank down until he was sitting with his back against the wall of the cargo bay. The voice said, "Damn, they always do that just before they disappear! Ah well, I might as well turn the mike and camera off."

CHAPTER 3

BALON WOOD ISLAND

IT WAS JUST after midday when to his surprise Kal saw that they were again overhauling the schooner 'Vrouwe Irene', this time she was down to her mizzen sail and all of her fore sails, stay-sail, inner and outer jibs, and flyer. Again, the sails needed trimming and again there was nobody on deck. Kal made an entry in his log and took a close look at the schooner. The vessel was forty-five to fifty feet long with a sharp clipper bow and fine lines, she even had a carved figurehead of a topless female holding a conch shell, and the vessel's round stern had the typical schooner, counter stern. A deck house sat in the middle of the main deck so she was not a trading vessel. The 'Stella Maris' passed the schooner close enough for Serah to notice that the spoked steering wheel on the aft deck had been tied down, so it was no coincidence that there was no one on deck. The why and what-for of the mystery, provided Serah and Kal with a subject for discussion for the rest of the afternoon.

Later that day the weather closed in and by nightfall, they were in a shrieking gale. The huge swells that had given them such a pleasant sleigh ride now became mountainous waves of fast moving water with foam streaking their sides like angry snakes. Kal took down the foresail, and the mainsail he lowered so that only the top three panels still caught the wind.

Every time 'Stella Maris' topped a wave the windblown spume would hit his skin like shards of glass. Kal tried to send Serah into the cabin but she would not hear of it instead she collected two blankets, one for Kal to wrap around himself and one for herself. Kal lit a stern light but after it blew out three times, he gave it up as a bad idea. Then the long wait for daylight began.

At about three am, Kal could hear, above the noise of the gale, the sound of rushing water. When he looked around to see where it was coming from, he got the biggest fright of his life. No more than ten to fifteen feet behind 'Stella Maris', he saw a huge black shape bearing down on them. He tried to steer out of its path but it was too late and with a horrendous crash of breaking timber, the bow of 'Vrouwe Irene' cut into 'Stella Maris'. Even Neptune would take notice of the scream that Serah let out. Next moment three heads appeared over the bow rail of 'Vrouwe Irene' quickly followed by a rope ladder and some grappling hooks. With a heavy heart, Kal realised that 'Stella Maris' was done for. Strangely enough, he also hoped that the 'Vrouwe Irene' was not breached in the collision. With a fair amount of trouble, he collected his ship's papers and his logbook then slid across the heaving and sloping deck to where Serah was clinging to the rope ladder. He gave her the signal to start climbing and she did. On deck of the 'Vrouwe Irene', three men and a woman were waiting for them. The woman wrapped a blanket around Serah's shoulders and told her to come with her to the galley where it was warm. Serah looked at Kal and he gave her the nod. Shaking with the cold and fright Serah went with the woman. There was no time for apologies at least not at that time, and the man in charge asked, "What else can we do for you?"

Kal suddenly realised that his whole capital, a box of precious stones and about one hundred and fifty grams of gold were still on board of 'Stella Maris' the treasure was secured in a leather bag inside a sail bag that was hanging near the cabin entry. He grabbed a line and tied it around his waist while he said, "I got to go back and get some essentials. Can one of you watch the line and drag me back should the need arise?"

The man who had spoken nodded his head and placed himself near the rope ladder. The wind was shrieking through the rigging of the two ships locked together, spouts of water and foam exploded into the air every time the two hulls were slammed together. Even though the tangle of the two ships moved about alarmingly, Kal made short work of getting back on the sloping deck of 'Stella Maris'.

He pulled himself up to the cabin hatch just as a wave washed over the stricken ship and which threw Kal off his feet. The line around his waist held him back from the boiling sea near the stamping dolphin striker[2] of the 'Vrouwe Irene'. Here Kal's unbending will came to the fore. The line was cutting into his waist and his feet were slipping on the wet and slanted deck. Crunching noises of timber being smashed into splinters came from within a welter of foam. His eyes were burning from the salt seawater and his vision was very limited and he was washed away just as he reached the cabin hatch. Giving up never entered his mind and once more he struck out for the open cabin hatch.

At the second attempt, he managed to lean into the cabin and grab the bag. It was not a moment too soon; he could feel 'Stella Maris' slide

---

[2]   The vertical spreader tensioning the bowsprit water stay

deeper into the water and only the grappling hooks in her rigging held her tied to 'Vrouwe Irene'.

The drag caused by 'Stella Maris' started to make 'Vrouwe Irene' sluggish and Kal advised his rescuer to cut the 'Stella Maris' free. The man gave him a grateful nod and soon after, Kal saw what was left of his beloved 'Stella Maris' slip away over the top of the next oncoming wave.

During the next twenty minutes, the men reduced the 'Vrouwe Irene' sail until she was running under a storm jib and reefed mizzen sail. The man who had talked to Kal obviously was the captain or leader and he came up to him.

"We have to prepare for the day." As he looked up at him Kal realised the man wore a key on a chain around his neck but before he could ask what it meant, the man continued, "My name is Dan Waverley and I am a wraith like all the others on board. During the day we lock ourselves in the main cabin so we don't get blown away. There is another cabin, a small one, in the bows. It is yours and your companion's for as long as you are on board."

"OK, that explains why we kept passing you during the day and you kept passing us at night. So what happened?"

"That is a story for another time. You and your companion have nothing the fear from our shape chances, we stay locked up until our basic instincts settle down and we can function normally."

"How is it that you can promise that with such conviction?"

Dan held up the key and asked, "What is going to happen to this key when I turn into air?" Kal shook his head, "It's going to drop on the floor?"

"Exactly and by the time I realise I need the key to get out of the deckhouse, my hunger and basic urges, have subsided to a controllable level."

Kal laughed and said, "Well, Serah and I will keep the show on the road during the day and you and yours can have the night watch".

Dan smiled and said, "That's a deal. The others have already gone into the deckhouse so I better send Serah to you and close up shop."

A few minutes later Serah came out of the deckhouse carrying an extra blanket for Kal and a plate of steaming food. Before Kal could say anything, Serah enthused, "You should see it! They even got a wood stove and all. It is a pity we cannot go in there during the day; it would be nice to be able to feed you hot coffee while we are on watch." Kal hugged her and said, "You don't have to be out here in the cold, we got our own cabin in the fo'c's'le."

"No way Hose, I'm not leaving you here by yourself."

The arrangement worked well and for the next two weeks, Dan and his crew kept the 'Vrouwe Irene' on course at night while Kal and Serah kept her honest during the day.

As night fell, Kal would wait for Dan to materialise so he could hand over the watch. This particular evening Dan said he wanted to discuss a few things, so Kal waited for Dan to organise the crew. They leaned against the taffrail and Kal watched the narrow wake left by the schooner. He was still looking at it when Dan said, "She is a fine ship."

"Yes that she is. Did you transfer with the 'Vrouwe Irene'?"

"No, she was adrift when I materialised on her deck one evening. There were three corpses on board, and old man, an old woman and a younger one. None showed any injuries but they may have poisoned themselves by accident because I found some strange, leafy plants in the galley that smelled like arsenic."

"How did you recognise the smell?"

"I am, or was, a food chemist."

"Where about?"

"Sydney, Australia."

For a moment Kal wanted to tell Dan that he himself came from the Core as well but he decided that unless Dan asked, he was going to keep quiet as it might seem unfair that Kal did not finish up as a wraith.

Dan never asked the question, but smiled knowingly; neither the name Australia nor Sydney should have been accepted without a demand for clarification by a Dimensioner.

After some reflective silence Dan continued, "That same night, or evening rather, another wraith materialised on deck. She was gorgeous but completely insane. By then I figured out that should I become gas the next morning, there was nothing to stop me from being blown away and that if I wanted to stay on board I would have to find a draft free place. The deckhouse was the place and I tried to entice Miss Gorgeous 2010 to enter the deckhouse with me. I like to think that she may have been worried that I might make a pass at her but; in all honesty, I think it was the presence of the three corpses that decided her to stay on deck. Anyhow she was gone come daylight the next day."

"How long ago was that?"

"Just over two years ago."

"Did you establish who those people were?"

"Yes, they were the owner, his wife and the daughter on a round the world tour. The paperwork to back it up is all in the deckhouse. Actually, that brings me to the subject I want to discuss. Where were you headed when we ran into you?"

"Rapa Nui".

"Oh, Easter Island[3], do you still want to go there?"

---

[3] The first European to see Rapa Nui was Jacob Roggeveen on Easter Sunday 1722; hence the name Paas Eiland (Dutch for, Easter Island). The name Easter Island did not come into use until James Cook visited the island AFTER the separation from the Core of the Dimension of Wind, Wood, and Water.

Kal shrugged his shoulders and remarked, "Priorities have changed somewhat, now I would like to get to a place where I can buy or build another boat."

"You can have this one."

"What do you mean? What about the others?"

"It is getting harder and harder for us to retain the reasoning power to stay focused enough to stay with her. Just this morning, we lost two more. At one stage there were twelve Wraiths on board, now there are only three left. The longer we are Wraiths the more our mental capacity seems to dwindle until in the end we no longer can function. The two we lost yesterday were Annie and Juan; both have been Wraiths for a number of years. At some point, I may forget to lock the deckhouse door. Anyway, before that happens I want to hand over the 'Vrouwe Irene' to you."

Kal did not know what to say until he at last asked,

"Why don't you sell her?" Dan laughed, "And how am I going to hang on to my pieces of gold during my next change?"

Kal saw the funny side of the problem and laughed with Dan, "You got a point there!"

After weighing the pros and cons, Kal said with some reluctance, "I don't think Serah and I could run her. She's just too big and tender for two people to handle."

For a while, they both stood and watched the stern light throw its weak light over the ship's wake. In the end it was Dan who broke the spell, "I know an island where the people would be only too willing to help you build your new boat. It is known as Balon Wood Island for the obvious reason that they grow the Balon wood there. That stuff is amazing; it weighs only a fraction more than balsa wood but has the strength and most of the characteristics of Australian hardwood such as silver ash. You build a boat using that stuff and it will last forever providing, of course, that nobody runs over you."

They both grinned at that and Kal said, "OK skipper let's head for Balon Island and I'll see you in the morning."

Next, he went to join Serah in the fo'c's'le, with loving on his mind.

The 'Vrouwe Irene' headed in a more northerly direction, away from the roaring forties and into the warmer and calmer South Pacific. Live on board settled into a routine where Dan and his Wraiths kept the schooner on course during the night and Kal and Serah managed her during the day. Gradually the sea turned from a grey mass of heaving water under angry skies into a deep blue expanse caressed by lighter winds. Then one day flying fish scooted away from 'Vrouwe Irene's bows and a pod of dolphins took up position on either side of her. Serah was spell bound by the dolphins and it was not long before she recognised individuals amongst them whom she promptly gave names.

The apparent leader of the dolphins, sported a massive scar on the right side of its head, and missed its right eye. Kal could understand why Serah called that one 'Scarface' but he was somewhat confused by Serah's logic when she pointed out another dolphin and told Kal that that was Bella. When he asked why the name Bella, he was told that the dolphin 'felt like a Bella'.

At that point in his life, Kal went and tidied up some lines that the night shift had left somewhat untidy.

During the days that followed Serah developed a rapport with the dolphins. The pod liked to swim off the starboard bows probably because that way Scarface could keep an eye, his left eye, on the 'Vrouwe Irene'. Serah would lay on her side on the foredeck and watch the antics of the dolphins as they rode the bow wave. She often would fall asleep and be all-apologetic towards Kal as well as Scarface. She would feel that she had neglected Kal and had not given Scarface the attention and respect he and his pod deserved.

Nothing much happened during the next fortnight except that Kal was getting worried about Serah; she seemed lack-lustre and slept a lot. Serah confided in him that she felt tired all the time and that at times her belly hurt. They both attributed the ailments to her pregnancy.

Then one fine day a group of three towering cumulus clouds stood out amongst some light wispy clouds above the horizon and Kal knew that beneath each of those cloud towers they would find an island. A few hours later three mountainous islands appeared on the horizon. Kal was excited because those were their destination. The largest island was Balon Wood Island.

From what Dan had told him, reefs surrounded the islands but each had its own lagoon and the plan was for Kal to sail about near the passage through the reef until Dan and his crew woke, and they could work the schooner into the lagoon together.

As they slowly sailed past the main island, Kal was surprised that Serah did not get up from the deck where she was lying on her side facing the dolphins. He assumed she was asleep and was not worried until Scarface suddenly came up alongside the stern where Kal stood at the wheel. The dolphin was shattering and making whistling sounds while breaching and slapping the water, next he would race forward to the bows, slap the water with his tail and race back to start the whole sequence all over again.

A sudden fear squeezed Kal's heart and after hastily tying down the rudder, he rushed to the foredeck where Serah was still lying on her left side. He bent over her and gently shook her shoulder while calling her name. There was no reply and Kal felt for a pulse in her neck. There was a pulse but it was very weak. Kal realised she needed help and she needed it now. Without thinking about it twice, he raced to the mainsail halyards and dropped the mainsail onto the deck, and then he rushed aft and spun the wheel to bring the 'Vrouwe Irene' about in the quickest way by gibing. He could hear the scream of stretching rope fibres as the mizzen came over and the boom collided with the back-stay. He dashed forward and threw off the jib sheets. Once the foresails came over to the lee side he tensioned the staysail sheet but left the others loose. With both the mizzen sail and the staysail now drawing, he ran back to the wheel and aimed the 'Vrouwe Irene' for the windward side of the passage through the reef.

As Kal steered the 'Vrouwe Irene' towards the passage he saw two canoes coming away from the shore. In the lead canoe, he counted seven people, four manning the paddles, one man standing in the bows of the narrow craft and two women squeezed side by side on the seat behind him. The standing man was middle aged and had an air of authority about him. One of the women was about the same age she could be his wife. The other looked a bit younger than Serah, and had a strong resemblance to both the standing man and the woman sitting beside her, probably their daughter.

The man spoke loudly but Kal could not understand him but from the tone assumed it was a welcome speech. He had no time for that and urgently gestured at the foredeck. The young woman spotted Serah, she immediately drew her mother's attention to Serah and the woman, with a 'cut the commercials' tone in her voice made her husband aware of the facts. He looked, saw, and ordered the rowers to bring the canoe alongside post haste.

A few minutes later and with the canoe in tow, the four rowers set the foresails and tidied the mainsail. The chief, that is what Kal had decided he was, stood at the wheel and piloted the 'Vrouwe Irene' through the narrow passage while his wife and daughter tried to make Serah as comfortable as possible.

Scarface and his mob, perhaps worried they might finish up on someone's dinner plate, stayed outside the reef.

As soon as the schooner came within hailing distance of the shore, the chief started bellowing orders to those on the beach and people ran off in all directions to do his bidding.

They took Serah ashore in the canoe and Kal went with her. Some people had brought a bed made of bamboo and covered in soft mats to use as a stretcher and they carried Serah towards the second biggest hut in the village. As he entered into the dimness of the hut, he could see twenty to thirty people sitting along the walls.

Kal suddenly realised that his concern for Serah's well-being had cured him of his claustrophobic fear of crowds. In a fleeting sense, he hoped the cure would be permanent.

Serah's bed stood next to an open fireplace where some young people were lighting a small fire. On the other side of the stone circle sat a very old woman, her skin was like that of a prune, both her eyes were pale white with cataracts and she appeared quite blind. The fresh hibiscus flowers in her long, grey hair created a strange contrast.

At first, she appeared to be mumbling to herself but her voice gradually became louder and a hush fell over the congregation. Her chanting became a rhythmic cadence and at different locations among the audience, rattles began to follow the rhythm. Then somewhere in the village, quite suddenly, one of the large hollowed out, wooden pahu drums took up the rhythm and the air vibrated with its booming sound.

While still keeping up her chanting the old Shaman sprinkled dried herbs on the smouldering coals and puffs of aromatic smoke filled the hut. Meanwhile two acolytes slowly wafted green branches above Serah's still body. After about two hours of this, the old woman suddenly stood up and all rattle shaking, and drumming stopped abruptly.

Unerringly the blind Shaman turned towards Kal and gestured for him to come close. When he stood next to her, she grabbed his arm and guided his hand to Serah's forehead. Serah's brow felt cold and clammy and Kal knew she had passed on. He was no longer aware of where he was or of the people around him, there was such an atmosphere of finality about the whole situation. He brought up his other hand and placed it on what both affectionately had called 'the baby bump' but there all life had gone too.

Leading the way the Shaman left the hut and quietly everybody followed her. How long Kal stood there he never knew but eventually, Dan's hand on his shoulder brought Kal back to the present. With a start, he looked about and said,

"Serah is dead. Did I kill her?"

Dan shook his head, "And how would you have done that?"

"By taking her away from her family?"

"Didn't she want to go with you, or, did you make her come?"

"No, it was her decision."

Dan tried to console Kal as he gently led him out of the Shaman's hut. He told him that he had spoken with the chief who insisted that Serah be buried on the island.

For some reason Kal's mind became fixated on Scarface's behaviour and after he told Dan of the dolphin's performance, Dan became very pensive. Secretly he was convinced that the dolphins knew that Serah was sick but that Kal failed to understand them until it was too late.

The bed used to bring Serah ashore now serviced as her bier. It was set up under a roof on posts and a finely woven mat covered Serah's body.

All evening people came and paid their respect by placing bunches of flowers or small parcels of food on the edges of the mat and on the ground around the bier.

The chief came over to Dan and spoke to him. After he left Dan turned to Kal, "Apparently it is custom for the husband of the deceased to place something of value to him or to her on top of the mat covering the body. Is there anything you can place there?"

With dull eyes, Kal stared into the distance but said nothing. Dan was about to repeat the question when Kal turned to him, "All that is left of the love we shared is this Sianksey Snake."

He lifted the pendant from around his neck and showed it to Dan. Dan bent over for a closer look at the circular piece of carved Abalone shell and remarked, "Is that a snake curled in a circle around itself?"

"Yes it is a copy of a tattoo her sister has around her belly button. Serah carved it and it had great significance to her that is why she gave it to me and I really would like to keep it as it is my only memento of her."

"Not quite, Kal, she remains in your heart and soul."

After another long pause Kal remarked with a sigh, "You are right; I will place this on her body".

Before Dan locked himself in the deckhouse of the 'Vrouwe Irene' the next morning, he told Kal that he could trust the people there. Apparently, Dan knew the islands in the Core as very exclusive tourist havens. The people were much the same and very trustworthy in the Core so he was sure the people populating the islands in the Dimension would be too. He also told Kal that the grave was to be dug on the next day and on the day following Serah's body would be lowered into the grave at the exact moment the first sun ray would rise above the horizon so that the sun would carry her soul to the after world. Kal thanked him and saw him off to the schooner. After that, he wandered down the shore and away from the village so he could grieve over Serah.

Kal wandered aimlessly along the beach, his mind was no longer in turmoil but a deadly stillness and a near fatalistic depression settled on his mind.

What was there to live for?

Serah dead! 'Stella Maris' destroyed! Marooned on an island thousands of miles away from anywhere surrounded by people whose language he could not speak and to top it all off he was in the wrong dimension.

Suddenly he stopped, spread his arms stiffly away from his body, threw his head back, and while looking at the fading stars he yelled, "Beam me up Scotty!", then overcome with the banality of the outburst he laughed hysterically as he sank to his knees. He bent forward and with his hands to his face the dam broke and Kal cried, as he had not done since he was a small child.

After a long time, he got up and walked into the sea where he flopped onto his back in the slight surf. He thought back to the times when he was convinced that Serah and he would sail to the end of the world and back with never a problem or a cross word. The thought that he would lose it all just like that had never entered his mind.

For a long time his mind just went blank yet still filled with despair, finally he just wanted the sea to carry him away. That was until a wavelet sloshed over his face and he sniffed up some seawater. Sneezing and spluttering he got to his feet and with a wry grin mumbled, "I can't even drown myself without making a mess of it." Next, he continued his trek along the beach.

Some distance down the beach, a rocky outcrop came right down to the water's edge and only at low tide was there a narrow strip of sand at the foot of the cliff face. It was low tide and Kal followed the sandy ledge at the base of the steep rock. When he got to the other side, he was in for a few surprises. He more or less expected the cliff to mark the end of the island. This was not so, another bay as big as the one where the village was situated lay on the other side of the headland. Two other markers vied for his attention. First up he realised that he was standing in the wide and sandy mouth of a river. Because of its width, the water from the river coursed down through a number of shallow channels the deepest of which only reached as high as his calves. It was an unexpected find, sure, but it did not lie outside the norm. What he espied up against the tree line and skyline did seem to lie outside the realm of the possible.

He saw what looked like the outlines of a section of a city, a collection of oblong, square and rectangular shapes that overlapped each other like buildings do when built in front and behind each other. The black squares were in the shape and size of windows and doors while the larger squares were coloured in subdued pastel colours ranging from creamy white, sandstone, yellow ochre, to several hues of blue and pink-purple. The whole seemed to shimmer yet it was dense enough to hide what lay behind it. The spectre attracted Kal like a moth to a flame.

As he came closer, another phenomenon became apparent. Floating rocks. Blocks of coral and other types of rock but all about the size of a football floated about three feet off the ground. Here and there, some stationary rocks hung suspended about two feet off the ground. The slight breeze did not affect the floating rocks; they floated down-wind, against the wind or at any other angle to the wind.

As Kal came within a hundred feet of what looked essentially a mirage, one of the rocks floated in his direction. Kal stopped and waited to see what would happen next. Adrenalin surged through his body and the fight or flight reaction tugged at his senses, yet he stood his ground.

As the clump of coral came within six feet of him, Kal became aware of a fuzziness shimmering about the rock. What really freaked him out was not the deep voice he heard in his head, but the sight of two disembodied hands holding the rock. The deep voice spoke again and this time Kal listened. *"This is a pleasant surprise; you are the first one in a very long time who has not fled in abject terror."*

"Should I?"

"I don't see why. As you can see I'm not a man of substance so how can I physically harm you, and what is more, what would I achieve by it?"

Kal played with that thought for a moment then asked, "Are you a day-time Wraith?"

The voice in his head chuckled and said, *"Oh I like that. That puts us in a new category altogether where in fact we are a failed experiment."*

"What are you talking about?"

"The true Wraith achieves complete dissolution during the day and complete solidification during the night. We on the other hand are half-Wraith during the day and half-Person during the night; we are never fully dissolved but also never fully solidified. What, if anything, can you see of me?"

"Well, your hands holding that rock and a bit of a shimmering haze behind the rock. By the way, tell me why are you holding that rock; as a weapon?"

"No", that chuckle again, *"the rock is to stop me from floating away on the wind of chance. Can you imagine the panic I would cause should my shimmering self, go yahooing through the village in the middle of the day? And can you imagine the indignity of being slammed upside down into the side of a hut or a tree by a wind that just does not care about how undignified that would make us spooks look?"*

A sad little smile crossed Kal's face and after a moment, the voice continued, *"You seem sad, is there anything I can do?"*

Kal sat down on the wet sand and poured his heart out, something he could never have done in front of a physical stranger but here he was dealing with a disembodied voice and one that spoke his own language at that.

With a shaken voice, he began, "My partner just died and our unborn baby died with her. What am I going to do without her?" Without waiting for an answer, he went on, "We lost our boat some weeks ago; that was hard enough but at least we had each other. But, now, there is nothing left."

After a pause he added, "Stuck on this island somewhere in the South Pacific with people to whom I feel indebted already but whose language I cannot speak so I can't even tell them how grateful I am!"

There was another long pause and Kal was just about to ask how come the voice spoke his language when the voice interrupted with, "*Oh, oh! Got to fly, there is somebody coming and it would do you no good to be seen speaking to a flying rock, now would it? Call back any time; I should be here unless I lose my rock.*"

Kal turned around to see who was coming. It surprised him to see the young woman who he surmised was the chief's daughter. She had just come around the headland and it was plain to see that she was well and truly out of her comfort zone. She came very slowly constantly looking to left and right as well as behind her. When she saw Kal looking at her she stopped and would not come any closer. She beckoned him urgently and Kal walked back to her. As he did so, he could not help but admire her young body, it was flawless; her skin had a natural pale tan while her hair fell in waves of black silk over her shoulders down as far as her slim waist. Her eyes were dark and bright. All she wore was a broad belt low on her hips with a tiny apron. From the apron, brightly coloured streamers reached as far down as her knees. The belt ensemble festooned with sewn on tiny shells appeared to be more of a decoration then a dress. Kal remembered seeing her and her mother as well as many more men and women and all the kids in the nude especially so when their activities took them into or near the water.

When Kal reached her, she grabbed him by the arm and started to pull him away towards the headland cliff while she kept up a constant stream of talk of which Kal did not understand a word. Finally, he got sick of it and he stopped suddenly nearly throwing the girl of balance.

"What is it you are trying to tell me?"

The girl had a "Huh?" look on her face that quite suddenly became a fearful expression. Kal wondered what she was scared of but then realised that it was he.

He could not understand what she said but neither could she grasp the meaning of his words. Add to that the size of him compared to her and the scary aspect of his many scars and Kal realised he owed her an apology. He took her free hand and placed it on his chest and in a much softer tone, he said, "Me Kal".

The girl looked up at him and asked, "Mekal?"

He shook his head and made an amendment, "Kal".

Suddenly her face brightened, she pulled her hand away but then came back and jabbed him in the chest with her index finger and with a voice dripping with understanding said, "KAL!".

Glad that a point of understanding had been reached, Kal was not surprised when the girl took his hand, placed it on her breast, and then said, "Mailiku".

To ratify this memorandum of mutual understanding Kal pointed at himself and said, "Kal" then he pointed at her and said, "Mailiku".

Quite happy with the reaching of this milestone in their understanding of each other, Mailiku took his hand and urged him on towards the cliff face. When they reached the narrow point, waves smacked into the rock face sending spray up into the air and at least two feet of water covered the sandy strip between waves.

If it had been up to Kal, he would not have attempted to cross but Mailiku was not prepared to spend a minute longer on the wrong side of the cliff face. They were about halfway across when an extra-large wave threw Mailiku against the rocks. She banged her head and dazed, slid into the churning foam. Kal who was right behind her saw it happen and grabbed her before the backwash could drag her into deeper water. He hoisted her onto his shoulder in a fire fighter's lift and completed the crossing.

Once on the dry sand at the other side he slid her off his shoulder and helped her to sit up. Still groggy she leaned her head against his chest and mumbled some words. From the tension with which she held onto Kal's arms, he knew that she had not yet recovered and needed to hear something from him as encouragement. With a soft voice he addressed her, "Listen Mailiku our mutual understanding at this stage is somewhat restricted seeing as how only the words 'Kal' and 'Mailiku' have any meaning to either of us but I do recognise your need for some reassuring chit-chat, so that is what I'm doing, plying you with meaningless chit-chat. Do you understand that?"

Kal of course did not expect an answer to his question but he just wanted to make the sound of his words convey an enquiry into the state of her well-being. His use of their names in close proximity also aimed at her understanding that he had her back, so to speak. It must have worked because gradually Mailiku released her grip on his arms and smiled wanly. She was still in a fair bit of pain and now that they were at the 'right' side of the headland she could have all the time she needed to recover.

While still dazed and in shock Mailiku relaxed completely as Kal held her.

After a while, he realised that he drew as much comfort from the feel of her body as she did from his nearness. So, they sat quietly until

Mailiku regained her senses and began to tense up. Kal did not want to scare her or be seen to intimidate so he pointed at her and himself and then in the direction of her village. She nodded her head and they got up. Mailiku must have received a decent smack to the head because she staggered and Kal had to support her for a while.

When they reached the village Mailiku indicated that he was welcome to come with her to her parents' hut but Kal noted certain hesitancy so he indicated he wanted to sit on the beach and wait for Dan to materialise, night was not far off.

As he sat in the sand and watched the sun go down, he went over the day's events when he felt a gentle hand on his shoulder. It was Mailiku and she brought him a wooden bowl filled with fried fish and boiled taro. She smiled at him as she handed him the bowl but she would not stay. Kal realised he had not eaten anything since arriving on the island and suddenly he was famished. He was still eating when Dan splashed ashore. Kal offered him some food but Dan refused saying he had eaten on-board.

Dan sat down heavily and Kal knew something was amiss. "What is wrong?" After a moment, Dan sighed and replied, "I'm the only one left. All the others are gone."

"Hmm, so what are you going to do? Wait here until some other Wraiths blow in?"

"I honestly don't know Kal, I find it harder and harder to lock myself in come morning. I mean, what's the use? Most people are scared of me and when at last they are not scared any more, they want to sleep at night not entertain some Wraith."

After a short pause Dan continued, "Anyhow what did you do today?"

Kal told him of his encounter with the half Wraith and how Mailiku, had come to drag him away. When Kal finished his story, Dan had a smile on his face, "That voice in your head must have been Abdullah. He was the manager of the 'Trade Winds' in the Core."

"Please explain".

"On these islands in the Core, there is, or was, a tourist resort called the 'Trade Winds'. I used to go there at least once a year. That is how I learned the language. Anyhow, one important South American politician-cum-drug-lord was hiding there when one of the North American agencies decided he had to disappear mysteriously.

They tried the inter-dimensional transfer thing at long-distance and it was only partly successful. From what I saw after arriving there, the Core 'Trade Winds' was burned to the ground with a massive loss of life of course, although they never found any bodies.

Having been one of the first ones on the scene I was hounded by the press, Interpol, CIA and a few lesser-known agencies. I must have let the cat out of the bag when I mentioned the lack of bodies at the scene and about two months later, I had my very own transfer."

For a while, Kal just stared at the sea then he turned to Dan, "The people in the village behind us are they too from the Core?"

"No, they are related to the villagers in the Core but they are native to this dimension. You know how the language used by the Westerners in this dimension is different from that used in the Core?"

"Yes".

"The same applies to their language; it is different but understandable."

"So, what do you think went wrong with the transfer of the 'Trade Winds'?"

"Well, for one thing the distance between the atomiser—or whatever it is they use—and the resort. Next, there is the fact that not only did they blast a whole heap of people and not just one, but they also tried to atomise the buildings."

"Is that what those shimmering squares are?"

Dan nodded his head. For a long time Dan was silent but then he seemed to come to a decision, he slapped his knees and said in a strong voice, "I suggest you visit Abdullah again and tell him that you are a transfer from the Core as well, he can give you a lot of useful information. I have to go and speak with the chief so I will see you later."

CHAPTER 4

TO BE OR NOT TO BE

Slowly Harry Knott noted a swishing sound and as he became more conscious, he knew he was lying on sand. It was dark but a faint moon glow allowed him to establish that he was on a beach. He sat up, rubbed his eyes, and stared at the swaying coconut palms above his head. Gradually his memory returned. The last thing he remembered was that Wilson and him were in the back of a large van listening to the voice of BB telling them they were about to be transferred into another dimension. The vibrations in the back of the truck combined with the hum of the frequency modulator, if that is what it was, made both of them weak and he must have lost consciousness because that is all he could remember. How they had come to be in the back of the van also was a mystery but going by his headache Harry suspected that when BB had gone to the bar to get the last round of drinks, he had slipped some knock-out drops in Wilson's and his drinks.

Just then Harry heard sounds behind him amongst some bushes. He jumped to his feet and spun around. He might have gotten a fright but the two men coming towards the beach got a bigger one. Harry decided to press his advantage and asked in his best 'no-nonsense-I'm-a-cop' voice, "And who are you and where did you come from?"

The younger of the two replied, "I come from Amsterdam that is in Holland."

"Yeah, I know that. And where does your mate come from?"

"I don't know. He woke up near me and has not said a word. I think he must have been a Wraith for a long time."

"Are you a Wraith?"

"Yes, worse luck. And you?"

"I suspect that I must be because I woke up on this beach and I have no idea how I got here, or where we are."

Thoughtfully the young man remarked, "Well, all I can tell you is that last night I woke up on a film set."

"What do you mean by a film set?"

"I woke up on a wharf in this harbour town and it must have been a film set because the place was jam-packed with all kind of sailing vessels from dinghies to four-masted square-riggers, but not a single motorised vessel anywhere! When I materialised I was leaning against a lamppost that sported an oil lamp right near a quayside tavern with the name 'The Gull and Grape', there was a brawl in progress so I did not ask them the name of the set or town."

A light went on in Harry's brain, he knew where 'The Gull and Grape' was. He had read about the place in the 'Sea Shell' journal. He told the other, "The name of that harbour town is 'Capricornia' and it is situated on the west coast of 'Antipodia'".

The young man gave him a funny look and said, "Never heard of either of those places!"

Harry smiled grimly and told him, "You are in a different world now and what you know as 'Australia' in our world is known here as 'Antipodia'. The harbour town you saw is not a film set but is reality."

"You must be kidding me! Right?"

Harry shook his head, "Nope! I wish I was."

While they spoke, the silent Wraith had wandered away in search of food and the young one flopped down next to Harry. "If you only just arrived, how come you know so much?"

"A friend of mine has been living here for something like four or five years now. He lives on a yacht and keeps a journal of his experiences. I was lucky enough to have a read off it"

After a while the young man asked, "How does he manage to stay with his yacht?"

"What do you mean?"

"Well, he must be a Wraith like us and dissolve at every sun-rise."

Harry shook his head again, "No, his transfer into this dimension was spontaneous and because of that he did not become a Wraith".

"What? Did he sign up for it or something?"

"No, it was not voluntary but it was spontaneous and not machine driven like your transfer and mine. The clowns that set us up wanted to get rid of us but did not have the procedure right. By the way who did you piss off to earn you this trip of a life time?"

"I am…was an auditor and had to have a look at somebody's taxation account. Let us just say there were a lot of big, very big mistakes and all in favour of the account holder."

"Let me guess that somebody was one of our Polies?"

"No, actually it was one of our bankers with 'connections' though."

Each steeped in their own morose thoughts the two men stared with unseeing eyes at the moon sprinkling shimmering patches of gold on the murmuring wavelets rolling onto the beach while the trade winds gently rustled in the palm leaves above them. Suddenly Harry stirred and asked his companion, "Are you hungry?"

"Yes, what have you got to eat?"

"Nothing, I'm afraid but I know where you can get some."

"Where?"

With a grin on his face Harry pointed at the coconuts in the tree behind them and said, "I'm too old and fat you are young and look as though you worked out in the gym, so up you go Sunshine".

With a doubtful look at the tree, the young man tried to get out of it by saying, "OK, so I go up the tree and bring down some coconuts …"

"Four will do at this stage".

"Yeah, OK, so how are we going to open them?"

"You just go and get the coconuts while I figure out how the Natives do it."

"What Natives?"

"Quite stalling and get up that tree."

While mumbling some dark words about wanting to audit Harry's last twelve tax returns, the young auditor approached the tree. Halfway up, the young man looked down at Harry and shouted, "Just in case I fall out of this tree and break my neck, my name is Paul."

"Ok Paul, should I have to sign your early-release form I'll sign it with Harry."

"Oh, pleased to meet you".

"No you're not. If you had not met me you wouldn't be stuck halfway up a bloody coconut tree."

"Ugh! That audit report is going to be a corker!" About five minutes later, the first coconut hit the ground two feet away from Harry.

"Careful! You nearly hit me!"

"What a pity I missed, I must have some of your bull dust in my eyes!"

Harry smiled glad to have been able to drag Paul out of his depressed mood. Actually, he quite liked the young but honest auditor.

Through the imaginative use of a few sharp sticks, some sharp rocks and their fingers and teeth, they managed to quell their thirst with the sweet water from the coconut before smashing them and eating the white meat. Afterwards they wandered aimlessly along the beach until they came to a place where some people must have had a BBQ during the day. While looking for food scraps Harry noticed some glowing coals in the BBQ pit, hurriedly he had Paul drag over some firewood and within minutes, they had a fire going. Paul was not happy about the fire and asked, "Why do we need a fire?"

"Are you scared of it?"

"Yeah, kind of."

"Well there is your answer."

"What are you talking about?"

"You're scared because you are a Wraith and Wraiths are supposed to fear fire."

On the defensive now, young Paul asked, "Yeah! So what?"

"Boy! You can be dense! You really don't get it do you?"

"Get what?"

"This fire my little friend is our protection! You see those two Yobbos coming down the beach; see the baseball bats they carry? They probably are what you call a Wraith patrol. They feel they have the right to bash up anybody they consider a Wraith. Now watch carefully, when they come closer and see us warming our hands over the fire, something will happen in the grey matter behind hose low brows. The question will pop up, 'Are they Wraiths, or are they not?' This is in fact the first question in the 'Wraith Detection Manual'. Now the ultimate answer is revealed after simply ticking the right boxes on a number of questions.

First question, 'Is it day or is it night?' Tick, 'night'.

Second question, 'Do they have tattoos?' Tick, 'Too dark to see.'

<u>Third question,</u> 'Is there a fire anywhere near them?' *This is the hard one and has a multiple possibility answer but the right ones to tick are of course,* 'Yes they are sitting near a fire. No, they are not ON fire. No they do not appear to be scared of the fire or us.'

<u>You have finished the questionnaire and the conclusion is,</u> 'SORRY BOYS. They are NOT Wraiths so be polite and keep going'.

After the men had passed and Paul got over his bout of the giggles, he asked Harry, "That's a neat trick why don't other Wraiths use it?"

Harry looked at him dumbfounded and answered the question with a question, "Duh. Could it be because they are scared of fire?"

After a moment, Paul came back with, "Yeah, but we are not."

"You were and by tomorrow night I might be too."

By following in the direction, the Wraith squad had gone they eventually found themselves in town somewhere near the wharfs. Just before daybreak, Paul found a small window that gave access to a cellar underneath one of the go-downs. They squirmed through the window and closed it behind them. The place was cavernous but empty. With a bit of luck they would not blow away and would still be in each other's company when they materialised in the cellar the next evening.

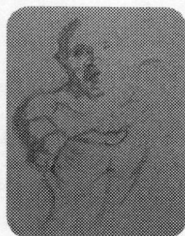

CHAPTER 5

IN LOVING MEMORY

WELL BEFORE DAWN, a canoe bumped into the side of the schooner 'Vrouwe Irene' and Mailiku followed by another woman climbed on-board. A third person, Mailiku's brother, handed some stuff up and then joined the women on deck. Together they approached Kal where he was leaning against the deck house. Kal did not know what they were up to but figured it had something to do with the funeral of Serah so he complied when Mailiku indicated that she wanted him to sit down.

First, they rubbed his body with coconut oil then they applied black paint in intricate designs on his chest, back, and arms. Last, they tied finely plaited bands around his upper arms and ankles. On his head, they placed a circlet with some rooster feathers that waved in the wind.

Besides feeling somewhat ridicules in this get-up, he also felt somewhat intimidated. He had no idea what they expected of him and there would be no one to ask. He did not want to make a fool of himself nor did he want to insult his hosts through his ignorance. The three-some did not give him any time to worry about it. As soon as they were finished, they guided him to the canoe and indicated he should get on-board. Standing stiffly in the bows of the vessel Kal was paddled ashore. A small group of people was waiting on the beach and followed when Mailiku's brother lead Kal to the graveside.

The legs had been removed from Serah's bier and the platform now rested on two bamboo beams suspended over the open grave. The mats on which Serah's body was lying had been folded open so that they covered the edge of the grave. Although some corruption must have sat in by that time, Serah's body did not show it. She had been bathed and her skin rubbed with coconut oil, her hair was spread like a halo around her face. The Sianksey's Snake carving lay between her breasts.

As the old Shaman began her litany, Kal noticed that two strong warrior types flanked him on both sides. For a moment, he wondered why they were there. Was he to be pushed into the grave as well or were they there to prevent him from jumping in after Serah. He did not care. While they stood there listening to the Shaman, Kal heard the whispering voice of Dan behind him saying, "Listen carefully, I've told the Chief that the 'Vrouwe Irene' is yours but that if they build you a boat to your design, you will give the 'Vrouwe Irene' to the village in exchange. He agreed to that and wants you to build a model of the boat you would like them to build."

After a short pause Dan continued, "I am so sorry for ramming your boat. Had that not happened Serah might still be alive. Watch carefully when the sun comes up over the horizon, Serah's soul will be set free and the sun will guide her into the afterlife. That is the essence of the message the Shaman is giving the people. I am about to dissolve and perhaps I never will come back or perhaps I may materialise on the deck of your new boat."

Just then, the first sun ray peeked over the horizon. With surprising speed, the old Shaman bent over the bier, took the Sianksey's Snake carving, placed a kiss on it, and briefly held the amulet against Serah's forehead. Just in that split second that the carving touched her forehead, Kal could swear that he saw a pink vapour rise above her. The moment was gone and the old Shaman stood up and gave a nod with her head. Just as the gravediggers lifted the bier to withdraw the bamboo beams, a ray of sunshine lit up Serah's face. She looked peaceful and Kal could not prevent a sob from rocking his body.

Silent tears coursed down his haggard cheeks as they gently lowered Serah into her grave. The mats that had covered the edges of the grave now folded over her body so hiding her from sight and falling earth.

Slowly the Shaman walked from the head of the grave to where Kal stood at the foot end. She stopped in front of him and said something in a kind voice; then she held up the Sianksey's Snake amulet, kissed it once more, and slowly placed its string around Kal's neck.

The two warriors turned him around and Kal noticed at once that Dan was no longer there. For an instance he hoped his friend had gone back to lock himself in the deckhouse of the 'Vrouwe Irene' but he knew he was hoping against hope.

The warriors guided Kal to the chief's house where they shouted a challenge while still outside. Two warriors who came rushing out of the chief's house brandishing war clubs answered their challenge. After some more shouting, the two warriors formed a guard of honour and Kal followed one warrior inside while the others followed him. Once inside he was lead to the head of the house where he was invited to sit next to the chief. There were at least forty to fifty people sitting against the walls of the house.

Placed in front of the chief and Kal there was a large wooden bowl filled with an ochre coloured liquid. Kal knew what that was. During his wanderings about the Pacific in the Core, he had plenty of opportunities to become acquainted with Kava, a root extract. Originally a ceremonial drink only for chiefs, dignitaries, and Shamans but in the Core, although still accorded a certain amount of ceremonial respect, the drink has become popularised. Commoners as well as those of other races who do not understand the ritualistic value of the drink partake freely now as it is slightly narcotic.

For quite a while there was silence in the house then an elderly man came forward and kneeled next to the bowl of Kava. Before the old man could say anything, Kal suddenly realised what was going on. The elderly man was to speak on Kal's behalf and should be offering a gift of Kava. Kava that Kal should have given him for the purpose of asking the chief for his hospitality. Kal was in a flap. He could not let the old man present 'make belief' Kava. He turned to the chief and said, "I know that you may not understand me but I must go to the waqa (boat in Fijian) to get Kava." He repeated himself and this time he pointed in the direction of the 'Vrouwe Irene' as he said 'waqa' and made a bringing back gesture with his hand as he uttered the word 'Kava'.

A murmur of voices went up but was stilled by a hand gesture of the chief. Kal looked at the chief and asked, "OK?" as he moved his head up and down. Kal could see that the chief only half understood him but the man nodded his head. Kal got to his knees and crawled behind the chief to get to the nearest door. Once outside he sprinted to the beach closely followed by Mailiku's brother, the chief's son. They jumped into one of the canoes and raced over to the 'Vrouwe Irene'.

Kal climbed on board but his companion stayed with the canoe. In the deckhouse, Kal had seen a big bundle of Kava roots all dried and gnarly; he split the bundle in half and went back to the canoe. The young man took one look at the bundle and shook his head. Kal spread his hands as though to say, "What?" The young man took the bundle and halved it again. One-half he kept the other he gave back to Kal. Hurriedly Kal took the surplus back to the deckhouse and locked it. In an aside he sadly noted that Dan was gone.

They raced back to the shore and ran back to the chief's house. Kal was about to enter when the chief's son stopped him. He took the Kava bundle from Kal and called out. A minute later the old man who was to speak for Kal shuffled outside and his eyes looked like saucers when he saw the bundle of Kava roots he was handed. The old man waited outside until the chief's son took Kal back inside and gave them time to regain their places before he entered.

This time when he kneeled before the chief, he sounded a lot more confident as he presented the Kava on behalf of Kal. As per protocol, the chief's representative accepted the Kava on behalf of the chief and officially welcomed Kal into the village. A cup-bearer then presented Kal with a full bowl—half a polished coconut shell—of the mixed Kava but Kal indicated that the honour of the first bowl should go to the chief. The chief refused and Kal had to drink the whole cup in one go. The mix was strong and Kal could feel his tongue go numb after the second cup.

There were two mixing bowls going, the one for the chief and a selected number of others, while the second bowl supplied the rank and file.

Even though Kal could not understand the discussions, the body language and tone of enquiry led Kal to belief that the chief had to explain Kal's presence to them.

In between grieving over Serah and trying to make sense of what was going on around him Kal wished he were somewhere else.

For a while, he had been hearing a dull, rhythmic, thumping, as that of a large pestle. Well that was exactly what it was. A large hollow rock and a hardwood pestle were in use to grind the Kava roots Kal had presented. It was not until Kal had drank a cup oh 'his' Kava that the chief nodded his head and at the same moment he felt a small hand gently pulling him backwards out of the circle of drinkers. Kal was grateful for this reprieve, the Kava was super strong and all Kal wanted to do was to go to sleep. Mailiku pulled him out of the circle after her father's nod of consent.

CHAPTER 6

BRUTUS

JUST AS THE sun was setting and shadows spread over the land, Harry became aware of himself. Next to him, he saw Paul in a haze. Harry had an overwhelming hunger and a stirring in his loins, as he had not felt for years. Somewhere in his cloudy brain, he knew that he should not give in to the desires associated with those sensations. It was hard but he held it together. Not so young Paul, he threw a bit of a tantrum with growls and throwing things. Harry let him blow off steam for a while until he told Paul that he looked like an extra in a caveman movie.

In the end he said, "Sit down Paul and let us access the damage".

Still muttering Paul sat down and asked, "What are you talking about?"

After a short pause Harry remarked, "You seem to be rubbing your eyes a fair bit. Anything wrong there?"

"Yeah, I think I lost my contact lenses."

"Anything else?"

"No, what else should I be losing?"

"What about that there?" Harry pointed at a small shiny object on the floor. Paul peered at it and asked, "What is it?"

Harry looked at him and said, "Looks like a tooth crown to me".

Paul ran his tongue along the inside of his mouth and said, "Oh shit! It is mine! Did you whack me one while I was out to it?"

Harry gave him a strange look, "Don't be daft! I could ask you the same thing because, look over there those are my false teeth."

Paul looked to where Harry was pointing then looked back at Harry and said, "Hmm, yes, your face does look as though it has collapsed. Blow us a raspberry Harry." (*Harry's reply had to be deleted*)

As Harry went over to pick up his dentures he asked Paul why he was not looking for his contacts but Paul just shrugged his shoulders and sounded quite depressed when he replied, "What's the use I will only loose them again in the morning."

"Not if you take them out and leave them in a safe place."

"That is assuming we find another place that is draft free. By the way didn't you tell me that anything that does not exist in the Dimension, like plastics and the like, will dissolve?"

"Yes?"

"OK so why do you still have your gnashers?"

"Oh I can feel that they are slowly disappearing but hopefully they will last me this night out."

"Yeah, you'll be sucking on baby rusks after that".

Harry chuckled at the doom-laden tone of Paul's remark even though he admitted that Paul was right, without his upper and lower sets of dentures, he would only have four teeth, and none of them lined up with each other in a meaningful way.

After making sure that the coast was clear, the two of them exited the cellar through the same small window and left it partly open, ready for future use. Then began the search for food.

They never had any luck until they scouted around the back door of a bakery. There they found some burned offerings that were still quite edible. Paul made some disparaging remarks about resembling a mangy cur when a deep growl came from somewhere near in the dark. Hastily Paul turned and offered his half-eaten bun.

The dog, a big brute of a thing, took the offered crust and suddenly became all nice and nearly fluffy. Paul at once became the dog's 'bestest' (*the best of the best* in Paul's dictionary) friend who would not leave his side after that. Harry, Paul and the newly christened 'Brutus' promenaded along the wharf looking at ships and taking in the local ambiance.

They met the Wraith patrol of the night before and were recognised. The patrol wanted to stop for a bit of a yarn. However, Brutus, perhaps basing her attitude on previous experience, did not like men with clubs and made her opinion quite clear. A growl promising impending doom and an impressive display of teeth and bristle could not be mistaken for anything else but a promise of severe pain. The Wraith patrol politely tipped their caps and kept moving at a slightly increased pace.

Harry and Paul spent the rest of the night familiarising themselves with the dock area and the immediate surrounds. Every now and then Brutus would bound away on secret business but never for long. They had just decided to call it a night and nurse their hunger in the cellar when Brutus came back from one of her forays with a couple of pounds of roast pork still hot and smelling like a dream. She laid it at the feet of Harry and disappeared again. Paul remarked dourly, "That dog is a thief and a smart one at that."

"Why do you say she's smart?"

"She is making sure she is nowhere around when the owner of this pork comes to accuse us of theft and proceeds to beat the living daylight out of us."

Harry shook his head and mumbled something about Paul being ungrateful for the things the good lord was providing and that if he was concerned about accusations of theft he had better help conceal the evidence by eating his share.

Paul could see the logic in that and soon they were scoffing the roast. Meanwhile Brutus came back with her meal, a raw but plucked chicken. Neither Harry nor Paul found it their place to ask where the meat supply came from. Paul did remark that the service was excellent after Brutus licked the oil and grease of their fingers.

After Harry mentioned that he would love to have a drink, Brutus stood up and both men felt that she wanted them to follow so they did. The dog lead them down some narrow alley ways and through one back garden until they suddenly came out on a small, cobbled square that had a hand operated water pump in the middle. Brutus walked over to it and looked at Harry as if to say, *"It's your turn, swing that handle so we can get a drink."*

Harry pumped up the water and watched Brutus drink her fill before he told Paul it was his turn. After they all drank their fill, Brutus lead them back to their cellar and dawn was breaking when Harry climbed down through the window. He tried to get Brutus to come with them but the dog plunked herself down and in doing so, closed the little window. Harry again felt that Brutus was much more than a stray that had adopted them. He was still standing near the window when he felt himself dissolve again.

The last light of day weakened as Harry and Paul materialised. Knowing what was to come they both were able to control their urges. Perhaps due to the late meal of the night before their hunger was manageable and there was no way that they could satisfy the other urges so the desires did not take too long to fade.

Harry looked for his teeth but they were gone. Paul felt sorry for Harry but did not say anything, which perhaps was just as well.

When Harry stuck his head out of the cellar window, a big, pink, slobbery tongue blinded his vision. Brutus was back on station and very proud of the fact that she had been able to resist the temptation to wolf down the two fried chickens she had liberated. Was that two chickens? Ah well, one and a half then.

Paul was delighted, "Gee Brutus you're such a good girl! Where did you get the chickens?"

Brutus said nothing but Harry could not help but mutter, "Always the bloody auditor! Where do you think she got 'em from? No, don't answer that one; you might expect me to arrest her."

Paul glowered at Harry then said with a shovel load of sarcasm, "Isn't it amazing how circumstances change the law?"

"If I were you I would not make that accusation with stolen chicken grease running down your chin." They both chuckled while feeding Brutus titbits.

For the next seven days the routine was the same, Harry and Paul would shelter in the cellar during the day and Brutus would be waiting for them in the evening. She always managed to bring them a feed.

Harry became worried about Paul's mental condition, the young man often faded away into a mind space that Harry could not understand. Paul would become so vague in his speech that he was no longer coherent but after a while, he would snap out of it and be his usual self again without any memory of his temporary 'absence'. Harry wondered why he was not experiencing the same mind wanderings and could only put it down to their age difference. His brain was a lot older than Paul's and more set in a pattern. With typical good-natured irreverence, Paul claimed Harry's brain had rusted itself into a closed circuit and that nothing could dislodge it. Then wistfully added he wished his brain had done the same.

On the evening of the eighth day, things turned bad. Paul woke up in typical Wraith fashion he screamed and raced about; he could not find the cellar window until Harry shoved him towards it. Once outside he saw a sexual partner in Brutus but that only earned him a painful bite. When he spotted the two fried ducks Brutus had procured, he grabbed them both and would not give Harry his share. Brutus who normally shared her affections equally now did not want anything to do with Paul; perhaps understandingly so.

By the time morning came, Paul had not spoken at all he was like an uncontrollable child and just shouted, groaned and moaned. Harry was glad when it was time to return to the cellar, he was tired.

When they reached the cellar Paul refused to enter and even Brutus tried her most intimidating snarl on him but Paul would not budge.

Harry was aware enough to realise that if he stayed with Paul they would both float away. In the end he climbed through the window and as he turned to try and convince Paul once more to come down, Paul shouted something that sounded very much like, "I'm gone" or, "I'm done" and then slammed the window shut.

CHAPTER 7

A'ANU

IN THE EVENINGS and at night, the 'Vrouwe Irene' was a lonely place to be but after some time had passed and Kal became used to Serah not being there he began to prepare himself for the making of the junk model the villagers were going to use to build the real one.

Then one day, while Kal was searching for suitable bits of timber, an old man came up to him. For a while, the senior citizen followed Kal about the place until Kal could no longer stand it. He turned to the old man and asked, "Can I help you?"

He expected one of those, 'Sorry but I cannot understand you' smiles but to his surprise, the old man in turn asked him in perfectly good Malay, "Can you speak Malay?"

Of course, Kal could! He spent his childhood in Malaya! Why had no one asked him that before! He could have kissed the old man! They promptly sat down for a serious confab. From their conversation, it turned out that A'anu as a young impressible lad had followed the call of the missionaries as they spread the Word and the white man's diseases across the Pacific. A'anu himself had a permanent reminder of that folly his whole face bearing the scars from chicken pox.

On their way across to the Solomon Islands A'anu disenchanted with the lack of respect for and the amount of ridicule his ancestral believes received from the missionaries, decided to jump ship as soon as an opportunity should present itself. This opportunity came one dark night when the ship approached an island in the Solomons and a fire lit on shore invited the missionaries to make landfall. What the missionaries did not realise was that the fire was a cooking fire and that they were on the menu. During the ensuing commotion, A'anu slipped away.

It took him ten years to make his way via a stint as a pearl diver on a Malay pearler to Malaya. There he fell in love with a Malay girl who was the daughter of a boat builder. He started from scratch in his father-in-law's boat building yard and after twenty years when the old man passed away, he became the new boss.

Two years later his wife died. They never had any children so there was really nothing to keep A'anu in Malaya. He refurbished an old *prau liar* (sailing ship) and with a crew of Malayans set sail into the Pacific to find his island home.

It took him a few years and by the time they found Balon Island, the crew was homesick. A'anu had foreseen this and as payment offered them the ship. The Malayans jumped at the change to have transportation with which to go home so everybody was happy.

While A'anu had been telling his story, Kal, on a number of occasions had to remind himself that he was no longer in the Core and that A'anu's memories related to a place in the Dimension that had not been touched by the industrial revolution. That meant no machines, no radio, slow communications, and isolation of island communities and so on.

Conditions in the places where Kal had grown up in the Core had already been subjected to some hundred and fifty years of post-separation influences. Where he remembered Belawan, the harbour of Medan on Sumatra, as a busy port where all manner of motorised vessels jostled for quayside space to unload their cargoes, A'anu described the same port in the Dimension as a sea of masts with some sails partly hoisted so they could dry. In his memory, the only pollution came from the smoke of many little cooking fires on which street vendors cooked their spicy dishes for sale.

Kal had to keep reminding himself that the places he knew in the Core were the same and in the same time-slot as those in the Dimension, the only difference being the influence of the industrial revolution was missing in the Dimension.

On a few occasions, he caught himself thinking of the Dimension as being behind the times. From a superficial Coreling's point of view, that might seem to be the case. The industrial revolution took place in the Core after the Dimension separated from the Core. However, to claim that the Dimension is a dead backwater of the Core is like saying that the branch on a tree is a dead appendage of that tree.

True, in the Dimension there are no new discoveries in technology, instead, there is a constant development and improvement of the existing technology of sail and all that pertains to Nature.

Quite unintentionally, man is far less destructive and the negative chemical footprint left in the Dimension is nothing compared with what is happening in the Core. It came as a bit of a surprise when they established that Kal actually left Malaya at roughly the time that A'anu first arrived there, the only difference being that Kal lived in the Core while A'anu arrived in the same area and in the same time slot but in the Dimension.

On board of the 'Vrouwe Irene' Kal found quite a few tools but a ruler was not amongst them. For some reason, Kal felt more at ease with feet and inches, probably because he used that measuring system when he built 'Stella Maris'. He decided to build the model 'three feet' long and the full size junk therefore would be thirty-six feet long (a 1 to 12 scale). A'anu was of the opinion that thirty-six feet was a tad small for a sea-going junk.

"Thirty-six feet is about all I can handle on my own."

"On your own, aren't you taking a crew along?"

"No, I may never come back here so how would they get home?"

"You'll have to find a crew that would not want to come back here."

"Oh yeah? How?"

"Get married!"

"Get married! Get real! Who would have me? All scars and no manners".

"The scars came with the package and therefore cannot be seen. The bad manners, if there are any, can be un-learned. Anyway, there is a young lady who has been mooning over you ever since you arrived. At present she is giving you time to get over the loss of Serah but mark my word, she'll come after you when the time is right".

"Who might that be? Mailiku?"

"I must say you are sharp."

"You know, sarcasm does not suite you! Anyhow Mailiku has the looks with which she can snare any man on this island so why should she be interested in me, I can't even speak her language."

"Well you could try to learn hers; she is doing her best to learn yours".

"Who is teaching her?"

"I am."

"How can you teach her my language, you don't speak it either?"

"I might not speak your 'white-man-tongue' but you speak better Malay than a lot of Malayans I know so that is what I'm teaching her."

During the next six months, A'anu and some other old men taught Kal everything there was to know about Balon wood. The adult tree stood some one hundred feet tall and had a straight trunk with no branches for about the first forty feet. The branches were small and densely covered with large, heart shaped leaves. Once dried out the wood itself was not very much heavier than balsa wood but had the strength of Silver ash. It had a creamy, beige colour with heart-shaped darker patches. The grain was so strong and so straight that the carpenters could set up a log of say, forty feet and then with wedges split planks of that log as thin as half an inch. By applying heat or steam, the fresh planks could be bend quite easily and would retain that shape once cured.

There was one drawback if that is what it could be called; once the wood had been milled, it had to be used straight away before the sap had time to dry out. The sap, a milky syrup, would dry into a film as hard and water proof as a coat of fibre glass resin. The boat building trade used this characteristic extensively where the careful, diagonal strip planking ensured a strong and water tight hull. The locally built canoes were laid up in two layers for the smaller ones and three layers for the bigger ones of up to forty feet long. When it came to the hull of Kal's boat, the lay-up would be in four layers of half inch thick by three inches wide planks. To ensure the freshness of the planking, A'anu organised three work crews, the first felled the trees while the second team reduced the trees to planks and transported the timber down to the slipway where the shipwrights would shape and use them before the sap could set.

Kal had been wondering what the ship builders were going to use for fasteners; he had not seen a single nail, screw, or bolt. In the end he could not curb his curiosity any longer. He asked A'anu and the latter laughed and said, "We just glue it together."

"You must be joking. Some things you just can't glue together."

"No, you're right. Come and I will show you."

He took Kal to a hut somewhat removed from the slipway. There he introduced him to an old man and his wife, a young man, and a young teenage boy. The old man and the young man were cutting and shaping a jet-black substance that had the appearance and density of petrified wood but was in fact seasoned wood of what they called the Masi tree.

The two men shaped lengths of the wood in what looked like pins of different size and diameter, some were straight while others had a slight taper. The old man's wife sat there with a short plank of Balon wood with various diameter holes drilled through it and did the sorting. She would find the hole that was a tight fit for a straight pin while the tapered pins had to match with the holes that would only allow half of their length to go through. Once the old man had approved a pin it went to the teenager, who then fire hardened it. Any reject went back to the old man who would then reshape it to fit a smaller gauge.

While they were talking to the pin-maker, a couple of neighbours came over with baskets full of pins ready for final quality and size control.

On their way back to the slips, Kal shook his head in wonder, "How come all this work is done by people who, in the first place don't know me and who, in the second place are not getting paid for their work?"

A'anu looked at him for a long time, finally, he said, "This is a cash-less society so the whole search for profit is different and far less mercenary.

Profit here is not a personal gain but a communal gain.

A section of the available work force goes fishing so the whole village can eat fish while another section of the labour force does the planting so the village can eat tapioca.

Those that have specialist skills or who have strong trade preferences usually can apply their skills in their chosen fields as long as their efforts benefit the community, the community will support their other needs in return."

"So no revenue collectors, union demands, and other forms of profiteering?"

"No, not yet, at least not here in the islands".

CHAPTER 8

TO SHIMMER OR NOT TO SHIMMER

ONE MOONLIT NIGHT some three weeks after Paul vanished; Harry and Brutus sauntered aimlessly along the beach. Perhaps their sauntering was not completely without a goal, after all, they were looking for food.

Sunday, the day of rest, had just passed and Harry was hoping that some of the families that came out for picnics on the Sunday had left some food behind but so far the pickings had been poor.

Trying to shake the funky mood he was in he walked into the sea and let the gentle surf rock him for a bit. Brutus came over to see what the story was. With her head tilted to the left and her tattered right ear upright while her unscathed left ear flopped about never having learned the art of standing at attention, she stood over Harry wondering whether he needed rescuing or that he was just doing some stupid human thing. Harry splashed some water at her and Brutus realised this was far more serious, a challenge to see who could churn up the most water had been issued. At high speed, she jumped and ran in a tight circle around Harry splashing water everywhere.

Eventually a majority of two votes, hers, and Harry's, made Brutus the winner of that contest. Harry laughed at her antics and he had the distinct impression that that made Brutus even more boisterous and happy. They raced each other to the shore and nearly bowled over an old, very dark, man. Harry came to a screeching halt and so did Brutus. To his surprise Harry noted that Brutus seemed to know the old man and gave him a third degree bum and tail wiggle (that is the fastest). Harry was still stammering out his apologies when a deep voice appeared to surround him, *"Your apologies are not necessary but accepted none the less. Please be seated so we may talk."*

Harry just could not help himself, as soon as they sat down near the fringe of coconut trees he blurted, "I am really surprised about Brutus—the dog I mean—normally she is quite stand-offish with people she does not know."

"Who says she does not know me?"

"Oh! Well does she?"

"Have you ever tried to touch her?"

"Come to think of it, she never really gave me a chance. But what has that got to do with it?"

"Let me ask you a question, does the name Tjitjira mean anything to you?"

"Yes, of course! You must then be the spirit elder who helped my friend Morgan Turbot".

"That is right and Brutus is my spirit dog. She has been sent to help you because you are connected with Morgan as well as Kal and also because there is no aura of evil radiating from you."

Harry sat down heavily and was silent. After a while, he looked up at Tjitjira and asked, "Is there any way that you can stop this shape changing?"

The old spirit elder shook his head sadly and said, "*If only I could I would.*"

"Ah well, can you tell me where either Morgan, or Kal are at this moment?"

Tjitjira gave a mirthless chuckle and answered, "*You could not have found a better time to enter the Dimension. Morgan is on his way to see Europe while Kal is on a little island somewhere in the south east Pacific. Therefore, you see, you have a choice. You are halfway between your two friends.*"

"Great! How am I going to meet up with either?"

"*Well, I came to offer you a ride to one of your friends. All you have to do is make up your mind as to who you want to see.*"

"I think I would like to meet up with Kal if I could. Did he get his boat back and what about the girl, what was her name? Serah! Did she make it all right?"

Tjitjira slowly shook his head, "*Serah has joined her ancestors. That to me is no more than a change of address but for Kal her demise from the physical world was devastating*".

"What happened?"

"*She never fully recovered from a knife attack by a jealous ex-boyfriend*".

"Did they get the bloke?"

"*Yes, her brother and Kal finished him*".

A brooding silence followed during which Harry's police officer's mind studied the angles finally he asked, "Was the death of Serah the reason for Kal to take off?"

"No, Serah took a long time to recover but seemed to get on top of it all and in the end they got married. It was not until after that they took off. Near Balon Island a schooner ran over them and sank Kal's boat".

"What! The 'Stella Maris'?"

Tjitjira nodded his head and continued, "The Wraiths manning the schooner fished them out of the water and brought them to Balon Island. Serah was seven months pregnant but she and the child both died on the day they arrived at the Island."

Harry was quiet for a long time while he processed what Tjitjira had told him, in the end Harry asked, "Where is this Balon Island or has Kal left there?"

"No, he is there. Balon Island is the main island in a small archipelago in the south-east Pacific; the people there buried Serah and are now building Kal a new boat."

"And, you can take me there? How?"

"Taking you there is no problem; just as you change shape and become gas, I breathe you in and you become part of me. Then when we get to where we are going I breathe you out just before a shape change and that is it."

"So why do you sound so unsure of yourself?"

After a long silence, the old man spoke, "The problem is not how to get you there but how to keep you there. The islands are quite windy and I know of no place where you could secure yourself through the day except…"

When the silence became too suspense-laden Harry asked, "Except…?"

The old spirit elder answered the question with a question, "Have you ever heard of the Shimmer people?"

"No, who or what are they?"

"They are different from the Wraiths they are the ones that got stuck halfway during a shape change. You could say that during the day they are half Wraith while during the night they are half Person. Day or night, when *one of the Shimmer people comes near, all you can see is something like the flickering of heat-haze above the dessert for instance. When you talk to them, you hear their voice in your head and that freaks out most people. What disturbs people even more is that if a Shimmerer wants to stay in the one place, he or she must latch onto something heavy enough to stop them from floating away. When they do that, the vibrational frequency in their hands takes on the vibrational frequency of the object they hold to such an extent that they, only their hands that is, become visible. Therefore, if you see a pair of hands carrying a rock and a shimmer near or surrounding it and hear a voice in your head, you know a Shimmerer is addressing you."*

"Why is that worse than being a Wraith?"

"There are a few reasons that Shimmerers have put forward, for one, they claim that the Wraith during the solid state has the option of suicide. What they forget is that the Wraith after a short period does not have the capability of making a decision on the matter. Another reason they put forward is that they, being half-lives, have to endure existence twice as long as a Wraith. However, perhaps the most common objection is the fear factor. Most Shimmerers are acutely aware of the fear they cause in normal people. The disembodied hands carrying a rock, the voice heard in the head, and, the shimmer image, can instil a large amount of fear in a person and that fear is reflected back onto the Shimmerer."

"That does not sound all that bad. What do the Shimmerers live on, like, food wise?"

"They neither drink nor eat and must absorb their nutritional needs directly from the air around them."

"Do they die?"

"Eventually but it takes a long time."

"Yeah, like what?"

"In the Dimension the average lifespan of people is forty to fifty years. The Shimmerer can live up to ninety years."

"Oh, anyway, what has all this got to do with keeping me in situ on Balon Island?"

"Should you wish to become a Shimmerer, I can only do that while you are within my breath. Therefore, you would have to let me know before we start the journey to Balon Island."

"So in other words I have about two hours to decide what to be for the rest of my life?"

"Yes Sunrise will be in two hours."

Harry got to his feet and with his head bowed, slowly walked to the surf. What was he to do? Stay as a wraith and slowly lose his faculties until he perished? That could take anything up to two years, or, should he become a Shimmerer and live for another forty years, during which time he would have his faculties but perhaps nobody to communicate with. Still undecided Harry came back to where Tjitjira was waiting. After Harry sat down the old man said, *"If you have made up your mind to become a Shimmerer, I have a surprise for you"*.

"And what would that be?"

"I will rig up a harness for Brutus, so she can be your counterweight."

"She is your dog so why would she be happy to be my Seeing Eye dog? Besides that, how would I feed her?"

"She is a spirit dog and does not need feeding. She will be happy to be with you as long as you will treat her right."

Brutus looked at Harry as though she understood every word spoken.

"Well, you could have fooled me about the no feeding bit!"

Tjitjira laughed and said, *"She had to keep up appearances!"*

After another pause, the old man said, *"Near the village where Kal is there is a colony of Shimmerers that would welcome you"*.

"It sounds as though you would rather see me become a Shimmerer than to stay a Wraith?"

"*I wish that I would have the capability to return you to your normal state as a human being. However, that is not possible because you were not the result of a spontaneous transfer. That being the case I can only influence the powers at work to transform you into a Shimmerer and I rather see you as a Shimmerer, at least that way you will retain your wits and your ability to communicate with Kal for a much longer time.*"

"OK, a Shimmerer it is. Brutus, it looks like you and I are about to begin a long and lasting friendship."

Brutus gave Harry her tilted-head—raised-ear look that said, '*That is fine by me, now let us play.*'

With the breaking of dawn Tjitjira got Harry to stand in front of him, he placed his hands on his shoulders, or so it seemed, and just as Harry began to experience the dwindling awareness, part of the normal shape change, Tjitjira's ghostly form appeared to absorb his melting image.

CHAPTER 9

THE RAIDING PARTY

IN ORDER TO recognise any building problems before they became problems Kal decided to build a scale model using the same building approach, as he wanted to apply to the real version. It was going to be a junk with an overall length of thirty-six feet[4] and a beam of twelve feet on deck but only ten feet on the waterline.

The bottom would have to be nearly flat to allow her ballast—forty percent of her total displacement—to be carried internally because there was no way the island could produce either lead or cast iron for a poured keel. The ballast would be sand and rocks in the bottom of the boat and held in place by wooden floorboards.

Above those floorboards, there would be six foot three inches of headroom to allow Kal to stand up straight.

---

[4] Kal did not have a ruler of any kind so he made his own. He cut himself a staff of iron wood that was his height plus about two inches. He then divided the staff in half and then in half again and so on until the smallest division was about a quarter inch. He marked his staff with notches of various length and depths and that was his "maatstaf" or measuring stick. A'anu then made a duplicate and using those two measuring devices, the junk was built.

The sail plan was that typical for a junk that size, two masts, the main mast just about dead centre, and the foremast close to the bow. Both masts would lean forward, the main mast by five degrees and the fore mast by ten. The sails would have battens and the sails themselves would be finely woven mats.

Kal was concerned about getting the cordage required for the full-scale rendition of his junk but A'anu assured him that one of the neighbouring islands was already preparing the raw materials for the required ropes and rigging.

For about six months gangs of villagers worked on the project until one day a young man came looking for A'anu. He seemed to be in quite a state and as he told his story to A'anu, other men dropped tools and headed for their huts. When the young man finally rushed away A'anu came over to Kal. "There is a raiding party on the way."

"A raiding party? What? To raid the village? Why?"

"They're after women. They'll steal young women to take back to their village as wives. Perhaps a bit barbaric but it prevents inbreeding."

"And the girls don't mind?"

"Some are not too happy about it, mainly because they do not know whose bride they will be but on the other hand there are quite a few who have made arrangement beforehand. They are all right, no, I feel sorry for those that are picked at random and may finish up with abusive men."

"What about the men of this village, are they just standing by to let it happen?"

"Oh no, they'll put up quite a fight because they want to prove that they can defend their women folk and also to test the mettle of the future husbands of their daughters. Our young men in turn will raid some other village."

"What about the young women who definitely do not want to play ball?"

"They hide and hope for the best. If caught, they will get an unholy hiding because they have insulted any prospective husband. Their behaviour has indicated that they consider the attackers as being so far below their standard that they would perish rather than become wife to one of them."

Just then, a shrill scream announced the arrival of the raiding party. Kal picked up his staff and headed in the direction of the chief's house.

The scene that met his eye made his blood boil. A very large and very ugly man apparently decided that Mailiku was his for the taking. He was hitting her with a closed fist while he held her by a handful of hair. Blood from her nose was running down her chin and covered her breasts. Her flailing arms were not strong enough or heavy enough to hurt her attacker.

When the man saw Kal stalk slowly but very determined towards him, he stopped hitting Mailiku but still held her by her hair.

Kal voice thundered when he told 'Ugly' to let the girl go and although 'Ugly' could not understand what was said, he did figure out that Kal was challenging him for the hand of the maiden. He shoved her to the side where she fell to the ground. Next, he adopted the traditional spread-legged fighter's stance. Wrong move. Kal slid his iron wood staff forward until he had a two handed grip on the aft end of it. Holding the point about half a foot above the ground, he rushed 'Ugly'. This being an unfamiliar step in the dance of death, 'Ugly' was expecting Kal to swing the staff left or right aiming it at either side of his head. He was so concentrated on the defences of his ugly head that he forgot all about the dangly bits between his spread legs. Kal did not. Once he was within striking range, he whipped the staff up as though he was throwing up hay and the point of the iron wood stick came to a violent and sudden stop in the groin of 'Ugly'.

A'anu who watched all this scrunched up his face in sympathy and at a later date told listeners that he fully expected 'Ugly's gonads to pop out of his mouth or eyes.

Kal knew that 'Ugly' would bend over to console the crown jewels so in a rare display of patience waited until 'Ugly' was bent over before he cracked him on the back of the head with the staff. 'Ugly' no longer wanted to play the game and quietly dropped to the ground.

By this time, her mother had taken Mailiku into her father's house.

Later that day after the marauders had left with their mostly willing captives; A'anu came and sat next to Kal on the beach. They discussed the day's events and Kal mentioned that he probably had made himself an enemy for live. A'anu shook his head and said, "No you did not. You'll never see that man again."

"And why is that?"

A'anu answered matter of fact, "He is dead by now".

"What!?"

"He tried to grab the chief's daughter and that is a taboo. Even though the chiefs are male, heredity goes through the females. Only the son of a chief's eldest daughter can become the next chief regardless of who the father is. "Consequently, the chief's daughter is the only female who selects her own husband but even then only with the approval of her mother and in a roundabout way her 'father' who in fact is her uncle because he is the son of her mother's sister. Only when the mother has no sisters will the brother of the next matriarch become chief.

"That is the custom right through these islands and everybody knows and respects that. The man who attacked Mailiku must have been some upstart who did not respect custom and could have caused an all-out war, a war that none of the islands wants".

"OK, let me get this straight. The chiefly heredity goes through the female line and only a male descendant from that female line can be chief?"

"Correct. On top of that, the women from that line will not marry a male from another chiefly line. Whoever fathers a son or the next matriarch must be a commoner."

"Why is that?"

"Two reasons, the first again is to prevent inbreeding, but the second one you might find interesting. By ensuring that any male chief has a commoner father, the general society feels closer to the chief, after all his father was one of them."

"Is this a matriarchal society or a patriarchal one?"

"It used to be matriarchal and I suppose it still is. The person held in the highest esteem is still the chief's mother and let me tell you that she yields the most power in any matter affecting the community except for war, then the chief takes over but his mother directs him from behind."

"So, Mailiku's father, the chief, is in fact the son of her grandmother and a commoner. Then that same lady, her grandmother, gave birth to a daughter, not necessarily from the same father, which is Mailiku's mother. Now, Mailiku's mother gave birth to Mailiku and her brother. The brother automatically becomes the next chief ahead of Mailiku's son. Right? So that means that Mailiku must marry a commoner to produce a son to become the next chief after her brother."

"Yes that is right."

A week later, a large number of canoes approached the village. Kal saw them coming and wondered what the occasion was. He drew A'anu's attention to them and asked what was what. With a happy laugh A'anu explained that it were the same people who had staged the bride raid and who now came back to show there were no hard feelings and that the women they took had been feasted and were quite happy in their new role.

As a consequence a number of pigs lost their life that day, the underground ovens were stoked up, kava flowed freely and the somewhat melancholy music of the islands could be heard everywhere.

The young brides happily showed off their new husbands to family and relatives. Those that were not happy with the happenings of the previous week did not come to the feast and had been kept in their husband's village for attitude adjustment.

Kal could not remember when last he was in such close contact with the life force of a community.

On the surface, it appeared that the islanders had an unencumbered life and that they could do whatever and whenever they wanted to do it. His enforced close contact with the people on Balon Island revealed that beneath the surface the islanders lived by a well-structured code of conduct much of which was not immediately apparent. Their willingness to live by that code further enhanced the image of a carefree existence.

Kal remembered an occasion, while still in the Core, when he travelled a long distance by car. He had been driving all day along isolated cross-country roads where the only other people he saw were a few travellers going in the opposite direction.

His journey was urgent so he drove through the night. After hours of driving with as his only companion a half moon and the dashboard lights, he finally came to a tiny township. There was nobody about and a few streetlights only increased the image of loneliness of the place. He was thinking at the time how picturesque the place would be in daylight.

As he drove along its thoroughfare, passing houses where an occasional forgotten porch light threw a small cone of light in the darkness, he wondered how much happiness, sorrow, and secrets lay hidden from the traveller, the outsider, within the dark embrace of the houses along the street.

He did feel like an alien visiting a planet of secrets and that the only secure place was the car, his private world. He compared that experience with how he sometimes felt in the village where his boat was being built.

Although at times he felt lonely and cut-off he realised that was not due to the attitude of the people around him but due to the fact that he did not speak the same language. He realised that the sense of isolation he felt on the road trip in the Core was not present here among the people of the Dimension or at least he did not experience it among the Balon Islanders.

One morning on his daily run down the beach towards the headland, Kal saw a lump of coral float above the beach moving about erratically. He suspected that a Daytime Wraith was attached to the coral and sure enough, when he came closer he saw the same two hands as before. "Hi Abdullah, what are you doing here?"

"Looking for you, can you come to the resort? There is somebody I want you to meet." After a slight pause the voice continued, *"Please don't bring the girl friend this time."*

"I didn't bring her the last time; she risked life and limb in order to protect me from your lot. She nearly drowned on the way back."

"Oh! I hope she is all right?" There was real concern in Abdullah's voice.

"Of course she is. I was there wasn't I? So why don't you want me to bring her?"

Abdullah's stone wiggled as though he wanted to scratch his head but was not game to let go of his anchor.

Finally, he said, *"Her appearance so close to the colony created quite a stir. The male population could not stop drooling over her while the female population could not hide their jealousies. It was quite tense there for a while. Some couples still have not buried the hatchet!"*

Kal laughed and began to sing, "The girl can't help it; the girl can't help it!"

"Yeah you can laugh. How would you like it if the younger ones of our male Shimmerers would start touching up girls in the village?"

Kal could see the comical side of it and chuckled, "Your boys would lose their rocks in more ways than one."

"Ha, ha! You forget that our esteemed guests think they are the cream of society and that therefore their slightest wish is my command! Telling them that it would be too expensive to organise does no hold water either. Their promise is that one day, after I have fixed whatever caused them to become Shimmerers, they will be able to access their bank accounts and pay for whatever they demand at present on credit."

"OK, so what do they want?"

"Hula-hula parties with extended entertainment, what else?"

"Oh I'm sure some of the older ladies in the village might be interested; do you want me to ask them?"

"You do and I'll drop this block of coral on your head!"

Suddenly a bit more serious, Kal remarked, "I noticed that you now call yourselves 'Shimmerers' was that your doing or voted for in council?"

"No, Tjitjira is calling us that."

"Tjitjira! Is he here?" Kal shouted excitedly.

Somewhat surprised Abdullah asked, *"Do you know him then?"*

Still excited Kal replied, "Do I know him? He is the one who helped me to get into this Dimension and he... oh never mind. Is he the one you want me to meet?"

"He asked for you, yes, but he has someone else with him."

"Who?"

"I'm not telling you, Tjitjira wants it to be a surprise. Just go back to the village and tell the girl friend to stay put and that you are going to visit Shimmerville and that you will be perfectly safe so that there is no need for her to form a posse of nubile young women to come to the rescue."

After a pause, Kal asked in a quiet voice, "Did he bring Serah?"

There was compassion in Abdullah's voice when he replied, "No Kal, I don't think even Tjitjira has the power to do that. Just warn the village that you are going for a visit and come over as soon as you can."

"OK Abdullah, I'll be round next low tide. You better go back now before you get caught on this side."

CHAPTER 10

THE 'VROUWE IRENE' TO GO ON A TRADING TRIP

WHEN KAL RETURNED to the village, he went straight to where he knew A'anu would be handing out the boat building jobs for that day. There seemed to be a bit of a dispute happening and Kal wondered what went wrong.

When A'anu came over to where Kal was waiting for him Kal asked, "What was all that about?"

"I think some of the boys been working on the one job for too long. In their lifestyle they are used to do a lot of work but all in small jobs, a day planting here another day fishing or building a house or whatever. None of their tasks take as long to show results as what it is taking for building the boat."

"So what, are they dropping the project?"

"It has not come to that but eventually it may."

"Does the chief know?"

"I doubt it. If he did he would be here reading them the riot act. He made a promise to Dan and you and intends to keep it."

"Good for him but I don't want to be the cause of a rift in the village."

Both were silent and deep in thought. Eventually Kal came up with an idea, "What if we organise a trading trip in the 'Vrouwe Irene'? She is just lying there at anchor so why don't we give them a taste of the inter-island trader's life?"

"That would work, I'm sure."

"You don't sound too happy about it."

"No, no, I think it is a good idea but how are we going to tell them without making the chief loose face?"

"That is simple; we let the chief make the announcement."

"He won't do it."

"And why not?"

"The schooner is still your boat so he can't tell you how to use it."

"Well isn't there something we need more of?"

"Oh we can always use more matting materials for the sails."

"What has the village got that they can use for trade without going short themselves?"

"Tobacco and rice, I think."

"Good, let's go and talk to the chief."

They arrived at the chief's hut while he was having breakfast and there was no way that they could refuse the offered meal of fried fish and taro.

The chief became quite agitated when he heard about the disharmony in the ranks and was all set to give a stiff talk to the rebels. At first the dialogue was between the chief and A'anu and it was quite clear that the chief saw the whole plan as giving in to a few troublemakers. Kal had a feeling that the conversation was not going in the right direction so he interrupted as gently as he could, "Talk to me A'anu, what is the problem?"

A'anu said something to the chief and the latter gave a short nod. "Like I said, the chief feels he has no right to commandeer your schooner and neither does he feel inclined to bow to the demands of a few impatient youngsters."

"Well tell him that I came to ask to borrow some of his young men to go on this trading trip. We need the sail matting and perhaps some more straight Masi wood? Tell him that as far as he knows everything is fine on the job. To the men you can pretend that you did not want to tell the chief about their grumbling because you know what he would do."

A'anu spoke to the chief and another debate ensued. In the end, the chief smiled and said something softly to A'anu. The latter smiled as well and translated, "The chief reckons that you should have been a chief yourself".

Kal showed him the 'No-no' shaking of hands and smiled at the suggestion. Suddenly the chief's face clouded over as he listened to something Mailiku whispered in his ear. He spoke to A'anu and it was evident from his tone that he was asking him a question and wanted a straight answer. A'anu suddenly looked unhappy and nodded his head. Kal, well aware of the sudden climate change asked, "What's up?"

"It may be nothing but Mailiku pointed out that a brother, or first cousin in your customs, of the man you stopped from attacking her is one of those grumbling and she has heard that he may have it in for you."

"Well, perhaps I should pick a fight with him before we leave?"

"No! Don't even think of that! All his mates and relatives would come to his aid. They would have to through custom ties."

"OK, so who is coming to my aid, should he start something?"

"The chief, me, Mailiku, and her brother."

"What, five against fifty?"

"Yeah something like that."

"So why hasn't he started anything yet?"

"There are too many in the village that he does not know whose side they are on."

"Why is that?"

"Mainly because his cousin broke a taboo."

"OK, well I may just have the answer to that. Does either of you know Tjitjira?"

A'anu shook his head but the chief said something that did not need translation because to all intents and purposes the tone of his voice and the mention of the name said it all, "What about Tjitjira?"

"The chief knows him does he?"

A'anu asked the question and translated the reply, "He does not know him, but he knows of him."

"OK, well Tjitjira wants me to come to the village of the floating stones where he wants me to meet someone."

"Who?"

"I don't know all I can think of is that somebody I know has become a Wraith or a Floating Stone. I have to go and find out and if it is someone I know I can take him on this trading trip. That should keep me safe enough."

Through A'anu the chief asked how Kal knew Tjitjira and Kal spent some time on telling them how his boat with only Serah on board had been transferred from the Core into the Dimension and how he had kept vigil near the spot where it happened until Tjitjira came and warned him that his own transfer into the Dimension was close. He also told them about the time Serah was attacked by her ex-boyfriend and how she nearly died of infection and that Tjitjira had come to safe her.

"Well, you should go and see him but take someone with you."

"That is fine by me but I'm not taking Mailiku." He looked at her crestfallen face, smiled and said, "I was warned not to".

"Why?"

With a big smile on his face Kal said, "She is too beautiful, her last visit caused all kind of strive, men going gaga over her, women becoming so jealous of their husbands that they wanted to kill them. You name it; she started a riot that still has not settled down and they only saw her from a distance. Can you imagine what would happen if she came close to some of those old codgers?"

After A'anu translated, and perhaps embellished some parts, Mailiku blushed and smiled prettily and Kal had to admit to himself that she was all kinds of gorgeous. The chief a hummed a bit but then to bring the serious business back on the table he asked if Kal needed an escort. Kal told him there was no need and suggested that while he was away the chief should announce the trading trip.

CHAPTER 11

REUNION

L OW TIDE WAS in the middle of the afternoon and Kal knew that
he would have to spend the night in Shimmerville until the low
tide on the next day.

Mailiku insisted on escorting Kal as far as the headland where she
nearly drowned. Uvula, her brother, came along because he wanted to see
Shimmerville. When he found out they would have to stay overnight, he
became less keen. So when Kal suggested that he escort Mailiku back to
the village just in case 'Ugly's cousin, Domo, was planning a kidnap, he
was not hard to convince that his duties lay in that direction.

After seeing the pair off, Kal negotiated the narrow strip of sand at
the foot of the cliff face. Again, the view of the wide and nearly dry river
mouth, its meandering gutters and the orangey tinted sand in its wide
bed captivated him. Shimmerville itself shimmered in the afternoon sun.

Kal was half expecting Abdullah to be waiting for him but when that
was not the case he decided to make his way towards the mysterious yet
non-scary mirage that once was a resort for the rich. As he came closer
he noticed a big, black, scruffy looking dog sitting about doing nothing.

By this time Kal could see a number of floating stones hovering about the dog and he wondered if the locals had cornered the unfortunate beast. He was about to go to the dog's rescue when he heard the now familiar voice of Abdullah, *"Ah, there you are, we were not expecting you until later. Come and meet some old friends of yours."*

"What are you lot doing to that poor dog?"

"Not a thing. Come."

Still suspicious Kal followed Abdullah's floating block of coral, a pink one on this occasion. As they approached the dog, there were several Shimmers near the animal and one began to solidify. Kal was not surprised when Tjitjira appeared; after all, he knew the elder would be there. The old spirit elder had a big smile on his face as he greeted Kal with, "So we meet again. One of the reasons for me to be here is to tell you that Serah is happy to be with her ancestors and wants you to be happy as well. The other reason comes with the dog."

He turned towards the dog and said, "Say something".

Suddenly a familiar voice sounded in Kal's head, *"Hi Kal! How are you doing? You lost a fair bit of weight. God it is good to see you again!"*

Kal frowned deeply as he turned to Tjitjira, "I know that sounds like Harry's voice but how come that dog acts as though he knows me?"

"It's not the dog talking, her name is Brutus, and she is now part and parcel of Harry Knott."

"Harry? Harry a Shimmerer now? How come?"

Tjitjira turned towards the shimmer near Brutus and said, "You tell him Harry." And with that, Tjitjira vanished.

Harry's voice sounded in Kal's head, *"Let's find a place where you can sit down and I will tell you all about it".*

As they moved towards some big rocks Kal asked, "Who decides where you go? The dog or you."

"That's a combined committee decision with me being the chairman but not always with the deciding vote."

Kal grinned; Harry had not lost his sense of humour.

Just then, Brutus' head and mane shook as though being ruffled by an invisible hand.

Soon after, they found a spot in the shade of a breadfruit tree. Harry told Kal the whole story from the time when Kal had made the transfer to when Tjitjira had sent Brutus to keep him alive as a Wraith, then how he had suggested that Harry would find the lot of a Shimmerer more bearable and rewarding, and how Brutus had become his anchor. In return, Kal brought Harry up to date with what was happening in his life.

Because there was no need for the Shimmerers to eat, there was no food available for Kal; on top of that, Shimmerers did not sleep in the normal sense where one lays down on a bed so Kal struck out there as well. Most of the night was therefore spent with talking.

CHAPTER 12

THE CYCLONE

KAL STOOD ON the beach and looked up at the lead grey sky. There was not much wind and the atmosphere was oppressive, it was as if the sea, the island, and even the people were waiting for something to happen.

Down the beach he could see Brutus aimlessly wandering about and Kal whistled. Brutus pricked up one ear and when she saw Kal, came bounding towards him. Kal knew that Harry would be cursing the dog because when Brutus was running Harry was dragged along like a loose lead. Sure enough, when Brutus came to a skidding halt in front of Kal, Harry let both of them have it, *"You bloody mutt! Why can't you walk normally! You drag me along like I'm nothing more than... than a... a bit of rope or something! And you Kal! You know what happens when you call her."*

"So how do you want me to attract your attention? Just wave? As soon as Brutus spots me she'll come running. You know I have that effect on her."

"Yeah, yeah! Anyway what is so all fired urgent?"

"Oh, we are testy this morning! Is Brutus in the same kind of funky mood? Do you think a game of 'fetch' would cheer her up?" Kal teased.

"Sorry, I'm worried about the weather. Do you think we might get a cyclone?"

After a moment thought Kal replied, "That seems to be a distinct possibility. How would Shimmerville handle something like that and, what about the Shimmerers themselves?"

"There are a number of caves not far from the resort and Abdullah told me they will shelter there. As for the resort itself the wind cannot get enough of a grip on the shimmering to destroy it."

"So? What are you doing here?"

"Well, actually, Abdullah sent me to tell you that the people of the village are more than welcome to come and shelter in the caves as well."

"OK, I'll tell them but they may have their own methods of wintering a cyclone."

"What will you do?" Harry asked and after a moment's contemplation Kal answered, "I've been thinking that I should take the 'Vrouwe Irene' out of the lagoon and into deeper water. That is if I can scrape a crew together."

"Well you can count me in even though I realise I won't be much good to you in my present condition."

"OK, well let's go and talk to the chief."

Although Harry had become semi-accepted by the village, mainly due to the efforts of Brutus, kids would still follow them and adults would still shy away. Kal and Harry went to find A'anu so he could translate Abdullah's message for the chief.

They found him at the building site where Kal's junk was starting to take shape. He was busily supervising the tying down of the half-completed junk. It was plain to see that he expected a cyclone.

When Kal conveyed the Shimmerville offer, he shook his head and said, "Thank you for the offer but we have our own cave. The villagers are already preparing to go and you are welcome to come with us."

Kal told him, "Thanks but I think there is a need to take the 'Vrouwe Irene' out into deeper water but for that we need a crew of eight men. Can you ask those you think would be good for the job?"

"OK, let me get the ball rolling and then we better go and tell the chief what we're doing."

Half an hour later they sat in the chief's house and A'anu spoke on their behalf. The chief confirmed that they had their own cyclone shelter and he agreed with the need to take the 'Vrouwe Irene' into deeper water.

They did not spend all that much time inside the chief's house but when they came out things had changed.

The winds were increasing and white caps were now crowning most of the waves inside the lagoon. The waves outside the lagoon had grown into rolling mountains of water that exploded and boomed on the reef. Huge plumes of spray and foam would shoot up into the air only to be torn away by the gale force wind. The whole sky was a roiling mass of green-black clouds that appeared to touch the tops of the coconut palms near the beach. Palm leaves as well as coconuts had become missiles that streaked through the air on a near horizontal trajectory.

Grim-faced, Kal and Harry—presumably grim-faced as well—made their way to the foreshore where they found A'anu, nine young men and Mailiku. Kal thought it nice of the girl that she had come down to see them off but was not impressed when informed that Mailiku was coming on the trip. When A'anu told him this Kal objected and said to tell her she could not come.

A'anu with a horrified look on his face said, "I can't tell the next mother of our people that she cannot do this. That should have been decided between you two in private!"

Mailiku pretended she was not aware of the discussion but Kal could see her look in their direction every now and then from under her eye lashes. He did not want her to lose face in front of her people and rather exasperated he asked A'anu, "What does she want to go and risk her fool's neck for?"

"To find out why you are risking your neck."

"Ah! You can be just as frustrating as she is so let's stop wasting time. Does her father know?"

"Oh yes."

"So why didn't he stop her?"

"Two reasons, firstly, until she is married only her mother can forbid her to do things, this has to do with what I told you about the matriarchal descendant thing, and secondly she is as capable as some of the best sailors among her people."

"Yeah, but she can still drown like anybody else!"

A'anu did not reply and they all boarded the canoe that would take them to the 'Vrouwe Irene'.

Once on board there was no more time to worry about what was right or what was wrong, the schooner was bucking on the waves and tearing at her anchor. Kal had the distinct impression that she was dragging her anchor.

The ever-increasing wind screamed along on a course parallel to the reef. This meant that the schooner would have the wind coming in over the port beam as she went through the channel. In a way that was good because all sails would draw but it did require the 'Vrouwe Irene' to sail as high as possible to counter act the sideways drift.

They hoisted the mizzen sail with all three reefs tied and a storm staysail. Under this heavily reduced canvas the 'Vrouwe Irene' set off well to windward of the passage through the reef.

Kal was at the helm as none of the others wanted to take the responsibility of getting the ship safely through the passage. He felt extremely vulnerable because he did not see the 'Vrouwe Irene' as his. In his mind he already had made her the village's property and he knew how much the schooner would mean to the village. Suddenly Mailiku stood next to him and she laid her hand on one of his. With the other hand she pointed straight ahead and warned, "Coral head. Go there."

She indicated the new course Kal should steer and five minutes later he could see the waves breaking on the coral head just to leeward of them. By that time they reached the passage through the reef.

Huge ocean swells covered in smaller waves pounded on the reef throwing water and spume everywhere. Through gestures, Mailiku told Kal to sail much further to windward of the passage then what he wanted. Nevertheless, he put his trust in her and headed straight for the cauldron that was the reef. Then right on the last minute a sideways current threw the 'Vrouwe Irene' on a heading that took her clear into the passage.

As soon as the schooner started bucking into the head seas a couple of the younger men under the command of Mailiku shook out one reef of the mizzen sail and the 'Vrouwe Irene' gained speed rapidly. For an hour the schooner stormed along with her lee deck under water until they were in deep water where the waves were huge and marble-streaked by foam but with nothing to run into for some thousand miles. They dropped the mizzen sail all together and set a larger storm jib. Under this triangle of sail they ran off before the wind.

Conditions improved slightly, the lee deck was no longer submerged, and the schooner's movements smoothed out a bit because she was now running with the waves. After a while, they had to set another foresail to gain more speed because the waves were still overtaking the 'Vrouwe Irene' and she would try to broach every time a wave lifted her stern. Dark clouds raced by at mast-top level and rain and spray hit their bare skins like needles. Waves higher than her tallest mast would sweep up behind her and threatened to swamp the schooner but every time, sometimes with her stern and taffrail submerged, the 'Vrouwe Irene' would shudder and raise her stern on and over the following wave. With terrifying noise the wind screamed and roared to intimidate even the bravest among them. Mailiku hunched on the deck with her arms wrapped around her knees. Her hair was wet but still blew all over the place. Kal tapped her on the shoulder then pointed at the ship's deckhouse but she shook her head and stayed by his side.

For the next twelve hours, the 'Vrouwe Irene' ran before the cyclonic winds. Some gusts were so strong that they would flatten the raging seas and at times like that, it was hard to determine what was water, what was spray, and what was up or what was down. Sometimes it was even hard to determine whether they were on the surface of the water or underneath it.

Twice the 'Vrouwe Irene' was thrown on her beam-ends but both times she recovered without taking in too much water.

All the men had tied themselves to lifelines not that it would have done any good if one was washed overboard. The drag of the body through the water would have been too strong to bring him back on board but it did allow them to stay on their feet by keeping tension on the line.

Brutus with Harry in tow decided their place was in the deckhouse where they might be tossed about a bit but from where they could not be blown away.

When they left the lagoon the wind came from a north-easterly direction but as time went by the winds gradually set through from the east and then south-east. Seeing how cyclones spin in a clockwise direction in the southern hemisphere, Kal knew that the centre lay somewhere to the north or north-west of their position and he kept a weather eye out for any changes from that direction.

On the third day when Kal came on deck he noticed a change in the cloud cover. The wind was still howling at close to one hundred and eighty kilometres per hour but the cloud ceiling seemed to be higher and now there was a sickly, yellowish green light in one area away to the north-west. He headed the schooner towards it because it might well be the centre or the eye of the cyclone.

A couple of hours later they suddenly had blue sky overhead, the wind dropped away to nothing and the waves were flattened although the swell was still there and quite energetic.

Mailiku came out on deck and stood next to him to watch in awe what nature had on display. The 'Vrouwe Irene' had sailed into the eye of the cyclone and the scene was awe-inspiring. Some two hundred meters astern a wall of angry white caps could be seen under a low and broiling mass of dark clouds, the white caps and the clouds appeared to be churning around the edge of the circle of flat water.

The sky above this circle was blue but not the sunny pacific kind of blue; it had a yellowish-brown tinge that gave the blue an unhealthy and slightly threatening quality.

The subdued light of the sun briefly lit up the bedraggled people and their ship but nobody took much delight in that because they knew they would be in for it again as soon as the cyclone centre moved away from their position. There was not enough wind in the eye of the cyclone to allow the 'Vrouwe Irene' to manoeuvre in any direction so they just had to wait. When the centre finally moved away and they were thrown back into the maelstrom it nearly came as a relief. It was far more frightening to watch and contemplate the conditions within the seething waves at the edge of the centre than to actually be in it. While being thrown about by wind and waves no one had much time to consider the 'what ifs' of the situation.

It took another eight hours before the 'Vrouwe Irene' was more or less spat out by the cyclone and all on board were glad to see it move away in a south-easterly direction. Everybody found a comfortable spot and went to sleep while the schooner crabbed sideways as she lay hove-to.

CHAPTER 13

TROUBLE IN PARADISE

WHILE THEY WERE fighting the cyclone, everybody on board the 'Vrouwe Irene' had done their bid, including Domo, the cousin of 'Ugly'. Now that the emergency was over and everybody looked for a spot to get some sleep, Kal noticed that Domo and four others did not seek shelter in the deckhouse but congregated on the foredeck. Kal found himself a spot near the steering binnacle on the aft deck so he would be at hand should a rudder adjustment become necessary.

He had been asleep for a number of hours when a sixth sense woke him. He maintained his steady breathing and did not move but slowly opened an eye to see what woke him. There, no more than three feet away, stood Domo. With his right hand raised, he held his short sword ready to strike Kal.

Kal's combat training took over and he rolled onto his stomach then catapulted himself up right. Just as he did so Domo swept his short sword down but because Kal had moved only the tip of the sword carved through the skin on the back of Kal's head. Before Domo could recover from the downward sweep of his right arm and body, Kal grabbed the man's sword arm and jerked it down. As he did so, he himself stood up and the top of his head smashed into Domo's face.

The move did nothing to improve the attacker's looks and his blood streaming from a smashed nose freely mingled with Kal's blood.

As Domo staggered upright Kal jabbed a straight fingered punch at the man's Adams apple while he snarled, "Just because our blood has mixed does not mean we are now blood-brothers!"

Domo once more bent forward clutching his throat, so, as he went past Kal rabbit punched him and Domo went bye-de-byes.

Kal well and truly in combat mode, had memory flashes of his time of imprisonment when torture had given him most of the scars on his body. When in that frame of mind he was dangerous and could not be relied on to show mercy. When Domo made a feeble attempt to get to his feet, Kal knelt down, slipped his right knee under the unfortunate's throat, and then came down hard with his right elbow on the back of Domo's neck. Domo slipped back to the deck not quite dead but anyhow no longer interested in the proceedings.

Grabbing Domo's short sword Kal advanced in a crouch on the other four young men while he roared, "WHICH OF YOU GIRLS IS NEXT!"

Three dropped their weapons and backed into the others who had emerged from the deckhouse behind them to see what all the shouting was about. The fourth stood his ground although he may have been too scared to move. Whatever it was that made him stand there while he wet himself is a moot point because when Kal jabbed him with Domo's sword just enough to draw some blood he dropped his own sword.

With Domo's sword in his left hand, Kal flicked up the dropped sword and caught it in his right hand. Pumped up on adrenaline and testosterone, Kal's muscles bulged with a short sword in each hand.

Suddenly everything that had happened to him, the death of Serah, the loss of his junk the 'Stella Maris', and everything else came to a head. He wanted nothing more than for someone; anyone, to make an aggressive move and all hell would break loose. Yet, even in his present state Kal would not attack an unarmed man.

Out of nowhere, Mailiku appeared by his side and tentatively placed a shaky hand on his arm. In the blink of an eye he drew his other arm back and launched a short sword at the schooner's mizzen mast. The weapon twanged when it embedded itself in the wood of the mast and then snapped off flush with the wood. Still angry he shouted, "Now any time you think you would like to have a go at me, look at that, and imagine that it could be your skull instead of the mast."

Without another word, Kal brushed past the men and went into the deckhouse. As he threw himself on one of the bunks, he told A'anu, "Stuff the trading mission. Let's go and see what is left of the village."

Later A'anu told Kal that when he came on deck all the young men, except for Domo who was still 'indisposed', were crowded around the mizzenmast. They compared the broken short sword with another and so determined that the section embedded in the mast was some three inches long. When A'anu translated what Kal had shouted just before he went below, the anonymous verdict was that none of them would give it a go.

None, except A'anu and Mailiku dared to enter the deckhouse. When Mailiku came in she silently went about looking for the things she needed to treat the cut on Kal's head. As she was about to start Kal turned to her and took one of her hands and said slowly, "Thank you for stopping me out there".

She may not have been able to understand all of the words but she could see their meaning in his eyes. She smiled and went to work on his injury.

A few minutes later Brutus with Harry in tow came aft from the forward cabin. Harry's voice sounded in Kal's mind, "*What was that ruckus about? I nearly sent out Brutus to give you a hand but she said, (big sigh) 'Nah, he can handle it!' Well, did you?*"

"Of course I did but you could have been out there to direct traffic, after all, that was what you were trained for at the police academy."

They both laughed and the tension was broken.

By next morning, the sea was calm and only a large swell was there to remind them of the cyclone.

The sky was a blue dome reaching down to the horizon in every direction with not even the suggestion of a cloud anywhere. Kal and Brutus, with the Shimmerer Harry attached, stood at the taff rail while Mailiku was giving directions to A'anu for a course change.

Once the 'Vrouwe Irene' had settled on the new course Kal asked A'anu why she was giving him directions, A'anu replied that the girl was one of the navigators taught by the master navigator of their people. He said that she was one of the best and could read the waves, the sea, the clouds any many other signs unrecognisable by most other people. A'anu said something to Mailiku who then went and looked at the sea to windward. A couple of minutes later she came back and spoke to A'anu. "Mailiku says that we will see the island tomorrow when the sun is at its highest point and the island will be just of the starboard bow."

She was right.

Before they got to the island there was yet another confrontation but of a different kind.

Domo, supported by his four henchmen shuffled from the fo'c's'le where he had been in hiding since the mutiny and approached Kal. Brutus, always on guard (of course), growled and flashed her pearly whites while her hackles gave a fair imitation of a scrubbing brush. The whole display lacked somewhat in sincerity because Brutus never got up off her fat tail.

The delegation stopped at a safe distance and Domo began to speak in a croaky whisper. Mailiku went over and relieved A'anu at the wheel so the latter could be interpreter. Frowning and with a stern voice Kal asked, "What does he want?"

A'anu translated for both. Domo offered his apologies but Kal was not letting him get away that easy, "Your act was mutiny and where I come from that is punishable by death. You knew that this vessel will become the property of your people so why try to take it by force?"

Even A'anu looked shocked but he translated both Kal's words and Domo's answer, "I did not want to seize the ship! I wanted to avenge my cousin."

"The one who not only broke a taboo but also molested and injured Mailiku, the next matriarch of the Balon people? Don't you abide by the rules of your people?"

"Yes I do!"

"So did you attack me because you wanted to kill *him* but I beat you to it? And if you had killed me wouldn't that be mutiny?"

Harry's voice sounded in Kal's head, *"You're confusing the poor lad."*

Kal continued, "'Ugly' had it coming but if you feel that he was treated unfairly and that the breaking of a taboo is insignificant we can always have another go but this time on land so that there is no possibility of confusion over the issue at hand, but, I promise you, you would still finish up dead."

"No! You will have no more trouble from me."

"Yes, well, I do not want to see you for the rest of this trip and we will let the chief deal with you when we get home."

"Why must the chief know?" Domo asked with a fear-filled hoarse whisper. *Obviously, his voice box was still dented.*

"Why must the chief know? Of course he has to be told! You tried to kill me while I am one of his guests!"

"But… it did not happen in the village… and you punished me already."

"No. I did not punish you; I only stopped you from killing me. If I wanted to punish you, you would be dead!"

Domo said not another word and shuffled back towards the fo'c's'le. A heavy mood settled on the rest of the people on board because all knew that in all probability the chief would hand out a severe and painful punishment.

During the night they sailed through a small group of atolls and the next morning they found Domo missing, presumably he had slipped over the side during the night and was now the only man on the island. Kal wanted to go back for him but after consultation with Mailiku, A'anu told him not to bother because Domo had banished himself from his people before her father would have ordered the same measure but only after a good trashing.

As predicted by Mailiku, Balon Island appeared over the horizon just before midday and everybody became anxious to see how the village had weathered the cyclone.

As the 'Vrouwe Irene' approached the passage through the reef, it already became evident that the full force of the cyclone had hit the island. Row upon row of coconut palms had their crowns ripped off by the wind and their trunks stood there like so many toothpicks. Most of the thatch and bamboo houses in the village were blown away or lay in shambles. The torrential rains had washed away whole sections of the hill behind the village and deep run-off channels scoured the beach. As soon as the schooner was at anchor half of the men on board jumped over board and struck out for the shore to find out how their wives and kids or elderly parents had come through the ordeal.

Even while he saw to the 'Vrouwe Irene', Kal could not see any sign of his half-completed junk and he had a bad feeling about it when he finally swam to the beach. A'anu was waiting for him and from his body language Kal could tell that the news was not good.

"The ground underneath the supports on one side became soft from the rain, the supports gave way and the wind did the rest."

Together they followed the trail of broken parts for half a mile down the beach. In the end Kal put his hand on A'anu's arm, "There is nothing we can do about it now, let's go back to the village and see what has to be done there before we worry about the junk. Ok?"

A'anu numbly nodded his head and they went back to the village.

Within a fortnight the village was rebuilt.

Each morning the chief called together every able bodied men and women, he would listen to the progress reports from clan leaders as well as selected family heads. After that he would prioritise the needs of the village and ask for volunteers for the different tasks, some would go fishing while others would tend to the food gardens while the rest would be set to building houses. Although never asked, Kal attached himself to whatever group was building the bamboo and thatch houses. The cyclone did track outside the reef on a course parallel to the island and so only the outer edge of the destructive zone hit the village. Still to get palm leaves for thatch and bamboo for walls and supports the people had to go inland for about two miles.

Much to Harry's chagrin Kal always went with the group that went for the bamboo and palm leaves. The problem was that Brutus followed Kal; *it was much more fun to run through the scrub, wade into water holes or to go wherever her nose ordered her to go.* Harry on those occasions complained bitterly about being dragged along by Brutus. Kal had no sympathy for him because in his opinion Harry could disengage himself from Brutus and hang on to the nearest tree while the others did all the hard work of cutting down bamboo and palm leaves. Harry was not having any of that after he tried it once and Brutus forgot to collect him when the work party went home. On that occasion Kal had returned to the village early with a load of bamboo, Brutus followed him, and both forgot all about Harry. When called to task over the matter, Brutus tipped her head sideways with her one standing ear upper most and looked at Kal as though to say, *"Well, you could have reminded me!"*

CHAPTER 14

SHIMMERVILLE

ONCE THE IMMEDIATE rush was over and most villagers had a roof over their heads, Kal began to wonder how Shimmerville had come through the cyclone so he and Harry decided to go and have a look. This time Kal made sure he took some food with him. Mailiku was not too happy about the proposed visit but she could not stop Kal. Through A'anu, he told her to stay home. Some mysterious 'family emergency' forced A'anu to decline the offer to accompany Kal and Harry.

After they had been walking towards the headland for some time, Kal suddenly asked, "How are you coping Harry?"

"This being a Shimmerer sucks and Brutus has a doggy smell!"

"Ok, we'll give her a salt-water bath when we get to the headland and a freshwater rinse when we get to Shimmerville."

Brutus' reaction, *"Like hell you will!"*

"No, seriously, Harry. You did not get much of an introduction to this dimension. Would you rather be back in the Core?"

"Well I seriously hope that this shimmer thing is only temporary and I also would like to have the choice concerning staying or going back. What about you?"

"While Serah was alive I had no intention of ever going back, but now, I don't know."

"I would have thought that this dimension is right up your ally."

"Yes in a way it is, but, living in my present rural setting among people has opened my eyes to some of the advantages we had in the Core."

"Such as?"

"Well here there is the higher mortality rate among the very young and also the fact that here a person of fifty years is considered ancient."

"To us that might seem pretty awful but don't forget that we base our judgement on what we are used to. In this society babies are not even given a name until they have survived the first year of their life, by that time they have developed enough immunity to stand a fair chance of surviving..."

"What do you mean?"

"Well for one thing, the parents believe that by not naming the baby, evil spirits—the ones that bring sickness—cannot identify the child, so it is a sort of protection. A more important aspect of this not naming custom is that both parents are less attached to the baby than if it was identifiable by a name. They believe that an unnamed child does not have as yet a soul while a name identifies the child's soul."

Kal shook his head slowly and said, "Hmm, I don't know."

Harry saw that his friend had to give the matter some more thought in his own time so he went on to further explain the second part of Kal's original statement, "You mentioned that here people over forty are old and those over fifty are considered ancient. Is that so bad? Again, people here are conditioned into expecting the older generation to swing away about the forty to fifty mark. In the Core we expect people to pass on around seventy or eighty. Are we shocked when somebody does not reach the age of say ninety? We may be shocked when a friend or family member cashes in their chips at forty but not at eighty-five, it was such-and-so's time to go."

They moved on in silence for a while until Kal voiced another thought, "Do you think people were only meant to live for say fifty years?"

"Personally I think that is a distinct possibility."

"What makes you say that?"

"Well look at it, all the serious illnesses in our society such as heart problems, high blood pressure, liver disease, kidney failure, diabetes, Parkinson's and... and... Ah! What's it called?"

"You mean Alzheimer's?"

"Yeah, all 'old men's' complaints usually not evident until after age forty."

"So you reckon it is ok for them to die at forty, forty-five?"

"Yes, that is what the people here are used to besides that it prevents a lot of suffering."

"So you reckon that should be happening in the Core as well; do away with all health care etcetera? What? As a means of population control and saving of the tax-payers' money as well, perhaps?"

"You are being facetious now. We cannot turn the clock back in the Core but at the same time we do not have the right to influence the natural progression of life in this Dimension."

While they talked, Brutus steadily led them away from the beach and eventually they found themselves about halfway between the surf and the high water line but facing the steep side of the headland.

Somewhat exasperated Harry said, "You dumb dog! Now we got to follow the headland back to the beach and we will miss the tide!"

Brutus ignored Harry's complaining and with new purpose dragged him further towards the rocky barrier in front of them. Kal always enjoyed the utter disregard Brutus showed for Harry's mutterings but even he felt Brutus had failed on this occasion. Not so Brutus. Moreover, with a complete disregard for the opinions of either of them, she dragged

Harry towards the sheer rock face. Just as Kal was about to assert his 'better' understanding of the circumstances and order Brutus to change course towards the beach, he spotted what looked like a track meandering through the rocks and up the side of the steep incline. The wily dog had known it was there all along. Even Harry was impressed but at once began telling Brutus that no way was she going to drag him up that narrow and steep goat track. Brutus treated the haranguing with the contempt she felt for it and began the climb.

Half an hour later they topped the escarpment, all three were puffing and Kal had to remark, "Harry I don't know why you are puffing, you got your private tugboat and you seemed to be floating in her wake without too much walking."

Brutus turned to Harry and with her head tipped sideways and her tongue lolling out of the side of her mouth she gave Harry the third degree, "*That better not be true Sunshine!*"

In complete denial, Harry muttered something about getting even with both of them and then changed the subject, "*I suppose there is a way down, or do we fly from here?*"

Kal looked questioning at Brutus who thought it was high time she sat down for a good scratch behind the left ear. Eventually she got up and led the way across the spine of the headland so they could look down the other side. Both Kal and Harry were in for a surprise. The last time they had seen the river it had been a wide sand expanse with some small channels carrying a small quantity of clear water to the sea. Now it was a turbulent stream of muddy water transporting trees and branches from the mountains to the sea. In many places water rushing over submerged rocks set up foam-crested waves that appeared to be trying to roll upstream but could get no further than where they were.

As soon as Kal looked in the direction of the resort, he knew there was trouble. Of the shimmering squares that indicated buildings only two small ones, one blue the other orange remained. Neither could he see any floating rocks.

They followed the headland towards the place where the resort had been hoping to find some survivors or a way to get across the raging river. It did not look very promising. As they came closer, Kal became aware of a sense reminiscent of someone moaning. He asked Harry, "Do you hear that?"

"Hear what?"

"It is not exactly a sound alone, more a sound and a feeling supporting each other. Together they convey a strong feeling of sadness and loss."

After they had gone a little further, Brutus suddenly sat down, threw her head back, and led out a long drawn out mournful howl. Harry said, "I understood that one!"

Not long after Kal heard the heart-broken voice of Abdullah, the maître de of the resort, in his head, "They're all gone! The hurricane took them all. I am the only one left."

Now fully aware of Abdullah's presence, Kal asked, "We can hear you Abdullah but where are you? I can't see your pink rock."

"I have sought shelter between the two rocks to your left."

"They are massive! You could not even lift one of them leave alone both!"

"I know but all the others were taken by the cyclonic winds and I only just made it here in time. Now my greatest fear is that I will blow out to sea and drown!"

Harry not always the most sensitive in those matters grumbled, "Stay there and you soon will have a tree growing through you!"

Somewhat peeved Abdullah came back with, "You can talk! You have Brutus to care for you!"

"Brutus care for me? Ha! It's more the other way round!"

Kal laughed and cut in, "Now, now girls that's enough. I'm sure Brutus can take care of both of you, hey Brutus?"

Brutus gave Kal a lopsided look and spoke, "Wuf?"

"What does 'woof' mean?"

"Not 'woof', 'WUF' and that means, 'What? That pair of moaners. I'll show you whom looks after whom! Hang on boys!"

Harry for all his big talk must already have grabbed Abdullah because in the next instance Brutus was off at full pelt back the hazardous way they had climbed onto the headland. Kal was in stitches as he watched the break-neck speed by which Brutus bounded from one narrow foothold onto the next. Both Harry and Abdullah were screaming and neither was yelling encouragement. To add insult to injury, when they reached the beach, a few seagulls were standing on the edge of the water some distance away. As soon as Brutus spotted them, she was off again. She raced towards them at full speed, the gulls only had just enough time to get airborne and out of reach of the dog who now bounced up and down on the spot.

Someone, either Harry or Abdullah, shouted, *"I'm going to hog tie this dog!"*

Even Brutus was tired now so the rest of the return journey to the village was without incident.

Some days later Kal and Mailiku sat on the beach at night. Harry, Abdullah, and Brutus had moved away from the village as they did every night. As far as the nervous mothers and kids knew, the threesome spent their nights on the 'Vrouwe Irene' where in fact it was too hard for them to get on board, so they just moved out of sight of the village.

By this time Kal and the girl could communicate quite well with a mixture of Malay, learned from A'anu and Kal and the local language learned from Mailiku and A'anu. With her hand on Kal's arm and her head on his shoulder, Mailiku asked Kal what the future held for them.

Kal felt he had to be completely honest with her and told her that he could not see himself living in a village, or any other communal setting. In a rare instance of baring his soul, he told her that people in general made him angry as well as in some ways frightened.

He had suffered too much at the hands of his fellow man and did not trust anybody. It took him a long time to begin to trust someone and when he finally did, unerringly a break-up would follow for which he always felt responsible. He told her that he had very strong feelings for her but, at this stage at least, for him to be happy with her; they would have to sail away.

Mailiku had suspected as much and with tears sliding down her cheeks, she nodded her head. Then she told him that to leave with him was not possible because of her obligations as the next matron of the village once her mother died. They sat for a long time with their arms around each other and each with their own sad thoughts. Was there really no hope?

CHAPTER 15

A STRANGE CARGO

THE TROPICAL HUMIDITY and heat lay over the sluggish flowing river. Near the middle of its brown stream, a large junk dropped her anchor. Usually reaching a destination was somewhat of a celebration but there was no sign of any such atmosphere. The crew looked suspiciously towards the muddy riverbank and the foreboding jungle crowding the banks. Were they were supposed to deliver their cargo at this forsaken place?

The captain of the junk stood on the high poop deck with him stood the man who had contracted the junk to take him and his cargo to this forlorn place.

As they stood there watching the shore something floated against the hull of the junk with a loud boink. The captain shouted to no one in particular, "What is that?"

One of the crew shouted back, "A floating tree. It's a big one too but it is floating free now."

The captain was about to voice his displeasure to his passenger when the latter grabbed his arm and pointed at a number of dugout canoes that came shooting out from behind a high bank in a bend in the river. Two men with long paddles drove each canoe. They were dressed in colourful-feathered headdresses, plaited and fringed arm and ankle bands but nothing else.

With relief showing in his voice the captain turned to his second in command and ordered, "OK, bring them on deck."

Soon after, ten men and eight women climbed out of the ship's hold. They were slaves. With their hands tied behind their backs and a chain connecting the iron bands around their necks they looked a miserable lot. Like everybody else, they wore no clothing but what made them appear naked as opposed to nude, was the fact that none wore any feathered head dress or arm, wrist, or ankle bands.

Among the men, there were two white men and among the women, there was one white one. The three were a father and his two semi-adult children.

It was evident that the middle-aged white man was most indignant at his treatment and he promised that God personally would bring down his wrath on those responsible for his family's ill treatment. Just as well that none of those present understood his language.

A swift smack on the buttocks from a rattan sweep convinced him to walk down the plank and into the waiting canoe together with two other slaves still chained to him.

Besides its crew of two, each canoe transported three slaves still manacled to each other. Because of this arrangement, there were three canoes with three male slaves as cargo and two canoes with three female slaves as cargo. One canoe carried one male and two female slaves. It happened to be the first canoe to head for the shore.

It was not unusual for both crew and passengers to stand in the canoe rather than sit so nobody took any particular notice when the first canoe took off with everybody on board standing.

About halfway to the shore the male slave said something to the two women who both nodded their approval and next thing they put their combined weight on the port gunnel resulting in the canoe capsizing. All three had their hands tied behind their back and the chain connected their slave collars. Without a sound, they disappeared in the muddy water and drowned before the startled eyes of the canoe's crew whose first priority it was to save their up turned craft.

As a result, all the other slaves had to sit down in their canoes.

The agent, or whatever, whose duty it was to procure ten male and eight female slaves went into hysterics and refused to leave the safety of the junk. He knew that his lord and master, the 12th Earl of Brine, would have him killed over this debacle. The remaining canoe crews also hinted to the captain that seeing how he received his payment in advance, it might be a wise plan to depart before the Earl would demand a part refund.

As the last canoe load of slaves slowly climbed the slippery yellow clay slope of the landing, the junk with the erstwhile procurer of slaves still on board quietly slipped out of the river.

After following a narrow and slippery path through the jungle for about an hour, the group of slaves and their minders, arrived at a clearing. Here they waited. The clearing appeared to be a level platform halfway up the side of a mountain.

There was a palisaded enclosure and a small bamboo hut. The male prisoners were locked into the enclosure while the females were herded into the bamboo hut.

CHAPTER 16

THE 12ᵀᴴ EARL OF BRINE

SOMETIME LATER, A strange procession entered the clearing from the opposite direction. Up front, marched two guards festooned with colourful feather headdresses and arm bands, each carried a spear rifle-style on the right shoulder. Behind them came the personage of importance while behind him there were another four guards each with a spear on the right shoulder.

The parade marched up to a raised dirt platform and following a bellowed command from the man in the middle, the cavalcade came to a shuddering halt. The person of interest left the formation and climbed the platform.

Even though he appeared to be of European descend, he wore the feathered headband. The only other item of clothing he wore was a red coat as worn by the British military around the time of the final separation of the Dimension from the Core. In addition, he wore feathered bands just below the knee. In his right hand and raised in front of his face he held a rusty cavalry sword.

When he reached the platform, he turned and with a wave of the hand dismissed the honour guard. He jabbed the point of the sword into the ground, folded his hands, and rested them on the pommel of the sword. In response to another shouted command, the guards dispersed to bring forth the slaves from the enclosure and the hut.

The nine men and six women were a sorry sight, their bodies covered in filth and mud, their eyes sunken and their shoulders slumped from pure exhaustion and loss of spirit.

They lined up—more or less—in front of the earthen dais and the man with the sword began, "I am your lord and master, the 12th Earl of Brine. The soil you tread was claimed by the first Earl of Brine—erstwhile member of His Majesty's Armies in India—. The first Earl of Brine made his claim in the name of His Royal Highness, King George III and therefore you are on English soil and subject to his laws." —*In fact, Herald Brine, the self-styled first Earl of Brine, hailed from the slums of London and had been gang-pressed into the Army and never made it above the rank of private before he deserted. After somehow reaching the Pacific, Brine the castaway and deserter roamed the island as a beachcomber for years. During that time he learned the language and made himself useful as a procurer of slaves. During the two hundred years that followed, nothing much changed except that the Brine dynasty was established. During the first Brine's time, a Portuguese family had to leave the Philippines in a hurry and eventually settled on the same island. Brine married one of the daughters and the rest, as they say, is history. Their son began the Earl of Brine tradition as the Second Earl of Brine. Probably due to the lack of other 'European' families the consecutive Brines first married cousins then sisters and aunts and the 12th Earl of Brine was the fruit of a liaison between a mother and son—.*

After catching his breath, the 12th Earl of Brine bellowed, "You stand here before me accused of unlawful ingress into the King's lands…"

The middle-aged white man interrupted, "I, the Reverend McDougall, demand to know by what authority you enslaved me, a messenger of God? Further, I demand that you return me and mine to our clothing so we may no longer be an affront to the eyes of the Lord our God. Lastly, I bring the word of Our Lord and therefore cannot be denied entry to any heathen land."

For a moment there was total silence, even 'the animals of the field' waited with bated breath but then the Earl exploded, "I AM THE LORD AND MASTER HERE AND IF THERE WERE A GOD HE TOO WOULD GO BY MY RULES!"

Not to be outdone the Rev. McDougall rose to his full height and roared, "YOUR BLASPHEMY WILL NOT GO UNPUNISHED AND MAY THE LORD OUR FATHER SMITE THEE WITH HELL FIRE! YE SPAWN OF SATAN!"

Red faced, drooling from the mouth and with his insanity blazing in his eyes the 12th Earl of Brine shouted, "I be the highest authority here and to prove it to be so, I condemn one of ye to death, make thy choice ye or yer son!"

With his head bowed, the reverend considered the matter but before the impatient Earl could demand an answer, he looked up and shouted, "If ye must, take my daughter she being descendant of Eve the temptress, or, my son but I must continue to bring the Lord's word to the heathens in this land."

In the silence that followed the white youth cried, "DAD!" but his sister remained silent. In a loud pulpit voice, the reverend admonished his son, "We all must make sacrifices to serve the Lord, me more than ye! Ye will shortly bask in the Glory of the Lord while I must continue His Work in the Valley of Tears!"

"Ye know what?" the Earl shouted, "I've changed my mind! I hereby condemn both, ye and yer son!"

He slid his finger across his throat and a moment later, the Right Reverend McDougall and his son had their throats cut by two of the Earl's guards.

With another wave of his hand, the Earl dismissed the prisoners who were then taken back into the enclosure for the men and the hut for the women while four guards carried off the two dead.

A short time later the screams started. The first came from the male enclosure but soon after, screams also came from within the hut of the women. The new slaves were being branded with the Earl's mark, a triangle on the back. Against the background of the screams, the Earl held court and adjudicated over matters brought before him. His judgements seldom were just; they usually were in favour of those that provided him with the greatest kickback.

With the court session completed to his satisfaction, he pulled his sword out of the ground and held it in front of his face. This was the command for the honour guard to form up and to have the prisoners brought out for transportation to his camp proper.

The cavalcade was something to behold. Up front, two guards with their spear on their shoulder goose-stepped their way up the narrow and slippery path, followed by the Earl who used his sword as a walking stick in the steep places. Behind him, in single file and chained together, came the slaves, seven males and six females. Bringing up the rear came the other four guards, they were supposed to be goose-stepping as well, but were slack about it.

The path followed a steep ridge so narrow that two people could not walk side by side. Eventually the procession reached a natural platform about the size of two football fields. An eight feet high palisade surrounded the whole area.

As the caravan approached, the gates swung open and that is when the Earl had a hissy fit. Screaming obscenities, he broke formation and stormed at the gatekeeper. The poor man did not know what was going on but he stood his ground. The Earl got right in his face and yelled, "Who gave ye the order to open yon gate?"

Confused the gatekeeper mumbled, "Nobody but I saw ye coming!"

"What if I be the enemy pretending to be me? Huh!"

By this time, the poor man was laying on his back while one of the guards stood over him with his spear ready to strike if so ordered. The hapless guard mumbled something and the Earl shouted, "What be that?"

"I said that nobody would have the valour to do that, Sire."

The Earl underwent a complete mood change and said with a smile, "Ye be right! Nobody be as audacious as to do that! Still next time ye await my order to open yon gate."

—*The 12th Earl of Brine was like a small child who has been cheated out of doing something he would have enjoyed doing*—.

As the prisoners entered the camp, they saw right in the middle and built on a man-made earthen platform, the Earl's palace. It was a large bamboo and thatch house on stilts. In the shadow underneath the house, women were busy cooking on open fires while children, dogs, and chickens fought each other for the best shadow spots.

A whole village surrounded the common in front of the Earl's abode as well as the mount it stood on.

The prisoners were marched to the platform and made to kneel on the parched earth. After a suitable lapse in time during which the Earl had refreshed himself, he came out on the veranda and gave them a rambling speech in which he told them that they now belonged to him and that their future would end in death should they run away as they could not escape him seeing how his ancestor had claimed the whole island in the name of King George III and he therefore represented the Crown and should he send a request to England for assistance in apprehending runaway slaves, the King himself would send him a warship at least.

He then allocated each male slave to a specific villager for duties in whatever trade that villager involved himself in.

Finally, he got to the women. He ordered the collars removed and the white girl kept aside—she was his for as long as he fancied her—the other women he set loose.

Then the race was on. The five young women ran for their lives while every able bodied man went in pursuit. Behind the men came a string of women hurling abuse at their husbands, they did not want to have another mouth to feed, but for most, the motivation was pure jealousy.

Meanwhile the Earl ordered two of his servants to give the white girl a bath before bringing her inside the house.

The two servant women, slaves themselves, at first were rather rough with the girl but when one saw the tears slowly running down her cheeks she asked in pidgin, "What name belong em ye?"

With her head bowed she answered, "Marigold Jordan McDougall".

The woman nodded her head slowly and said, "Ah! Jordie! Good name. Why ye cry?"

Her green eyes flashed and she shook her mane of dark auburn hair as she snarled, "That man! That Earl Something, killed my brother… and my father!"

While the second woman went to collect some more water from another cistern, the one who spoke before said in a whisper, "Him very bad man, kill many people but him brother of King George! Ye be careful, very careful! Him no good, Jordie"

While she was untangling and washing the girl's hair the woman looked at the branding on Jordie's back. In the next instance, she spat on the burn and with a not too gentle finger rubbed her saliva into the wound. It hurt and Jordie blurted, "Ouch! What did ye do that for?"

"Burn go bad already! Ye wait, Ono bring medicine."

After giving the other woman some terse instructions, the older woman hurried off towards a hut on the other side of the common.

While Ono was gone, Jordie stood there as the other woman poured water over her. It was the first opportunity that the girl had to unwind a little bit.

A wry smile curled her lips; up to some months ago, her life had been one of pious obedience in a cloistered community of a fanatic religious group on the island of Viti Levu. Her father had been part of the power triangle at the top, but felt he should be the leader. When he was told unequivocally that he was dreaming, he decided to start his own commune somewhere in the islands.

They travelled from island to island but nowhere could they find a niche for an evangelist whose brand of enlightenment centred on hell and damnation.

On top of that, wherever they went in the greater community people stared and laughed behind their hands at the chin-to-ankle covering of the heavy black clothing they wore. Then about three weeks ago, a man who had listened attentively to what the Rev. McDougall had to say approached her father with a proposal to take him to a community that sorely needed the guidance McDougall so clearly could provide. He did apologise that the village was situated on one of the more remote islands but that he was in a position to offer them free transportation. Her father of course immediately saw the hand of God in the whole situation and accepted the offer with open arms.

That same night the man took them down to the waterfront where they boarded a large Chinese Junk. Within ten minutes of boarding, a motley bunch set upon them. Their clothes were torn off them, they were fitted with slave collars, and their hands were bound behind their backs.

At first she had been appalled at their nudity but then, for the first time really, did she take note of the fact that most people went about in the nude or nearly so and that nobody actually took much notice. She had drawn more stares when she had worn the outfit her church, through her father, had insisted she wore.

The first time she was out in the rain, she felt so good; the raindrops were clean water that cleansed the skin with freshness, without contamination from being strained through her sweat soaked clothing. The feeling of air flowing past her skin all over and not just her face or hands was another exciting experience plus the absence of the rancid body odour so prevalent among her people who wore the heavy woollen clothing of the homeland. She decided she loved the tropics and would never go back to the cold climate of northern Europa. Cynically she concluded that train of thoughts with, *'I hope I'll live long enough to get away from here to enjoy my life in the tropics.'*

Just then, Ono, the women who went for the medicine for Jordie's burn, returned. She made Jordie kneel on some matting and told the other woman to dry the burn area carefully. After having blown on the wound to dry it further, she produced a wad of mashed green leaves with a pungent smell. The woman squeezed the mash and let the juices drip into the open wounds. The initial contact stung quite severely but then the pain subsided and soon after, Jordie became dizzy. She would have fallen had not Ono supported her limp body. Together with the other woman, they carried the unconscious girl to a partitioned corner under the house.

Moments later the Earl appeared on the veranda and bellowed for Ono, "Where be that white woman?"

"She very sick, cannot climb stairs today!"

"What's wrong with her?"

"Bad spirits go in burn on back, man he no clean burn iron! Now girl sick and cannot come to you!"

"Well, ye damn well fix her quick!"

"Ono give medicine OK but girl may die."

"That is no option! She dies you die! She must produce the heir to my kingdom!"

Under her breath and in her own language Ono whispered, *"Yeah whatever, you moron."* Aloud she asked, "How can next Earl be son of slave girl?"

"Not that it be any of yer business but the boy never need know who his mother were."

Later, when Jordie heard what the Earl told Ono she, involuntarily squeezed the woman's arm. Ono looked at her and whispered, "Of what ye be scared?"

Quietly so the Earl could not hear her Jordie asked, "Ono where're you from?"

The woman said she came from Viti Levu (Fiji) and that was the first time Ono saw the girl smile. Ono slapped her hand over her mouth in pleasant surprise when Jordie told her that she learned the Fijian language while growing up in Levuka and later in the interior of the main island in a village called Nandrau. Her Fijian was not faultless but it was a lot better than Ono's English.

After the Earl had ordered another young woman to his quarters in order to 'satisfy his needs', Ono relaxed a bit and as she tended to Jordie's burns she told Jordie how she had been 'raided' together with three other women and one man. The others had all died through one cause or another and Ono was the only one left. After they had familiarised further with each other, Ono asked, "Why did you squeeze my arm when that man was talking about you being the mother of his son?"

For long moments Jordie's eyes searched Ono's. In the end she looked down at her hands and whispered, "I cannot make babies. If he finds out he will kill me like he did my father and brother."

"Why do you say you cannot have a baby?"

"My father, may his soul rot in hell for all times, saw to that!"

Venom dripped of her words as she spat them out and Ono knew she had to tread wearily. She stroked the girl's head and asked, "Will it help to talk about it?"

Suddenly penned up emotions burst free and with sobs that seemed to come from the bottom of her being Jordie buried her face against Ono's neck and with her arms around the woman's shoulders she started to say things in between the sobs and tears.

At first Ono could make head nor tail of what Jordie was saying but gradually a picture of what the girl had suffered at the hands of her own father began to emerge.

Jordie had been brought up in a fanatically religious enclave somewhere in Viti Levu (Fiji). The Brethren as they called themselves must have thought that their ways were the only ways; even to the extent that their buildings were replicas of their dwellings in a cold northern European country. Even in the tropics they still wore their heavy woollen clothing and except for the hands and the face, it was a sin to expose the skin. As a result their women were kept indoors from an hour before sunset until an hour after sunrise. This may have reduced the risk of Wraith attacks outside the home but did nothing for the attacks by Wraiths who had wafted into the home during the day when windows and doors had been open to attract some circulation. Ono had some second hand knowledge of this sect and could confirm that the group was tolerated by her people but not loved or listened to when they were preaching.

Anyway, gradually a story unfolded that shocked Ono to the core. Apparently two days after Jordie turned twenty her father hopped into bed with her and raped the young woman. The next day he berated her for being a temptress and made her feel that she was guilty of seducing him and that the Lord God would surely punish her for it. Quite cynically Jordie had wondered whether the weekly return to her bed and the scolding the next day by her father had been the Lord's way of punishing her, after all, He works in mysterious ways.

Then one day Jordie became ill with a mysterious malady that she could not recognise, nor could their 'doctor' a staunch member of dear old Dad's flock. Her father suddenly all full of concern went outside the norm and pressurised the local Fijian 'witch doctor' to come and see the sick girl. The woman came and laughed in the Reverend's face when she told him that his little girl was pregnant. Apparently the Reverend's first reaction was to pass it off as a case of 'spontaneous' conception. He was reluctant to accuse his daughter of playing around, for one there was no suitable victim available, and two, it would indicate that the infallible servant of God could not control his own daughter. Therefore after a nasty argument the witchdoctor brewed an herbal concoction that would terminate the pregnancy. She warned the father that the herbs were extremely powerful and that under no circumstances the girl should be given a second dose.

Unbeknown to the witchdoctor, the father palmed one stem of the herb and hid it. As soon as the witchdoctor left he sent one of his minions out to find more of the herb. When he got them he brewed another dose and fed it to his daughter. Within two hours the poor girl was screaming and writhing on the floor of her bedroom with agonising abdominal cramps.

She never had another menstrual period since.

A week later the 'old man' was back in her bed.

"What about your mother Jordie?" Ono asked during a break in Jordie's story.

"I think she knew but was too scared to face him and his temper. Don't forget she was brain washed into believing that all women are an abomination in the Lord's eye."

"Are they?"

"If they are why did He create us in His liking?"

"Is that what you believe?"

"Not any-more! If He is so almighty why does He allow so much misery and pain?"

"Isn't that the Devil's work?"

"If that is so then He either is not almighty or just does not care!"

Ono just held the girl and slowly Jordie regained her composure. Finally she asked, "What is this Earl going to do when he finds out I cannot produce his heir?"

"He would want to kill you but he is not going to find out. Every month when I go into the women's house you go a day before or after me."

"How many kids does he have already?"

"Who knows, every time some young woman in the camp falls pregnant she'll claim it is his. He sleeps with all of them so only the mother knows—perhaps—but she'll claim it to be his in the hope of currying some favours or protection from being put to death for 'loose moral behaviour'."

Some months passed and Jordie slowly adapted to her new life but there still was something depressing her. Then one day Ono sat her down and asked what it was. After some to and fro talk Ono asked, "Is it that you are a slave?"

After a long time of introspection Jordie shook her head slowly and replied, "No, it is not that I *am* one but that I'm *marked* as one."

"Why is that?"

"Nobody can force me to think like a slave, inside I am still my own master even though I got to pay lip service. No, it is that cursed triangle burned into my back, it proclaims to the world that I am a slave. What galls me is that I am marked for life!"

Slowly Ono turned around so Jordie could see the tribal tattoo on the woman's back. With a sudden burst of insight Jordie realised that for the first time she became aware that the tattoo covered the triangle brand burned into Ono's flesh. Before then she had only ever noticed the ink. Ono turned round and smiled, "We can cover your slave mark as well."

"What kind of tattoo could I use, there are no tribal markings among my people."

"We'll think of something. One of the old men here is very good at covering the accursed triangle."

Good to her word Ono introduced Jordie to the old tattooist and he sat down with her and with Ono as an interpreter he started to ask her all kind of questions.

At first Jordie thought he was a bit too nosey but after a while she began to understand that he was taking stock of her inner fears and hopes. Eventually he suggested a bird with its wings spread as though the bird was getting away from it all, not just her current conditions but also those of her childhood. When he showed her a sketch of what he had in mind she immediately fell in love with it.

The application of the design was a slow and painful process but, probably because it took so much effort and caused so much pain, it was far more precious to Jordie than a mere skin decoration. To her it was the symbol of her will to be free of oppression of any kind and it showed in many small but liberating ways. One of her more subtle acts of deviance was that she renamed herself and henceforth would only react to the name given to her by Ono, 'Jordie'.

Another good example is the day she stood in the main room of the Earl's house. He had called for her and there was no doubt in her mind what he wanted. Where before she had meekly done his bidding, after all her father had taught her that, this time she made it different.

She stood in the middle of the room and stretched, fully aware of her firm breasts standing out from her chest. She revelled in the cool breeze caressing her flat stomach and thighs and was aware of the flow of air gently moving her hair over the tattoo on her back. The Earl lay on his couch flat on his back with his hands under his head and looking at her with lust in his eyes, "Come here I want ye and I want ye now!"

"Yes I can see that! That be an erection to be proud of, however ye must wait a while I am not ready yet and ye always complain when I be too dry."

"Well come over and suck on it while ye be waiting!"

Jordie shook her head and said in a no-nonsense tone he had never before heard from her, "I don't suck my thumb and I don't suck yer dick!!"

Before he could complain she impaled herself on him rather violently. The unexpected fierceness he accepted as passion but nevertheless it subdued his libido to the extent he nearly lost the erection. The young woman kept riding him hard until she could feel him coming up again and when he was about halfway to his climax she suddenly withdrew and got off the divan. In agony he cried out, "I be not done yet!"

"Well I be."

And with that she walked out of the house. She expected she would be punished for what she did but she did not care for once she had stood up to the tyrannical demand for sex, first from her father and then from this pompous little turd.

Half an hour later he came down to where she was cooking underneath the house and without any preamble he hit her on the back with a riding crop. She clenched her teeth and even though tears streamed down her cheeks she refused to cry out.

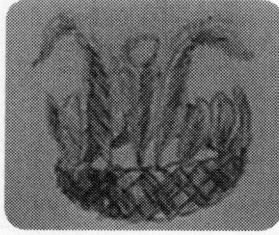

CHAPTER 17

THE RUN FOR LEAD

SEVERAL MONTHS PASSED and life on Balon Island returned to normal after the repair of the cyclone damage. The taro and dalo plantations were bearing crops again and the fishing was good.

A'anu and Kal had marked the trees they needed for the rebuild of the junk. Seeing that they had to start from scratch, Kal decided he wanted to ballast the vessel with a lead keel or lead ingots. To get the lead he would have to make a trip to Antipodia. The trip would take about two to two and a half months.

He would have to sail the 'Vrouwe Irene' north until he could pick up the south equatorial current that runs from east to west just below the equator. A'anu felt sure they could get lead in Malaysia but, at that stage, Kal was planning to get the metal in Antipodia because he did not want to be caught with a fully laden ship in the light wind areas on the equator where they were also likely to encounter pirates from the Maluku Islands.

They would have to come south anyway to pick up the westerlies on the edge of the Roaring Forties, south of Antipodia, to bring them home again.

Once he made his plans known just about every able bodied man volunteered for the trip. He selected the ten best ones amongst them and preparations began to ready the 'Vrouwe Irene' for the trip. Kal was sorry he could not talk A'anu into coming on the journey but the latter felt the start of the rebuild of the junk was more his strong point.

Mailiku wanted to come however both her mother and the chief said no to that one. Her mother was getting old and even though the journey was planned to take two months, one never knew what lay ahead and the voyage could well last much longer. Mailiku was next in line for the Matriarch role should her mother pass away and therefore should not be off somewhere she could not be reached. A tearful Mailiku watched the schooner glide out of the lagoon.

With a crew of ten young and able sailors in the crew, life soon settled into the routine of making miles.

Both Harry and Abdullah spent a lot of time in the deckhouse where the wind could not blow them away. At such times, Brutus would come on deck to spend some quality time with Kal for whom she had developed a strong attachment.

On a number of occasions when his passengers were safely ensconced in the deckhouse, Brutus would come on deck, stand next to Kal and suddenly fade away. The first time it happened Kal worried that the spirit dog had gone back to Tjitjira but after some time Brutus materialised and came bounding up to Kal for a bit of a tussle and a good ruffle behind the ears.

After a couple of weeks of plain sailing the south-east trades weakened and they spent a few days becalmed but thanks to the south equatorial current, they still moved in a westerly direction. In this area it is often a case of making use of whatever wind may accompany localised squalls that never last long except if they are storms and part of the monsoonal trough.

The only discord came the evening before they reached land, Kal decided from his noonday sextant readings and his dead reckoning that they were nearing one of the southernmost islands in the Solomon Island group. They had not seen land yet by the time it became dark but Kal was confident that they would make landfall the next morning.

Just after sunset there was a hellish commotion on the foredeck, men were screaming and an unearthly roaring tried to overpower their screams. Kal rushed forward to see what was happening only to come face to face with a materialising Wraith.

The Wraith was a man with an ebony black skin and he was hungry. The white of his eyes nearly seemed luminous and his pink gums and large white teeth did nothing to remind the kids of Father Christmas.

The Wraith had latched on to one of the crew and his mates were trying to stop the Wraith from eating him alive. Someone threw a machete for Kal to catch and with that, he stormed towards the Wraith. Before he could get to him, Brutus flew past him and went for the Wraith's throat. The Wraith let go of the hapless crewman and concentrated on Brutus instead. The dog took no notice of the punches the Wraith threw at her instead the dog snapped and bit wherever she saw a biteable surface until she made it to his throat. With a loud snap of her jaws, she sank her teeth in the side of the Wraith's neck and hung on. No matter what the now distressed creature did, Brutus hung on.

At first Kal thought that the dog was injured internally because even though she had a lockjaw hold on the Wraith, blood sprayed from her nose with every breath she exhaled. Kal suddenly laughed and shouted, "Shit! You are such a poser, Brutus, you are a spirit dog so how can you bleed?"

As if to proof the point, the Wraith wrapped his arms around the dog to try to pull her away but all he grasped was air. There was an image of the dog for all to see but it was an illusion. The only things real were the jaws clamped on the Wraith's neck.

One of the canine fangs had punctured the carotid artery in the side of his neck and the Wraith was rapidly bleeding out. In due course, he collapsed on the deck and after a bit more twitching he lay still.

When Kal told the men to toss the body over the side they seemed very reluctant and Kal reconsidered. He knew the men were deadly scared of the Wraith, even in death, and anyway at sunrise, the body would become gas and blow away. For the rest of the night nobody ventured anywhere near the foredeck.

By morning, the 'Vrouwe Irene' was sailing under the brow of a steep, volcanic island. Its sides were clad in dark foliage and the rising sun highlighted the streamers of morning mists rising from the dense jungle.

For most of the morning the 'Vrouwe Irene' sailed along the coast looking for a place to make landfall, they were in need of fresh water and hoped to find a fresh water source. Beaches were few and those they did see consisted mainly of narrow ledges covered by black, volcanic sand. It was not until late in the afternoon that the ship sailed into a brown slick in the otherwise clear sea. Kal knew that the slick indicated the run-off of a river so he edged the 'Vrouwe Irene' into the current and followed it to the shore.

Hardly visible from the sea they were surprised to find a large river mouth with on the south bank a landing that appeared to be in use although they could not see any people. The 'Vrouwe Irene' dropped her anchor in the deep water near the opposite river bank, a safe distance away from the landing, to wait out the night.

The night was dark and strange sounds came from the shore, some were definitely animal sounds but others begged identification. The men who were not used to this kind of dense jungle, wanted to light a fire but Kal put a stop to that. Until he knew what the locals were like, he saw no need to advertise their presence. He and Brutus spent most of the night on deck and it was with relief that they watched the sunrise in the morning.

As soon as the day watch came on deck, Kal ordered the ship's longboat launched. While on that task, a canoe with four people on board came around a bend in the river. The men in the canoe stood upright while they drove the craft forward with long paddles. They were all ebony black and naked except for the colourful, feather headbands, armbands, and leg bands. A couple also wore necklaces of boar tusks.

They swung the canoe around so it was facing upstream and then held station at a safe distance from the 'Vrouwe Irene'. When they shouted, it did not sound like a challenge but more like a question. Kal deduced from this that they were not antagonistic and put on a pantomime. He picked up a small cask and showed it to be empty, he then grabbed a cup one of the crew had brought him, and made the universal sign of drinking.

The canoeists at first looked somewhat confused until Kal made the motion of dipping the cup into the cask and then moved it to his mouth with a drinking motion including the wiping off of excess fluid after the drink. The resident bright light in the canoe frowned but then cupped his hands and made the drinking sign. Kal enthusiastically nodded his head and the canoeist's face exploded in a bright and toothy smile. He then indicated that water was to be had somewhere around the river bend upstream. With gestures, he indicated that the canoe would show the way.

With four men, Kal manned the longboat and cast off to follow the canoe. At the last minute Brutus jumped into the longboat as well. The canoe led the way into a tributary of the main river to where a mountain stream cascaded clear water over the lip of a low cliff face. All they had to do is position their water casks under the stream to catch clear mountain water.

While the men were busy filling the casks, Kal tried to communicate in every language he knew but without success. Although the men did not appear to be confrontational at all, Kal noticed that one was missing and wondered if he had gone for re-enforcements. Therefore, when the casks were filled Kal did not waste any time and got the longboat under way. The three remaining canoeists stayed on shore and actually waved as they left.

Any feelings of relief vanished as soon as the longboat turned the corner into the main river. There, strung out across the stream were six canoes. Each craft had six men in it of which at least three brandished a spear or a machete of sorts.

In the lead canoe, he saw a man, obviously the leader judging by the greater amount of parrot feathers decorating his hair and legs, who was waving an ancient and rusty cavalry sword. He had on a threadbare red coat with the sleeves torn out, and he yelled something. It took a while before Kal realised the man actually spoke English but with a quaint accent that at time sounded more Spanish than English, "Ye have violated the sovereignty of Greatest [sic] Britain by crossing her borders. Ye have further violated said sovereignty by setting foot on her soil without having permission to do such. Ye have further stolen water belonging to the Crown. For this and other, as yet, undetected crimes ye are hereby ordered to handover one of yer men to serve as a slave for as long as it pleases me."

Kal could not believe his ears and would have laughed in the man's face if it had not been for the deadly serious intent showing on the faces of his retinue.

Perhaps a bit of diplomacy might be in order here so he asked, "And who do I have the honour to address?"

With a surprised look on his face, the man in the red coat muttered, "The savage speaks the King's English!" In a louder force he announced, "Ye, sir, have the honour of addressing me, the 12th Earl of Brine, representative of King George III in whose name these lands were claimed for the Crown by the First Earl of Brine anno 1751".

By this time, Kal realised that the good Earl was somewhat loopy so he tried to humour him a bit. Instead of telling him straight out that he was an idiot he said with a straight face, "Excuse me, but I know nothing of such annexation, in the first place and in the second place the good King George III died around 1820. That is quite a while ago and I wonder if the present queen knows anything about this annexation."

"It be of nought concern to me! All this talk about who be what, and queens, does nay alter the fact that this here island belongs to His majesty's Crown and that ye have trespassed and shall pay the fine due!"

"Oh yeah, that's another matter, the British crown outlawed slavery in 1833, more than a hundred and fifty years ago"—Kal hoped the Earl was not aware of the fact that he no longer lived in the Core where the abolishment had taken place well after the final separation—. "Didn't you get the government gazette on the subject? It was quite an extensive issue complete with colour pictures."

"Yes, yes I saw that, (*a blatant lie*) but circumstances here, in His Majesty's dominions, be extenuating and require the practice to be continued for some time. Anyhow, I need nay explain myself to ye!"

"Perhaps you do!"

Kal's voice had taken on an authoritarian and threatening quality that did not go unnoticed by the Earl who suddenly came down a few rungs on the ladder of self-importance. Before he could recover Kal continued the bluff with, "I, Kalahari van Straaten, hereby must inform you that as a special envoy of Her Majesty, the Queen of England, I have been sent to determine whether in fact you have disobeyed Her Majesty's forefather's command to abolish slavery. And should that be true, which by your own admission it appears to be the case, I am to order you, by force if necessary, to set free the slaves and to further desist the practice."

As if to divert attention from a painful subject, the Earl suddenly asked, "How be it I only note South Sea Islanders in yer crew?"

"I came into the Pacific by way of the Horn in order to bring the same slavery abolishment message to an island in the East Pacific. My own crew was sick from the long and arduous journey round the Cape as well as a severe bout of scurvy..."

The Earl interrupted with disbelief toning the timbre of his voice, "Scurvy? That be done with a century ago!"

"Yes well, the bureaucrats back home failed to supply us with the preventative medication! Don't worry the last word has not been spoken on the subject. But, to get back to your question why the crew is native to the South Pacific, they are all slaves that have been set free and to a man they volunteered to bring the message to you and having first-hand experience of the abhorrent practice, they are willing to use force to carry out Her Majesty's dictates."

While this palaver was going on the river's current swept the whole gaggle of canoes and longboat downstream towards where the 'Vrouwe Irene' was riding her anchor. Just at the right moment, Pinnie, one of the crew silently gave the order and with a few strokes of the oars the longboat came along side and tied up to the schooner.

Kal watched the Earl carefully, it was clear that the man was not used to be questioned and it was also quite plain that he was certifiable. He was just about to continue the charade while he still had the upper hand when the Earl spoke up, "Ye being the envoy of His Majesty"—*he refused to accept the Her Majesty bit*—"you better come ashore so I may take ye to my seat for further discussions."

Harry's voice in Kal's head groused, *"He did not mention anything about you returning here."*

Kal mumbled, "With you, Abdullah and Brutus to help me I have no doubt I'll be back."

Striding back to the quarterdeck of the schooner Kal shouted loud enough to be heard in London, "Samu, prepare a landing party. Semi ceremonial. Five men only, all volunteers."

Samu who only recognised the mention of his name reacted by coming on deck in full view of the Earl and by saying, "Huh?"

Before the Earl could become curious about the dead-pan expression on Samu's face, Kal called to the Earl, "Our preparations may take some time so I suggest you appoint one of your men to remain on the landing to guide us while you return to the comfort of your garrison."

Meanwhile Abdullah's voice went ballistic in Kal's head, *"What are you doing!? Samu does not have a clue of what you want and neither have I! What do I tell him?"*

Kal turned away from the men in the canoes as though they were no longer of any import until his landing party was organised. Quietly he said, "Samu did his job just fine. Did you notice how his 6 feet 7 inches stature of all muscle and mean looks impressed that worm of a make-believe Earl and his cronies? Anyway we got to find something for me to dress up in so I can look just as ridiculous as the Earl and please brief the men on what was said especially the bit about them being released slaves hunting for slave masters."

Harry now joined the conversation, *"That should be fun! Give me my body back, I would just love to drag the right Earl's ass through his own shit!"*

Good naturedly Kal replied, "Language, language, my wild Colonial Boy!"

Abdullah remarked, "*That must remain an insider joke, in this dimension Antipodia, or Australia, was never used as a dumping ground for what the British government considered to be undesirable malefactors. I assume Harry's disregard for his Betters comes from that historical travesty of justice?*"

Harry just grunted he realised that they were in a bit of a jam and that their only way out was to convince the 12th Earl of Brine that they were what they claimed to be. In a sober voice he said to Abdullah, "*Come on grab hold of Brutus and let's go talk to the men to put them in the picture. You're going to have some fun convincing Samu that he is the enforcer. We also must dress up our puppet here to look the part. Got any ideas?*"

The only reply from Abdullah was a mincingly sweet, "*Oh goody, goody, let's dress up our poppet like a Mardi Grass queen complete with rhinestone tiara and Magic wand.*"

Kal could swear that even Brutus was 'snorting with mirth' as she dragged the pair away.

Left alone on the aft deck, he leaned on the taff rail and wondered what he had gotten himself and the others into.

CHAPTER 18

THE END OF A DYNASTY

Two hours after the 12th Earl of Brine invited Kal in his capacity as the envoy of the British Crown to come and discuss the abolishment of slavery, the ambassadorial party assembled on the aft deck of the 'Vrouwe Irene'.

There was Kal with a large British flag draped over his shoulders like a cape, a klewang—a four feet long and narrow machete/sword with an offset handle—in a wooden scabbard tied to a leather belt around his waist. On his head he wore a conical contraption hastily fashioned from part of a sleeping mat. He felt ridiculous with the head gear but was told by a crew member who apparently hailed from this area, although not the same island, that all self-respecting wizards wore one of those things. When Kal remonstrated that he was not a wizard both Harry and Abdullah talked in his head at the same time and even Brutus gave him a lopsided look that said, *"I'm coming too and not just to play fetch! The boys and I have a few plans of our own!"*

At this point Abdullah appointed himself master of ceremonies. He had to because Kal was about to flop down in the stern sheets of the longboat which of course was the last place for a dignitary to be. Abdullah ordered him to stand in the bows with his sword hand on his hip and the other by his side.

Kal had to brace his knees against the tiny foredeck to keep his balance as the boat was briskly rowed to the landing.

As soon as the bows scraped the beach, Brutus jumped out to establish the beach head, in the process of which Abdullah and Harry fell flat on their faces in the mud. In the confusion of the disembarkation Harry and Abdullah had to have a quick dip to wash off the mud.

With Brutus on point duty and disinclined to make like a pup and play in the water, the two Shimmerers hung on to an oar each while they washed themselves. The guide left behind by the Earl saw the conical hat of Kal and had he been of the right persuasion he would have crossed himself when he saw two of the longboat's oars jiggle about with nobody near them and water being splashes about without an apparent cause. Surely witchcraft.

Samu as the maître de barked some orders and the others lined up behind Kal. Pinnie, the local lad in Kal's crew, was put in the lead behind Kal so he could translate for the Earl's man.

The yellow clay slope of the landing was fairly dry but steep. Once at the top of the bank the incline became less acute and they moved into the shadowy world of the jungle.

After about fifteen minutes' walk through the steamy jungle they arrived at the place where the reverend and his son had been dispatched but there was nobody there now so they kept going.

Just before the party came out of the jungle onto the narrow spine, Brutus propped and growled. Her companions, the two Shimmerers, knew the signs by now and urgently sought new anchor points. Just as well. A few moments later Brutus appeared to leap straight through some dense foliage and her growl was drowned out by the screams of two men now flushed out of hiding and with bleeding bite marks on their arms and legs. Neither introduced themselves but both took off in the direction of the Earl's palisade.

With a wide grin on her snout Brutus came from the scrub dragging a spear and a blow pipe. With one swipe of his klewang Kal chopped the blow pipe in halves and then told Pinnie to arm himself with the spear and to use it if and when he needed to.

There was a certain satisfied swagger in Brutus' step as she once again took her place in the procession with her two charges in tow.

When the procession eventually arrived at the palisade, the gates were already thrown wide open and the 12th Earl of Brine was there in full regalia and waiting. Samu bellowed the parade to a halt and the British envoy solemnly shook the Earl's hand.

Kal followed the man back to the front veranda steps and gingerly climbed the single log that had treads cut into it. Not something one would want to negotiate with a skin full of booze!

Even the Earl was surprised when they got up onto the veranda to find Brutus waiting for them. The wily dog had come up the back steps and had checked out the house as they climbed their way to the veranda. Kal could see that the Earl was not too happy about Brutus being present but exaggerated reports of what the dog had done on the way up had already circulated the camp, obviously, and even the Earl was inclined to address her with 'Sir'.

Kal was at a loss. The 'Vrouwe Irene' had only called in to look for fresh water and no one on board even knew of the existence of the 12th Earl of Brine or the far flung outpost of the British Empire that he claimed to have established. It was very doubtful that anybody in the British Empire knew of this out post either.

In as formal tones as he could Kal repeated his demand that in conformity with the Slavery Abolition act of 1833, all the Earl's slaves were to be set free and that he was to compensate them in some manner for the hardship and indignity suffered. Of course there were great outpourings of 'poor fella me' by the Earl and Kal was sure that if the Earl should at all comply he would only do so because he was superstitious and feared what the supernatural could do if he refused. Kal also knew that as soon as he and his party, in particular Brutus, had left things would be back to normal. Just to make a point Brutus got up and casually faded straight through a wall and then returned from inside the house through the main door. The Earl gaped and turned all kinds of pale when next he heard Harry's voice in his head, *"See what I just did then? How would you like me to drag you through that wall? The bamboo splinters would give you hell especially if I drag you forward and backward a few times!"*

The Earl now as white as a sheet, rolled his eyes up into his head and fell backwards in a dead faint. Harry snorted with pleasure and Brutus sat down for a satisfying scratch at some pesky flea behind her right ear.

Pinnie, the local lad, called out to the women downstairs that the Earl might need their attention and Ono together with Jordie heeded the call to arms.

It was while they fussed over the Earl that Kal saw Jordie for the first time. He saw the whip marks the Earl's riding crop had left on her back and although he never said anything he decided that the girl was one slave the Earl was going to lose.

While Jordie and Ono were, half-heartedly, trying to revive the Earl, Kal never the one with the snitchy pick-up lines asked, "Does either of you speak English?"

Ono gave him a look that conveyed the message that she did not know what he was talking about but there was a somewhat different reaction from Jordie, she asked him, "Is the pope a Catholic?"

"I guess the answer is 'yes'. OK, let's try it again. My name is Kal, what is yours?"

The girl sounded quite snide when she replied, "It used to be Magdalene McDougall but in my guise as that of a slave it is now Hey-you and I am no longer to respond to Jordie." Then she broke down in tears and sobbed, "Has that bastard sold us to you?"

"No, far from it, we are here to tell him that it is against the law to have slaves and to set you all free."

There was scorn in her voice when she retorted, "Yeah? And who's going to make that law stick? The moment ye 'set forth on yer crusade', the old bastard will have us all flogged and I'll be his play thing again until a younger and fresher toy comes along."

Not quite knowing what to say Kal made the mistake of speaking at all and to top it off he said the worth thing he could have set under the circumstances, "You don't like him do you?"

Jordie sneered and cried at the same time when she shouted, "What be there not to like? He slayed my father and brother in front of me, he branded me for life with his branding iron and he uses me as a sex slave. If you ask him he probably let ye have me for the night. Would that be pleasing? Like I said what be there not to like about that degenerate?"

Abdullah's voice sounded in Kal's head, *"You are getting nowhere for some reason she is suspicious of you. Let me try."*

Kal was disappointed when he communicated to Abdullah, *"For the life of me I cannot think why she should be, my scars, my conical hat and my regal dress should convince her that there is nothing wrong with me!!"*

On a sudden impulse Kal put a hand on Brutus' head and told the dog, "Go and talk to Jordie, perhaps she will listen to you; after all dogs are either good or bad, cannot lie or pretend to be what they are not."

"You wanna put some money on that?" That was Harry's voice for Kal's benefit only.

Suddenly Jordie's full attention was focussed on Brutus because of what Kal had said to the dog she now believed that Abdullah's voice actually came from the dog. With eyes as big as saucers she grabbed one of the other woman's hands and clung to it. Ono was petrified she had witnessed the kaleidoscope of emotions reflected in her friend's face but not being able to understand the language spoken she had no idea of what was going on. Meanwhile Abdullah patiently explained the whole situation and a contrite look came over Jordie's face. Then the dam burst and Jordie rushed Kal while tears streamed down her face. She wrapped her arms around his neck and sobbed, "Please hold me I need to feel safe."

Well aware of her young body against his, he complied with her demands and suggested, "Perhaps you should let your friend know what is going on because in the next few minutes she is either going to attack me or run for the hills."

Through her tears she smiled, "Her name be Ono and she comes from Viti Levu (Fiji) and yes ye are right she does nay have a clue of what goes on."

She turned towards Ono but while still staying in Kal's arms she rattled off in Fijian thereby causing Ono to smile hugely.

While all this had been going on nobody really kept an eye on the recovering Earl. When the latter came to his senses and saw Jordie in the arms of Kal something snapped in his overtaxed brain.

Suddenly in a flurry of movement he was at them with a dagger that he plunged towards Jordie's back. Right on the last moment Kal whipped the girl around to the side and the dagger instead of sinking in her back finished up in Kal's left arm. With a roar that even made Brutus yelp— *although she would never admit to it later on*—Kal pushed Jordie out of the way and grabbed the first thing that came to hand, the Earl's rusty cavalry sword. In all the excitement he forgot that he had the klewang on his hip. That was probably just as well because with it he would have decapitated his opponent. As it was he only half decapitated him which made it a bit easier for the clean-up crew.

Harry recited, *"Being the ONLY representative of the law it is left to me to find out what happened.*

Question. Were there any witnesses to the alleged unprovoked attack on Miss, eh, anybody, what's her name? Oh yes, thank you sir, Miss Jordie?

Answer. Yes plenty.

Second question. Did anybody witness the alleged counter attack by Mr Kal van Straaten?

Answer. What counter attack? There was a blur and then, and then, the Earl's head kind of fell off.

Question. What do you mean by kind of? Did it or did it not fall off?

Answer. Well you see, it did not fall off completely but he is still dead though.

I repeat my question. Did anybody see Mr van Straaten attack the Earl? The fact that the Earl is now deceased has nothing to do with my question as to whether anybody saw the counter attack or not. No? In that case due to the lack of evidence it must be concluded that the demise of the 12th Earl of Brine was due to misadventure and that the injury that allegedly caused his premature entry into Valhalla was self-inflicted in view of the fact that it was his sabre that done it."

Harry had not only cast his voice into Kal's mind but also into Jordie's. She looked into Kal's eyes and said soberly, "It be him or me and I believe that I be less evil than what he were."

For no apparent reason except for Jordie's nearness an urgent desire in Kal began to manifest itself in his loins. Jordie noticed the rise in the tide and with a challenging expression that at the same time was a fatalistic look she asked, "Well? Art thou going to serve yer need?"

With a mixture of anger and pity—anger at the man that had been her father and anger at the worm that had been the quasi Earl—and pity for the girl's subjugated state of mind, he said, "You are no longer anybody's slave or property. From now on the desire must come from both sides and now is not that time is it?"

With her eyes downcast she murmured, "Thank ye."

Suddenly the tension broke or the reality penetrated her thinking, whatever it was, she turned away from Kal and sobbing quietly fell into the embrace of Ono. The two women sagged to the floor and talked through their tears and at the same time.

Abdullah quietly suggested, *"Let the women be, they need to straighten out their emotions. You better pull that dagger out of your arm, and, by the way what are you going to do with the Earl?"*

"Me? Why is it always got to be me?"

"Hey! You chilled him."

At this point Harry got involved, *"Let's not go there, we got a stiff on our hands and we got to get rid of the body before he stinks out the place."*

Abdullah again, *"OK, I know what. We tell the boys to get rid of it before we tell them they are no longer slaves and do not need to obey the great white master any longer."*

"Good plan. I wonder if they'll eat him."

"Well if they do they better not come to us complaining of indigestion, I did not bring any Mylanta, did you?"

"Will you pair just shut up and let me think!"

Somewhere in the back of Kal's mind a fading voice asked, *"Did you know he could think?"*

Kal turned to Pinnie who had been watching the proceedings from near the top of the single log ladder, "Pinnie can you ask some of the men to come and take the body away?"

In broken English Pinnie replied, "No can do Boss. Boys scared come in house, they say bad spirit protect Big Boss."

"You scared of bad spirits?"

"Me? No, me not come from here."

"OK, come and give me a hand and we will show them that this bad spirit is not strong at all."

Without waiting to see if Pinnie would follow, Kal walked over to where the corpse lay. Although somewhat reluctant, old habits die hard, Pinnie crossed the forbidden territory of the veranda and got hold of one of the body's arms. With Kal on the other arm they dragged the Earl to the front of the veranda where the gathered population of the palisade could see their erstwhile master.

Pinnie asked, "How we take him down? Me no carry him down log step! Too narrow."

Without a word Kal pushed the body off the veranda and watched as it flopped like a sodden rag doll onto the dusty ground below.

Kal had to give Pinnie his due, after one look at the horrified faces of the former slaves he began to orate—something his people are good at. Kal withdrew out of sight, he wanted Pinnie to be the people's new leader until they had decided whether to stay or go back to where they had been shanghaied from.

On his way into the house to look for something to bandage the stab wound in his arm, he walked past the two young women and Jordie touched his hand he looked at her and she asked, "Would you mind telling me something?"

"Anything you want to know."

"Those voices I keep hearing, are they angles?"

With a smile he replied, "No they are not although sometimes they would like me to believe that they are. Do you know what a Wraith is?"

With a suspicious look she answered with a long stretched out, "Yes!"

"Well, they are kind of the same but different, they are Shimmerers. During the day they are half wraith and half person, during the night they are half person and half wraith."

"Isn't that the same thing?"

"I wish it was! Quite often when I tell them something during the day, they forget it as soon as they change at night. Next day they may remember what it was if they want to that is."

"Are...are they living...inside you?"

"No, don't worry, they are so light that any puff of wind could blow them away..."

"Like a Wraith at sunrise?"

"Yes, so normally they carry something heavy to keep them on the ground but this pair, Harry who is an old friend of mine, and Abdullah, who I met about a year ago, are lucky, they got Brutus the dog to tow them around and to keep them on the ground."

"Be Brutus a ghost, I saw her fade straight through that wall."

"Brutus is a spirit dog who can materialise in part or wholly. She was sent by one of the spirit leaders to protect Harry and me."

"So when Brutus went through the wall did they get pulled through as well?"

"No they are too smart for that! They were hanging on to one of the veranda posts."

"Will I ever meet Harry or Abdullah?"

"You have already met Abdullah. When you thought the dog was talking to you in your head? That was Abdullah. Did you hear the rubbish that was said about the fight?"

Jordie smiled and said, "Yes."

"Well, that was Harry, he thinks he is something because he used to be a copper."

"What be a copper?"

"He would tell you that he is 'a servant of the people and an up-holder of the law' in other words a policeman. Nothing special in fact."

From the direction where Brutus was having her siesta a disgruntled voice said, *"Don't listen to him I saved his bacon too many times to count. He is a full-time concern and needs constant watching! Doesn't he Brutus?"*

"GRUFF!"

"Oops! That means, 'shut up and let me sleep' OK, the law is on your side."

The nonsensical banter had the desired effect, Jordie became visually more at ease and the two young women even giggled when Jordie translated what had been said for Ono.

Suddenly Jordie became aware of the blood dripping steadily from Kal's arm, with her hand over her mouth and big eyes she said with a voice full of concern, "Oh! I'm so sorry! You are bleeding!"

She turned and said something in Fijian and Ono disappeared down the back steps of the house.

"Ono is gone to get some stuff to stop the bleeding and, hopefully, stop any infection."

She made Kal sit down and elevate his arm. As they waited for Ono to come back a somewhat embarrassing silence developed between them.

Kal felt a strange attraction for the girl as though she was familiar. There was a vulnerability about her that made him want to protect her but at the same time he could feel a strength radiate from her that told him she was tough when it counted. He wanted to talk to her and make her feel at ease but he did not know where to start, there were so many things to say.

On her part Jordie was tongue tied now that he was so near. She could still feel the steely strength in his arms from when he held her and swung her out of the way of the mad Earl. Obliquely she studied the many scars on Kal's body and suddenly for no apparent reason she touched the nasty one that ran from his left ear to the bottom of his jaw, "Why dost ye nay grow a beard?"

For a few moments Kal studied her face, he was intrigued by the fact she did not ask him how he got the scar but just why he did not try to hide it.

Not unkindly he replied her question with, "If I grew a beard, that scar would stand out like a highway through a forest."

After a longish pause Jordie asked, "What be a highway?"

For a while he studied her face then he realised that Jordie could not know what a highway was because she did not come from the Core nor had she ever been there. "A highway is like a very long and very straight path but only much wider."

"Perhaps like the trails left by an ox cart?"

"Yes more like two or even three ox cart trails next to each other."

"That be a bit fanciful!"

"Not where we come from."

"Who be WE?"

"Myself, Harry and Abdullah."

"What about Brutus, and why dost she be named a boy's name?"

"Harry named her before he asked her if she was a boy or a girl. And no, Brutus is a local."

"Just so! That still dost nay tell me where ye come from, but if ye dost nay want to tell me that be all right too."

Just then Ono came back with her magic herbal juice, the same she used on Jordie's burns. She squeezed the juice into the open wound and Kal involuntarily moaned, "Shit! That hurts!"

Ono muttered, "Ah! Sa levu na mene-mene."

With a grimace on his face Kal asked Jordie, "What does that mean?"

Jordie giggled, "She reckons ye be a sook and that ye be laying it on thick, but she dost nay really mean it."

Kal decided to stay overnight in the camp and he was surprised how subdued the people were. In a way he had suspected that there would be celebrations instead the inhabitants seemed stunned by their sudden freedom. He guessed that for many it would be hard to imagine what life would be like without the, although tyrannical, guidance of the Earl to make the decisions for them. There would be those quite happy to remain where they were because of their plantations. They probably worried about what would happen to them if the majority of the ex-slaves left thereby exposing them to attacks by raiders or those who claimed the land belonged to them or their tribe.

Every now and again a bubble of laughter or singing would erupt somewhere in the village where a small group of people suddenly realised they were free, free to do with the rest of their lives as they wanted. Each eruption of frivolity died down quickly when the participants realised the responsibilities their freedom brought with it.

Kal drifted in and out of a strange state of euphoria that at times made him feel as though he was losing consciousness. One part of him felt he should talk to Pinnie about problems the ex-slaves might have to face. On the other hand, probably due to his strange state of mind, he felt he should stay out of it and should let them solve their own problems. He was still battling with those conflicting thoughts when Jordie came to his side and asked him how he felt. She did not really have to ask, the glazed look in his eyes was enough of an answer. Gently she explained that it was Ono's medication that made him feel that way and that when Ono applied the same medication to her back she had actually passed out.

Towards the end of the day when the mosquitoes came out, Jordie came back with a potion of herbs and coconut oil that, when applied to the skin, kept the mosquitoes and sand fleas at bay. Kal was laying down still feeling rather out of it so she applied the lotion.

With one arm resting on his chest Jordie sat next to him and they talked in a relaxed manner about all kind of things. In the end Kal with his good arm resting comfortably on her hip finally fell asleep and Jordie, not wanting to disturb him, slowly lowered her head on his chest as well and she too fell asleep after an emotional day.

Before breakfast the next morning, a delegation with Pinnie as its leader knocked on the trunk ladder and asked for an audition.

Kal told the three men, two women and Pinnie to come onto the veranda. At first the ex-slaves were rather reluctant to come up, after all, the erstwhile Earl would have killed anybody game enough to come on his veranda. After Kal told them it was too hot out in the open under the blazing sun they nodded their heads and made the climb up the ladder.

They came to ask him what he wanted them to do.

Through Pinnie, Kal told them, that what they wanted to do from here on was their own responsibility. He himself would be leaving either later today or tomorrow at the latest because he had his own responsibilities after all he only came here looking for fresh water. Through Pinnie he was asked if anybody could come with him. He told them that the ship was fully crewed and that the only people he could take were Ono, because she came from Viti Levu (Fiji) and he would be calling in there on his way back, and Jordie because her people were at the place he was going to.

"So what would you advise them to do?" Pinnie asked.

"Have you offered to lead them while they get on their feet?"

"No, not yet, I was hoping you would."

"I take it those five people are 'section leaders' chosen to be the delegation?"

"Yes they are."

"Well, I suggest that you tell them that just now you asked me if I would release you from my employ should they want you to oversee their efforts to rehabilitate their sections. I want it to come from you, so it will not sound as though you are doing it on my orders. I want them to know that you fight your own battles and are not just another white-man's flunky."

"You never treated me like a flunky! But I understand what you are saying. Wish me luck, here goes."

While Pinnie began to orate in the ceremonial manner of his people, Kal could feel the caress of Jordie's body as she stood close behind him and whispered, "I dost nay know that a 'sinner' could be so considerate. My father, the right reverend McDougall never would have thought of such things. He were dead sure God created black people to be slaves and loved to quote Genesis 9, 25, '*Cursed be Canaan! The lowest of slaves will he be to his brothers.*'"

Kal did not know how to react to her statement but then she whispered, "Don't worry I nay quote bible and verse to ye every time I get a pleasant surprise."

Before she went back inside the house she squeezed his arm, "Breakfast be ready whenever ye be."

Harry's voice sounded in his head, "*She had us all worried there for a moment, including Brutus.*"

"Whaf?"

"*Nothing, go back to sleep.*"

Soon after the assembly broke up and silently the five representatives left.

"What's happening Pinnie?"

"It is hard to say, they told me that they now must go and bring the proposal to their people and that they will be back later this afternoon. They will stage a general assembly and a kava ceremony to either accept or reject the offer."

"What do you think will be the outcome?"

"None of those people is used to be in command so I think they will accept me but probably with certain conditions."

"Oh well! Come and have breakfast."

Later that day Kal took Jordie down to the 'Vrouwe Irene' to show her around and to relief the crew that had remained on board. The men that had accompanied him into the lair of the Earl replaced the ones that looked after the ship.

CHAPTER 19

THE JOURNEY CONTINUES

I T WAS LATE in the afternoon when Kal, Jordie and the crew on shore leave approached the palisade along the narrow track on top of the razorback. To their surprise they heard singing and guitar strumming coming from the enclosure. The gate stood wide open and Kal smiled from ear to ear when they entered the village common and saw what was going on.

True to Pinnie's predictions there was a full scale kava drinking session in progress and the music would stop while the bowls of kava were handed to Pinnie and the five 'section' leaders. As soon as those six had drank their bowl, the music and dancing would start again.

From the festive atmosphere Kal deduced that everything was sorted out and he was curious as to what the final outcome was.

Pinnie wanted to vacate his place of honour at the head of the gathering for Kal but the latter refused and instead sat down with the five sub-leaders. This move further established Pinnie as the person in charge.

Kal found it interesting that the different styles of music from the traditional chanting recitations of the Micronesian and Melanesian to the hula and tamure as well as the melodious but often melancholy Polynesian guitar and drum music, were all in the mix.

Much later Pinnie told him what had come out of the ceremonial meeting. It had anonymously been decided by all concerned that Pinnie should be the leader but then the debate had started about who should be second in command. Pinnie as the leader was an attractive proposition because he had no ties with any of the groups and therefore, it was felt, he could be impartial. They wanted this same impartiality to apply to the second in command. There was the traditional and typical nonsensical political rhetoric coming from all sides until Samu, the giant Balon islander with the mean face, stood up and announced that he was to be the second in command. Who was going to argue with him?

Surprised Kal asked, "Truce up? I would never have guessed he would want the job."

Pinnie grinned and said, "I don't think he really wants it. He was just sick of listening to all the pomposity being aired. In the end Samu is going to be Samu and follow his own star."

"Do you think it will work?"

"Oh yes. He is going to keep me honest too."

"How is that?"

"Samu is a good follower for as long as he cannot see any duplicity in what is asked of him. He is a man not only of a few words but also with an alert brain. On top of that he has a good heart and would sooner put me in my place than let me make a fool of myself or hurt anybody because of stupidity, greed, or arrogance."

"For how long are you planning to run the show for them?"

"For as long as it takes I suppose. After all I come from one of those islands so, really, I'm home. I don't know for how long Samu will want to stay though."

"If he finds himself a wife he may well be prepared to stay for good."

It was early evening and Kal stood on the veranda of the ex-Earl's residence. He was leaning on the balustrade while he stared into space without seeing anything. He had been on land and among too many people for too long. He knew it and the only remedy was to set sail. He would have left the day after the slaves had been set free but Harry, Abdullah and Brutus had dug in their heels, they wanted to stay longer to make sure the people were OK. Had it not been for his friendship with Harry, he would be gone.

Suddenly Kal became aware of somebody standing quietly next to him, he looked down and saw it was Jordie. She smiled up at him and asked, "If I be interrupting yer thoughts, tell me and I will go."

"No, stay, but I may not be very entertaining as company."

"I didst nay come to be entertained. Yer aura speaks of sadness. Why?"

Kal looked at the girl for a long time but finally he spoke, "Yes I am sad because I am lonely. I miss my wife who died about a year ago and I miss a lot of other people who once meant a lot in my life but who are all gone. Gone as in dead."

After a pause during which Jordie came closer and put her hand on his, she said, "As long as somebody be remembered they be nay really gone. I dost nay know whether ye can see this but everything be a form of energy. Now, energy can change the form in which it presents itself but it can never be destroyed. So ye see those we miss nay be gone, they only changed as energy expressions."

For a long time Kal looked at the young woman before he asked, "Wasn't your father some kind of missionary or something?"

With a scowl on her face she said, "Yes he be, or claimed to be."

"But?"

"He represented the devil more than God! He be a selfish, evil man who thought of nothing else but his own gratification! He used the guise of that of a man of God so people would fear him."

After a brief silence she added softly, "In many ways the Earl be more honest."

"How do you mean that, what is the comparison you see?"

"The Earl lived by the sword and, shall we say, his 'charming' personality; while my father used the bible as his sword in much the same way, they both achieved their selfish goals by intimidating simple people."

"OK, but where does the honesty bit come in?"

"Any person in the know to overcome the power of the Earl's sword would win. There be no example in history that tells of someone winning over God."

Suddenly there were tears on Jordie's cheeks and Kal understood that she had come to a conclusion that rocked her beliefs.

After a sob she said, "I suddenly realise that when my side wins, we say that God be just and therefore on our side. What about the side that be defeated? They must be as convinced as we be that their side be right and ours be wrong therefore they must believe our God to be evil because God always be on the side of the just. But how can any of this be true, there being only one God?"

"Do you think God feels emotions?"

"How could He? If that be true how could He let my father, one of His ordained servants, rape me a few days after my twentieth birthday? And allow it to go on until we came here. Once here that task were taken over by that worm, the 12th Earl of Brine. Well at least he didst nay pretend to be innocent."

"Do you belief though that God is everywhere?"

"Yes I do, I just can't see how He can watch over us as well as our enemies. That appears to be a conflict of interests!"

"Yes it would seem so, but, what if God is everywhere but cannot influence our personal emotions?"

"Do ye think God be just an observer?"

"I would not go as far as that, an observer watches and bases actions on the observations made. I think that happens but not in the way we would like or expect it."

"What dost ye mean?"

"We tend to ascribe so much importance to our self and our species that we see ourselves as even more important than God…"

"I nay see myself as of more importance than God!"

"Oh but you do. Here is God the most important force in creation, by the way, I agree with you there, yet we expect Him to be aware of our personal suffering and on top of that we would dearly love it if He did something about it. Don't worry before I got all those scars I was of the same opinion until one day while I was strung up like a slab of fly-blown meat, blood dripping from fresh cuts and pain so severe it had me on the edge of sanity and after He did nothing about it, I realised how presumptuous it was to think that the greatest power of all would even be aware of my existence. I too fought with the dilemma of why He did not come to my assistance in the first place and why he allowed the others to do this to me."

"So what be the answer? Be there no God?"

"Oh there is a power that is everywhere and that does sustains us but, in human terms, that power is emotionless."

"So what dost ye call it?"

"To me it is the manifestation that we call Nature. Nature is everywhere, in everything and always has the last word. We can clear the jungle that is around us but as soon as we leave Nature reclaims it. I can suffer a knife cut, but provided I survive it is nature that heals my wound…"

"What if ye did nay survive? Would nature have deserted ye?"

"No, the part of nature that you recognise as Kal would morph into other expressions of nature, or, as you said yourself, energy. My flesh would feed insects while my bones would become nutrients in the earth. Everything is on a continuous spiral of birth and rebirth."

"Doesn't that frighten you?"

"What?"

"To think that ye are on yer own without a higher power to guide ye?"

"No, nature is that higher power and it does guide those that are willing to understand it. What frightens me is that so many people try to bend nature to their will rather than make responsible use of the powers that are available for our benefit."

"Such as?"

"In my life wind and sea are important and I not only constantly try to learn more about those forces but also I am starting to learn that those forces although highly complex and diverse always behave in accordance with nature's laws and that it is up to me to learn to recognise those laws in their diversity so that I can make use of them to my benefit. A farmer learns the different laws pertaining to when to plant, where to plant and when to harvest. The grain, or whatever he grows, is used by us as food to give us what? Energy."

Jordie was a bit sarcastic when she asked, "Should we praise the Lord in the shape of a grain stalk then?"

"No Jordie, although that has been done, we do not have to kowtow to nature, we owe it to ourselves to try and understand the powers of nature and how to apply them without expecting it to bow to our demands. We of the superior intellect should learn something from the 'dumb' animals in the field. We should go with nature, not fight it."

"But dost that nay mean that we be nay responsible for what we do, like, dost the fear of God nay keep us in line?"

"Did the fear of God keep your father, or, the Earl in line?"

"True it nay didst. So what will?"

"Ignorance is the greatest evil there is and it will not be overcome until all people realise they are their own keeper and that everything, in the final analysis, is their own responsibility. To understand the laws of nature and to feel comfortable in their embrace is the highest state of mind we can reach."

"Have you?"

"Sometimes when sailing a ship and it is making the most of the prevailing wind. When ship, wind and sea are in harmony, I can stand at the taffrail and watch the wake sliding away from underneath her stern and know a limitless sense of freedom and contentment. During those moments when no other problems or worries plague my conscious mind, I think I have."

Kal did not realise that somewhere during their conversation his arm had crept around Jordie's shoulders and hers held his waist as she said dreamily, "Yay and at such times the moon's reflections on the waves will show us the stairway to heaven."

The next day Kal finally got permission from the three musketeers, Harry, Abdullah and Brutus, to announce their leaving.

It was a bitter-sweet farewell, some of the slaves had become very attached to Jordie and Ono and would have loved to come away with them but it was not possible. As it was, Jordie and Ono would have to travel with Kal to Antipodia. Once he had bought his lead, he would sail to Viti Levu (Fiji) and drop them off.

He wished both Pinnie and Samu well and told them that if they decided that they rather would go home to Balon Island, to meet him at Suva Vou in three months' time, that being roughly the time he expected the 'Vrouwe Irene' to be at the island Viti Levu to drop off Jordie and Ono.

Now with Pinnie gone, Kal lost his interpreter and had to rely on Abdullah to perform that task. It led to some strange situations, at first some of the men could not accept that even though they could only hear Abdullah's voice in their head, they could not answer him by thinking the answer but had to actually speak up. Most were convinced that it was Brutus who spoke in their head, after all they could see only the dog and not Abdullah, but felt silly talking to the dog.

One day, through Abdullah, one of the men was told to do something. The job miss-fired and the poor man got that upset he decided to go to the top with his complaint. As he approached Kal he stated, "Him Marie dog him bugger up true!" (Meaning, that female dog stuffed up!)

During the first days back at sea things were a bit chaotic, mud had to be swabbed off the deck, sails had to be set and trimmed to their optimum and the men had to get back into their sea-going routine. But then the ease of running with the trade winds brought back peace in the hearts of those on board.

Harry and Abdullah spent equal time between arguing with Brutus, talking with Kal and arguing amongst themselves. Brutus with canine indifference and with the, 'me no speaky the English' shrug of her shoulders did what she wanted to do anyway. Kal refused to be drawn into their good-natured squabbling and spend far too much time getting to know Jordie. It must be said though that he did not neglect his duties as skipper and navigator.

On a beam wind he steered a southerly course towards the coast of Antipodia. The largest city on the continent is located were Sydney is established in the Core. In the Dimension the town is called New Hoorn, after a Dutch town on the sheltered shores of the Zuider Zee.

New Hoorn was established on the shores of what in the Core is known as Sydney's Circular Keys and the Rocks. Here in the Dimension sailing ships from all over the world constantly sail up to the town to deliver their cargoes and to load their return shipments as they once did in the Core.

Since its establishment around 1650, the town has grown from a shanty town to what in the Core would be a medium sized town where the original tents and bark huts have been replaced by solid sandstone buildings with cobblestone and brick paved roads. In the centre of town there is even gas burning street lighting maintained by the council. However, since the increase in Wraith attacks many of the street blocks now have Wraith gutters encircling them. The burning gas in them does not only keep the Wraiths at bay but also provides light for those that venture out after dark.

Kal did not look forward to the hustle and bustle of New Hoorn but he knew there was a thriving boat building industry and lead for ballast should not be hard to get. Jordie on the other hand was excited about visiting New Hoorn, she was born on Viti Levu and had never been off the island until she got shanghaied. Now her scornful mantra was, 'Become a slave to see the world', and every time she said it, Ono would scold her, "Don't say that! You're attracting the evil powers that landed you in that situation in the first place!"

They were four days out from New Hoorn, the day had been pleasant with a steady easterly breeze of fifteen knots and the 'Vrouwe Irene' sang her song of swishing bow waves, gurgling wake and creaking rigging.

A lone albatross that must have lost its way or that decided to visit the milder climes, circled the schooner for some time but then caught a thermal and glided away preferring her own company or solitude. Jordie who stood next to Kal watching the bird said, "There be something not many people know."

"What about?"

"The albatross."

"Oh yes? What is it?"

"It be the only bird that can glide down wind and gain height whilst doing so."

"I knew that!"

"Ahg! Every time I try to impress ye with superior knowledge ye shatter me!"

As he grabbed her and tickled her sides he said, "Oh Diddums, here let me put the shatters pieces back together again!"

Squealing she fought free and darted away from him and ran straight through Brutus. The dog just looked at her and said "Ruff", it was Abdullah who complained, *"Hey lady watch where you going I might start to like this and then you'll be not safe anywhere!"*

Jordie challenged him by sticking out her tongue and saying in a sing-song voice, "Catch me if ye can."

"Brutus go fetch!" Abdullah commanded. Brutus looked at Jordie, shook her head and said, "Grruf." (*Go get her yourself, I don't play fetch on my day off.*)

Harry just sniggered which of course started another quarrel.

Moments later Jordie was back by Kal's side and the latter asked, "Did you know?"

"Know what?"

"That you scream like a girl?"

As she placed a well-aimed punch on his arm she hissed in mock anger, "That's because I be a girl! What did ye think, that I be a dictionary?"

"Yeah one of those old ones with the wooden covers and iron bindings! You must have hit me with the lock."

Life was good on board the 'Vrouwe Irene'.

Just on sunset Brutus became restless and walked the deck. It was too much for Harry and Abdullah and they temporarily found themselves alternate hand holds so the dog could do her own pacing. Kal felt a certain disquiet as well but could not determine what it was.

They did not have to wait long, right on sunset and with an animal like roar a Wraith began to materialise on the after deck. As soon as Kal realised what was happening he ordered Jordie and Ono into the deckhouse with instructions to lock and barricade the door and likewise lock all the hatches from inside.

After barging about for a while the Wraith rushed up to the man at the wheel and threw him aside like he was no more than a bag of rice. The poor man hit his head on a deck fitting and was knocked out cold.

Before Kal could react the Wraith spun the wheel and 'Vrouwe Irene' began to turn to starboard. At the time she was on a broad reach with the wind coming in over the port quarter. Before anything could be done the schooner turned so far down wind that the wind now came in over the starboard quarter and the sails gibed. The huge mizzen sail with its heavy boom came whistling across, smashed through the port back stay and pulled up short against the port standing rigging. The main sail and fore sails all came across as well and the total outcome was that the ship lurched from her starboard beam onto her port beam with such force that Kal was sure she would capsize.

Everything happened so fast and with so much noise that a few of the men sleeping below decks screamed in panic but when the schooner slowly righted herself, they settled down.

The girls must have told them there was a Wraith on deck so they had to stay below. Meanwhile on deck it was organised chaos. Stay sail and jib sheets had to be untangled and the large mizzen sail had to be nursed while Kal inspected the rigging, boom and mast for damage before allowing full wind pressure in the sail again. He could not just swing the ship back to port to resume his previous course because that would mean the sails would have to gibe back. A manoeuvre too risky with a sail the size of the mizzen sail and in the wind force they were experiencing. He would have to wear the ship around by continuing the turn until the 'Vrouwe Irene' was pointing directly into the wind, once there the ship would come 'in irons' meaning that all forward movement would stop because all the sails just flapped in the wind and were no longer driving her. Eventually the wind would start to push her backward. Then, to get back on the port tack, the helm would be laid to starboard so that the rudder was pointing to port. The ship would then drift back, slowly turning her stern to port until the wind once more filled the sails and she would be heading forward again with the wind coming over the port side. The ship could then fall off the wind until she once more was on course.

One of the men was already in the rigging of the mizzen mast trying to disentangle the broken back stay while another hoisted the new stay in place.

Because of all the excitement the Wraith had been forgotten but now he let his presence be known with a not so loud grumble. The flying mizzen boom must have just grazed his head, had it hit him full on he would have been dead. As it was, blood was streaming down one side of his face.

For some reason he was fixated on the schooner's helm and just as he again made a lumbering grab for it Brutus seemed to appear out of thin air and just in front of his face. Before he could even raise a hand to brush her away the spirit dog clamped her not so ethereal fangs around his throat. His wind pipe was audibly crushed and blood gushed from his carotid arteries under pressure.

As the Wraith ended his wretched existence by bleeding out on the nicely holy-stoned and bleached deck, Brutus quietly withdrew to her spirit world for some quality time-out without her two hangers-on.

It took Kal and two of the men to dump the expired Wraith over the side. Kal was not leaving him on deck till morning because he was in the way of the man at the helm besides that he stank to high heaven.

There was no further trouble that night but the innocent holiday mood was gone.

CHAPTER 20

PIRATES ON THE WAY

THE 'VROUWE IRENE' fetched the antipodean coast near what is now known as Coffs Harbour and Kal was pretty pleased with himself. Harry had to point out of course that it would be nearly impossible to miss the continent but Kal ignored him and instead basked in the glory of Jordie's admiration, at least she said he was smart.

As soon as they came near the coast they also entered the shipping lanes and a constant watch had to be kept.

The tall ships with their towers of sails were in the business of making miles while the wind was right for them and did not get out of the way of a small schooner like the 'Vrouwe Irene' but then too, Kal did not expect them to. The tall-ships were visible from a long way off and giving them plenty of sea-room was no problem.

Most of the crew including the two young women were like kids in a candy store, they had never seen ships that big and the fastness of the land that stretched from horizon to horizon filled the islanders with awe.

Late in the afternoon of the day following the day on which they first saw land, Kal was watching a hybrid schooner a bit larger than the 'Vrouwe Irene'. The hybrid had her foremast rigged with square sails rather than the usual fore-and-aft configuration like on the 'Vrouwe Irene' and running with the wind she was making good use of them.

Idly Kal was still debating the pros-and-cons of the two different rigs, when he noticed a slight course change by the other ship. It did not take him long to figure out that the two vessels now were on a collision course. According to the give-way rules of the sea, the hybrid had the right of way so why did she change course? Kal had a funny feeling that not everything was as it should be and kept a close eye on the other ship while, through Abdullah, he ordered all hands on deck. The girls he sent below decks.

Suddenly Brutus was standing next to him bristles up like a razorback and a bit of drool dripping from a fang. Kal had to laugh at the drool bit because that was a new act. He made the motion of patting her head and for a moment she looked up at him with an adoring look, her one standing ear flopped in the down position and her bristle laid flat. As soon as she felt she had acknowledged his gesture she re-assumed her 'bring it on' stance and Kal knew for sure the other ship meant trouble.

Quietly he told Harry and Abdullah to find themselves hold fasts in the deckhouse but they would not hear of it. They would find anchoring points on deck in case Brutus was going to be busy. He was glad the Shimmerers decided to stay on deck and Kal started to give orders through Abdullah again. "Tell two of the men to stream the sea anchor on the port side so the other boat cannot see them do it and don't let them set it until I give the order."

Harry then asked, "*What are you trying to do?*"

"I want us to slow down but so that they don't notice it until it is too late."

"Too late for what?"

"You watch them, when they think the time is right they will angle to port and aim to come onto our starboard bows. That way the wind will push their ship against the 'Vrouwe Irene' and their sails will take the wind out of ours so then they can board us. As soon as I see them turn we will stream the drogue but leave the sails untouched. It will take them a while to realise that we are slowing down and they will have to alter their course again. When they do that we will release the sea anchor, turn into them and hope they will overshoot us. Once we are on their weather side they will have no hope of catching us. With their square rig they only have advantage while running down wind. Meanwhile, Abdullah, can you instruct the men to arm themselves but to take no obvious notice of that boat's approach but have them standby for some sudden course changes and they may have to repel boarders."

The minutes passed slowly, the hybrid schooner was now squarely aimed at ramming the 'Vrouwe Irene' and in an attempt to further intimidate what they thought to be some rich man's fancy yacht, they ran up the jolly roger.

When Harry saw that infamous flag go up he started laughing, *"They must be joking!"*

"I'm afraid not! I can see some musket barrels! I know they are peashooters compared to an M16 or even an AK47, but they can still kill you!"

"Only if you stand still long enough for them to get ready."

Kal gave Abdullah the nod and swung the bows of the 'Vrouwe Irene' so that the two schooners were rushing head-on to each other. The men adjusted the sheets so the sails were still at their most efficient. Next the drogue was set and with only a hundred yards to go the 'Vrouwe Irene' slowed down and turned even further to starboard and into the wind.

After a tense few minutes it was clear that Kal's strategy would only partly succeed.

The hybrid tried to compensate for the last minute course change but it did come too late and instead of hitting the 'Vrouwe Irene' on the starboard bows, which would have given the pirate the upper hand, the ship struck a glancing blow on 'Vrouwe Irene' port bows and that allowed her to scrape along the hybrid's port side. As a result the 'Vrouwe Irene' had the upper hand as far as position was concerned, now it just depended on the crew as to whether they could defeat the pirates.

The pirates threw over grappling hooks and pulled the two ships together, this resulted in the two ships turning to 'Vrouwe Irene's port until she was side on to the wind. Her sails still pushed the ship forward which meant that the pirate was being driven backwards and her sails became even less effective. Not a good position for a would-be victor to be in.

The first attacker to jump over from the hybrid schooner did not even hit the deck before he had Brutus as a necklace. Again the dog's body was visible air but the jaws and fangs were real enough.

Brutus was not playing this time and a snap of the jaws and a good hard shake of the head were enough to leave the man draped halfway over the bulwark and bleeding out at a rapid rate.

Four men jumped over from the pirate ship one had a musket and was menacing Kal with it when Brutus sauntered over and nonchalantly stood between the two. When Brutus with an ominous growl, sparkling white ivories and a near Mohawk bristle stood in front of the attacker, Kal new the man was about to experience severe pain.

It will remain a point of debate whether the man meant to shoot Kal, or Brutus or that the musket went off by accident. The fact remains that the weapon discharged with an almighty report that scared the wits out of not only Kal's crew but also those of the pirates located anywhere aft of the main mast. In any case the projectile discharged from the musket disappeared over the side and may have hit Antipodia at some later date.

In the meantime the man dropped the now redundant musket and drew his broad sword. In the interim Brutus had not been sitting still and was on her way over to get closer acquainted with the rogue. Her demeanour promised excruciating pain and impending doom and that was what she brought him. Some was self-inflicted because when the man tried to hack Brutus in half with his short sword, it met no resistance in the mirage of the dog but the weapon swung through and he just about amputated his own leg. He fell to the deck screaming in agony and Brutus stood over him with what looked suspiciously like a malicious grin before she casually removed his voice box and disconnected his carotids. Kal shook his head and said, "God, I hate it when you do that," as he patted her mirage head.

Meanwhile, the noise made by the musket shot had an unexpected response. Just after the shooter collapsed to the deck, the deckhouse door flew open and Jordie burst forth, her auburn hair swinging wildly about her face and shoulders and in her hands she held a blunderbuss. As she purposefully strode to the foredeck it was evident she was looking for someone.

Kal was speechless, in the first place he was not aware they had a blunderbuss on board and in the second place the reverend's daughter showed courage and determination he had not expected. She did not appear to be about to turn the other cheek.

Kal rushed forward to protect her but he was not really needed. Brutus 'had her back' and anybody in front of her and the weapon, got out of the way fast. Standing on the foredeck of the 'Vrouwe Irene', Jordie was level with the aft deck of the pirate ship. She stood there and looked at a man standing at the helm and issuing orders to others. He had a red bandanna, or whatever, wound around his head and Jordie was sure it was the pirate captain. She pointed the blunderbuss in his direction and shouted,

"Hey ye! Yes ye with the red rag around yer head. Be ye the captain of this tub?"

The man glared at her and moved over to grab a musket leaning against the railing. Jordie brought the blunderbuss to her shoulder and shouted,

"If ye thinks ye can get to that thing faster than I can pull this trigger, go ahead and try it! Please!"

There was something in Jordie's voice that made quite a few combatants stop and take notice. The captain, because that is who he was, froze for a long moment but then when he saw the eyes of most of his men on him, he decided that he needed to lead by example and that some slip of a girl could not tell him what to do.

Mind you even if her aim was right there was no guarantee that the projectile would hit anywhere within six feet of the point the blunderbuss was aimed at.

History does not record what the not so good man was thinking when he made a lunge for his musket, however, he never got there. Jordie pulled the trigger, the flint hit the primer and the blunderbuss exploded but not before it sent a solid lead ball through the forehead of the hapless pirate. The girls had well and truly overloaded the black powder charge and by the time the smoke cleared Jordie stood there with a black face and the barrel of the blunderbuss looked like the skin of a half peeled banana. Jordie looked at the defunct weapon and said, "Oops!"

Upon seeing their leader reduced to shark bait the remaining three pirates gave in gracefully they were more scared of Jordie and her blunderbuss than of the other crew members. Their apparent motto being, 'We don't fight girls.'

In a matter of moments they were trussed up like turkeys and Kal wondered what to do with their schooner. He had no use for it and anyhow he did not have the man power to run the two ships at once. He was half decided to scuttle the vessel when they heard voices calling from below decks. Upon investigation they found four men and a young girl shackled to a bulkhead. Slaves on their way to a market.

Kal soon found out that the five prisoners came from east Java and he had no problem communicating with them.

They told him that the Arab captain and his henchmen had captured them and four others. The Javanese had been on board of their inter-island trader when they had been attacked. The pirates sank their boat after robbing it of anything of value to them. Of the nine would-be slaves four died from the injuries sustained in the fight and Kal surmised the 'Vrouwe Irene' was attacked in an attempt to fill the vacancies left by those four.

Kal was still talking with the obvious leader of the Javanese when Jordie put her hand on his arm and said softly, "Will you have a look at that!"

Kal looked over to where Jordie was pointing and a big tension-breaking smile slid over his face. There was Brutus with the young girl, Brutus the killer hound from hell was laying on her back, tongue lolling out of the side of her mouth and tail wagging in the same slow rhythm by which the girl stroked the dog's belly. Brutus winked at Kal but did not get embarrassed neither did she report back for duty.

Kal's crew wise in the ways of ships and the sea meanwhile had lowered the sails on the 'Vrouwe Irene' and were busy lowering sails on the pirate and sorting out the tangled rigging.

Kal asked Jordie and Ono to see to the feeding of the starving ex-prisoners while he went to where Harry and Abdullah had latched on to the taff rail while Brutus was 'otherwise engaged'.

While leaning on the railing Kal asked, "Harry what are we going to do with those people and that schooner?"

"Well the right thing to do would be to sail the price to New Hoorn and to let the authorities decide."

"Yes well, you know what will happen, the authorities will see that schooner as their property and those Javanese will never see their homes again!"

"I didn't say the right thing to do was necessarily the right thing to do. There are more ways to skin this kitty! I agree with your summary of what would happen and may I therefore suggest that we send those people home using that schooner as their means of travel?"

"See? That's what I like about you. Even though you are a public servant you do come up with an original thought from time to time."

"I was a public servant in a land far, far away where a firm hand and a dogmatic approach to the rules was the only way to survive and, by the way, got me in my present travail."

"Yeah, yeah! Why aren't you talking Abdullah?"

"I don't see any cause for me to interfere, the planning and discussions are in total agreement with what I would suggest under the circumstances hence my voiced opinion would be surplus to requirements and therefore a waist of my time as well as yours."

"Jeez you were quick on the take with that one!"

Kal smiled and said as he walked away, "I'll leave you two love-birds to it while I will go and appoint a captain and give him his ship."

At first, to Kal's surprise, the Javanese did not appear all that keen on taking over the pirate ship. It took a bit of probing but eventually it came to light that the ex-prisoners were worried that if they arrived in any port in charge of a 'white man's' ship, they could be in trouble. After Kal explained that should he take them in to New Hoorn, the authorities would take the ship for sure. In the end the authorities might try to get them passage on a ship going to Java but it was far more likely that they would be walking and swimming home. They were still debating the matter when Kal had an idea, "I will write you a letter that will explain to whoever stops you that I have hired you to deliver my boat to Batavia for me."

Just then the little girl came over to show her father what a good dog Brutus was and could she keep her?

Brutus gave her a lopsided look that said, "How am I going to break it you gently? But I don't think so, Sweetheart."

Abdullah must have re-attached himself to Brutus now that the immediate violent action was over and he said in Kal's head, "*This pirate ship may be known on this coast or in the Java Sea. It may be advisable therefore to not only alter her appearance but also her name.*"

"You're not just a pretty face are you?"

In a matter of a few hours the pirate ship was renamed to, 'Java Belle', her square rig was replaced by a fore-and-aft mainsail with the compliments of 'Vrouwe Irene' whose spare mizzen sail was swapped for the 'Java Belle's' square sail and spar. A spare gaff on the 'Java Belle' was brought into play for her new mainsail and no boom was required.

Kal wrote an impressive looking letter with a lot of difficult words in which he said that the Javanese crew were delivering his vessel, the 'Java Belle', to Batavia for him. He signed the letter and then added both Harry's Abdullah's forced signatures. Harry signed as a Sergeant of Police in the capacity of witness to the legality of the document while Abdullah supposedly signed as the ship's previous owner. By late afternoon the two ships separated with the 'Java Belle' heading north and the 'Vrouwe Irene' heading south. Before the ships parted company Kal collected the slave irons used to hold the Javanese and in turn used them to imprison the three pirates. He had no idea what he was going to do with them. After one of them leered at Jordie and made some very lewd remarks, both the girl and Kal were tempted to see how well the pirates could swim while shackled together.

CHAPTER 21

WELCOME TO ANTIPODIA

THREE DAYS LATER and early that evening they sailed through what is known in the Core as the Sydney Heads.

When the lights of New Hoorn came into sight, they stood out like a welcoming beacon and all looked forward to some time on shore. The wind dropped to a light breeze and progress became agonisingly slow especially now that their goal was in sight.

Suddenly the peace was shredded when two Wraiths materialised on deck. They did their roaring and screaming act until they spotted the three hapless pirates who were shackled to the ship's railing. With a deafening roar they attacked the men who had no chance to either defend themselves or to escape the attack. It was over in a minute after the two Wraiths tore into the ill-starred men.

By the time they were finished there was not much more left than blood, gore and some bones. For some reason only known to themselves the Wraiths shied away from the encroaching crew. Perhaps once satiated the Wraiths had lost the will to fight and instead jumped overboard to swim for the shore.

Nobody on board felt that the Wraiths would be able to swim that far and even the islanders, excellent swimmers themselves, doubted very much that the Wraiths could reach the shore. No-one would shed a tear if they did not make it.

From time to time Kal would descend into a black cloud of depression and usually those bouts were associated with crippling back pain and migraine headaches. He did not know what came first the chicken or the egg, the depression or the migraine.

The first time Jordie experienced Kal's dark mood she thought it to be her fault but Harry assured her that she was not to blame and that it had to do with all the scars Kal had. Naturally she was curious as to how he had got them and got so many of them. Harry at first was reluctant to divulge the past but when she started asking questions that indicated she suspected Kal had been a price fighter of some kind he decided the girl should know the truth, after all there was nothing shameful in Kal's past.

As soon as Harry and Abdullah sat down on the cabin seat next to Jordie, Brutus realised that this was going to be one of those lengthy discussions so she released herself from her passengers and faded through the deckhouse door to be with Kal who had the deck watch.

Besides, she was of the opinion that Kal could do with a bit of TLC.

Harry related to Jordie how he and Kal had been in the army together and what happened and why. He was somewhat surprised when he realised that Jordie did not know Kal had come from the Core like himself and Abdullah. He then had to explain how in the Core the natural vibrations are faster nearer to the top than the bottom of the Core and that those different vibrations inspire people to 'discover' new technologies. It took a bit of explaining that each technological era had its own vibrational frequency. It was Abdullah who succeeded in making the penny drop when he said, *"Imagine a reed stalk rising out of a still pond.*

It is the only one there and the water is as smooth as a mirror.—have you got that picture in your mind?"

"Aye."

"The reed stalk is growing out of the earth at the bottom of the pond. Now something makes the stalk vibrate. What happens to the water?"

"It ripples."

"Right, what can you tell me about those ripples?"

"I suppose they go on and on until they run into the edges of the pond?"

"Correct again, but what I did want to hear is that the ripples stay on the water's surface, the horizontal plane. Now imagine that the reed stalk is the Core, where do you think the vibration causes the most movement, at the base or the top of the stalk?"

"At the tip the base being thicker and stiffer than the tip?"

"Right again. Now, the rate of movement at any given point along the length of the stalk we call it's frequency at that point. The higher along the stalk the greater the movement and therefore the frequency. Can you follow that so far?"

"Aye, what ye be saying is that the reed stalk be the same as the Core and that it grows upward, away from the Beginning and that the higher it grows the higher the frequency of its vibrating?"

"Precisely, now anything alive on or in the Core vibrates at the same frequency as the Core at that point. It is this frequency rate that affects people's brains and causes them to discover and develop new technologies."

"Aye be that like the discovery of the art of printing in the 1400s by the Germanics and the Chinese only fifty years apart?"

"Yes that is a good example. In our case what happened was that at a certain point in the Core's growth it produced the vibrations that made people develop the technology of sail. It took hundreds' of years for the Core vibrations to increase and give gradual rise in the development of the technology of sail.

One of the problems with the Core vibrations is that they mainly find resonance in younger brains.

The older people become, the harder it is for them to change with the Core vibration until a point is reached where the new vibrations are so different that those that could not keep up with them, reject the Core and peel off into a Dimension where the vibrations remain the same as what they were when it separated from the Core. This is where the surface of the pond comes in, we can compare that with the Dimension of sail. After that instead of growing UPWARD with the Core, a Dimension grows OUTWARD at right angles to the Core like the surface of our pond and technology does the same by lateral improvement.

When our reed stalk broke the surface of the pond the technology of sail was no longer the highest technological advancement because at that time the Core was already involved with the technologies driving the industrial revolution. Steam took over from sail and the combustion engine was not far away."

"Begging yer pardon. Ye now speak of things of which I have no ken, like steam replacing sail, and what be a combustion engine?"

"Don't worry about that just yet."

"I be born in this Dimension of Sail but I be young does that mean my vibration still rises with that of the Core and I be unhappy here in the Dimension? Or be my brain now slow and stiff like an elder?"

"No. Your vibrations are no longer influenced by the growth of the Core, instead they now respond to the frequency of the Dimension and that allows your creativity to be expressed in the further improvement of all technologies relating to wood and sail. Those that were caught up in the final separation were older people because they spent their life working techniques that suited their vibrational frequency, and that is what made them happy in the first place. When those people are faced with a new technology for which their own vibrational frequency is too low, they opt to follow their life's pre-occupation and follow the technique into its dimension. In that Dimension the upward development ceases and the outward development, or call it the further improvement of the specific science—in our case that of sail—becomes the goal. In this Dimension of sail and wood for instance, the Balon wood was developed, the flax and cotton grown here for the purpose of making sails, for instance, is far superior to anything grown in the Core."

Abdullah looked over at Harry and said, "Hey, it's about time you take over again."

"No, you're doing fine and anyway it serves you right for butting in in the first place."

Abdullah smiled, not that Jordie could see that of course, but before he could continue, Jordie asked, "Be there any more of those 'peel away' dimensions?"

"Yes there are, there are many small ones at all levels along the Core but the big ones are those where a completely different technology erupted and what was the current technology became obsolete quite suddenly. The first one may have been the Dimension of Stone and Fire. The next big one would have been the Dimension of Bronze and Copper."

"You said there be many little ones along the Core. How does that work?"

"Ok, imagine it like this, at a certain point in time a stone-age man found out that the buffalo skin he hung up to dry on a tallish branch on the tree trunk he was pushing home through the water became a lot easier to push with the wind coming from behind. In fact it was so good, he could stop pushing his fire wood and clothing raw material and could actually relax by climbing on the log.

The first sailing raft was born. At that point in time a 'technology ring' grew around the Core.

Our caveman and his mates sailed happily downwind on their logs while drying their buffalo hides. Then the Core vibrations inspired somebody to hollow out a log and the first canoe was born.

Next some smart-ass came along and plaited a mat to use as sail. 'Boris and the Originals' wanted nothing to do with all this newfangled technology and they pushed off from the Core to create their own little mini dimension.

Every time something new was added to the knowledge of sail and some more brains could not understand the vibrations that caused this enlargement of the technique, the budding dimension of sail would widen but still grow along with the Core.

This two dimensional growth—upwards and outwards—continued until the time the main push created by the vibrations in the growing Core dumped the technology of sail in favour of a completely new technology and from that point on the growth in the Dimension of Sail only went outward and that means that anything new is strictly concerned with the ESTABLISHED technology of Sail."

"So, in the Core there be no more Sail technology? What about trade between the islands? How be that done?"

"There is still some sail technology in the Core; it is just no longer a necessity for trade and commerce. There still are ships crossing the oceans and seas but most are no longer propelled by wind."

"How do ye mean? Slaves in gallows?!"

"No, the ships are driven by what is called an engine. The engine converts fuel into energy and that energy can be used to turn a propeller which in turn pushes the ship through the water."

"Ok, no slaves rowing, no sails drawing?! Yeah, whatever! Anyway how come ye knows so much about it?"

"Because I, we, come from the Core."

"Who be 'we'?"

"Myself, Harry and Kal."

"Oh yes! I knew that! But tell me why Kal be flesh and blood and ye pair are of so little substance?"

In mock anger Harry grumbled, *"Watch how you put that, young lady!"*

Before the exchange between Harry and Jordie could degenerate into one of their friendly slinging matches, Abdullah continued with, *"On occasion someone is born 'too late' and does not fit into the Core society. If that person has the typical characteristics of a bygone age, he or she may be spontaneously transferred into their right Dimension. Kal is such a person and his transfer was spontaneous. Harry's and my transfers were the result of meddling by people in the Core who think they have discovered and easy way to get rid of unwanted people."*

With a slight smirk on her face because Jordie could not imagine why two people like Harry and Abdullah could be labelled 'a danger to society', she asked, "And what crimes against humanity earned ye a trip to the Dimension of Sail?"

"In Harry's case the list is endless but let us say the one that cooked his goose, was his attempt to expose the people directly and indirectly responsible for Kal's injuries and the suffering he experienced on their behalf."

Harry muttered something under his breath the gist of which gave Jordie a clear understanding of what Harry would do to each and every one of those people if he ever got hold of them.

"And what about ye Abdullah?"

With a bitter little laugh Abdullah replied, *"I was an innocent bystander. I was the maître de at the 'Trade-winds' island resort on Balon Island. A South American drug lord was in hiding there when the powers that be, decided society would be better off without his presence so they tried to transport him—and the resort with him—into this dimension. A lot of innocent people became part of that package. Something went wrong and even though we did not finish up as Wraiths, we became what is now known as*

Shimmerers, half person—half wraith by day and half wraith—half person by night."

"Begging yer pardon, but what be the difference?"

"During the day I can remember what I did yesterday but not what I did last night. At night I can remember what I did the night before but no what I did yesterday during the day."

"That be a bit tricky."

"Yes, it is daytime now so you can ask me all about what happened yesterday but not about what happened last night."

"Ooookay, so what about ye Harry, how come ye be a Shimmerer if you nay be part of this 'Trade-winds' thingy?"

"I was not always a Shimmerer you know, I got talked into it."

"Bull-dust! He asked to be made into a Shimmerer so he and Brutus could become inseparable but then Abdullah had to come between them."

It was Kal who had come into the deckhouse and could not resist to tease his friend.

"Hmm! Yes well, perhaps we best nay go there." Jordie joked and then asked Kal, "When be we dropping anchor?"

"That's what I came to tell you. The Port Authority cutter is about to come along-side. Harry you and Abdullah better lay-off the bickering and Brutus you better get your 'Trespassers may be eaten' look to keep them at a safe distance."

Somewhat nervous Jordie asked, "What about me, Kal?"

With a quasi-frown and rubbing his chin, Kal looked her over and said, "You're a nun we are giving a lift to your mission headquarters in the Fidji Isles."

With a haughty look over her shoulder and a little wiggle of her hips she remarked, "Amongst the faithful as well as the converted we are known as 'sister' and not 'nuns'! But I belong to neither group."

Suddenly serious Harry interrupted, "*I would not let on that you are an ex-slave on the lam.*"

"That despicable little toad had no legal claim over me or Ono!"

"*I know that but we don't want to pique any public servant's curiosity. The 'Earl' is dead and his reign of terror is over and it serves no worthwhile purpose to arouse any official interest in us or what we have been up to.*"

"Harry, spoken like a true public servant, but Jordie, he is right the least attention we attract from the 'authorities' the better it is."

"Alright but we hast nothing to hide, like, we didst nay wrong!"

"That may be so but I do not want to have to explain what happened to the 'Earl' or the pirate ship for that matter. So we'll just be polite and a tumbler short of a full jug of wine so they can leave us alone."

It was Abdullah who sounded disappointed when he remarked, "*Oh G! And I was so looking forward to telling them how Jordie blew that blunderbuss apart and the look on her face when that pirate captain sprouted a red flower on his forehead and could not make it to his musket!*"

"Yes, well, ye better behave and do as the CAPTAIN ordered! We do nay want any unnecessary attention dost we now?" Jordie retorted with a schoolmarm voice.

Shortly after the 'Vrouwe Irene' reduced sail and the Port Authority cutter came alongside and two men jumped across onto the deck.

"Good evening to ye all! Who be the Master?"

"I be the Master of the 'Vrouwe Irene'. Kal van Straaten, how can I be of service?"

"Whence dost ye hail from?"

"Balon Wood Isle via an unnamed island in the savage isles North-north-east from here."

"Didst ye encounter any savages there?"

"Nay, we only called in to replenish our dwindling water supplies."

"Didst ye encounter any pirates?"

"Nay. Why dost ye ask?"

"We noted blood stains on the deck and suspected a violent encounter took place."

"Aye upon approach of yonder headlands, two Wraith materialised and attacked one of the crew."

"Aye, so noted. What be the where-about of said Wraiths?"

"That be the curious happenance! Both devoured the hapless man but then jumped ship together!"

"Yes that be curious behaviour but then again, who knows what goes on in the brain of a Wraith?"

One of the Port Authority officer spotted Jordie and asked, "And who may be the shapely wench?"

Kal laughed softly and confided, "Much to my dismay I must tell ye that she be a nun on her way to save the heathens in Fidji."

"What a waste! Anyway, what be the purpose of yer visit?"

"We came to obtain lead for ballast for a ship being built on Balon Isle."

"In that case ye be advised to drop anchor over yonder where the ship builders ply their trade. If I may suggest a man by the name of Amos is a trader with extensive knowledge of the boat-building trade and an honest trader to boot."

The helpful official pointed to an area where Kal could see a row of boats in various stages of construction sitting on slipways. A few other sailing vessels were riding their anchors there as well.

After some more palaver the Port Authority officers wished Kal a safe journey and withdrew to their cutter.

Kal ordered some more sails set and changed course towards the anchorage the officials had indicated.

Jordie came over and asked, "What didst those men wanted to know about me?"

"Gee you have a high opinion of yourself! What makes you think they wanted to know anything about you?"

"The way they be leering at me!"

"You better get used to that. They wanted to know who you are and I told them that you are a nun on her way to the Fiji islands. They were disappointed."

She briefly touched his hand and then walked away. Kal noticed something sad in her behaviour and wondered what it was but then the needs of his ship took over and he directed the crew to ready the 'Vrouwe Irene' to come to anchor a safe distance away from a brigantine already swinging on her anchors.

It was a warm summer's night and seeing how the twilight hours during which the Wraiths normally materialised were well past, most of the crew found comfortable spots on deck for a well-earned rest.

Kal retired to the divan bed in the deckhouse seeing how that was the only resting place long enough for his tall body. Brutus and entourage preferred to stay on deck and so did Jordie and Ono.

For a long time Kal lay there thinking about the journey so far and as to how to best tackle the next step towards getting his junk afloat. He was impressed with the sailing ability of 'Vrouwe Irene' as a ketch rigged schooner but he preferred the somewhat slower but more comfortable and forgiving characteristics of a proper junk.

He must have been dozing off because he did not hear or see Jordie coming until she quietly lay down next to him. She placed her head and right arm on his chest and Kal automatically wrapped his arm around her shoulders. Neither of them spoke and Kal had a feeling that speaking would disrupt a certain harmonious spell.

Much later she snuggled into his body and whispered with wonder in her voice, "I never thought I could want it and on top of that enjoy it so much."

After a pause she whispered with sadness in her voice, "I can never give ye a baby. Ye knew that didst ye not?"

"Whether I did or did not does not change anything Jordie, my feelings are for you not for any unborn babies."

After a while Kal continued, "Before you get too attached to me you should consider the fact that I am fourteen years older than you and with all my scars I am nothing much to look at."

"Do ye want me to call ye 'daddy'? And what of the scars ye talk about, I nay see any, I only see thee."

Rather morosely Kal said softly, "I hope you will never have to compare me with your father."

Jordie realised she must have touched a sore point in Kal's self-esteem and whispered, "I be sure I won't! Now hold me and go to sleep."

CHAPTER 22

NEW HOORN

An hour after sun-up, Kal ordered the ship's long boat to be launched and a short time later Kal, the girls and the crew bar one, were on their way to shore. Brutus and co plus one crew member stayed on board.

Before going ashore Kal, through Abdullah, instructed the shore-going crew members to suss the place out for merchants that could supply the ship with food and other stores, he himself was looking for a merchant that could sell him four tons of lead in ingots.

The girls were going to do what girls do best, they went shopping.

On the waterfront itself there were a number of slipways and almost every one of them had a ship on the stocks.

Kal went from yard to yard asking where he could find Amos, the trader recommended to him by the Port Authority officer.

It was not until midday that he found him at one of the slipways overseeing the delivery of spars for a nearly completed brig. When Kal approached him with his request for lead, Amos took him to his office down one of the narrow cobblestoned alleys.

On their way there Kal could not help but compare what he saw in New Hoorn with the same area of Sydney in the Core. Here the place although a hive of activity the feel of 'go-go-get-it' so prevalent in the Sydney water front was missing. To start off with, the smell of diesel fumes was absent, people although not dawdling were not in too much of a hurry not to greet each other or even stop for a quick enquiry of some kind.

People came across as being confident and less harassed then their fellow men in the Core.

As they walked the side-walks of narrow streets past warehouses and go-downs, Kal luxuriated in the smells of spices from the far-east, the smell of teak, camphor and other exotic woods from Asia.

One shop had beautifully carved trunks and a ward robe made from Djati, a black iron wood from Borneo, on display on the side-walk. In Kal's estimation it would take four men to move the ward robe in and out of the shop. "Does the merchant leave his wares on display out here over-night?"

Amos shook his head and grinned, "Nay, his daughter be a levitator and it be her that dost the transportation of his goods. As a matter of interest, it be her to levitate thine lead on board should a deal be struck."

The mention of a levitator took Kal back to when he met Moana the spouse of Kees, both were dimensioners he met in his early days in the Dimension. Moana was a powerful levitator and between her and Kees they introduced Kal to this typical dimensional art.

A few are born with the ability to move heavy objects with the touch of a finger and an inordinate amount of concentration.

The levitator, always a female and one that has never born a child, learns through meditation to concentrate anti-gravitational forces in every fibre of her body. In order to expose the maximum surface of her being to act as antenna for the cosmic forces, the levitator never wears any clothes at all and many will not even wear bangles, arm bands, necklaces or rings.

One might say that the art of levitation is a technology never developed in the Core and could be seen as an upward development.

The counter argument to that is that the same forces are present in the Core but were never developed except perhaps by some fringe-dwellers like the generally ridiculed witchdoctors, Magicians and other dabblers in the occult. In the Core there never was the time to develop this science. While in the Dimension this and other esoteric sciences are pursued because they were already there and just needed lateral development.

The individual levitator has limitations to weight and size of the object to be moved, she must at all times be in contact with both the object and the ground. To this end she shuffles her feet never lifting one or the other off the ground. Where the weight and or size of the object to be shifted lays outside the capabilities of a levitator a second and even a third may come together to achieve their aim.

Eventually Amos stopped in front of a shop where the shop front consisted of a glass and lead window that held some hundred and twenty squares of glass held together by strips of lead between the individual panes. Seen from the inside of the shop it became evident that each pane of glass although mainly clear, had its individual shade of clear. Amos noticed Kal's interest and wistfully remarked, "That window ones held the image of a galleon under full sail and in full colours."

"What? As a painted window?"

"Nay! It were a proper leaded window of coloured glass, as one sees of saints and such in the better cathedrals!"

"What happened to it?"

"What else! Vandals smashed it! At least their leader a ruffian by the name of Hendrik be no more, he be feeding the fishes at the bottom of the harbour."

"Did you put him there?"

"Nay, he were caught setting fire to one of the buildings on the water front. Some raw justice was met out that night to him and two of his cohorts."

"Perhaps a bit drastic?"

"May-haps but it were effective, there be no further vandal activity for near on two years!"

"Didn't the Port Authority investigate?"

"Yes, some two weeks gone by. Memories fade and the general recollection were that there be quite some Wraith activity that night. Who's to say with any assurance what transpired on that dark and frightful night?"

While they had been talking, Amos showed Kal into an office that reminded Kal of places he had seen in old Europe, the walls were covered in wainscoting up to five feet from the floor. The panelling was in natural wood colour and the sandstone walls above that had their natural sandstone colouring. Although the years of people smoking cigars in there had stained the walls towards the ceiling a rich brown.

Near one wall of the office stood a large mahogany desk with a comfortable looking leather upholstered chair behind it for the operator of the desk.

The light from the large window fell onto the desk from the left so a right handed person using one of the nibbed pens would not be writing in his own shadow.

On the other side of the room a stood a small round table with three comfortable looking leather upholstered chairs. In the middle of that table stood a silver coffee pot with steam coming from the spout. The smell of freshly brewed coffee was very inviting. Kal wondered if Amos had sent off a carrier pigeon to warn his wife to have the coffee ready.

There was nothing business like about the way Amos went about his business, he began by offering Kal one of the easy chairs, next he asked Kal if he wanted coffee and if he did how he would like it assuming in advance that he wanted it in a cup.

Once seated, business was not mentioned until both had sampled their coffee then Amos started the proceedings by laying down the rules of business as he called them, "My way of conducting business be not to the taste of some but I found it to be the quickest and least tasking. Thy inform me of what thine requirements be and I will tell what can be done and what the costs be to thee. There be no haggling back and forth. Does that approach meet with thy approval?"

"Let me get this straight, I tell you what I need and you will tell me what you can do and how much it going to cost? And should the price be too high in my estimation, I just say thank you and walk away?"

"Aye. In that manner thy never hast to wonder whether thee might have missed the opportunity to obtain the merchandise for less. While this one-price-only approach on my side assures thee that the price asked is the minimum I can offer thee."

"That sounds fair enough to me. What I hope to get is four tons of lead in twenty pound ingots."

"Aye, presumably delivered 'on board'?"

"Yes."

"Let me see…"

Amos got busy with a silver-point and a piece of much used and erased parchment. The tip of his tongue described little circles in front of his lips and a concentration frown wrinkled his brow. Kal sipped the excellent coffee while he waited.

Eventually Amos surfaced, put his tongue away and sighed, "Thy requirements be eight thousand pounds of lead in ingot form of twenty pounds each. The price of lead, pure lead, at present being a quarter of a ducat per pound, the total price be two thousand ducats delivered on board."

"What is the exchange rate for the Ducat?"

"The present gold value of the Doubloon be seven point six grams."

"A Doubloon equals two Ducats, right?"

"That be correct so the total cost in gold be seven thousand six hundred grams or seven point six kilograms."

"Right, is there a bank or something like that where I can exchange some jewels and free gold for Doubloons?"

"Aye there be. The Royal Bank of the VOC[5], be represented by the New Hoorn Exchange Bank."

Kal reached his hand out and shook Amos', "It is a deal then."

A few more pleasantries were exchanged and Amos produced an excellent Portuguese Port and a glass for each sealed the transaction.

Kal was about to leave and with his hand on the door knob he asked, "How safe is this town?"

"In what manner?"

"Well I must find the New Hoorn Exchange Bank to trade some valuables for doubloons and I would not like to be ambushed on my way there or on my return."

"When would ye need to conduct said transaction? Would on the morrow suit ye?"

"Yes it would."

"That being the case, I be honoured if ye allow me to provide escort to the Bank seeing as how I too must do my banking."

On that note they parted and Kal returned to the waterfront where his crew would be waiting with the longboat.

---

5   VOC. Vereenigde Oostindiesche Companie. [United (Dutch) East India Company]

Just as Kal arrived at the jetty he saw Jordie and Ono coming back from their trip to town, both were chattering and giggling while they tried to control a number of mysterious parcels and packages.

"Good afternoon ladies, how was your shopping? All shopped out?"

"Never!" Jordie laughed.

"What did you get?"

"Oh, ye know, girl things!"

"So they are secret are they?"

"Sort of."

"What does that mean? Sort of!"

"Don't be impatient!" She laughed as they all climbed into the longboat.

As soon as they climbed on board of the 'Vrouwe Irene', the girls shooed Brutus and retinue out of the deckhouse as well as one of the crew who had been asleep and who was not too impressed with the female stand-over tactics.

Brutus came up to Kal to greet him and next Kal heard Harry's voice, "*Hey! Aren't you the skipper AND owner of this tub?*"

"Yeah, so?"

"*Well how come you let that snip of a girl chase us out of the deckhouse?*"

"Probably because she told me too to stay out as well."

Even Brutus then chipped in with, "wooF"[6]

Seemingly there was nothing they could do about it so Kal informed them of the trade with Amos. He was quite happy with the deal and actually had expected a higher price.

Soon some delicious smells of frying onions and meat and other unidentified but seemingly very appetising culinary aromas came wafting

---

[6]   Brutus speak, wooF, *What the hell!*

from the deckhouse and it was decided that the girls were cooking up a storm and to leave them alone.

Knowing very well that neither Harry nor Abdullah required any food, Kal nevertheless was not surprised when Harry grumbled, *"You see that Abdullah! Everything for little Kallie here! Those women know very well that we do not eat but still they have to go and tempt us with those smells all because they want to get in the good books with Kal."*

Abdullah gave a sly cackle and said in a doom-laden voice, *"Do not worry my friend! We will suck off the delicious aroma and that will leave the food tasteless but Kal will still have to eat all of it to show his appreciation."*

"I wonder if Brutus will be on our side." Harry asked in a hopeful tone.

Kal bent over and patted Brutus on the head and asked, "You wouldn't would you Brutus?"

After a few moments Brutus lifted her head and howled.[7]

Kal groused, "Bloody traitor!"

It took a long time but eventually the moment arrived when it seemed that Kal's grumbling stomach would get some satisfaction.

The deckhouse door was thrown open and a smiling Jordie presented herself for Kal's inspection. All Kal was interested in at that moment was to still the gnawing critters in his stomach and he was just about to thank Jordie with a winning smile and to dash past her to the table when a momentary look of disappointment on Jordie's face caught his eye.

A more critical appraisal of the girl informed Kal that there was something different about her.

He stopped his headlong rush not because he was awe struck but simply because he could not figure out what it was that was different. Was it her hair? No. Did she wear new bangles, or a necklace? No. Then what was it? Suddenly he saw it! The narrow belt and small apron Ono

---

[7]   Brutus speak, *"I feel your pain as though it is mine but what can I do?"*

had plaited for her was gone, instead she now wore a broader, leather girdle that sat low on her hips and dipped down in a 'v' below her belly button. At the bottom of the 'v' thin leather thongs extended into an apron and each thong had a wooden bead at its end. The belt was of fairly thick but supple leather and was finely tooled with an array of mythological dragons, birds and other decorative symbols. Jordie twirled around to show off and with a big smile she asked, "Do you like it?"

Jokingly Kal folded his left arm over his chest while he rubbed his chin with his right hand. He tipped his head to the side and studied her while inwardly he marvelled at the fact that Jordie seemed to be as excited as a girl in the Core would be showing off a new evening gown.

When the pause dragged out a bit too long for Jordie's liking she asked with a frown, "Well?"

"Yeah, it is gorgeous but…"

"But what!"

"I still like the looks of the girl inside the belt better."

"Argh! Men!"

With her arm through his she lead him to the cabin table where a selection of Malayan type spicy dishes was awaiting his attention.

As Kal was getting stuck into the food of his childhood he asked Jordie, who was daintily sampling some of the more harmless looking and or smelling dishes, "Did you or Ono know how to cook this stuff?"

"No…"

"Just as well! If either of you had I now would have to keelhaul you for holding out on me!"

Jordie laughed happily and told him, "We were looking for a way to thank ye for what ye didst for us but we did nay know how to until we arrived at the Chinese food market in town and I remembered that one of the people ye rescued from the pirate ship didst tell me that ye sorely missed the food from the Indies. So we enlisted a kind old Chinese lady who be selling spices and she gave us all the recipes and some we have nay tried yet."

"Well, thank you very much aren't you going to join me?"

"That were the intention but because neither Ono nor I have ever cooked those dishes before, we had to sample each one and we be satiated. Those fried bananas be yummy be they not?"

CHAPTER 23

MARIGOLD JORDAN MCDOUGALL

"STILL NAY SIGHT of the lass?" Amos asked as he looked concernedly at Kal as the latter sat with his head in his hands staring at the cobblestone pavement at his feet.

Kal shook his head and replied, "No! And I got no idea where she could be! I just hope that she did not meet with foul play."

"Were Jordie in a sad or subdued mood?"

"No! That's just it, she seemed happier than ever! That is what makes me fear she may have been abducted but why?"

"She be a comely lass and we may need to consider that although rare, she may have been waylaid for the purpose of enslavement."

Kal did not say anything to that even though the thought had infected his mind ever since Jordie had failed to return from a trip into town to do some shopping. There had been nothing in her demeanour to indicate that she was planning on leaving and only the night before her and Ono had been talking about what Jordie was going to do once she got back to Fiji.

The question had been would she get in contact with the Brethren, the religious zealots her father had belonged to? Her answer had been an emphatic, 'Nay ever!'

When Kal told Amos about this the latter became quite agitated, "Ye be amiss by nay mentioning that happenance earlier!"

"Why?"

"The Brethren be represented here in New Hoorn and them may be the abductors!"

Kal jumped up and balled his fists, "Where do I find them?!"

"Calm thyself, there be no profit in thy charging off to confront them, they would merely spirit her away. Let me send out one of my spies, a man skilled in the arts of observance without being seen."

It took a bit of convincing but in the end Kal was persuaded to let Amos' man scout out the Brethren enclave to see if he could establish Jordie's presence there.

Within an hour Amos despatched his man and the long wait began. It was late in the afternoon so they did not expect to get any report from him until at least the next morning.

Ono was the last to see her, on the day in question the girls went to the market to get fresh produce like they did every second day or so. When they got to the market Ono went one way while Jordie went the other and they planned to meet at the Chinese lady's stall where they bought their spices.

Ono got there first and had been talking with the old lady for quite some time before she became worried about Jordie's failure to show up.

After a feverish search of the market Ono rushed back to the ship and reported the matter. Kal together with the whole crew searched the market and immediate environment for hours but without success.

They continued their scouring of the town for another three days before Kal decided that with the cyclone season coming on it would be in Ono's interest if he send the 'Vrouwe Irene' to Fiji to take her home and then return for him and, hopefully, Jordie.

Now Kal had the choice to do what he had been doing for the last fortnight and wander along the waterfront visiting taverns in the hope he would meet someone who might have seen or knew the whereabouts of Jordie, or he could accept Amos' offer of a meal and a jug of rum.

After the 'Vrouwe Irene' left to take Ono to her home in Fiji Kal had accepted Amos' invitation to stay at the trader's house.

The journey to Fiji and back was not expected to take more than twenty-five days and Kal thought it unlikely that he would find the girl if he had not done so within that time. So far fourteen days passed without seeing hide nor hair of her and Kal was getting desperate. In his search for a reason for her disappearance he even played with the notion that she might have been transferred into the Core.

After breakfast, Kal was just getting ready for another search of the water front when Amos' man rushed in. The man was out of breath and took a while to slow down his breathing so he could speak. He rattled off something in a dialect that Kal could not understand—the local common language in fact a mishmash of mainly Dutch, Portuguese and Malay—. As the man made his report Amos became quite excited and finally told Kal, "He thinks he saw her in the Brethren's compound!"

A shot of adrenalin coursed through his veins as Kal asked, "What did he see?"

"He observed three people, two men and a women between them, enter the chapel. My man at first saw nothing strange in that until he noticed that each man had a hold of one of the woman's arms."

"Ok, but what made him think that the woman was Jordie?"

Amos put the question to the man and he replied at length. Finally Amos turned to Kal, "My man observed that although she wore a bonnet and her hair be cut short, he noticed some hair be outside the bonnet and that hair be orange like Jordie's."

"Ok, let's go!"

"Nay, my friend, my man will show ye the location but neither he nor I may be seen there. Trust me to ensure that no troopers be in the vicinity of the Brethren's enclave during yer visit there."

"What are you going to do?"

"Do not be concerned with that matter but bring back the girl safely if it be her."

Half an hour later Amos' scout pointed at a gated yard, nodded his head and was gone.

Kal's army training took over and he spend quite some time observing the place. An ornate iron piquet fence between brick pillars every twenty feet or so closed off a gravel and grassed yard from the road. The side fences were of wooden palings and no more than seven feet high. The three storied sandstone building set back from the road looked like it once had hosted balls and other occasions where the rich had escorted their ladies up the sweeping stairs leading up to the balcony in front of the massive wooden doors.

Off near the right hand boundary of the property stood a smaller building with a domed spire and Kal assumed that to be the chapel Amos' man had spoken about. Over on the left hand side of the yard there were some stables but none seemed occupied. A Wraith gutter encircled the property just inside the boundary fences and another was visible nearer the old mansion while a third encircled the chapel.

Whether the occupants of the property to the right of the Brethren were of an opposing religious philosophy or just not into gardening is of no importance. The fact that their property, especially on the boundary with the Brethren's was overgrown afforded Kal plenty of scope to approach the chapel un-noticed.

It was getting towards sun down when Kal climbed the fence.

He hid behind the chapel and waited. He was not quite sure what he was waiting for but hoped the Brethren would make the next move. He did not have long to wait. One of the faithful, *we'll call him 'Bro One'*, came outside to light the Wraith gutters.

Kal let him light the one encircling the house but when he came over to light the one surrounding the chapel, Kal came up behind him and hooked his left arm around the man's forehead and eyes. In his right hand he wielded the klewang and placed its razor sharp edge against the man's throat.

After he had dragged him into the dark shadows of the chapel he instructed the petrified man, "You call out for the new wench to bring out more oil for the Wraith gutter."

"Wh…what be the, the purpose of that?"

"Yours is not to ask why, yours is just to do or die."

"Th…that be nonsense, the Lord be my shield."

Kal was done talking, he dragged the klewang across the man's throat leaving a shallow but profusely bleeding cut.

"Every time you do not follow my instructions I will drag this sword through the same cut but deeper until at last I cut your throat. Now tell the new wench…What be her name?"

"Sis…Sister Marigold, Marigold McDougall."

"She is not your bloody sister! Now call her!"

"With her will be a guard who will overcome thy."

"And why would he overcome me?"

"Because the Lord be on his side."

"Well, call her and let's see whose side He is on. Oh by the way you say any more than what I told you to say and they can pick up your head out of the Wraith gutter."

To make his point the klewang made another pass across the nervously bobbing Adams apple.

"Now be as good a time as any to call."

After a very brief hesitation the man called, "Have Sister Marigold bring me more oil for the Wraith gutter..."

He was going to extend his request but thought better of it when the klewang made another gentle pass through what must have felt like the grand canyon of blood.

Suddenly the heavy wooden door of the mansion flew open and two men holding a squirming person dressed in the long black skirt of the order and the white neck to ankle gown that was both under garment and blouse.

As soon as the trio started coming down the steps, the girl tore away from the men in more than one way.

In their haste to grab her, they took hold of her shoulders and as she tried to shrug them off their hands slipped and only latched on to the white garment. The force with which she struggled tore the garment and as a result she finished up bare to the waist. Her bobbing breasts distracted her wardens to the extent that Kal had the time to render his captive, 'Bro One', unconscious by a well-placed blow to the temple with the handle of the klewang. That done he stepped out of the shadows and nearly jumped right back when the struggling female took one look at him and shouted, "KAL!!"

Yup, that's my Jordie!

She dropped the can of oil and charged forward and easily out ran her two guards.

Kal admired her presence of mind when she did not try to fly into his arms and thereby hamper him in what was to come. She tore off her bonnet as she ran and Kal confirmed what he suspected earlier, they had cut off most of Jordie's long auburn hair; the one aspect of her self-image she had been so proud of.

The first of the escorting Brethren, we'll call him 'Bro Two', to reach him came full pelt and probably hoped to knock Kal to the ground. Kal waited for him and just when the man put his left leg down to commence the last step to reach Kal, the latter jumped up and landed stiff legged on his opponent's knee. There was a loud crack and then an even louder scream when the knee joint collapsed and the man suddenly had a double jointed but useless knee.

The second man, 'Bro Three', on his arrival at the scene did some fancy goose stepping fearing Kal would somehow do the same to his knee but he did not need to have worried because Kal had something different in mind for him.

On his way to where the action was 'Bro Three' had picked up the container of oil and this he now hurled at Kal. Kal ducked and the container went sailing off in the distance spilling its oil on the way. Realising his only weapon was gone 'Bro Three' started yelling about Kal fighting an unfair fight unbecoming a gentleman.

Being of a gallant nature Kal replied, "Huh? What are you babbling about?"

"Ye be armed with a sword! Yet, dost ye intend to fight me, an unarmed man of the cloth?"

"No. The matter is in your hands. I will state what I am about to do and it is up to you whether or not you want to make an issue of it."

The brother seemed to grow taller in statue and less frightened, "And what, pray tell, dost ye aim to do?"

"I am taking this girl away from here to where she wants to be."

"That be impossible as she belongs to the Brethren. Praise be the Lord."

"Says who and to what purpose?"

"Says I and she must, in the name of the Lord, provide me with all my needs."

"Spiritual needs?"

"Nay! She being a mere woman could not provide such!"

"So, in other words you want her as a slave to do your menial work and to warm your bed! And on whose authority do you claim her?"

"Mine. As the leader of the Brethren in Antipodia and the Pacific."

"And which part of her do you claim to own, her body or her soul?"

Now quite angry 'Bro Three' roared in his best hell and damnation voice, "Ye blaspheme! She be Marigold McDougall, daughter of the Right reverend Elijah McDougall a servant of the Lord and born under the umbrella of the Brethren. The good Brother McDougall was called unto the Lord and therefore all that belongs to him shall be returned to the Brethren."

"Well sorry your Lordship but that makes no bloody sense at all."

Suddenly Jordie spoke up, "Ever since the *Right Reverend Elijah McDougall, servant of the Lord,* deflowered his own daughter, said daughter does nay recognise his claim to be the father of her."

"Ye have no right to denounce yer father!"

Kal had enough and he rudely interrupted, "You have less right to claim her as your property. She is coming with me that is if she wants to."

"Of course I want…" Jordie got no further than that because 'Bro Three', or whatever he called himself, made a sudden dash towards her but Kal was just that little bit quicker and tripped the man. He went down hard and on his way he grabbed a couple of handfuls of Jordie's skirt. The skirt came down and Jordie stepped out of it while she said, "Thank you now I'll just get rid of this night gown thing!"

When that dropped around her ankles as well she finished her statement by remarking, "Ah, that feels so much better!"

With his face pressed down into the gravel and Kal's foot on his neck, 'Bro Three' could do nothing but listen when Kal quasi-official said, "Well me-lady behold the head-honcho brother of the Brethren, grovelling at thy feet begging for yer forgiveness."

"Let me hear it from him. It would have so much more meaning."

"Having a mouth full of gravel makes that somewhat difficult me-lady."

"My gallant knight, it behoves me to inform ye that yon knave be returned to a conscious state and be on the point of flight me-thinks."

"Right, play time is over! We are out of here. Hang on, where is your girdle?"

"Those bastards took it!"

Kal stomped down on the neck of his captive and ordered, "Tell Brother 'Just Awake' where to find it and to bring it here. You can also tell him that if he brings anything or anybody else he will be the cause of your death! You both understand that last bit?"

Brother 'Still Groggy' nodded his head emphatically and scurried away before his fearless leader even told him to do so.

As they waited Kal was well aware that the man under his foot was a volcano ready to explode.

As he handed his klewang to Jordie he told her, "Bro' here complained before that I am ungentlemanly because he was under the impression that I would not meet him in a fight under equal terms. Here is my klewang, please hold it for me. The only time I want you to use it, and use it to your best advantage, is when you are in danger of re-capture."

Her hand was shaking when she took the sword but there was nothing shaky about her voice when she said, "This probably be the last time I ever speak to ye 'Brother', but I just want ye to know that I have renounced the Brethren and what they stand for, my father for what he done to me and my name therefore be no longer Marigold McDougall, but Jordie..." and in perfect unison both the girl and Kal added, "van Straaten."

Just then the brother under Kal's heel with a valiant effort freed himself.

Kal could have kicked him back in immediate submission but he decided to give the man a sporting chance to experience some more pain and let him get to his feet. Kal knew the other would not take to his heels because his world was shattered to such a degree that rage was the only escape left to him.

Kal soon realised that the man might claim to be a peace loving devotee but he also had in his past a history as a street fighter. Bro feinted with a right hook and as quick as a flash kicked Kal in the gonads. Kal went down and before he even hit the ground received a kick to the side of the head that set some bells ringing and they were not the bells in the chapel either.

A flurry of kicks aimed at his ribs and stomach followed but there was nothing much Kal, in his dazed state, could do about it. He rolled with the battering as much as he could while one part of his mind was waiting for the other part to get its act together so he could do something constructive towards hurting his opponent.

At last he managed to get one of his legs to obey the command and he stuck it between the kicking feet of his adversary. Apparently the move was unexpected and the 'bringer of enlightenment and pain' tripped and went down.

Kal was aware that the man had started to sit up when suddenly all movement stopped and he heard Jordie's voice, it had a nasty snarl when he heard her say, "Ye stop right there! Kal were prepared to face ye without a weapon so there be no need for ye to now come up with a dagger."

Kal wondered what power enabled the girl to control the holy thug so he lifted his still woozy head and looked a bit closer. His opponent had risen from laying on his back to supporting himself on his left elbow. In his right hand he held a nasty looking dirk with which he had been about to attack Kal but Jordie had placed the razor sharp point of Kal's klewang on the Brother's forehead. Just the slightest bit of stabbing pressure and his obstinacy in applying counter pressure had allowed the point of the klewang to penetrate the skin high on the man's forehead. Scalp wounds often bleed quite profusely and there was no shortage of blood running down his forehead.

Rather than being intimidated by the sight of blood, the man's rage was rekindled, he dropped the knife and grabbed the blade of the klewang. Wrong move, as he realised too late when he wrapped his fist around the blade to push it up and away the sharp blade sliced through the mouse of his thumb like it was butter. His reaction was to pull his hand down, away from the sharp part slicing into his hand. Wrong move again! He pulled his hand down so quick that he forgot to straighten his fingers so they, like four hooks, dragged the sword down with them. A witness, had there been one, might have asked, 'so what?'

Well, the point of the klewang was still embedded in the man's forehead and a moment's contemplation would reveal what happened next. The razor sharp point was dragged down by the man's own efforts and in the wink of an eye he lost one, eye that is. After that the point tracked down the side of his nose so cleaving one nostril away from it centre attachment before slicing through the man's lips leaving him with a double hare-lip.

Wondering whether God was still on the side of the just, the sliced and diced Brother crawled away. Meanwhile the other devotee, 'Bro One', had returned with Jordie's girdle. He should have just handed it to her and then he should have gone to provide solace to his leader, instead he decided to make one more plug for the cause, "Ye be damned for eternity!"

Kal could not help himself and had to answer with, "Is that curse *your* take on the situation or God's?"

"It be the Lord our God's because He be on the side of the just."

"So if you believe that you are right and God is on your side how come you just got a whopping whipping?"

"That be the Lord's way to teach us humility! Our cause never be wrong."

The man had already handed her the girdle and had partly turned away when his fanaticism must have reasserted itself and he lashed out with a vicious back-hander that caught Jordie across the face. The girl cried out in pain and surprise and Kal snapped.

Now years of handling ropes and sails had made Kal's large hands very hard and very strong. In a reflex to what just happened Kal's right hand shot out and grabbed the whole of the man's face. As Kal squeezed his hand two cracks were heard. The first snapping bone was the left cheek bone that gave way, the second was the god-botherer's lower jaw breaking. Before he could stop himself Kal chopped down with his left hand on the man's right collar bone and broke that.

Suddenly the berserker's gleam left Kal's eyes and from between clenched teeth Kal snarled, "Let's go before I rip one of those fanatic pigs apart and kill him!"

Jordie slipped on her girdle while Kal sheathed his klewang and then they left hand in hand leaving the gate wide open behind them.

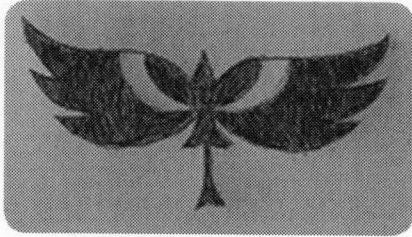

CHAPTER 24

INTERLUDE

By the time Kal and Jordie left the Brethren's enclave it was dark and nobody was about, or nearly nobody. Every now and then a furtive shadow would slip into the dark mouth of a narrow alley way but Kal did not give them any more than a fleeting glance to make sure the shadow was moving away and not towards them. He could not care less whether those shadows were people engaged in a criminal act, or, Wraiths trying to stay out of sight. It was well past the hour when the Wraiths were their most dangerous driven by hunger and lust.

Twice they themselves ducked into a dark lane and quietly stood in the shadows to see if anybody was following them.

Kal did not expect any of the Brethren to track them after the licking they got but one never could be too careful with fanatics.

Satisfied that nobody had tailed them, they entered Amos' house through the back door. Amos wrapped Jordie in his arms as though she was a long lost daughter and it was not long before they sat down to a mug of rum while somebody cooked a meal.

Amos' wife was full of concern over the way Jordie's hair had been hacked off and it was not long before the combs and scissors came out in an attempt to make the short haircut at least presentable.

Kal had loved Jordie's long dark auburn hair, especially the way she usually wore it with the two 'side panels' tied together in a ponytail on top of her head and the 'back panel' cascading down to the small of her back. He knew that her hair had been the girl's pride and joy and just hoped it would grow back quickly.

Kal inspected the many bruises Jordie showed on her body and asked what caused each one of them. Most were on her arms and shoulders and were caused by rough handling but one was on her lower back and he was concerned about that one. She told him that she got the bruise from falling backwards against the edge of a table when she was wrestling the Don, which is what she called 'Bro Three', the head honcho.

After a moment Kal gritted his teeth and asked. "I can imagine what the Don was after!"

"Yes but he did not get anything except sore nuts where I kneed him!"

"That's my girl!"

The next morning over breakfast Kal an Amos calculated that if everything had gone right, the 'Vrouwe Irene' should be back in eight or nine days, just in time to take delivery of the lead ingots.

Amos offered Kal and Jordie free lodgings for the rest of their stay. They accepted the offer gratefully and Kal insisted on providing the food while they were there.

At first Jordie was disappointed that Ono was no longer there but she could understand why Kal had sent the schooner to take her home. The hurricane season was rapidly approaching and by the time the lead would be ready for shipment the waters north of what is now Brisbane could be under the influence of the tropical lows coming from further north.

She was more than grateful that Kal decided to stay behind to look for her.

At times she would sit and quietly study his face. At such times she marvelled at the fact that a man had done so much for her. Up to that point in her life men had only used and abused her and at times she wondered whether it all was only a dream and that Kal would turn and abuse her as well. In a way it was frightening.

Did he come looking for her because he saw her as his property and would not let somebody else take that away from him or did he come because others had no right to own her?

But then he did say to the Don that he was taking her away to set her free, his exact words were burned into her memory, 'She is coming with me *that is if she wants to.*'

Those words indicated to her that he was giving her free choice then, but what about the moment when he had said that her name was 'van Straaten'?

Yes, what about that? I myself said the same thing at the same time! Do I want to be his? Yes! But not as slave and master! As husband and wife then? That would be nice.

A couple of days later they, Kal and Jordie, were in the market buying the daily store of fresh food when the old Chinese spice merchant lady came looking for them. When she spotted them over near the fish monger's she rushed over and hurriedly drew them behind one of the stalls and whispered urgently, "B'ethlen, they bad men, velly bad men! He come, he look fo' Miss, he velly angly." She looked furtively about then passed Jordie a small parcel wrapped in banana leaves, "You wash hai', hai' go black, men look fo' gi'l with olange hai'. Me go now. Neve' help Miss, B'ethlen bad vely bad!"

As soon as the old lady disappeared among the market stalls, Kal took Jordie's hand and said, "Come along, we're going to arm you!"

"What ye mean, 'Going to arm me'? Ye're not going to stick me in a tin suit or strap a whopping big sword to my side!"

"Close, you'll see."

Kal took her away from the market which was there to provide the citizens with fresh produce.

The traders selling more permanent goods tended to sell their wares from established shops.

It was not long before he found what he was looking for, an armourer. He steered the girl inside and when the store owner came to the counter Kal told him, "I want you to supply this lady with a weapon suited to her build and temperament and it has to be of the best quality available."

Much to Jordie's surprise, the elderly shop keeper had her doing all kind of arm and hand movements like making slashing motions, stabbing over hand and stabbing under hand as well as a few quick spins around, both left and right, as though she was being attacked from behind.

By the time he was satisfied, Jordie had worked up a sweat and was looking at Kal with a 'you'll keep' look in her emerald eyes.

The old armourer now lost interest in her and turned to Kal, "She be nay suited to wield a slashing weapon nor a heavy stabbing knife. The best weapon to suite her needs would be a poniard of medium length."

A tad cynical Jordie asked, "What be wrong with a short one?"

As quick as a flash the old man came back with, "Were thee only to clean thy finger nails with it, a small poniard would suffice, for anything more serious and keeping in mind thy muscle mass a medium poniard, in my opinion, be best suited."

Before they could turn this into a full scale tit for tat, Kal cut in, "A medium poniard sounds good. Can you show us some?"

"Aye that I can. What quality would thee like to inspect?"

"The best you got."

"That be this one, worked and engraved Toledo steel."

With loving gentleness he lifted the dagger from its display case and showed it to both Kal and Jordie. Even the girl was impressed and whispered to Kal, "That will cost a fortune!"

"Only the best for me-lady."

Kal was not in favour of the more common way the poniard was carried. With a twig and an idle tray of sand he made a drawing of what he wanted the armourer to fashion for him.

It was a sleeve of heavy, raw leather. At the centre of the two inch wide rawhide tube he wanted a heavy bronze stud fastened so it stood proud. The rawhide sleeve would shrink as it dried and the poniard's scabbard would be held tight. The head of the stud was to be shaped like the cap on a mushroom. Another strip of leather with a length wise slit in its centre was to be sewn onto Jordie's leather girdle so the poniards scabbard would be held between the leather strip and the girdle and the mushroom head would protrude through the slit in the sewn-on strap like a button through a button hole.

By placing this attachment slightly forward of the centreline of Jordie's left hip, the dagger could be drawn with the right hand for a normal upward or forward stabbing motion, or, it could be drawn left handed for a downward stabbing. That position was also the least inconvenient for the wearer.

The armourer was impressed with the design and asked whether Kal would allow him to use it in his trade. Kal jokingly told him that was fine by him as long as the armourer did not apply it to the weapons of Kal's enemies, the Brethren.

The trader laughingly opined that the Brethren would not be able to afford the weaponry that he would reserve the design for.

More serious, he promised to have the scabbard frog ready by the next day and Kal and Jordie left.

Later that evening Kal was watching Jordie as she dyed her hair black with the old lady's Chinese concoction the main ingredient of which appeared to be octopus ink. She was seated on her knees in front of the basin and when she finished she wrapped a towel round her head and sat up straight. Next she began to rub her hair and to do that to her satisfaction, perhaps not quite realising that her long hair was gone, she canted her hips forward to counter act the weight of her torso as she arched her back and bend her head back. With her elbows in the air her breasts and tummy were stretched tight. Kal could not help but admire her alluring lines. He got up and knelt behind her. Gently he cupped her breasts and then slid his hands down the tight curve of her firm belly. Jordie forgot all about the towel and wrapped one arm around his head as he bend down to kiss her neck.

The towel got lost during the ensuing proceedings and the next morning Kal was at a loss to explain the black dye stain on his right cheek.

At first Jordie thought it was funny until Amos invited her to explain the corresponding black stain on her left cheek. Yes, well, the subject was dropped after that and breakfast continued in an orderly but happy fashion.

Later that day Kal and Jordie went to the armourer's to collect Jordie's poniard.

The old man had done an excellent job on the scabbard frog and even decorated the leather with smoke-curl tooling.

It was plain to see that the old man took pride in his craft and was keen on knowing who he entrusted his wares to. Kal had the distinct impression that should the old man have taken a dislike to either of them Jordie would not have gotten her poniard. He asked her, "Hast thee named thine poniard yet?"

The question was put as though there was no doubt in the old man's mind that the girl would give the weapon a name. To Kal's surprise Jordie smiled shyly and looked at the ground as though saying the name out loud was in some way admitting to the world that she indeed had thought deeply about it and that up to that moment it had been her secret.

"His name be Reginald" after a short hesitation she continued, "Reggie were my little dog and, until Kal came along, the only male to ever defend me. It cost him dearly though, my father kicked Reggie to death for it!"

"It sickens me to hear that but the name be well chosen and I'd be proud to tool the name on the scabbard."

"Oh! Could thee?!"

"Aye, be it 'Reginald' or 'Reggie'?"

"Reggie!" she answered as she hugged Kal's arm.

In order for the armourer to stitch the keeper strap onto Jordie's girdle she had to take it off. She did so without a moment's hesitation but when the old man looked her up and down and then shook his head, she asked, "What?!"

He smiled and replied, "If thee change the curtains, make sure they match the carpet!"

Kal had trouble keeping his face straight when Jordie asked, "What on earth he be talking about?"

Kal said nothing but first pointed at her black hair and then at the auburn flash of pubic hair. All Jordie said was "Ooooh!" as understanding dawned.

Half an hour later the incident was forgotten as Jordie proudly showed off the poniard 'Reggie' on her left hip.

Just as they left the shop Jordie turned smiling her most evil smile and hissed theatrically at the armourer, "Rest assured Sire, for anybody to come close enough to compare the carpet with the curtains they would need to overcome 'Reggie', an impossibility I can surely promise thee!"

"That be thy promise to me mi-lady" the old man laughed as he patted her gently on the shoulder.

As they walked back to Amos', Jordie could not stop fiddling with the poniard, she was so proud of it. Just to tease her Kal remarked, "You know, the way you are waving that dagger about people may think that you are on the warpath. Come to think of it, even I may be in mortal danger!"

She gave him a cheeky look and he expected a smart-Aleck reply but instead she became very quiet.

They nearly reached their goal when Jordie put a hand on Kal's arm and stopped so suddenly that Kal spun round and was facing her. He was about to ask her what the idea was but when he saw the expression in her eyes he became very quiet and waited. He could not quite make out what her eyes were saying. They seemed to reflect an internal turmoil and Kal placed his free hand on her hand and waited. Slowly big tears welled up in her dark emerald eyes and in a small voice she asked, "What be thy price?"

"My price for what?"

"For all the things thee done for me?"

"What on earth are you talking about Jordie? I don't expect any kind of payment!"

Suddenly she bent her head and softly head-butted his chest a couple of times then looked him straight in the eyes and her voice was pure despair when she said, "Ye be the only man ever who has given me things, saved me from slavery and the Brethren yet has not stated your price. What be it thee will demand in payment?"

Kal was gob-smacked, his first reaction was anger. Who or what did she think he was? Had he ever given the impression that he was after something? What could she possibly give him? The circumstances of her life had left her without any worldly wealth or possessions so what could she possibly give him and in return for what? In the end he asked, "Why should I demand anything?"

Her eyes were blazing when she looked at him and said, "My father took my virginity and my ability to have a baby as payment for nurturing me through childhood. I had to become a sex slave belonging to the Earl to do with whatever his sick and depraved mind came up with, as payment for unwanted attention and sustenance to stay alive. The Don of the Brethren told me that I be the property of the church having been born to one of the faithful and as such I be his to use and I may add, abuse, for the term of my life."

She was silent for a while but when Kal opened his mouth to say something she held up her hand and said quietly, "Let me finish before I lose the courage to do so. As thee can see three men have taken and taken from me for very little or no return! Oh yes! They made me into trash not fit to be seen in the light of day! Yet thee dragged me out of the gutter and thee be trying to give me back some self-respect! I just needs to know what it's going to cost me."

Jordie was sobbing by this time and people started to look at this scarred man trying to hold on to the beautiful young woman clearly in distress. *Should they try and rescue her? Perhaps better to let things be, that man looks rather ferocious and with all those scars, he must be a fighter. So give him a disapproving frown but keep going.*

Kal was well aware of the passers-by and he coached Jordie into a quiet corner before he asked her, "Jordie if you saw an infant in distress would you try to rescue that child or would you let it be because the infant would not have the means to pay you for your services?"

"Of course not! What a thing to say, I be not that much of a slut!"

She saw the anger flare in his eyes, "I hope that is the last time I will hear you call yourself that! So tell me why is it that you can help somebody without thought of payment but I can't?"

"Well, for one you be a man and in my experience men expect payment for services rendered, and second, I be no longer a child and supposedly be able to function independently!"

Suddenly a horrible thought came to Kal and his voice took on menace when he growled, "I thought you had sex with me because you have feelings for me. Was it just for payment...?"

He stopped talking because he wanted to shock an honest answer out of her and not one just to pacify him or because she was scared.

The beautiful girl looked the scarred man straight in the eyes and in a voice that left no doubt she replied, "Nay! I sleep with thee because I love thee! What be of more importance, should thee ever again voice doubts on that score, 'Reggie' be the one to speak for me!"

Kal wrapped her in his arms and bend over so he could whisper in her ear, "Thy love, me-lady, be more than what I ever hoped or expected to get for my services."

Suddenly blushing like a teenager on her first date she whispered, "We better go, people are looking."

Kal looked up and suddenly stiffened, "Yes, let's run down this alley and hide. One of the Brethren is watching us!"

As they sprinted away Jordie whispered, "So much for dyeing my hair black!"

Kal could not help it, "It must have been the carpet that gave you away."

He got a punch on the run for that remark and the effort made Jordie fish-tail for a number of paces.

They hid in the dark shadows of a low wall and sure enough shortly afterwards one of the Brethren ran past. Jordie shook her head and Kal asked, "What's wrong?"

"I just cannot understand those fools. Their black and white garments!"

"You mean their black trousers and white shirts? What about them?"

"Duhhuh! In a place where nobody else wears much of anything they stand out a bit on a stake-out don't ye think?"

"Yes, but don't forget God is on their side. And, to believe the rubbish they believe in, they can't be too bright, now can they?"

"I hope you be right because I just saw another one peeking around that corner over there and it be not the one that just ran past!"

"Looks like they got us boxed in. They don't give up easy I must say!"

"Should I pull 'Reggie' out?"

"No, try not to draw any attention to your weapon until it is absolutely necessary. That might give you a slight advantage if they think you are unarmed. Ok let's go and talk to the boys. Come with me but stay in the shadows as much as possible so they don't see your 'Reggie'."

Kal started walking in the direction where they had seen one of the Brethren peek around the corner.

Kal kept to the left side of the alley so Jordie could keep her left side, the side on which she carried her poniard, in the deeper shadows.

When they reached the corner it did not come as a surprise when from around each, the left and the right corners of the T intersection, one of the Brethren stepped forward. One was brandishing a wooden club while the other was swinging an axe about in a way that was endangering him more than anybody else. Neither appeared too enthused about taking on Kal and one said quite lamely, "Sister Marigold McDougall belongs to the flock and thus be required to return with us."

In quite a reasonable voice Kal replied, "Can you relate to me when 'Sister McDougall' chose to become a member of your faith?"

"She were born to the faith!"

"In other words you are telling me that she had no say in the matter?"

"That be so I suppose but..."

"My question is; did she have the choice to join the faith through her own will?"

"Yes, but..."

"NO BUTS! DID SHE JOIN THE FAITH THROUGH HER OWN FREE WILL, YES OR NO?"

Now the other one joined in, "Having been born into the faith, she may nay have had a free choice but she be property of the Brethren by virtue of the fact that her father be a well-respected elder and missionary and she owes it to his memory to carry on his work!"

That was the wrong remark to make and before Kal could lay a restraining hand on her arm she blurted, "You want me to be like him?! What, the Brethren need another person to scare the bejezus out of poor unsuspecting folk with threads of hell and damnation and if that be not enough I could always do to their kids what he did to me I could..."

Her tirade was cut short by a rough hand on her shoulder, it was the first of the Brethren they had seen spying on them. He had snuck up behind them and on a sign from him the other two launched an attack on Kal while he made a grab for Jordie.

As soon as she felt the hand on her left shoulder she spun round to the left at the same time she pulled 'Reggie' from his sheath and with the momentum of her spinning body she stabbed blindly at her attacker. There was a surprised "Agh?" and the hand slipped of her shoulder.

Jordie brought both her hands up to her mouth as she looked down at the body on the ground, the red spreading on the white shirt and the handle of her poniard sticking defiantly up out of his chest.

Kal had just grabbed hold of the axe handle that axe-man was steering towards his head. The speed with which Kal pushed back overcame the grip axe-man had on the handle and as a result the axe reversed its trajectory and the back of the axe head came to a sudden stop between the eyes of axe-man. He lost all further interest in the reclamation of the wayward Sister McDougall and slowly and silently went to ground where he stood.

The third attacker suddenly decided that perhaps he should leave in a hurry, Kal had just started a beautifully executed swing of his klewang when the unworthy turned around to depart but, alas, he was too late. The tip of the klewang sliced through the back of the man's neck, cut the muscles that keep the head looking up as well as one of the vertebrae. Result? Half decapitated man goes nowhere, bends head onto chest and makes gurgling sounds after hitting the cobblestone road with forehead.

When Kal realised there was nothing more to discuss with his two opponents he turned to see what Jordie was up to.

The girl stood there in a state of shock, she still had her hands clutched in front of her mouth and her shoulders were hunched as she looked down.

Her would-be attacker was quite dead so Kal said, "Ok get your poniard and let's go before the cops get here."

She shivered as she turned to him and said in a small voice, "I tried but I can't get 'Reggie' out."

Kal bent down and jerked the poniard from between the man's ribs. "Sometimes it is quite hard to pull out a dagger because of the suction of the flesh encasing it but in this case you jammed it between two ribs.

It was a good shot though, he died of a torn heart. See what you do to a man?"

"Ha-ha very funny! We better do as ye said and leave."

Without further review of battle technicalities they left and approached Amos' house through a back alley just in case there were more Brethren watching the front door.

Quite early the next morning they heard the plodding clip-clop of many iron shot hooves on the cobblestone street. With a shouted "Whoa" the clip-clop stopped and Amos rose from the breakfast table saying, "That be the first load of lead. Let's go to the warehouse to oversee the unloading."

Both Kal and Jordie were not going to miss out on that event so while still scoffing down the last mouth full of food they rushed after Amos.

When they came outside they were greeted by two heavily built drays each being pulled by six Friesians[8]. The powerful horses had no interest in the excited calls of the street urchins scattering about dangerously close to their massive hooves and stood there quietly waiting for the next order of the wagoneer.

The occasional swish of a tail to shoo away flies or the stomping of a hoof for the same purpose were the only indicators of their presence.

Kal always had a soft spot for the gentle giants and went over to pat one on the nose. With a tone of surprise the wagoneer exclaimed, "Well! I'll be! That be the first time I seed a stranger touch that horse on the face and didst nay get his hand bit off!"

Kal gently laid his hand across the animal's broad nose and replied with a laugh, "We be kindred souls and know each other."

"Yeah, mayhap but be advised nay to turn thy back on her."

---

[8] Friesians are Dutch horses black in colour and used to drag heavy loads, such as beached fishing smacks off the North Sea beaches. To drag the smacks back into the water the horses often would work up to their necks in the surf.

When the wagon train was ready to move on, Kal stepped back from the horse and she threw her head up in the air as though she was waving farewell at Kal.

With a crack of the whip the horses threw themselves into their harnesses and the cart rumbled away down the road towards the water front and Amos' warehouse.

On their way there Kal told Amos what had happened the previous evening. Amos had been out and they had not seen him until at breakfast. Amos was not surprised and could only hope that the Brethren would hold back a bit now they had lost three of their ilk but he doubted that would stop those fanatics. He shook his head and meant it when he turned and said to Jordie, "Ye surely must be born under an evil star!"

"Aye but Kal be there to see me out from under it."

She said slowly and with complete conviction in her voice. Kal just squeezed her hand.

When they arrived at the warehouse the first dray was pulled up in front of the double doors. Waiting for them there was a young woman of generous proportions. She had piercing black eyes that sparkled with an inner fire. Her raven black hair hung down her back and was somewhat untidy.

In a hushed voice Jordie asked, "Who should that be?"

Amos answered, "That be Flo, the furniture maker's daughter. She be the levitator and she be here to unload the drays."

Jordie had never seen a levitator in action before and she was awe-struck when she saw Flo touch the first pallet of ten lead ingots with just one finger of her outstretched hand and the whole pallet rose above the floor of the dray. Two men guided the pallet by gently pushing it this way and that so it would not foul the sides of the dray. Once it was manoeuvred off the wagon Flo started to shuffle towards the warehouse making sure her feet never left the ground.

Apparently it was of the utmost importance for the levitator to stay grounded that way.

Some of the horses must have been aware of the force field surrounding Flo because they became restless but after Flo had touched each one of them and with some soothing words added they settled down and she could resume her work.

Kal had to explain to Jordie that the levitator has the ability to concentrate anti-gravity forces within her being and then has the gift to use them to negate the magnetic pull of the earth on the object she touches lightly with a finger.

She can counteract the weight of an object but needs outside help to move it horizontally because she touches the object with only a feather like touch of a fingertip. Too much or too little pressure of her finger and the object regains its weight and flops down on the ground. The people helping her by steering the object to where it has to go have to be trained as well. Both the levitator and the guides must keep both feet on the ground at all times and the guides must be well aware that any sudden move will break the connection between levitator and the object.

Before moving any load that way the exact route is surveyed so that the levitator knows what to expect and the guides are aware of any obstacles to be evaded. In the case of Flo her guides were her father and her brother.

Before each pallet would be levitated Flo would stand at the edge of the wharf legs slightly apart, arms stretched stiffly downwards away from her body. With her head thrown back she would breathe deeply.

Jordie asked in an awed whisper, "What she be doing?"

Without thinking Kal replied, "She's recharging her battery."

"Oh…" after a short pause, "what be a battery?"

"Perhaps the wrong word to use. She is like a dried out sponge and she is soaking up the energy required to levitate the next object."

"Where be that energy coming from?"

"Nature, or God, if you like."

"I begin to understand yer ability to equate God with Nature."

"In what way?"

After a thoughtful pause Jordie said hesitantly, "I see how Nature represents all energies and that they be available to anybody who knows how to ask for them. I can also see that those energies in themselves be neither good nor bad, they only become either through their application." After another short pause she added, "A scary thought really!"

"Why scary?"

"Don't ye see? It means that we be responsible for how we apply that energy, and that guidance towards what be good or bad does nay come with it! That must come from inside ourselves. It be entirely dependent on how well we understand the energies at play and how adapt we ourselves be at using them!"

"Welcome to the real world." Kal said while he hugged her to his side.

They watched in silence as Flo levitated the second pallet off the dray. Two down and eight more to go just on this wagon alone.

After Flo had unloaded the last pallet off the dray, Amos came over and told the girl to have a rest. Flo silently nodded her head and went to stand on the edge of the wharf again. Jordie asked if it was alright for her to go and talk to Flo and Amos smiled and nodded his head. Before Jordie approached Flo she said to Amos, "It probably be my imagination but it appears to me that Flo be slimmer now than when she came here this morning."

"Aye! It affects different levitators in different ways. Our Flo loses about two kilograms in weight for every bushel she transports."

"That's a lot!"

"A weight-watcher's dream." Kal could not help himself.

Jordie gave him a quizzical look but said nothing. Instead she walked over to where Flo was sitting on a bollard and soon the two young women were chatting and giggling as though they had known each other for years.

Later while Flo was unloading the second wagon, Jordie stood next to Kal and said in a confidential tone, "I found out why Flo wears nay girdle nor any other form of adornment, nay bangles, and ankle or arm bands, nay necklace nor hair combs. All those extras interfere with the energy vibrations that become her strength and that she absorbs through the uncluttered pores of her skin."

"I knew that."

"Arrgh! You did it again! Know-it-all!"

"Very early in the piece just after I arrived here in the Dimension I met a levitator. Her name is Moana and between her and her husband, Kees, they taught me a lot about levitators."

"Husband? I thought they could nay marry!"

"They can get married but if they want to retain their levitation powers, they cannot produce any children."

"Can they adopt a child?"

"I don't know, but…"

"Ah! Finally I got you!" Jordie sang as she did a little fist swirl and dance.

Pretending he was peeved, Kal asked, "Well do you?"

"Nay, but…"

"Yeah, yeah, you don't know either."

"Still!"

With a smile on his face Amos had been listening to the exchange and interrupted with, "If ye like I be willing to go and ask Flo but mayhap the question may break her away from her concentration thus delaying the unloading of thine lead."

Kal turned to Jordie and said in a doom-laden voice, "Let that knowledge remain her secret!"

They were silent for a while until Kal mused, "Perhaps this will help; I see the whole thing as *fact and fiction*.

The *fact* is the unalterable presence of a natural power, take for instance the wind. The wind is there no matter from what direction it is blowing or how strong. Does it have the capacity to be *good* or *bad*? No, it just is and therefore it is a *fact*. The *fiction* part comes in with our ability to use it to *our benefit* in which case it is *good*. Should we want to go in the opposite direction or should it blow too strong or be too light for our purpose does that alter the wind and make it *bad*? Of course not, that is just our expectation and is therefore not in line with the nature of the natural power in evidence at that time and thus must be seen as *fiction*."

Jordie stuck her arm through Kal's, rolled her eyes at Amos and whispered with exaggerated huskiness, "Oh I love it when ye talk dirty like that! Take me home and let us…!"

"Fact or fiction?"

"Fiction!"

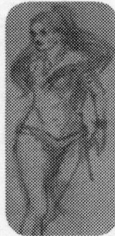

CHAPTER 25

THE 'VROUWE IRENE' IN PORT

TWO DAYS AFTER the delivery of the lead ingots, the 'Vrouwe Irene' entered the port of New Hoorn. Kal, Jordie and Amos stood on the wharf and watched as the schooner dropped anchor. Shortly thereafter the longboat was launched and some of the crew started rowing in the direction of where Kal was waiting for them.

The first to jump onto the wharf was Brutus, of course, and Kal roughed up the imaginary head of the dog. Kal knew it was only an illusion but the illusion had sharp teeth and was not pleased if ignored. So, Kal rubbed air and Brutus wagged her illusionary tail and said, "Ruff!" meaning, "Good to see ya and don't believe a word of what those two moaners will try to sell you!"

"Where are Harry and Abdullah?"

"Auwhoohoo!"

"That sounds like you are accusing them of deserting you! Is that right?"

"*Too right that's right!*" That was Harry's unmistakable gritty voice.

"What happened?"

"You see how that mutt got on the wharf? The way she first jumped into the boat and then onto the wharf! She would have ripped our arms out!"

"Gosh Harry! You can be such a pussy-cat sometimes! Where is your sense of adventure?"

"Yeah, and hello to you too. By the way, what happened to the hair of our fair maiden?"

"Long story we'll tell you later. Hello Abdullah I presume you didn't trust our leaping hound either?"

"Indeed I most assuredly did not. Coming back to the subject of the missing locks of she-who-blasts-a-pirate-captain-with--one-shot-from-a-blunderbuss, I sincerely hope that the malefactor responsible is suffering incredible pains for his efforts?"

Jordie butted in, "He most assuredly dost. Yon knight came to the aid of this damsel in distress and transferred the distress onto the scoundrel and his cohorts."

"Well done that man."

Amos had a pained expression on his face and asked with a tremulous voice, "Be it me or dost ye all hear voices where there be none to speak?"

Kal laughed and said, "Jordie, you explain it to Amos…"

"Oh, it is Jordie now, what happened to Marigold?"

"Harry! You can be such an insensitive sod! Is that your training or is it just you?" Kal asked.

"Sorry. I'll just go and sulk somewhere."

"Good idea but don't go too far. In your present condition it may be too hard or too much effort to come looking for you."

"Who is the insensitive sod now? Huh!"

Whether Harry really was hurt or not is not known but he left the reporting of the 'Vrouwe Irene's trip to Abdullah.

The short version of the report was that they had arrived in Fiji without any mishap and had dropped off Ono at her village on Suva Bay.

Much to their surprise Samu, the heavyweight Balon Islander they had left with Pinnie to lead the ex-slaves, had canoe-sailed his way to Fiji because he wanted to go home to Balon Island more than wanting to stay on as second-in-command of an ex-slaves colony.

Kal was happy to have him back, he was a quiet powerhouse of a man and could be relied on in the most harrowing of situations.

It was just then that one of the crew, the oldest man in fact, stepped forward with a face full of trepidation.

Kal could see that the man was shivering with nerves and that he obviously would have preferred to be someplace else. Kal turned to Jordie and asked her to translate or rather to make use of her knowledge of Fijian to see if she could make out what the man wanted to say.

In the end she turned to Kal, "I don't really understand what he is trying to say but it has something to do with the 'Vrouwe Irene' and something that is broken, but what I don't know."

Before Kal could reply Abdullah came back on line, "*He is trying to tell you that the 'Vrouwe Irene' hit the reef on our way out of Suva Bay.*"

"How come? What happened?"

"*There was a sudden drop in the wind just as a larger than average comber surged across the passage through the reef. It pushed the 'Vrouwe Irene' sideways and we scraped the reef.*"

"Did she spring a leak?"

"*No, nothing like that. She may have lost some of her copper sheeting but that would be all.*"

Kal smiled at the old man and patted him on the shoulder to indicate that he did not hold him responsible. It was nearly comical to see relief flood the man's eyes and bearing. He bowed his head and then withdrew to the longboat.

With a sigh Kal said to Amos, "I suppose that means a trip up the slips for the 'Vrouwe Irene'. Can you recommend one?"

"Aye. I be honoured if ye be of a mind to use that slipway over yonder."
He pointed at a large slipway not far from where they were standing.

"It looks all right from here but who owns it?"

"Would ye be surprised to find that I be the owner?"

"Nah, not really. Have you got room to slip the 'Vrouwe Irene'?"

"Most assuredly. It be a bit late in the day now but she can be slipped
on tomorrow's early morn tide."

It was decided that Kal and Jordie would go on board of the schooner
for the night to discourage any last minute attempts by the Brethren to
abduct Jordie.

That evening Jordie leaned against Kal as together they looked at
the shore lights of New Hoorn. With his arm around Jordie's waist Kal
mused, "This is the best way to look at any city."

The girl heard something in his voice that she had not heard since
coming to New Hoorn, he was at ease and in control of his own little
world.

She was glad that she now was part of that world and sure that he
would do anything to protect her.

Well before daylight and before the land breeze would flow towards
the cold sea, the 'Vrouwe Irene' raised anchor and under mainsail alone
she ghosted towards the buoy Amos had indicated the evening before.

The schooner tied up to the buoy which was located at the end of
the slipway's trolley tracks. From there a cable led to the large capstan
at the head of the slipway. Well before the tide turned workers on the
slipway allowed a ship's cradle to run down the trolley tracks on the slip
and the crew on board the 'Vrouwe Irene' centred the schooner between
the four corner posts, leaving the tie-up buoy behind her stern and free
from the cradle.

When the tide was at its highest four men strained at the spokes of the capstan while the crew and other slipway workers pulled on lines attached to the cradle. Slowly the boat was pulled from the water.

Ropes leading from the top of the main mast then were tied off and kept the schooner in an upright position.

As soon as the tide had dropped enough so the men could stand on the bottom, they went overboard to scrape off any growth from the hull. There was not all that much because of the excellent anti-fouling properties of copper sheeting. What little there was, was eager to let go.

The damage done by her encounter with the coral reef was limited to a strip of six feet long and a foot wide where the copper sheeting had been ripped away and the timber underneath had been scoured.

The damage was not sufficient to require replacement of the planking and the repair to the copper sheeting could be done easily in one day so the 'Vrouwe Irene' could be re-floated on the next high tide.

That afternoon Kal gave each man a doubloon and told them they could go into town. He knew that most of them would exchange their doubloon for a smashing head ache while others would hang on to their money not knowing what to spend it on. One ducat, half a doubloon, would give a heavy smoker enough tobacco to see him through for the trip back to Balon Island. Some of the men had no interest in visiting the town and remained on board. Samu was one of them. Since he had come back on board in Fiji it was nearly impossible to get him to leave the deck. The 'Vrouwe Irene' was his ticket home and he was not letting her out of his sight.

The night was overcast and dark, at times rain drizzled down wetting the deck but not enough to run down the scuppers. There was a fair bit of wind that made strange moaning sounds among the buildings and other paraphernalia cluttering the boatyard. Many sounds were strange and Kal was restless. Jordie was fast asleep in the crook of his arm and Brutus lay asleep on the foot of the couch. Suddenly Kal heard something hitting the side of the boat. It was not like the wind threw something against the hull, it was a furtive sound and Kal instantly took notice. So did Brutus.

Not wanting to wake Jordie, Kal disentangled himself from her and was about to open the deckhouse door when he heard a meaty smack and a groan.

He raced out of the door just in time to see Samu in action. The huge man had hold of the shirt front of, you guessed it, one of the Brethren. With his other fist he gave the man a quick tap on the noggin that left the worthy unconscious and sprawled on the deck.

Next Samu leaned over the railing and plucked another of the Brethren off the ladder. This one Samu gave a fairly convincing blow on the top of his head. Kal could hear the breaking of bone and the luckless zealot finished up two inches shorter and quite dead. One mighty fist on the top of his head had broken his neck and driven his spine into his skull. He too was one of the Brethren. Samu was about to toss them both overboard but Harry told Kal to stop him. Kal did but then wanted to know why.

"It is proof that they came aboard illegally and met their demise because Samu, your faithful servant, tried to detain them."

Just then the first man came to and silently got up with a dagger in his hand. He attacked Samu from behind but right on the last instant Kal spotted him and tried to push Samu out of the way. The dagger tore into Samu's shoulder as he spun around. At least it had not finished up in his lungs. With one sweep of his left hand the big islander pulled the dagger out of his shoulder, spun it round and planted it hilt deep into the top of the man's skull. He looked grotesque with the dagger's grip sprouting out of his head but he did not care he was well past the point of vanity.

"Leave him on deck too?"

"*Yes, you better organise Goldilocks to have a look at Samu's shoulder though.*"

This time it was Brutus who had a five seconds' sulk because she had come on deck too late and Samu had all the fun. So she just had to be satisfied with standing over each vanquished miscreant and growl and drool some spittle.

As soon as it became daylight and the workers arrived at the slipways, Amos sent one of them to fetch the local constabulary and the undertaker to cart off the Brethren.

With that problem solved the 'Vrouwe Irene' was allowed to trundle back down the slipway for as far as gravity would take her. Once at that point they had to wait for the rising tide to float her off the cradle and then the crew could haul on the stern line still attached to the buoy.

Two work boats each with six oarsmen then towed the schooner to the wharf in front of Amos' warehouse for the loading of her cargo of four tonnes of lead ingots.

Flo was again engaged to do the levitating and by the time the cargo was loaded on board the erstwhile rather plump girl was downright skinny. When Jordie remarked on the fact Flo laughed, "Aye, whenever I've over indulged in mother's pies and cakes I just go out for some serious levitating. Like, levitating further afield than the dockside inn of course."

The next few days were taken up with the hustle and bustle of getting the 'Vrouwe Irene' provisioned and made ready for her trip into the Pacific.

Kal felt that the mainsail and two foresails, the stay-sail and the outer jib, needed replacing.

Where originally he was to have matting sails for the junk, he now took on board enough spare canvas to equip the junk with canvas sails.

Two barrels of half inch anchor chain were stood up and lashed to the main mast.

Lamp oil and other combustibles for light and cooking hustled for space with food stocks such as rice, sugar and other non-perishables.

Perishables such as vegetables, potatoes, tubers and fruits were accommodated in the deckhouse where they resided in hammock style nets over the galley bench. The water barrels were filled and four extra full water barrels were taken on to later find a berth in Kal's new junk.

Kal had the two top spars for his junk sails made and they were lashed to the inside of the deck railing.

By the time they were ready for sea, the 'Vrouwe Irene' was heavily laden but not over loaded.

On a bright and crisp early winter's morning the schooner set sail and bore away from New Hoorn. Once the initial rush was over Kal came to stand next to Jordie who stood at the taffrail looking at the rapidly disappearing town.

Kal put his arm around the girl's shoulders, "A penny for your thoughts?"

"They probably be not worth it but I were just hoping that this be the last we see of the Brethren!"

"Yes, parting is such sweet sorrow."

In a thoughtful mood Jordie mused, "Whenever ye leave a port, do ye miss the good people ye met?"

"Yes, I do but I make myself believe that we meet people, good ones as well as bad ones, because we must. Once the lessons are exchanged, we learn from them and they in turn learn from us, our ways must part. If at a later date we have further knowledge to exchange we will meet again."

As she nestled herself closer into Kal's embrace Jordie said, "Well I nay be leaving ye any time soon because it is going to take me a life time to learn all the lessons ye can teach me."

CHAPTER 26

ENCHANTED ISLE OF
THE DOOMED

FROM NEW HOORN the 'Vrouwe Irene' steered a southerly course in order to pick up the stormy westerlies and for about two weeks they skated along on the northerly fringes of the Roaring Forties.

On the thirteenth day out the wind suddenly backed into the southeast and the schooner was forced to take an east-nor'-easterly course.

On the morning of the second day the horizon all-round the vessel appeared as a narrow band of vertical nearly white shimmers like a narrow horizontal band of electrical discharges. The spectacle cast a glare so bright it was impossible to determine where inside that band lay the horizon. The sky overhead had a hard metallic blue colour but the wind remained fairly steady.

Kal drew the attention of Harry and Abdullah to the phenomenon but neither had ever seen it before. Abdullah questioned the members of the crew but none had ever seen anything like it either. There was nothing that could be done about it so they sailed on.

All day long a close watch was kept on the band of vertical electrical discharges. The 'Vrouwe Irene' was sailing along at four to five knots but never seemed to get any closer to the shimmer in front of the bows nor did she appear to travel away from the shimmer astern.

After dark the ring of flickering coated the night and anything in it with an eerie pale blue light that was far more threatening than total darkness would have been. The pale light was so strong it made the full moon appear like an off-white pancake floating in the sky above them.

Although Kal was tempted to remain on deck all night, he let Harry talk him into taking his watch below while Brutus with Abdullah in tow took the first watch on deck followed by Kal's watch and then the dog-watch by Brutus with Harry.

Towards the middle of Kal's watch he started to get an uneasy feeling as though he was being watched.

He toured the deck thinking that perhaps one of the crew was having troubles with the unusual phenomenon that surrounded the ship.

Although he found at least half the crew on deck unable to get to sleep, none of them appeared to radiate hostility towards him. He had just taken up his position near the stern again when Jordie came out of the deckhouse crying. Kal took her in his arms and asked her what was wrong. In between sobs she said, "I don't know! It feels as though I be violated!"

"How do you mean?"

"I feel the same filth and disgust as I used to experience after my father or the Earl were done with me!"

"Did you dream about them?"

"Nay. I woke with a feeling as though somebody be leering at me and then I started to get that disgusting feeling."

Just then two things happened. Brutus charged from the deckhouse in full battle mode and the lookout yelled, "Island dead ahead! Three miles."

Both Kal and Jordie jumped and Kal shouted, "What the hell! What is going on? Harry, Abdullah?"

"We're still in the deckhouse that bloody mutt took off without us! Something really got her spooked this time!"

"What's this island!? There is not supposed to be any land for hundreds of miles!"

"Are you sure we are where we're supposed to be?"

"What's that supposed to mean, Harry?"

"Ah, you know, perhaps you held the sextant upside down or something?"

"No Harry I did not and perhaps I should hold you upside down for a bit!"

Harry did not react to that statement because he could hear from Kal's voice that the latter was in no mood for jokes.

Kal spoke up again, "You two better come out here, there is something going on and I don't like it."

While saying that Kal spun the wheel but to his surprise the 'Vrouwe Irene' did not respond to her rudder and kept heading straight for the high and forbidden mass of the island. Kal was still grappling with that singularity when Jordie suddenly shrieked with a high-pitched scream and started hitting her thighs and belly.

"What is wrong!?" Kal shouted in alarm.

"Something be touching me!"

"But there is nothing the... Damn it! There is!"

"What it be?"

"Just a streak of black shadow but it seems to come from the island!"

"Get it off me! Get it away from me!"

By this time Brutus was snapping at the shadow but to no avail. Just then a crew member rushed aft and told Brutus—Abdullah—that the black shadow was in fact towing the 'Vrouwe Irene' backwards to the island. Abdullah translated the message and Kal thought for a moment then said, "Tell the men to launch the longboat."

Abdullah conveyed the message then asked Kal what he had in mind.

"It appears to me that whoever is on that island wants to get hold of Jordie so badly that he or they are using black magic to draw her to them, 'Vrouwe Irene' and all. Let's try this; Jordie and I will go and sit in the longboat I am hoping that the pull is on Jordie and not the schooner. By us sitting in the longboat the pull hopefully will be transferred to the longboat. That way the 'Vrouwe Irene' will have steerage again and may be able to pull us all away from the island and whatever is there. Make sure that the towing line is a stout one!"

"What makes you think they are pulling the boat rather than just Jordie?"

"I don't know Harry. Perhaps she is too small an object or they might do too much damage to her."

A few minutes later Kal, closely followed by Jordie climbed down into the longboat. A line as thick as a man's wrist connected the longboat to the schooner. It was not until the line was paid out to close to one hundred feet that suddenly the schooner regained her steerage and Samu began to alter the boat's course away from the island. At the same time the longboat began to crab sideways in her attempt to go to the island. Kal had his arms wrapped around Jordie who was crying hysterically, still slapping at invisible hands on her upper thighs and belly while she cried out, "Go away! Leave me be! Oh Kal I feel so dirty, just let me go! I never be clean again!"

Grimly Kal told her, "It will only be over my dead body that they'll have a chance and even then I will have hacked them about so much they no longer will be capable or willing to molest you."

The 'Vrouwe Irene' turned downwind but she was only making very slow progress. The heavy towing line between the ship and the longboat stood as tight and straight as a steel bar and the stem post of the longboat creaked alarmingly. Kal was grateful that the pull was on the boat rather than Jordie she would not have been able to withstand such forces.

Gradually all forward movement stopped but neither was there a reverse movement. It was a Mexican stand-off.

Suddenly Brutus went berko on the aft deck of the schooner but she appeared to be shadow boxing and there was no sign of what she was attacking.

Kal did not have long to study the commotion because suddenly a series of small light specks, some red others brilliant blue and a number of orange ones slowly rose and fell near the centre of the longboat.

Both Kal and Jordie forgot their problems and were mesmerised by the lights display. Slowly an old, dark man materialised. Kal knew who it was. Tjitjira the Elder had helped him on a number of occasions. Jordie began to shake violently and turned to Kal, "Dost he come to take or possess me?" she asked in a shaky voice.

Before Kal could answer Tjitjira's voice was heard in both their heads, "*Nay, Jordie, I be in attendance to expedite your release from the dammed souls on the isle of the doomed witchdoctors. I nay be in a position where I can effect your immediate release and ye needs to submit to the pull of your father, an inhabitant of the Enchanted Isle of the Doomed. Ye will need to submit to their dictates however it is within my powers to erase any memory within ye. Ye must now release your attachment to Kal as otherwise all on board yon vessel will perish."*

Everything happened at once, Jordie and Tjitjira appeared to dissolve into a black cloud of smoke that seemed to be sucked away towards the Enchanted Isle of the Doomed.

In utter consternation Kal looked at Jordie's girdle as it hung loose in his hand, she had been dissolved out of it.

The island itself began to fade out of existence and the pull on the longboat was lifted allowing the boat to shoot forward and forcing Kal to hang on for dear life. The 'Vrouwe Irene' suddenly released from the same pull began to surge forward and it took a number of men to drag the longboat alongside of the schooner.

Kal was devastated and although he felt that Jordie somehow was alive, he did not really know whether or not that was a good thing.

He wondered what the doomed on the island wanted with her. Then he remembered Tjitjira saying that it was the presence of her father's afterlife form that was doing the pulling and that made him grind his teeth. What did that pervert want of Jordie? Kal could imagine!

He wondered if Tjitjira had hinted at that when he said he would make Jordie forget all that happened to her while she was a prisoner of the Doomed.

It was not until then that Kal realised that not only had the island disappeared but the shimmering of the horizon was gone as well.

With a heavy heart he ordered the resumption of their course towards Balon Island.

Kal sank into the depths of a depression Harry had not seen him in since just after their adventures in an Asian country where Kal had withstood months and months of torture only to find out that not only had he and Harry been sent on an illegal action, but the same people who ordered the ingression had also sold them out to the 'enemy' because as a result of some political skulduggery that promised greater profits.

Even Brutus with a, for her rather embarrassing cutesy-cutesy puppy impression, could not get a smile out of Kal. In the end she too became downcast and just stayed close to him.

In private, Harry brought Abdullah up to speed as far as the reasons for Kal's sometimes sudden depression was concerned.

Abdullah in turn told Harry that he knew a few things about the Enchanted Isle of the Doomed but that the information might not be what Kal wanted or needed to hear at the moment.

One of the characteristics of the mini dimension of the Doomed that Abdullah mentioned to Harry was that time stood still, or at least appeared to stand still.

"Why is that?"

"The island is eternally cloaked in dark clouds, everything is grey and dour. Like us, the people there are all shimmerers so do not eat, prepare food or have to stick to a timetable of any kind. They have no need to be going out on the farm to plant or harvest or to go to the office or any job to earn money with which to satisfy their needs. They have no needs that must be satisfied. Their only wish is to get away from the place."

"What then? Do they die of boredom?"

"That's just it, they are aware and mobile within their confinement but they cannot 'wear out'."

"Does that mean that you and I are going to be living forever as well?!"

"Yes and No. We still have the mental stimulus of the changes in night and day, things still happen around us, like we need to hold on to Brutus or something so as not to blow away, we still have to circumvent attempts by people to treat us like Wraiths. All those things require brain activity and any activity in an organic system causes wear and tear eventually resulting in the breakdown of that system."

"You mean to say we are still organic systems?"

"Yup at least partly and that is why it is going to take a long, long time for us to break down."

"So the more I think the quicker all this will be over?"

"If you mean your existence; yes."

Harry was silent for a long time but finally he asked, "What does all this mean for Jordie?"

"Let's hope that Tjitjira can find a way out for her otherwise she'll out live both of us."

CHAPTER 27

JORDIE

ORDIE CLOSED HER eyes at least that way she felt a little normal. Everything around her felt spongy. The floor, the walls, the bed she sat on, all were of a drab grey colour and felt like wet sponge except that it was not wet. Not that it really mattered all that much because she herself felt as though she weighed only a few pounds. When she looked at her hand it seemed to be translucent yet at the same time opaque but not definite in outline or substance. Unexpectedly it hit her, was *she a Shimmerer now? Did Harry and Abdullah feel the same way? Pity she could not ask them.*

With tears sliding down her cheeks and a heavy sigh she went over what Tjitjira had told her.

He explained to her that the Enchanted Isle of the Doomed had been created by the Council of the Wise[9] to imprison those that used the occult powers to gain selfish goals. In order to deprive rapists and

---

9   Wise, see Adjunct

paedophiles, by far the greater percentage amongst them, of victims, the Wise created one section for males and another for females.

Once an after-life form was sent to the Enchanted Isle of the Doomed it could no longer make contact with the citizens of the main dimension. It was in fact a mini dimension within the dimension of Wind Wood and Water.

Next he told her that her father's after-life form had been imprisoned on the Isle because of what he did to her. It now seemed that that transgression had established a connection from him to her that survived his banishment. Even so, Tjitjira surmised that others on the island were giving him a helping hand and he wondered what the low-life promised them as payment. Jordie knew what it was instinctively—her body! She said so to Tjitjira and he agreed with her assessment as a result he placed his hand on her forehead and muttered words she could not understand.

After a while he removed his hand and told her the best he could do was to fix it so that whenever she was forced into submission with an after-life form and it was without her consent, she would have no memory of the happening afterwards.

If she were able to retain the purity of her heart Tjitjira felt the Wise could come up with a solution to set her free from the Enchanted Isle of the Doomed.

Just before they parted—Tjitjira himself could not enter the Isle of the Doomed—she had asked if there was even a remote chance that Kal could attempt to rescue her. He told her never to give up hope. He would give Kal all the assistance he could.

So far nobody had come near her and she curled up on the spongy bed and cried herself to sleep.

She dreamt that when the Doomed came for her while she was still on board of the 'Vrouwe Irene' she had grabbed the taff rail and held on with all her might. Kal encouraged her not to let go because that would be her doom so she hung on. In the end she had torn the stern out of the schooner and it sank with everybody on board cursing her. The only one not to condemn her was Kal.

As she floundered in the boiling sea a great claw plucked her from the water and was still shaking her when she woke.

The claw shaking her shoulder was the hand of her father. As soon as she saw the animalistic intent in his eyes a faintness overcame her and a shudder of revulsion shook her body.

True to his promise Tjitjira's spell put her in a mind space where she had no memory of her father's 'visit' nor of any other visitors that may have followed him.

When she woke, there was a pleasant surprise awaiting her.

There was a tall mirror in her quarters and when she stood in front of it she was surprised to see that her hair had grown down past her shoulders. She could see the shimmering image of her body and her hair but when she touched either she could see her action in the mirror but she could not feel it. She even tried to pinch herself but again, she could see her doing it in her reflection, but could not feel it. Mildly curious about the regrowth of her hair, Jordie realised that she had no way of knowing how long it had taken her hair to grow back or for how long she was 'asleep'.

There appeared to be no difference between night and day and the island was cloaked in an eternal dense, grey fog. The air was always hot and there was not even the slightest breeze.

She had no need for food so hunger could not be used to establish a time line either. All other bodily functions had shut down as a result as well. What a dull existence!

Jordie soon found that she could go anywhere she liked on the island but what was the use? Everything was dull, grey and spongy to the feel. The others she saw about all were shimmerers, all male and all were drooling after her. Cynically she reflected on the power her father and his cohorts must have over the rest of the population of sex-starved males. None of them was brave enough to approach her but all ogled her off. She returned to her room and stayed there hoping Kal would somehow come for her.

The mood on board became rather sombre and everybody except Kal perhaps, sighed with relief when Balon Island hove into view.

As a result of their arrival there was a lot of singing, dancing and storytelling that promised to go on at least until the next morning and quite probably for a few days to follow.

Halfway through the night Mailiku came over to Kal and wrapped her arms around him. Initially Kal stiffened a bit because he was at a loss how to make the girl understand that Jordie occupied his thoughts from morning to night, but then Abdullah's quiet voice sounded in his head, *"Relax Kal, she is not reclaiming you; she is trying to comfort you as a friend."*

That evening over several basins of Kava, Kal told his story to the chief. Abdullah and A'anu did the translating.

Much to Harry's disgust, he and Abdullah were left to hang on to posts during the Kava session while Brutus was away, 'visiting friends'.

At some time during the proceedings Tjitjira's form appeared and after the first consternation settled down Tjitjira began to speak in people's heads. His words automatically translated into the language each understood best.

"The lot that has befallen the girl, Jordie, has never happened before. Nevertheless it behoves us to set the matter straight and to close the loophole that allowed it to happen. For those of you who were not directly involved with her transfer I will briefly explain what happened.

"Many years ago there was an unusual epidemic of occultists, wizards and sorcerers, using their occult powers for nefarious purposes including paedophilia. The Council of the Wise decided to permanently remove such despicable persons from public life. To that effect they created an inner dimension that can be compared with a large foam bubble. Inside that dimension they created an island to which the wrongdoers could be banished. In order to keep them there the frequencies of the energy vibrations was lowered to such an extent that once there a person becomes a shimmerer. As such, should they escape into our dimension they would take the next step towards total annihilation, they would become a Wraith.

"What happened in the case of Jordie was that her father's after-life form was banished to the Enchanted Isle of the Doomed for raping his daughter over a number of years. What extenuated his case was the fact that he purported to be a man of God! What the Council did not realise because it never has happened before, was that the girl's father has a supernatural hold over his daughter. We suspect that with the help of some evildoers already on the island he was able to extract her from our dimension into that of the Isle..."

Kal could not help himself and blurted out, "Can't we extract the pair of them together? I'll soon put an end to his influence over her!"

Tjitjira slowly shook his head and replied, "Indeed we can bring them back but there are a few problems associated with that. The main one is time.

"There are a great number of holding spells associated with the Enchanted Isle of the Doomed. Some of those spells must be lifted while others must be modified and yet others must be set in place to ensure that only Jordie is extracted and that something like this will never occur again. Once we have succeeded with that we would be able to bring her into the Dimension but she would be a wraith. Because she was not banished to the Island of the Doomed but was an involuntary transfer we will be able to revert her back from wraith to shimmerer but not from shimmerer to solid."

"Why is that?"

"To do that we require to accelerate her vibrational frequencies to a level higher than what we can achieve in this dimension!"

"Well how long do you reckon before she will be back in this Dimension?"

"At least six months."

"Six months!"

"Yes, and we still would have the problem of her being a shimmerer!"

Kal fell silent but eventually he asked in a brooding voice, "So, is there anything I can do?"

"No there is nothing at this stage. I have to leave shortly to put the case before the Council of Elders. In the meantime I suggest that you finish building your junk. You must keep yourself busy or go mad."

Jordie lost all concept of time her life was a repetition of being half aware or not aware and in a vague way she saw it as her cycles as a shimmerer between being half person alternating with her being half wraith. At first she tried to keep a tally of the cycles but it soon became all too much and she just drifted. She was vaguely aware of shimmerers coming to visit but she could never recall what occurred during their visits or when they left.

One dreary patch of half awareness rolled into something that she knew was the end of that patch of semi awareness and that at the same time became the start of the next patch of part awareness, she could never determine the duration between the one and the next, or, if there even was an in-between at all.

At some point during her existence on the Enchanted Isle of the Doomed, Jordie experienced something that was different from the norm. It was as though a pleasurable pull wanted her to move in the direction of the beach.

At first, fearing it was one of her father's enticements, Jordie resisted the pull and tried to ignore it. However, the pull kept coming back a little stronger each time, never longer but just a bit stronger. After fighting the urge—who knows perhaps for weeks —Jordie gave in to it and made her way to the bleak beach where the murky waters lazily rolled grey foam onto the grey sand.

At first Jordie could not get her bearings and really did not know why she even came to the beach. The pull that made her come had vanished and after spending time there she decided to go back to her bedroom.

Just as she turned some bright red, green, blue and orange fire flies lit up the greyness in front of her.

The display of these bright sparks was so unusual in her dreary environment that Jordie was completely captivated by them. In the next instant she heard a familiar voice in her head and she realised that Tjitjira was near but invisible. He spoke in a rush and Jordie had trouble following him. He had to repeat himself and that became their undoing. What he told the girl went something like this, *"Jordie I am here to take you away. There is very little time because I cannot shield my presence and I must withdraw before the Doomed become aware that I am..."*

With a clatter and rattle as of dry bones a number of black shadows suddenly encircled Jordie. Many were in the form of black males in 'highly aroused' states. Later she recalled the touch of one black shadow but then her memory went blank and as per usual she had no recollection of what happened next. Instead she found herself back in her room and on her bed with no idea of elapsed time.

She did remember Tjitjira's being there and what he said. Suddenly she realised that the urges to come to the beach had been his calling her. What was she to do? Go back to the beach? No the Doomed probably were watching her. But then, how long ago was her meeting with Tjitjira? Perhaps she should wait until he called her again, that is if he would come back.

In the end Jordie decided that she would go back to the beach so as to be near and ready should Tjitjira return. Just as she was about to get up her father's black shadow together with a few others wafted into her room. Upon seeing them Jordie shut down. That is what normally happened.

For how long she was 'away' she could not say but when she was herself again she became aware of a shimmering pain in her belly. When she looked down at herself she saw the shimmering image of a stake protruding from her stomach. It was not until she tried to get up that she realised the stake had been driven through her and into the substance underneath her so she could not get up off the bed. Panic gripped her then. She wriggled and tried to push herself up to get off the stake but all to no avail. As a shimmerer she just did not have the strength required. In the end she gave up and cried herself to sleep.

CHAPTER 28

'BINTANG BALON'

EVEN THOUGH KAL could not see Jordie as more than a vague shimmer in the air, he could feel her wispy touch and he heard her clearly in his mind, *"Be honest with me Kal, what would ye have me do? Stay with ye as a shimmerer or go with Harry and perhaps never come back?"*

"That must be entirely your own decision Jordie. I do not own you nor am in a position where I am at liberty to make decisions that could mean life or death for you."

"I would like to have your advice though."

"What would make you happiest? No that is the wrong question, what I really want to know is, is your desire to be solid again important enough to risk two transfers, one from the Dimension into the Core and the other from the Core back into the Dimension?"

"The whole prospect scares me silly but the way I be now be no good to either of us. I want to feel ye when ye hugs me and I imagine that ye don't get much pleasure out of hugging a sponge. Do ye?"

"Jordie of course I do have preferences but at this point they are of no importance. As part of you throwing off the yoke placed on your shoulders by your father and the Brethren you have to make this decision yourself. I will back you whatever you decide to do."

"*What if my decision be wrong and ye can see it? Would ye let me go ahead and do it?*"

"What if, what if. You are procrastinating my girl."

Jordie became silent and went over the whole thing in her mind.

Even though Tjitjira did have the backing of the Council of Elders it had been touch and go when he had extracted her from the Enchanted Isle of the Doomed. Her father with some of his cronies had gone as far as driving a stake through her shimmer body in an attempt to keep her on the Isle of the Doomed. Only through Tjitjira's quick thinking had he turned her into a wraith just long enough for her to become gas within the pocket of still air created by a blanket wrapped around her. As soon as she became gas he dragged her and the blanket away from the stake and transferred her out of the mini dimension that was the Enchanted Isle of the Doomed. Moments later she then returned to be a shimmerer.

Afterwards Tjitjira told her that at the time he did not think he could save her and it was just lucky that it was day-time when all this happened because if it had been night she would have become a solid wraith and the stake would have kept her pinned in the Enchanted Isle of the Doomed.

The memory served Jordie to realize that Tjitjira was not infallible and that what he proposed to do with her in an attempt to make her solid might not work so well either.

He explained that to revert to being solid she had to go into the Core where the higher vibrational frequencies would cause her to spontaneously become solid again. That part he seemed pretty sure of, the part that was perhaps not such a foregone conclusion was whether she could transfer back into the Dimension and not revert back to be a shimmerer.

Jordie's initial worry was what would happen if she materialised somewhere in the Core where she knew no one. Tjitjira put her mind to rest on that score because Harry would be her companion and they would most likely revert back to where Harry originally had come from.

Tjitjira further explained that Harry needed to be her companion because he was a shimmerer and for him to become solid again he not only had to return to the Core but also he would have to find a place in the Core where the vibrational frequencies were higher than those of the surroundings where he was born. At that point Jordie lost interest because all she could think of was that Kal would not be going with her.

In the end Tjitjira asked her, "*Do you want Kal to come with you knowing that more than likely you will not be able to return to the Dimension?*"

Jordie had replied, "*We would be together and I will follow him anywhere.*"

"*Jordie, remember that in the Core Kal virtually was an outcast with perhaps even a price on his head and that if the WSA[10] found out his whereabouts they would chase him remorselessly.*"

Jordie had heard enough stories from Harry to know that was true. Besides if there was a possibility for Harry to become solid again she was not going to stand in his way. So in the end it was decided that through the machinations of the Council of Elders and Tjitjira, Harry and Jordie would be transferred back into the Core where Jordie would be solid upon arrival. The next problem was to find a point in the Core that had enough significance for Harry to act as a drawing point to home in on.

His old water police launch qualified nicely.

---

10   WSA. World Security Agency

Once there they would seek a venue with higher vibrations than their normal surroundings so that Harry too could revert to the solid state. Next they would have to wait in the hope that there was enough of a pull between Jordie and Kal to bring both her and Harry back into the Dimension. Having no great desire to be on the run from the WSA for the rest of his days Harry was quite keen on returning to the Dimension.

Perhaps the most frustrating aspect of the whole business was that nobody could predict how soon conditions for a spontaneous transfer into the Core would present themselves but all knew that when they did arrive there would be very little or no warning.

Tjitjira who became a frequent visitor, at some point asked Abdullah whether he would want to go back to the Core to become solid again but the latter declined the offer.

For one he was sure that the powers that be would be after him in order to silence him on the whole subject of the disappearance of the Trade Winds resort and the presumed loss of life involved. Secondly he had a sneaking suspicion that the drug cartel would be more than interested in hearing his take on the happening as well.

Besides he had no relatives mourning for him in the Core. There was no guarantee that if he became solid in the Core that he would be able to transfer back into Dimension. Therefore he felt safer to just stay with the status -quo, besides somebody had to give Brutus a reason for being.

In anticipation of an indefinite wait, the village built a hut for Kal and his entourage of shimmerers. To the casual observer Kal appeared to live a lonely existence where in reality the only time Jordie and him had some alone time was when they went for a walk with Jordie hanging onto Kal's arm or hand.

The junk was reaching completion and A'anu was getting rather excited about the approaching launching date. So were the boat builders for that matter and festive preparations were taking place all through the village. *Any excuse for a party!*

As the day came closer Kal was seen hiding behind a screen set up near the bows of the junk. He told people to stay away because he was painting the name of the junk on her bows and it was bad luck for anybody to know, to hear or to read the name before the launching day. He did allow people to see the black and white stylised eye carved and painted on either side of the bows and looking slightly downwards so the craft would see any reefs in her path.

The junk was built in a cradle and underneath the cradle there were rails made from the hard wood called Masi. Those rails were now lathered with a mixture of tallow and condensed coconut oil. Next every man, woman and child in village took up the towing ropes and the drag began.

An unexpected help was provided by an old man who in his younger years had been involved with the levitational movement of the Moai from their quarry sites to their placing's on Rapa Nui. Due to age his concentration was wavering resulting in short jerky movements of the vessel but eventually she got onto the greased rails and the haul-out became easier and smoother.

It took the best part of the day but by late afternoon she was in the water and afloat. The inevitable speeches took place followed by Kal giving the honour of revealing the junk's name to the head builder, A'anu.

With a shaky hand A'anu pulled the piece of canvas away and shouted for all to hear, "The ship's name is 'Bintang Balon'[11]"

Kal's use of the Malay word for 'star' and the island's name was a double tribute from Kal to A'anu whose twenty years of living and working in Indonesia as a boat builder not only had enabled the building

---

[11] 'Bintang Balon' translation, 'Star of Balon'.

of the junk but also made it possible for Kal to communicate with the people on the island. Naming the vessel after the island as well was a tribute to the effort the island population had put into building the boat.

With the ceremonial part concluded the dancing and singing and the 'this and that' of partying started. After a while Kal noted that hardly any of the island's alcoholic palm wine was being drunk. He asked A'anu whether he should feel insulted and A'anu told him that he should feel flattered instead.

"Why should I be flattered?"

"You, or rather I, told the chief on your behalf that you want to hand-over the 'Vrouwe Irene' tomorrow because you felt that doing it on the same day as the launching of the 'Bintang Balon' would perhaps seem to reduce the appreciation and gratitude you feel for what the village did for you. Right?"

"Yes, but..."

"Well, the village feels that attending the hand-over ceremony while supporting a hang-over would reduce their show of appreciation for the gesture you are making."

After a moment he added with a happy grin, "Don't worry, the day after tomorrow there will be plenty hang-overs!"

And hang-overs there were on the day forecasted. The majority of the villagers suffered hang-overs because they had a good time and now felt to be part owners of a schooner that was going to bring trade to their island.

Kal had the granddaddy of hang-overs as well but his was the result of feeling a painful loss at the sudden disappearance of both Jordie and Harry. It happened very stealthily and just after sunset on the day the 'Vrouwe Irene' changed ownership.

Partying was in full swing and everybody had a good time until suddenly Kal felt the feathery touch of Jordie's hand on his arm disappear. In the flickering light of the fires it was not possible to see the girl's shimmering form. In a bit of a panic he called Brutus over and when she came to him he asked, "Harry is Jordie with you?"

It was Abdullah's voice that replied, *"Kal, they are gone!"*

"Did you see them go?"

"Harry was saying something to me when, in mid-sentence, he shimmered away."

"Did it happen just then?"

"Yes about a minute before you called Brutus."

"Well they must have gone into the Core! Would have been nice of them to say good bye though."

"Yes, I'll miss them, let's hope it won't be for long."

After that Kal started to worry about all the things he thought could go wrong and he drank to make the pain of loss less gripping. It did not work until he was that drunk that he could not form and/or retain a complete thought.

CHAPTER 29

TRIP INTO THE UNKNOWN

T HE CRACKLE OF static electricity and a peel of thunder still echoed through her head when Jordie suddenly heard another voice from somewhere behind her. The voice said with a great amount of bewilderment, "Who the hell are you? Where the hell did you come from? What are you doing here and why are you naked?"

The first thing Jordie said was, "Can you see me?"

"Off-course I can see you and I must say you are an eye full but that is not answering any of my questions so let us start again, "Who are you?"

"Jordie."

"Jordie who?"

"Jordie van Straaten."

"I've heard that name before."

"*Off-course you have heard that name before!*"

"Who said that? Am I going mad? Are you a ventriloquist?"

"*Wake up Jeffrey! You ever heard a girl ven… what you me-call it, with a man's voice?*"

Jordie could see that the young man was getting flustered and she did not want him to lose control because they were on a boat like she had never seen before, it had no sails and a deep rumbling noise she had never heard before seemed to come from underneath her feet. She decided she better do something or say something to try and control the situation.

"The voice ye heard in your head be that of Harry Knott, he be a shimmerer but a good man all the same."

"How do you know my name? Harry? But Harry disappeared over two years ago!"

"That's right young Tomkins and now I'm back. By the way, Jordie is betrothed to Kal so don't get any ideas."

"Oh, this is all too much!"

With a resolute movement he turned the ignition key of the Police launch off and let the boat drift. They were over two miles away from the nearest rocks so there was no danger of a stranding. Now Temporary sergeant Jeffrey Tomkins leaned against the coaming of the well-deck and shyly looked at Jordie.

"How come I can hear Harry in my head but I cannot see him?"

"He be a shimmerer that be why…"

"I'll tell him Jordie. OK Jeff, remember when you read Morgan Turbot's journals of his travels in the Dimension of Wind, Wood, and Water, when he was talking about Wraiths that were people who got hung up, so to speak, halfway through a forced transfer from the Core into the Dimension?"

"Yes, as opposed to people who went over during a spontaneous transfer?"

"That's right. The Dimension is mainly guarded and to a certain extent administered by what they call the Council of Elders. Those venerable, and I mean venerable, people cannot become Councillors unless they have a lot of experience, a strong desire to help others, a will to safeguard moral standards and to top it all off, are prepared to tender their services for free. Well those

Councillors many of whom have supernatural powers, have the ability to transform a Wraith into a Shimmerer. A Shimmerer is half Wraith and half Person during the day and half Person and half Wraith during the night. It is the best they can do for those that in their eyes did not deserve the fate of the Wraith.

"Well to make a long story short, they made me into a Shimmerer and now they sent me here in an attempt to give me back my body beautiful."

"So what do we need to do to achieve the impossible? Your body beautiful? Be real!"

"I'll ignore that last remark for the moment. First things first. We need to take care of Jordie. She comes from the Dimension and all this is very new and strange for her. We really got to make sure she understands all the, for her, new things she'll encounter."

"Like what?"

"Anything to do with technology developed in the Core since and including the Industrial Revolution. You'll be in for some surprises."

"Shit! Where do we start?"

"Let's start with getting her some clothes."

"Right! Let me see. Oh, hang on, I got a pair of coveralls here that might fit her."

Hastily Jeffrey scuttled into the launch's cabin where some serious clanging and banging went on until he rushed back on deck with a pair of Police issue blue overalls in an outstretched hand. Without delay he offered them to Jordie who looked somewhat nonplussed.

Harry could not help but laugh, "You may have to help her getting them on. She's probably never seen a set before."

"Oh sugar!"

"Yeah, sugar and spice and everything nice. Just don't get any ideas young fella!"

By the time Jordie was dressed in the somewhat too big overalls all three of them had the giggles and the whole exercise was a good ice breaker.

Without thinking Jeffrey hit the starter button of the twin diesel engines of the launch and fear gripped Jordie. She started shaking and went as white as a sheet. Jeffrey saw the girl's distress and asked, "What is wrong?"

"What, what be that noise!? Be it that this boat be breaking up?"

"Huh? Of course not, that is just the sound of the engines."

"What be an engine?"

"Do you know what a machine is?"

"You mean like a windmill that grinds corn, or that pumps water?"

"Yes, you could call that a machine. In this case it is a mechanical device that turns a propeller. A propeller is like a small windmill that only has three sails and is fixed to the bottom of the boat. The engine makes it turn and that pushes the boat forward through the water."

"Oh."

"Does that make any sense?"

"No, but if ye can control it, it be all right with me."

Jeffrey Tomkins could see that he could be in for a torrid time trying to explain his world to the gorgeous but seemingly not too bright girl.

In an attempt to change the subject he asked, "When you just materialised, or, got here, you asked me if I could see you. Why was that?"

"Well after Tjitjira, he be a spirit elder, got me away from the Enchanted Isle of the Doomed, I be like Harry, a shimmerer and Tjitjira told me then that I would need the higher vibrational frequencies of the Core to become solid again. I didn't realise that it would be immediate."

Forced to revise his opinion of the gorgeous but not too bright girl, Jeffrey mumbled somewhat chastised, "Yeah, whatever."

Harry's voice was a quiet chuckle as he whispered, "*You might know your world but she knows hers.*"

The noise of the engines, the bashing of the waves as the powerful launch forced its way towards the coast and the harbour made it hard to conduct a conversation. Harry in his shimmer persona hung on for dear life while Jordie was unnerved by the violence of the boat's progress towards shore. In her experience boats moved in harmony with water and did not bash their way unfeelingly towards their goal. At the same time she was enthralled by the many lights the town on shore displayed to the night sky.

As the launch idled into the inner harbour towards the jetty in front of the yacht club, Jordie could not help but say, "What a waste of fuel be all those lights! Many illuminate areas where no people appear to be."

Before Jeffrey could come up with a perhaps snide remark at his world being criticised, he heard Harry's whisper, "*She has no knowledge of electricity or our paranoia over security so just nod your head and smile lad.*"

As he brought the launch alongside he asked, "Right Harry, what next?"

"*Can you take us to my house?*"

"Your house? The WSA appointed an agent whose sole task is to run you and or Kal to ground. He lives there now."

"*You are kidding me! It was the WSA that sent me off in the first place so why should they appoint an agent to hunt me down?*"

"You'd be surprised! The world's largest watch dog organisation has got more flaws in it than a second grader's spelling test! You were sent off by one section and now another is looking for you. They hounded me for ages until at last I had to take out a court order against them. Officially the WSA does not exist so I had to take the order out against Buster himself. He is now living in your house in the hope that you will return there. The neighbours think he is a relative who is looking after the place for you."

"*Hmm, I may have to go and haunt him out of the joint.*"

"Yeah well, while you're planning that move you better come with me to my house. Sandra who you used to call 'the girlfriend' and I got married about a year ago and we have a place now near the foreshore. You're both welcome and Jordie might find some answers to girly questions that I cannot help her with."

Sgt. Tomkins suddenly stopped speaking and with a strange, nearly haunted expression he turned to Jordie and said, "Listen to me! I'm talking as though Harry is here!"

Jordie replied, "Well he be here!"

Harry was a bit less subtle, "*Course I'm here how else can I be talking to you!*"

"Well I can't see you! All I hear is your voice in my head so how do I know this isn't all a big con?"

"*By who? Yourself? Are you asking the questions and then answering them yourself? You haven't flipped over my disappearance have you?*"

"Well, I thought perhaps it could be the WSA trying to trick me into revealing where you are or whatever."

"*Yeah? And what about Jordie in her birthday suit is that just window dressing or is she the reward? Well, let me tell you, don't try it on with her because where she comes from they take a very dim view of any man trying to put the hard word on any woman, married or otherwise. Anyway I am digressing. I realise that it all seems a bit strange but let me assure you we are genuine and we do so need your help.*"

"A bit strange? I'll say. I just thought of something that might tell me whether or not you are Harry. You once saw something that was embarrassing to me and I swore you to keep it a secret. What was it?"

"*How can I tell you that? You swore me to secrecy!*"

"Stop mucking about! If you are Harry tell me."

"OK, you got that silly little love-heart tattooed on your butt. By the way, did you get the initials changed because they belonged to a flame pre-Sandra?"

"Yes, you are Harry all right. As for the tattoo, I had it removed so Sandra knows nothing about it and I hope you won't mentioned it either. She thinks I got the scar in the line of duty and I want to keep it that way."

"I would not want to destroy the image of her hero being shot in the butt by some old lady armed with a spear gun! My lips are sealed but I don't know about Jordie's."

Rather anxiously Jeffrey asked, "Jordie?"

With a bit of a smirk on her face she feigned not to have followed the conversation and asked, "Huh? What were all that about?"

Jeffrey was about to explain it all to her when she said with a cheeky grin, "I won't tell her if ye promise not to relate to her ye had to wrap yer arms around me to help me get dressed in this garment."

"OH no! I can promise you *that* for sure!"

Harry got the giggles. Poor Jeffrey, he usually finished up being the butt of Harry's jokes and it looked as though Jordie was getting in on the act as well. Nothing much had changed, Jeffrey just was that type.

Sgt Tomkins was suitably impressed when he brought the launch alongside the low pier and without being told, Jordie secured the vessel dockside.

He had to smile when he saw that the girl was obviously hampered in her movements by the coveralls she was wearing. For a guilty moment he wondered how Sandra, his young wife, would fare in a society where clothes were optional. He would have to broach the subject and see if he could talk her into going there for a holiday on a 'when in Rome do as the Romans do' ticket. Yes well, pigs might fly too!

The next hurdle presented itself when they approached the parking lot where Jeff's car was parked. Jordie was holding back a bit and asked Harry, "What be those boxes on wheels?"

"*They are called cars and people use them to go from one place to another.*"

"How?"

"*They sit inside them and they drive to where they want to go.*"

"Where be the horses?"

"*No horses just another engine, or machine, like in the boat but this time the engine makes the back wheels turn.*"

"Be they safe?"

"*If you know how to control one.*"

"Does Jeffrey know how to control it?"

"*Oh yes, he was born behind the steering wheel of one.*"

"Really?"

Sgt Tomkins interrupted, "Harry! Stop confusing the poor girl! Jordie, we have special driving schools where people learn how to drive and what rules they must obey on the road. Anyway, hop in and we'll go to my house to meet Sandra."

The trip to Jeffrey's house was quite an experience both for Jordie and for Jeffrey. It was just as well that he had put her in the back seat because when another car approached them from the opposite direction, Jordie went into a flat spin. By this time it was dark and the headlights form the oncoming car mesmerised the girl, she had never seen lights that bright, and on the last minute she screamed convinced that they were going to collide. Jeffery got a fright as well and none to gently muttered, "Shit! Harry! Can you explain things to her? It must all be rather frightening for her!"

"*Yeah, sorry. I was miles away!*"

The rest of the journey went smoothly enough with Harry explaining what traffic lights were for and what the solid white lines and the broken ones on the road were in aid of. Not long after that discussion, Jeffrey, a bit of a lead-foot, crossed a white line and Jordie told him, "Ye just breached a law! What be the penalty for that transgression?"

"Sugar! You're as bad as my wife! I am the law so I can break it when necessary!"

"Who decides when it be a necessity?"

"I do!"

"And why were it a necessity?"

"Harry! Do something!"

"*Nope, it was you who crossed the line!*"

Before things could come to a head and Jordie and Harry could be asked to vacate the vehicle, Jordie saved the day by exclaiming, "Oh look at that! Be that a palace?"

"No dear, that is just a Woolworth Supermarket."

"So many lights and so many glass walls!"

"Yep, the lights are there to stop thieves from breaking the glass walls and steal things."

"Would it not be a lot cheaper to have stone walls and less lights?"

"You should apply for a job as a town planner or as an economist!"

"What be an economist?"

"I'll have to tell you some other time because we are home."

As they turned into the drive of Jeffrey's house Jordie took one look and asked, "How many families live here?"

"What, in this house?"

"Yes."

"Just my wife and I."

"But it be so big!"

"No bigger than most of the houses in the suburbs around here."

Before she could ask the obvious question of what a suburb was, Jeffrey vacated the vehicle and opened the car door for her. He was about to slam it close when Harry yelped, *"Hey let me get out before you slam that door, it is bad enough trying to hang onto Miss Jumping Jelly bean here! She is worse than Brutus!"*

"Who is Brutus?"

"Oh, his guide dog in the Dimension."

"So why does he need a guide dog, is he blind?"

"No, he be mostly hot air and might float away unless he hangs onto something or somebody."

"You wait! I'll get even or might even tell Kal on you!"

"Go ahead, Kal be on my side anyway. Now hang on to me, it be a bit windy dear!"

Sgt Tomkins shook his head as he walked onto the veranda of his house.

They were halfway across the veranda when the door opened and Sandra came through.

As Jeffrey introduced them the two women took stock of each other. Jordie was not very tall but well-proportioned and with her dark auburn hair was quite a looker. Sandra who was a head taller could be forgiven for the twinge of suspicious jealousy creeping into her eyes. There was however no need for her to compare her looks in an unfavourable light with those of the girl her husband had just brought home. Sure she was a fair bit taller and her hair was 'sensibly short' but she had a good and willowy figure with long legs and a good tan. She envied Jordie for her dark green eyes while hers were brown with hazel flecks.

Her mouth had a determined set to it but that was caused by her conviction that as a woman in a man's world there was no option for failure. Not that she had ever failed, she was a brilliant physicist who not only worked in a lab but also taught as a visiting lecturer at two different universities. Quite the opposite of Jordie but after the initial circling of each other, the women got on well.

Jeffrey entered the door and Sandra stood aside to let him and Jordie in. As soon as Jordie was over the threshold Sandra let go off the screen door. The spring loaded door closed and caught Harry half way through. Up to that point Harry had not uttered a word and Jeffrey had been so nervous about the meeting between the two women that he had forgotten all about Harry. Things changed rapidly at this point.

"Ouch! Jordie! I told you! You are worse than Brutus!"

On hearing Harry's voice in her head, Sandra lost the plot. She began to shake and went a deadly pale. In an aside to Harry, Jordie told him to zip it.

She grabbed the young woman by the arms and spoke softly,

"Sandra, ye're not going mad. I hear his voice in my head as well. The first time it happened to me I thought Harry were some evil spirit too."

In an attempt to lighten the tension she jokingly added, "I still be not too sure about the evil bit but he definitely be nay a ghost."

On a more serious note she continued, "Just be assured that he be here and that ye be nay going mad. Let us sit down and Harry and I can explain everything to ye."

Somewhat re-assured Sandra let Jeffrey and Jordie lead her into the kitchen where they sat around the kitchen table.

While her husband prepared a pot of tea, Harry explained to Sandra how he had been transferred into the Dimension by the WSA and how he had become a Wraith. Of course he had to explain at length what a Wraith is. Next he explained how he had been altered into being a Shimmerer. When he told her to look at where he was standing near the kitchen table, she could see the slight shimmer in the air and when he made her move her hand through the air she could feel his presence as a slight breeze on her own skin. That gave her the shivers and she went for a hug from her husband.

For the next hour Jeffrey and Sandra were spellbound by the stories Harry and Jordie told them.

The next crisis came when Jordie related how she had been branded as a slave and to show Sandra the tattoo and the branding on her back shrugged out of her coveralls.

Aghast Sandra stammered, "What are you doing?"

With a 'Huh?' look on her face Jordie replied, "Showing ye the burn and tattoo."

Harry then chimed in to explain the dress codes prevalent in the Dimension. Much to the relief of Jeffrey and Harry although the latter would never admit it, Sandra accepted the situation and studied Jordie's back. When she was done she remarked to Jordie, "I noticed you fidgeting before, are those coveralls bothering you?"

"If ye mean to ask whether this garment be annoying and chafing me, the answer be yes!"

Sandra looked at Jeffrey with raised eyebrows and much to the surprise of the latter, answered, "I have no objection to you taking it off as long as you promise me not to go out of the house or let people outside see you."

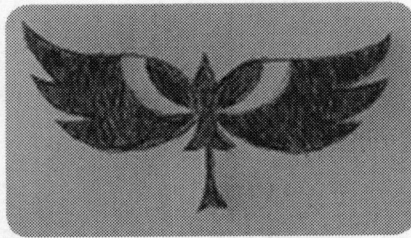

CHAPTER 30

SANDRA TOMKINS

HEARING HARRY'S VOICE in her head still freaked Sandra out but she soon took a liking to Jordie. Sandra shooed Jeffrey and Harry out of the kitchen with the excuse that the women had to do the cooking.

Gratefully Jeffrey grabbed a beer from the fridge and led Harry to the sitting room where he could bring him up to date as far as the hunt by the WSA was concerned. Meanwhile the girls were in the kitchen comparing notes, but that is not until after Jordie understood the machinations of the kitchen stove, a gas one in this case. She remained suspicious of the electric light, she could not understand how touching a little knob on the wall could produce a light in a tube stuck to the ceiling. When Sandra turned on the ceiling fan to disperse cooking smells, poor Jordie ducked for cover and even after Sandra had reassured her, Jordie still cast a suspicious glance at the spinning blades above their heads.

Sandra was full of questions about the status of women in the Dimension and some of the answers she liked while others she did not.

It surprised her that at least in the Pacific—Jordie referred to it as the Quiet Ocean[12]—the societies appeared to be mainly matriarchal.

Once she found out that it was a moral obligation for any man to come to the aid of any woman who felt she was being threatened by either a Wraith or a human male and that such intercession usually resulted in the death or serious injury of the offending male, Sandra began to understand why Jordie supported such a minimal dress code; she felt secure in the normal environment of daily life. As a matter of fact her nudity might help fool the Wraiths into thinking that she was a levitator. And finally there was the added fact that Jordie strongly believed that a person devoid of any garments would find it hard to support a pretence as to status or importance. All this had to be explained to Sandra and the food preparation consequently was not as fast and proficient as it could have been.

However, it gave Sandra a bit of an insight into the different standards and norms prevailing in the Dimension of Wind, Wood, and Water.

Another point of interest was what Jordie had to say about tattoos. She told Sandra that a tattoo in a clearly visible place was nearly a necessity in most places but was a definite 'must have' in the more populated areas where the incidence of Wraith attacks was much higher than for instance in the islands. This meant of course that a woman without tattoos could easily be judged to be a wraith, which could have dire consequences for the woman involved.

Sandra bared her left shoulder and showed Jordie a small tattoo of a bright red rose, "Would that do?"

Jordie smiled and said, "Nay if ye were to cover it with a garment. Wraith attacks in the main occur during the hours of darkness so a larger tattoo be of more significance.

---

[12] Quiet Ocean translated from Dutch 'Stille Oceaan'.

"The norm be that upon the birth of an infant a tattooist be commissioned to encircle a wrist or an ankle of the child with an unobtrusive tattoo by which it can be determined that the child nay be a Wraith. It be nay until the child comes off age that that person be allowed to commission a larger tattoo. That way it be hoped that a person will nay finish up with a tattoo that may be an embarrassment at a later age."

"I don't see a bracelet tattoo on you. How come?"

"I were born among a fanatic as well as fatalistic group of religious zealots who be sure that the Lord looks after His children and that therefore we be immune to Wraith attack. I were just lucky I suppose."

"Ah well, you now have an impressive tattoo on your back."

In a sudden move of female independence perhaps, or out of solidarity with her guest, Sandra whipped off her sweater and Jordie gasped in horror. She pointed at Sandra's bra and asked, "Art ye injured?"

"No! Why?"

"What be that harness ye be wearing?"

"That? That's a bra, a garment to support my breasts."

"Why do they need support? For vanity? To make them look larger, higher or firmer? Men be more impressed by the real natural look. Shed the thing and feel free!"

Sandra hesitated for a long time while she gave Jordie a questing look. Eventually she raised her hands and hovered her fingers over the clasp at her back. Then with a resolute gesture she unhooked the bra and she muttered under her breath, "Jeffrey will be sooo pleased!"

For a moment she fiddled with the buckle of her skirt but that was still too much for her so she left it alone.

Jordie watched with interest as, over the next half hour, she saw Sandra change from being very self-conscious to secretly enjoying the freedom to a full-blown celebration of emancipation. At that point the high-heel shoes came off as well.

When Jeffrey walked into the kitchen his jaw just about hit the ground. He looked at the empty beer bottle in his hand and cried out, "But I only had the ONE!"

Sandra gave him a cool look and said, "Equal rights Buster, you can walk about without a shirt, so can I."

"Hooray! Hooray! Female liberation and equality at last! I'll have another beer to celebrate this momentous occasion!"

"Yeah, but by Dimension rules you'll be in serious trouble if you molest me."

"I promise I won't molest you provided you feed me. Please!"

"You kids just go right ahead, don't mind me while you molest and feed to your heart's content. I'll just hang around."

As Sandra dished out the food she remarked as a matter of fact, "That's right we still got to find you some higher vibrations. Any ideas where we can find some?"

"Hey! That's what we came to you for, you're the physicist in this family!"

"You mean to say that it is up to me to leave you as you are or to change you back? Oh! Feel that power over a mere male! What is it worth? Huh?"

Jeffrey now got into the act and said in a patronizing tone, "Ah, don't be like that, honey, generally speaking Harry means well."

Sandra remarked in a mean voice, "I just wonder what concessions we can force him to agree to."

Harry sounded hopeful, *"Does that mean you know where to find vibrational frequencies higher than normal?"*

"Hey! Who is the scientist here? Of course I do! While you were playing spin-the-bottle with Jeffrey, we girls were hard at work on the problem."

"Yeah. Right! Gossiping is more likely!"

"Careful! Being a bachelor and all that you may not be aware of the fact that women are exceptionally good at multi-tasking."

Before Harry could come back with some cutting remark, Jeffrey butted in, "Harry, if I were you I would give it a rest now; unless you want to listen for the rest of the evening to women's lib propaganda."

"OK kids go ahead and enjoy your deliciously smelling food while I'll just hang around here near the ceiling."

"Hey, while you are up there floating about doing nothing, if I give you a feather duster can you dust the top of the ceiling fan?"

"Sure, would you want the dust on your dinner or sprinkled on your desert?"

"Are you suggesting that I am a bad house keeper and have dust on my ceiling fan!?"

With an exaggerated sigh Jeffrey mumbled, "Give it a rest Harry. You're only getting yourself deeper in the poo. Her first year at uni was entirely devoted on how to verbally destroy males."

They all had a bit of a laugh and after some more banter Sandra said, "Now let us get serious. I have some friends in the electronic side of the uni. Perhaps we can set up some experiment with high frequency sound. I'll have a talk with them."

"Can you trust them? Don't forget that the WSA is still very interested in me. For the life of me I cannot understand why."

After a pull on his bottle of beer, Jeffrey remarked, "I can tell you why, it all has to do with their program of 'assisted transfers' of which you were a victim yourself. If now you suddenly pop-up and spill the beans on their little transgressions, there is no way they can deny it and heads in high places would roll."

The Tomkins only had the one car and Jeffrey used to take it to work with him because he worked irregular hours. Whenever his schedule allowed, he would pick-up Sandra from either the laboratory where she worked or from the university where she taught. On this particular day he picked her up from the uni. As they drove away he spotted a black SUV pull out from the curb a few cars back. At first he did not take much notice of the other car but when it kept trailing him, he became suspicious. He turned yet another corner and when the SUV followed he said to Sandra, "Don't look back, I think we're being followed."

A shiver of fear went through Sandra but she tried to make light of it, "You've been a Cop for too long!"

"You may be right but this one has been following us since leaving the uni."

"What? Just because a car drove the same route as us? That does not necessarily mean that they are following us with criminal intent."

"Perhaps not but it sure looks funny considering that we have been going in circles. Have you seen any strangers hanging about at uni?"

"Not that I noticed but then again I'm not there full time and outside of a handful of teaching staff I know no-one. On top of that, why would anybody want to follow us?"

"Because, my dear, by now they all know that we are in the 'Anti Assisted Transfers Club' and they would love to show-off with a bit of muscle."

"I hope you're wrong but how could they know?"

"I would say our friendly local WSA agent Buster has been keeping an eye on us. He probably spotted Jordie somewhere in our yard or something. We'll soon find out!"

With that Sgt. Tomkins flicked on his emergency lights, pulled up in the middle of the road and jumped out of the car, pistol in hand.

The black SUV pulled up with squealing tires but well back from Jeffrey's car. Jeffrey waved the vehicle on but there was no reaction. Still with his pistol at the ready he began to walk towards the SUV. Suddenly the vehicle lurched forward and with squealing tires and burning rubber it performed a U-turn and sped off. As Jeffrey walked back to his own car he holstered his pistol but perhaps he should have kept it out.

As he opened the door of the car his first impression was that a huge wildcat was attacking him. The ferocious hell-cat turned out to be Sandra his loving spouse who did not approve of her husband's approach to what could have been a rather confronting situation.

Jeffrey's contention that he was in no real danger. His view that the WSA would think twice about taking on the Police Department was rejected outright. "Look what they did to Harry! You're deluding yourself! Just because you wear a blue uniform you think you're untouchable and bullet proof!"

Warily he slid behind the wheel and tried to gingerly place a placating hand on her arm but she wasn't having any and gloomily stared out of the window for the rest of the drive home. When they got there, she stormed out of the car and into the house. She barged into the kitchen where she spotted Jordie and demanded, "Where is Harry? Is he here?!"

"*Hey! Don't bite the girl's head off. It is not her fault that you can't see me. What is your problem?*"

"Our hero here just single-handed took on what he thinks is the WSA. He made like the 'stranger with a big-iron on his hip' the way he walked down the street with his gun in his hand… OK Corral all over again!"

"*Whoa girl, back up and tell us what happened from the start.*"

Harry spoke in his 'no-nonsense-I am-the-Police-and-in-charge' voice and it had a calming effect on Sandra. Before she could respond, Jeffrey reported, "After I collected Sandra from the Uni I noticed a black SUV pull away from the curb behind us. For some reason I got suspicious and kept an eye on it. It stayed a few cars back. I really got interested when it followed us around three corners in a row. So the time had come to find out whether this was a fair dinkum case of stalking. We took the scenic route and drove past the Uni twice more. They followed and by this time I realised why the vehicle had drawn my attention, it is the same make and model as that driven by Buster, the WSA operative living in your house, Harry. Next I turned into a one lane alleyway and the SUV followed. After I stopped the car diagonally across the alley and switched on my stick-on pursuit light, the SUV stopped a fair distance back but in the alley. I got out of my car to let them know I was not fooling. Next I waved them on towards me but they did not budge so I started walking towards them…"

"You keep hinting that there were more than one person in the SUV, what do you base that assumption on?"

"This had the markings of an observation stake-out and they usually are carried out by two operatives. If it had been an elimination mission there would have been some serious shooting well before then. Mind you all this is only summation because the window tinting was so dark that it was impossible to see inside the vehicle. I doubt that the window tinting was legal that's how dark it was. Anyhow, a bit of bluff would go a long way towards establishing top-dog status so after they would not come any closer, I drew my gun up into the attack mode and walked towards the SUV. They did not wait. With squealing tires and burning rubber they backed out of the alley, did a U-turn and were off. The only time I was in any real danger was upon re-entry into my vehicle." He had a big smirk on his face as he threw a kiss at Sandra.

Harry was quiet for some time before he remarked, "Why the sudden interest from the WSA? They did not see either of us. Even if they saw Jordie, they should not be able to tell that she came from the Dimension or that she knows me."

"Humph," Sandra said somewhat subdued, "It could be because I have shown interest in the vibration tests being conducting at the Uni."

"What? Did you mention me to somebody in the lab?"

"Of course not! The WSA uses vibration to get rid of their enemies but they don't really have much of an idea on how it works. They are trying to learn how to control it better."

"And why would they want to do that? They get rid of their undesirables so why would they want to learn more about how to do it?"

"They want to learn how to use the vibration technology more effectively. My guess though is that they want to control where 'in the past' those undesirables were dumped and whether they could bring them back again. Once they master that procedure they could very well use their advanced skills to denude the dimensional environment of ores, minerals and possibly oil."

Jeffrey now asked his wife, "How would that work?"

"Well, say that they found out how to go back to the year 1200. And say that they had a map of Australia showing all the places where gold was found in the 1800s. They then could send clean-up crews to dig up part of the gold and bring it back for their use in the present time."

"But if they rob the gold before it was found, where would they get the map that shows where the gold is? And, why if they are going to what must be considerable effort to get it, would they only take part of the deposits?"

"Because, my dear Jeffrey, if they took the lot, no gold would be found in that location in 1800 and no one would draw a map as to where to find it in the first place."

"But say they took half wouldn't the map show double the amount?"

"No, I can see it now; the map drawn in 1800 would show the amount found in 1800. And the amount found at that date is what was left after the robbery in 1200 using the locations indicated by the 1800 map in the present."

"OK I can follow that reasoning, sort off, but what do they want with the vibration frequency manipulation?"

"They're after the ability to modulate and control the vibration frequencies and that is what they are spying on. As soon as I showed an interest in the process they became suspicious and now they want to know why I'm curious. Instead of coming straight out and ask me, they must have decided that their method of cloak and dagger is more productive."

Sandra was quiet for a while and then mused, "They can't be aware of their transferees becoming Wraith and I wonder if that knowledge would reduce their interest?"

"Whether it would or not, they are not going to find out from any of us because both Harry and Jordie would become guinea pigs and would never be heard of again!" Jeffrey sounded pretty determined and his voice was like a direct order. Sandra came back with, "Who said anything about me dobbing in either of them? I'm not that stupid you know!"

"OK, OK, what are we going to do about the nosey WSA?"

"We might have to look for another location where we can beef up vibration frequencies to the required level. By the way, do we know the frequencies required?"

Sandra shook her head and said, "In a round-about way that is what I was trying to find out in the lab. I did not ask straight out what it would take to make a person disappear. My question was that seeing how the higher frequencies could affect mass, would exposure to those high frequencies affect living tissue and would that be dangerous.

"Dr Franklin, the head honcho, assured me that there was a strong possibility that the higher frequencies would affect living tissue but that it would be to the extent of complete destruction and that, therefore, every precaution was taken in the lab to shield the experiments.

"The reaction I got from him convinced me that he knew nothing of any experimentation by the WSA. In hindsight I now wonder about one of the lab rats. While we were talking she moved closer and closer to where we stood and now I wonder if she is a WSA spy!"

"Yes that could explain the sudden interest in you. You better lay low for a while. Perhaps we should look for higher frequencies outside the lab."

Quite unexpectedly Jordie entered the conversation, "The Good Book relates how Joshua marched his army around the city of Jericho once a day for seven days while blowing their 'bazuinen'[13]. On the seventh day they repeated it seven times in a row and the walls crumbled."

"Yes, and?"

"Be that not an indication that sound be of a higher, or mayhap a lower vibration frequency? And, if that be so, perhaps our search could be among minstrels and other music makers?"

For a minute not a sound was heard but then everybody at once started to talk excitedly. Where Jordie had in mind trumpets and the like, Sandra straight away jumped on the bandwagon belonging to the electronic barons of sound. Jeffrey having heard some of their more recent oeuvres which he called an unhappy mating between a seagull and a whale could just imagine Harry's reaction when the latter found out what he was in for. Much to his surprise Harry immediately agreed to the experiment even after Jeffrey explained the nature of the sound, he refused to call it music, and the fact that his hearing probably never would be the same afterwards.

It was Harry who asked, *"If we are being watched by the WSA, won't they think it sus if we suddenly go trooping off to a sound lab?"*

"Ah! I may be able to fix that!" Jeffrey said, "I have a few contacts on the docks who may be of assistance that is if what you need is what I think it is."

"Oh good, but what do you think we need, oh husband dear?"

---

[13] Trumpets or trombones, translation of Dutch: 'Bazuinen'

"A sound proof place where you can fiddle with your ghetto-blaster?"

"OH! You're such an observant man!"

"I am trying, dear."

"Yes you can be! But tell us what your friends can do for the greater good of man and woman kind?"

Jeffrey let the plug for women-equality slide because, in his mind she outranked him by miles anyway but she would never accept that and he was not about to tell her. Instead he stayed with the subject and said, "I imagine that you want a sound-proof facility and I think I can arrange that."

"How?"

"Well I imagine a ship's cargo container inside a larger one and with sound proofing material in the space between them."

"That could work but how are you going to arrange that without the WSA boys finding out?"

"My acquaintances can make whole containers, and the odd person for that matter, disappear so hiding a container in plain view is not going to be a challenge for them. The main thing you have to establish is how much sound proofing you need."

"Well, we can only establish that through experimentation with sound at different strength and frequency levels. To prevent lasting damage to the hearing, we'll have to use sounds that are outside the hearing range of grown people. We'll have to travel up and down the frequency scale until we find a sound with the right frequency strength and or volume. We'll only find that when we can see Harry re-emerge."

"In other words you want a lot of sound proofing. Leave it with me."

"Yes the funny thing is that the sound of the right vibrational frequency and volume will lay outside the band of 20 to 20000 Hz, or the band of sound within the human hearing range. However before we can establish the right sound level both in Hertz and volume, we will be making a lot of noise."

Jeffrey suggested that they would have their supper after which he would go and see some 'contacts' as he called them. Harry was very silent; as silent as a matter of fact that Jordie asked, "What be thy concern, Harry? Be ye concerned that the process may be detrimental?"

"I'm just wondering, that's all."

"What be thy concern?"

"Well, what did the WSA do to make me into a Wraith, did they lower my vibrational frequency or did they raise it? And, what will happen if we go in the wrong direction?"

"Didst Tjitjira nay tell thy vibration were to be raised in order to effect thy return to normal? Do nay forget that my vibration was raised by coming to your dimension and thus brought about my return to normal."

Sandra joined the conversation and mused, "If Harry's vibrational frequency was lowered to make him a Wraith, and Jordie's was raised to make her solid, that would suggest that we have to increase Harry's vibrational frequency to make him solid again."

CHAPTER 31

SOUND PREPARATION

JEFFREY DRESSED IN a pair of black jeans, black singlet and loose black jacket with a hoodie got Sandra to drive him into town. She dropped him off in a dark part of town after they had circled the block twice to make sure they were not being followed.

With the hood pulled low over his face Jeffrey looked just like many a junkie looking to make a purchase or a sale. It was not long before a shadow detached itself from a dark corner and quietly glided to intercept Jeffrey. The shadow said something to Jeffrey but the latter shook his head and made to move on. This apparently was not to the liking of the afore-mentioned shadow. The worthy drew a dirty big hunting knife and made preparations to do a number on Jeffrey. Jeffrey not to be outdone drew his police revolver and snarled, "You're a looser! Who brings a knife to a gun fight? Would you like me to show you why you should have stayed at home?"

"Sorry Mister!" and the shadow was gone.

Without any further encounters of the nasty type, Jeffrey walked onto the docks and slipped into one of the waterfront pubs. Upon his entry many conversations stilled and some suspicious glances were aimed in his direction. Jeffrey took no notice and looked around until he saw the man he was looking for. He leaned on the bar next to the man and ordered a beer. With a gravelly voice the man asked, "How you're doing mate?"

"Yeah, not too bad, I have a bit of a problem you may be able to help me with."

"Oh dah, and wat would dat be?"

"You ever done any business with the WSA?"

The man got a fierce look on his face and grunted affirmation before he said, "Look mate, I did but I won't ever again! Dah!"

"So what happened?"

"I ain't telling, you being law enforcement and all. You are OK but you hav rules to follow and you would hav to stir up too much shit if I told you. Dah?"

"Fair enough, but I take it that you are not exactly overwhelmed with tender feelings towards them?"

"You might say dat. What is all dis about?"

"Would it bring back that warm fussy feeling if you could sock it to them?"

"A distinct possibility. Dah!"

"OK I'll get us another beer and then let's find a quiet corner where we can talk."

When the man stood up Jeffrey was reminded of the reason why this giant was feared and respected on the waterfront. The 'Russian' as he was known, stood six feet and eight inches tall and was built like a country you know what. He could rip the seams of his shirts by just tensing his shoulder and arm muscles. He was not the waterfront boss but nobody was game enough *not* to carry out his 'suggestions', not even the proper authorities.

As soon as they sat down in the 'Russian's' office, a secluded booth near the back of the pub's public bar, he asked, "Ok lad wat is on your mind? Does it involve killing?"

"No it does not involve killing but it does involve secrecy to keep the WSA out."

After Jeffrey stated his requirements the 'Russian' surmised, "So you want two containers, dah? One inside de other and space between dem to be filled up wiz sound proofing materials. Dah? How we test dat de amount of sound proofing is enough?"

"My wife, who is a scientist will device some way of testing that."

"Where would you want containers?"

"The safest place would be here on the wharf as though they are ready for shipping. Don't you think?"

"Dah! I'll set dem up in a row dat has others looking de same. I assume you want electricity on job site? Dah?"

"That would be wonderful, now what do we owe you for this?"

"You said dat dis is to help Staff Sergeant Harry Knott? Dah?"

"Yes it is, and, if successful it will be a solid smack in the chops for the WSA."

"Dah, well Sgt. Harry has done us a few favours so let's call it quits. Dah?"

"Fine by me! How are you going to contact me?"

"From now on you better start reading junk mail in your letter box because when I got something for you, you'll find message inside your junk mail. Dah?"

It was near midnight when Jeffrey reached his home, as he passed his neighbour's house he spotted some movement near some shrubbery in his garden. He froze on the spot and when he was sure that he saw a figure observing his house he quietly drew back behind the neighbour's clapboard fence. The man in his garden was observing his house and was about to move closer when Jeffrey came up behind him and whacked him on the back of the head with the butt of his revolver. The man fell asleep on the job so to speak. Jeffrey, being a good boy scout was prepared and slipped a pair of handcuffs on Sleeping Beauty. He next dragged the poor man rather un-ceremonially to the house.

The girls and Harry were in the kitchen when he came through the back door. "Hi girls, and Harry, did you miss me?"

"Not particularly." Sandra announced in a teasing voice.

"Spoken like a true wife! What about you Harry, did you miss me?"

"Yeah like a hole in the head!"

"Well, I am happy that all is as normal as can be. By the way, I brought a friend home so you girls better cover up or make yourself scarce while we have a yarn with him. I found him spying on the house."

Sandra slipped into her blouse and passed a housecoat to Jordie then they all sat down and waited.

After another ten minutes the man groaned and looked cross-eyed when he opened his peepers. He looked rather startled when suddenly a voice boomed in his head, *"DON'T YOU JUST HATE IT WHEN YOU WAKE UP AND DON'T KNOW WHERE YOU ARE?"*

The worthy with a more than startled look on his face looked at the three stone faced people surrounding him and asked, "Who said that?"

Sandra gave him a cold stare and asked, "Who said what? Are you trying to confuse the issue? The question is not 'who said what' but more like, 'what are you doing in my kitchen and who are *you?*"

Except for a smashing head-ache the man became more aware of his predicament and started to tug on his handcuffs. "Listen here bitch, you better get them cuffs off-a-me, or wear the consequences when they find out!"

The same thunderous voice filled his head with, *"OH, OH, YOU'RE IN THE POO NOW, SONNY! YOU SHOULD NEVER HAVE CALLED HER THAT!!"*

Again the man looked at each of them but he had no time to make further enquiries because Sandra had jumped to her feet and had she been a kettle she would be blowing steam like it was going out of fashion. She walked over to the unfortunate baddy who was sitting up on the floor by now and without any preamble drove one of her stiletto heels into his thigh. While he screamed she warned, "The next time you use that word on me I'll drive this same heel through your face!"

She was convincing and he believed her. Now it was Jeffrey's turn, "Who sent you to spy on my house and why?"

"Aw man! I'm bleeding that b… lady stabbed me and I'm bleeding! Do something, man."

"Yeah well you should use your manners. I bet your mum would have warned you that that is not a nice thing to say to a lady unless your own mum was a bitch and was used to being called that. Anyway you're in my house and that lady is my wife and you are in her kitchen so you better make sure none of your bad blood spills on the floor. OK, back to my original question, why are you spying on my house and who is your boss?"

"I ain't saying!" He defiantly looked in Jeffrey's face and the terror reappeared in his eyes when once more Harry's voice boomed through his head, "WE HAF WAYZ TO MAKES YOU TALK!"

The poor man was terrified and asked Jeffrey, "Who is doing that!?"

"Doing what?"

"There is a voice hollering in my head, man!"

"You must have been smoking too much happy-weed! I hear nothing and I still want an answer! What are you doing in my garden and who sent you?!"

"Look man, if I tell you they'll kill me!"

"And I should care about that. Why?"

"Aw man. They just wanted me to keep an eye on who came or went from the house. That's all!"

"OK, we're nearly there, who is 'they'?"

"You're condemning me to death, man."

"Would you like my wife to give you a matching heel print on the other thigh?"

"No, man! They showed me a picture of some geezer in a Staff Sgt's outfit and told me that if I saw him enter the house to give them a call, or if I saw him leaving the house, to follow him. Nobody told me nothing as to what all this is about."

"Did they tell you his name?"

"No."

"Well describe him for me."

"Tall, fat, I mean heavy set, in his forties and with a mean look."

"You ever heard of Staff Sgt. Harry Knott?"

"Is that the one who went on the lam in the middle of an enquiry?"

"He was made to disappear and yes that description fits him."

After a moment's silence Jeffrey added, "The WSA sent you out to look for the man in whose house you are living. Let me assure you that if ever he comes back and finds you living in his place he'll shoot you on sight as being a felon caught in the act of unlawful entry into and squatting on his property. So Buster you stand a good chance of getting it from both ends, from Staff Sgt Knott if he returns and finds you in his house or from the WSA for stuffing up your task and for giving away their identity."

"You're a copper, I demand protection!"

"The only protection I can give you is to throw you in jail but I can't really do that because you did not actually enter my house, I brought you in. No the best thing for you is to disappear before the WSA gets suspicious, so, off you go."

Jeffrey dragged the man to his feet, "Say good bye to the ladies and I'll see you to the door."

In a rare display of manners Buster nodded his head and said, "It has been a pleasure to meet you."

Caustically Sandra replied, "I can assure you the pleasure has been all yours."

Jeffrey pushed the man to the front door and it was not until they stood on the front porch that Buster asked, "Hey man, what about them bracelets?"

"Oh you can keep them as a souvenir."

"Hey take them off me, man! I can't walk downtown in cuffs!"

"Sorry, I lost the key and it's amazing what you can do when you try." And Jeffrey slammed the door shut.

Buster had no choice but to scurry down town where he might have an acquaintance with bolt cutters or a hacksaw. He was a pathetic sight with hands cuffed behind his back and limping on his stabbed leg. But hey, perhaps that was a WSA operative's lot.

Jeffrey looked gloomy when he returned to the kitchen. Sandra's mood had changed and he could hear in her voice that she was scared, "What was that man doing in our garden?"

Her husband was ready to give her a smart reply but thought better of it in view of the concern he could hear in her voice, instead he replied, "It seems that the WSA is getting real curious and we may have to do something about that. I spoke to the 'Russian' and he is setting up a couple of ship-containers for a sound lap. He wants to know how much sound proofing you need."

"We'll have to crank up the sound probably as high as 30 to 35000 Hz to get the required increase in vibrational frequencies. Once we get above 20000 Hz we no longer can hear it or only as an ear-piercing squeal that, while still within our hearing capabilities, would drive us mad."

"Does that mean that Harry is going to be coo-coo but solid?"

With a wicked smile and while wringing her hands, Sandra cackled, "We can make it so!"

"No. Seriously, can you control it?"

"That's what we need a new-age composer for, preferably one who is involved with the new electronic music. Those composers, more electronic sound engineers, tread a very thin line between what sound frequency is on the edge of what can be heard and what will scramble our brains. I imagine that the frequency required, if we can find it in sound alone, will be higher still. But like I said we need an academic to lead the way."

"Do you know somebody like that?"

"I think so, you remember me telling you I went to see Dr Franklin?"

"Yes, the bloke in charge of the sound lab at Uni?"

"Yes, he is a bit eccentric but he likes to push the envelope when it comes to electronic sounds made into music of the modern kind. If there is anybody who can help us, it's him."

"But isn't he in cahoots with the WSA?"

"No, not Dr Franklin, his hate for politics and politicians is on par with Kal's sentiments! He just is naïve when it comes to dealing with them and their agencies. Don't worry once he knows that the WSA is spying on him he will either kick their agent out or he will feed the WSA false information. I just got to work out a plan to get him away from the lab and talk to him."

"You want to pay him a visit at home?"

"No they may be watching his place. Day after tomorrow there is a department directors' meeting, I'll speak to him then."

True to her word, two days later after the directors' meeting, Sandra managed to get Dr Franklin aside. As per usual the most noise generated by the delegates was after the meeting and Sandra used that as an opener to her question as to whether increased levels of sound had a higher vibrational frequency and that such higher vibrational frequencies could lead to new insights. The good Dr Franklin considered that an interesting proposition in view of the fact that quite often progressive ideas and insights were not born in the board room but during times of mental stimulation afterwards. He did warn though that the mental stimulation at least in part was due to the more relaxed environment and the 'lubricating' influence of alcohol. However he thought it a fascinating subject. He really got hyped up over the idea that music brings pleasure because it raises the vibrational frequencies of sound and excites the brain. From there it was not hard to get him curious and 'marginally' interested in Sandra's proposed sound experiments. Being a conspiracy proponent from way back, it was not hard to swear him to secrecy. He promised to meet her at the water police's office the following day after uni. Well pleased with herself Sandra drove home but not before driving once round the block and waving at the WSA operative who was following her in a not too stealthily manner.

Surprisingly Dr Franklin arrived at the Harbour Police's office at the appointed time even though he drove an ancient Skoda. The Skoda had once belonged to his long-gone Dad but the old car kept marching on. Various attempts by the highway police to ban the vehicle off the road had failed much to their chagrin because although it frequently slowed down traffic—a combination of its lack of power and the good Dr Franklin's absent mindedness—the vehicle was in an immaculate condition due to the fact its appointments were so basic and simple that nothing could go wrong with it and the servicing mechanic was an old cars nut from way back.

As soon as he had parked his car, Sandra invited him to get into her car and they drove around to where the shipping containers were sitting on the wharf.

The 'Russian' was waiting for them in the wharf-manager's office and after some introductions he took Sandra and Dr Franklin to a shipping container halfway down the back row. When he opened the doors of the container both Sandra and Dr Franklin were gob-smacked. Inside the container a smaller container was suspended in such a way that there was a two feet wide gap right round the smaller container. The all round two feet gap was filled with solidified liquid foam suspended in which the edges of layers of sound proofing material could be seen.

The 'Russian' in his gruff voice asked: "Will dis do Missus Tomkins?"

Before she could reply the Russian continued, "We suspended inner container from de ceiling and den sprayed foam underneaz. Once dat set we cut de chains from de ceiling and filled de whole lot wiz spray foam. So very little of de vibrations are passed from de inner container to de outside one. Dah."

Sandra turned to Dr Franklin, "Is this what we need?"

"Oh yes, this is exactly what we need!"

Sandra turned to the 'Russian', "How are we going to clean all this after we're finished?"

The 'Russian' laughed, "Dat's something de Japs can worry about. We just send de whole shebang to Mafia address in Tokyo."

"Oh you wouldn't would you?!"

"You just watch! We'll even send dem a hint suggesting drugs are hidden somewhere in foam and dat containers were originally bound for Sydney. Dah!" He gave an evil chuckle.

A few moments later he told Sandra, "There is fifty amp switchboard wiz five power outlets on back wall next to dat air-conditioning unit and an emergency switch on de right hand outside wall."

"When we switch on, won't the sudden power drain trigger an alarm?"

"No, we rigged it so dat when you fire up, de outside flood lights on dis end of de wharf go off, dat way one cancels out de other. Dah?"

When both Sandra and Dr Franklin started to thank the 'Russian', he became all coy and shy and suddenly had urgent business elsewhere but before he left he told them that if they had any requirements for special sound equipment he might be able to help with that as well, "Just tell me what you want, is amazing how long stuff can be held up on wharf! Dah!"

After the 'Russian' left Dr Franklin remarked, "Your Staff Sergeant Knott must have been a popular fellow."

"Oh yes, his obsession with giving everybody a fair deal did not only keep the 'Russian' out of jail on a number of occasions but also saved his life at least once. Don't forget that diplomacy is not exactly a characteristic in the circles that the 'Russian' moves in so quite often he waves the fists instead of waggling the tongue."

CHAPTER 32

THE JUNK 'BINTANG BALON'

IT WAS TWO months since the 'Bintang Balon' was launched and Kal was getting restless. He did not want to impose on the people of Balon Island any longer. He knew that he was welcome to stay for as long as he wanted to but the lure of the open sea was getting stronger by the day. He missed Jordie but was loath to admit it to himself.

Even though a relationship had been growing between Mailiku and him, before his departure to get the lead from Antipodia, they both decided at that time that there was no happy outlook for their relationship. Mailiku had her obligations as a future matriarch of her people and, being honest to her and himself, Kal realized he would not be able to give up his wandering ways. They had parted good friends and Mailiku had gone on with her life, found a suitable male and now was pregnant, yet, there still were wisps of feelings of guilt.

In view of all this and because he dearly wanted to try out his new junk, he decided to go for a cruise in her. Brutus, with Abdullah attached, decided to accompany him and on the last minute Samu, the silent giant, announced he would come to keep an eye on Kal in case of pirate attacks.

At least that was the reason he gave but the truth was that two young ladies had nominated him as the daddy of the infants growing inside them. Poor Samu could not for the life of him remember having had any dalliances with one and only a vague recollection of a possible encounter with the other so decided the best thing for him was to disappear for a while.

A slate grey cloud cover reached from horizon to horizon on the day the 'Bintang Balon' ghosted out of the lagoon. There was no sign of breaking surf on the exposed reef and the heaving sea looked like a breathing giant at rest.

Most of the islanders stood on the beach in a rather subdued crowd, they were sad to see Kal go. A'anu stood apart from the crowd and stayed long after the others drifted back to the village to resume their daily grind. Mailiku now heavy with child and two of her minders stayed on board until the 'Bintang Balon' was safely through the reef passage.

When the time came for her to go back she looked up at Kal with tears in her eyes and through Abdullah she told Kal that he always would be welcome on Balon Island. They hugged for a short time then Kal helped her down into the canoe and watched her as she was being canoed back to the beach and her people. To Abdullah he said, "It would be nice to feel as connected to a people and place like she does."

"*She might think that it would be nice to be free and unattached like you. We often tend to hunger for the opposite to what we have. Perhaps that is our nature and causes us to be forever seeking.*"

The initial sea trials of 'Bintang Balon' failed to reveal an unpleasant habit of hers. In a choppy seaway and at a specific angle off the wind she had a tendency to 'hobby-horse'. The junk was too light in the forward section and as a result the bow had a tendency to jump up and down too much. Kal laid the junk hove-to and he and Samu shifted some of the internal ballast forward. It was a hot and tiring job but the rewards were well worth the effort. 'Bintang Balon' became much calmer and easier to handle after that.

For a fortnight they sailed in a north-north-westerly direction towards a group of islands lying to the north-east of Pitcairn Island.

Wind and weather fluctuated between broiling hot days on an ocean as smooth as a mirror where the sun stood in the sky like an avenging god bent on cooking or baking all that dared to move. On such days white cumulus clouds stood like castles on the horizon and often were reflected on a black mirror sea. On other days and nights when scudding clouds appeared to have but one aim; to squash that little sailing vessel between leaden clouds and roiling waves. When that did not work the sea would try to wash people overboard and the wind would do its best to try and capsize the craft. 'Bintang Balon' took it all in her stride and soldiered on with a fine display of disdain which made the weather gods only angrier until they hissed and roared themselves out of existence, at least temporarily.

After a rough night the seas were still tumultuous but the sky had cleared except for a bank of thunderheads down wind. The wind which had been screeching during the night now dropped to a sedate fifteen knots and all was peaches.

Samu lay sprawled on deck taking in the sun while getting some shut-eye. Kal was at the helm and Brutus with Abdullah in attendance sprawled as his feet. The occasional hiss of escaping air, as the bows speared into a higher than average wave and flooded the shock-absorber compartment built into the bows of the junk, would temporarily shake Kal out of a semi-conscious state. After a quick look to make sure everything was still alright he would relax and drift off again to dream of the two loves in his life, his wife Serah who passed away, their unborn child and then Jordie who seemed to have all the characteristics he had loved in Serah plus a few more that he had never come across before.

At some time during the morning Kal was brought to full awareness by a tail-slapping sound near the boat. Kal rushed to the railing and saw a pot of dolphins acting strange, a number of them would surface, slap the water with their tails and then dart off in a north-easterly direction. At first Kal tried to discover if there was something they wanted him to see but he could not spot anything out of the ordinary. Kal still blamed himself for not taking more notice of dolphins and sometimes still wondered whether he could have saved Serah's life when she lay dying on the foredeck of the 'Vrouwe Irene' and a dolphin had tried to tell him. Resolutely he changed course and followed the pod.

Some twenty minutes later he saw what looked like two coconuts bobbing up and down in the waves ahead. He had woken Samu and the latter now had the helm while Kal went forward for a better look. Suddenly he saw something that clamped his heart in a cold vice, between the two heads for he was sure they were castaways, he saw a glimpse of what looked suspiciously much like the back of a large predatory fish. He shouted a warning to Samu and pointed the swimmers out to him. Samu nodded his head and steered straight for them. At the last minute he steered the junk into the wind and she came to a stop just upwind of the man and woman in the water. Kal was relieved to see that what he suspected to be a shark was no more than their wrecked canoe.

The pod of dolphins was doing victory laps around the whole scene and twittered and chattered as though they were celebrating. Kal stood at the side of the junk while Samu lifted the survivors out of the water as though they were weightless. They were in a bad state but Samu had them drinking water and eating cassava in no time while Kal got 'Bintang Balon' back on course. But before he did so, he called out a Polynesian blessing while facing the dolphins and waved his thanks. The dolphins stayed with the junk for a short time but then sped off towards the west.

Neither Kal nor Abdullah could understand the language the man and woman were speaking. However, Samu appeared to understand them well enough to figure out that they came from an island somewhere under the heavy thunder clouds on the horizon.

It was late in the afternoon before the 'Bintang Balon' reached the island home of the two castaways. The island rose as a forbidding mountain range. This side of the mountain was craggy and steep cliffs rose thousands of feet. Between the cliffs and the sea miles of flat, flood plains stretched out.

The rescued male stood in the bows and piloted the 'Bintang Balon' through a channel that ran through marshes and tall reed beds.

Here and there low islands covered in mangroves and other shrubbery seemed to close in only to reveal another channel just at the right time.

Eventually they reached a small jetty and the 'Bintang Balon' was tied up for the night. Kal was not going to risk grounding by blundering about in the dark. He had an unsettled feeling and declined the offer to go with the survivors to their village about two miles away on slightly higher ground.

Before they left, they had a long conversation with Samu who later told Kal, through Abdullah, that he had not understood much of what was said but he got the impression that the two were very surprised and grateful that Kal had gone out of his way to rescue them and then take them home as well. When Kal asked why that was so surprising, Samu said he had the impression they told him that there were white people living in the coastal swamps but they were not very nice at all and would rob and kill as soon as look at you. On the strength of that information Kal decided to stay on-board and to set watches. Just as well he did.

Around midnight Kal heard what sounded like a rip tide coming down the river. He knew immediately what it was. Somewhere high up in the mountains the thunder clouds they saw earlier in the afternoon must have dumped their load and so created a flash flood.

A brown torrent glittered menacingly under the light of the full moon.

After a quick inspection he realised that the bamboo jetty the 'Bintang Balon' was tied up to would not stand the pull of the junk once the flood waters reached it. He decided to cast off and hope that the flood waters would take him over any shallow spots they might come to.

At that time there was no wind to speak off so the junk would have little or no steerage. He spotted two long bamboo poling poles on the jetty and he felt it was better to steal them than to destroy the jetty by staying there.

When the flood came, there was a wall of water twelve inches high that came roiling down the river. Kal and Samu threw off the mooring ropes just before it reached the 'Bintang Balon' and next they were surging downstream side-ways. By jabbing at the river bottom with the bamboo poles they managed to turn the junk so that she at least faced in the direction of their drift. A couple of times the junk grounded but the pressure of the flood ably helped by the bamboo poles would refloat her and the run to the sea continued.

At one point they passed a scrubby island and Kal saw fire light among the shrubbery. He wondered if the light came from the settlement of one of the swamp people they had heard about. He did not have to wonder for long for next thing a flat-bottomed punt was launched into the swollen river. Not everybody on shore agreed with the action taken and some rather abusive and threatening language was exchanged between the two youths in the punt and some older sounding people on shore. Perhaps the two youths should have taken notice of their elders because they never made it even halfway before a floating tree trunk capsized their punt.

Fortunately for them, they had enough luck to reach the shallows at the end of the island but their home-coming without the punt may not have been very pleasant.

Towards morning heavy clouds moved in from the sea and torrential rain made it impossible to see more than a boat length ahead. Both Kal and Samu stood on the fore deck with their poles ready to push-off. After the night's activities and the need to be constantly on the alert, their arms were like lead and so were their eyelids. Both men were, wet, cold and bone tired but neither would give in. When daylight finally forced the inky blackness into a dull grey day, Kal was relieved to see a small island he had spotted the day before just before the 'Bintang Balon' had entered the river delta.

An hour later they set sail to the south west on a beam wind. Both men flaked down on the deck and with Brutus and Abdullah to keep an eye on things they fell asleep.

CHAPTER 33

ISLAND OF THE HEALER

ABOUT A WEEK later the 'Bintang Balon' arrived at an atoll. Had it not been for the palm trees growing on the low island Kal might have missed the island all together. Among a small stand of coconut palms they could see two huts but no people came to greet them when the 'Bintang Balon' sailed into the atoll's lagoon.

The only reason for calling in was that they needed water and where there are coconut palms there usually is fresh water but they might have to dig for it.

Once at anchor in the lagoon Kal and Samu launched the dinghy and cautiously approached the beach. Brutus stood in the bows of the dinghy but gave no indication of anything being amiss but still Kal had his klewang—a long and narrow cross between a machete and a sword—close at hand.

Cautiously they approached the two huts. The first palm they came to Abdullah deserted Brutus and found safe anchorage there by hanging on to the tree 'to give Brutus the freedom to move swiftly should the need arise' or that was the excuse but evil tongues at times hinted at a certain lack of 'gumption' on Abdullah's part.

The first hut they came to had partly collapsed so they moved onto the next one. There they came onto a grisly sight, in the middle of the floor a person had been staked out between four stakes driven into the ground. What was left of the unfortunate soul was a skeleton partly covered by desiccated skin and a large number of armbands, necklaces and leg bands. Remnants of a feather headdress still encircled the grinning skull.

Some strange masks were suspended from the rafters while others hung on the walls. It did not take genius to figure out that the remains belonged to an erstwhile witchdoctor and that the unfortunate must have really upset somebody to be staked out like that and left to die from hunger and thirst. If that is what happened.

Kal was all set to go back to the 'Bintang Balon' but Samu had discovered a variety of dried herbs in a row of clay pots. Samu seemed far more interested in the herbs than in the skeleton and Kal wondered why. He told Brutus to go and fetch Abdullah in the hope that the latter could throw some light on the lack of compassion shown by Samu.

After Abdullah took in the scene he told Kal, *"Those people are very pragmatic, the witchdoctor is dead and now is one of the ancestors. As such she will pass on her knowledge to a person chosen by her. If you ask Samu he will tell you that he was meant to find her otherwise we would never have found this atoll."*

"What, you want to tell me that it was divine guidance that brought us here?"

"Yes. Well at least that is what Samu will tell you."

After a pause Abdullah continued, *"It appears that this witchdoctor was a healer and that those pots contain the herbs needed to prepare the herbal medicines she used. By touching each herb Samu believes that she teaches him what that herb is used for. Some he might know already but others are new and he believes that she will teach him what their uses are."*

"Does it work?"

"In a way it works, whether or not her ethereal persona teaches him or because he believes that to be the case, knowledge he already caries in his subconscious as part of a racial memory perhaps, comes to the surface."

"Interesting, but what if he is wrong and his insights do not work?"

"If he is wrong and his advice leads to the death of a person of equal or higher standing than him he may well finish up the way this poor woman did."

"Oh, that would make one a bit more careful!"

"Healers are normally held in pretty high esteem so I would say that a chief must have died because of or in spite of her ministrations!"

"Not a very nice note to finish your life's work on, is it?"

"Don't worry too much about that. She was dead before they staked her out."

"Huh? What makes you say that?"

"Have a good look at her neck, you'll see that her neck is broken and the bottom of her skull is smashed. While you were in here, I went and had a look inside the other hut. It looks like that that hut was a hospital ward and I assume that a high ranking patient died in there so the healer got the blame and was liquidated. The body was staked out so the soul could not escape and raise havoc."

"'Do as I say not as I do', might be applicable here!"

A search of the island revealed a shallow well, more a soak actually, that held water that was only slightly brackish. Kal decided to only fill one of the empty water casks. Even that took two hours of waiting for the soak to refill.

While they were filling the cask the wind dropped and by late afternoon the sea was like a lazily undulating mirror. The sunset was spectacular with not a cloud in the sky the sun as if fighting the approach of the night, shot spears of orange across the indigo sea to the white coral beach. Just as the sun dipped below the horizon a green flash momentarily lit the spot where the sun disappeared. Samu saw this as an omen that he was indeed the chosen one to receive the past witchdoctor's knowledge. The twilight time in the tropics is short and soon it was dark enough for the first stars to wink on in the heavens.

Kal was confident that the 'Bintang Balon' was secure in the tiny lagoon and that no undesirables could bother them. He decided to sleep on the beach. After the evening meal they all went back ashore, Samu withdrew into the healer's hut while Kal decided to stay on the beach. Brutus found many objects and smells of interest along the high tide line and Abdullah had to find an anchor point near Kal or be dragged through the flotsam and jetsam of the sea.

Later Kal could never decide whether it had been his conversation with Abdullah while they sat on the beach reminiscing about their lives in the Core or the effect of seeing the skeleton in the hut, but that night he had a vivid nightmare. This is how he related it to Abdullah the next morning:

> "I stood on a high dune overlooking a deep blue sea. From where I stood the waves did not seem high even though there were many white caps. On the beach I saw a small, open sail-boat and I knew I had to take it down the coast.
>
> "Next I was sailing about half a mile off the beach, heading south towards my goal that was not as yet in sight. Upwind to my right, heavy clouds were forming and lightning could be seen throwing glare among the black thunder heads. Bad weather in the offing! It had me concerned because an open sixteen footer is not the ideal vessel in which to encounter the foul weather I saw coming.

"To my left, downwind, I could see low-lying mangrove swamps with many channels. Perhaps I could find a safe haven there until the bad weather had passed.

"I must have made it safely to the marshes because the next memory of the dream is that I am fleeing from rising flood waters. I am up to my chest in crocodile invested water. Because of the restricted water ways I cannot sail the boat but must pull it along behind me in a frantic attempt to stay ahead of the tempest released by the thunder clouds that are now overhead. The wind is gale force and some of the higher trees are toppling. The water around me is whipped up until it looks like horizontal rain and steam, the drops sting as they hit my skin.

"Under water I am knee deep in oozing mud that sometimes reaches as high as my groin. I need the boat to pull myself out of the mud and for some reason I am fascinated by waving heads of grasses just below the surface of the muddy water.

"As I move deeper into the coastal swamp I find some land that is not yet flooded and my progress becomes a little easier even though the mud still reaches to just below my knees.

"After hours of dragging the open sailing boat behind me, I reach an area that has not been effected by the storm. I can see open, calm water and have a rest before dragging the boat towards it. Between me and the open water there is a channel on this side of a steep earth bank, the open water lays behind that.

"As I watch a large schooner disappears behind bushes to my left and I assume that it is sailing in deep water, like perhaps a river mouth. I'm still looking in that direction when a man on a converted jet-ski comes flying past and he has my sailing boat in tow but he appears to be going in the wrong direction, away from the river mouth where I expect to find deep water.

———

"The man on the jet-ski obviously is one of the swamp people and carries all his worldly possessions on his ski. He is dressed in black and there are so many items and parcels tied to the jet-ski that it is hard to determine what is man and what is machine, they appear to be a single life form.

"Now I see that much of the swamp is a ship's graveyard. There are skeletons ranging from coastal tramp steamers to medium sized freighters and large tankers. I am standing near a wreck that at one time may have been a heavy duty machine such as a harbour wharf locomotive. It is a large lump of rusty iron whit bits of canvas and corrugated iron attached here and there.

"Next to me stands a man, all I can remember of him is that he had a big white belly and a large bald head.

"I voiced my dismay at seeing my boat being towed in the wrong direction but he assures me that that is not the case and that his friend is towing it to a place from where I can sail on. Next he calls two skinny lads and tells them to escort me to the meeting place.

"I am convinced that the two young men are mentally challenged they jump around me and make strange and loud sounds. Yet they seem to herd me onto higher ground and in the direction of where I suspect is the river mouth into which I saw the schooner disappear.

"A bit further down the track we came to a derelict set of train wagons that obviously had been there for a long time. Trees had grown from underneath them. There was sign that those wagons now were somebody's home.

"Like I said, they were herding me! Just after I had been forced into a yellow clay pit on the track with one of them in front of me and one behind me, they both were on firm ground but I was up to my knees in the sticky yellow mud, two other youths sprang from the scrub and with a lot of loud screams that made no sense to me at all, they performed a kind of goose stepping dance around me.

"After a while the new-comers paid my guides a number of coins and I realised I was being sold! I expected my guides to disappear but that did not happen, the new-comers drew hunting knifes and gestured me to proceed down the track. One against four were unacceptable odds at the time so all I could do was continue along the track.

"After some time my entourage quietened down and we puffed up the steep path. By this time I was getting pretty tired and did not really take too much notice when two more youth stepped from the bushes. Then something happened that seemed weird.

"The last pair to join us paid the second pair a fair amount of coin, they in turn gave half of that to the first two youths who then gave half of that back to the third pair.

"One of them must have seen the curiosity on my face and decided to explain it all. He told me that it was their way to assure solidarity, the first pair sold me and got paid, they then continued on with the second group knowing that they would get half of what the second group would be paid for me. The first group then paid half of what they received from the second group back to the third group. This way everybody received some money and all would be happy."

"Yeah well, like I said, it was a dream."

"After a while we passed another swamp home, again it was old and rusty but I failed to recognise its original configuration. No youths joined us on this occasion.

"Next all of us are standing on the edge of a natural pit. Some fifty feet below us a yellow clay pan can be seen. At high tide the bottom might be covered with a few feet of water but now it was nearly dry. I was not really surprised to see the spread-eagled form of a person covered by a thin layer of yellow clay, face-down in the bottom of the pit.

"The leader, one of the youths of the last pair to join us, now said, 'That is where you are going unless you can buy your freedom back.'

"I said something along the lines that the father or leader of the first two told me that they were charged with taking me back to my boat. His answer was pretty glib when he said, 'Oh yes and they did, if you look over there you can just see the stern poking out of the mangroves. But to get to the boat you must jump into the clay pit, or if you pay us the amount we paid for you, we will show you the way to get down there without having to jump.'

"Then the panic struck me, I did my utmost not to show them how I felt but I don't know what I must have sounded like when I asked, 'Oh yes? And where on this naked body do I carry a coin purse?'

'That ain't no concern of us. You want to live, you pay us the coin due otherwise you can join him down there. He too claimed he had no coin.'

"Just then with a lot of noise of breaking branches two burly men stepped forward. The first man on the scene grabbed the youth that had made the demand for money and hurled him over the edge and into the clay pit.

"He turned to me and I could see in his eyes that he was as mad as the others but he seemed to be on my side or perhaps not. The second man had grabbed the money pouch from the youth *that had been holding it, then he held out his hand and said to the others, 'Hand over the coin unless you want to join your mate down there.'*

"*As one of the first two handed over his pouch he said defiantly, 'You wait until he climbs back up here!'*

"*The man who had tossed the youth over the side, looked into the pit and shook his head, 'He ain't be doing any climbing or much of anything else, not unless he can do it with a broken neck.'*

'*How does you know his neck is broke?'*

'*Well, his head is turned around and he can kiss his self between the shoulder blades. Don't you belief me young Harrison? It be my pleasure to send you down there so you can ask him yourself.'*

"*The second man now turned to me and shook about half of the confiscated coins into my hands while he said, 'Take this coin and give all of it to the man who is watching your boat. For it he will give you back your boat and lead you out of the mangrove isles. Don't keep back any coin for yourself as that will give those louts a reason to chase you.'*

"*My rescuers and I watched as the remaining youths withdrew with their tails between their legs. Their memories were short though because not long after they withdrew they could be heard to holler and shout unintelligibly.*"

"*The next scene in the dream is where I see myself as a passenger sitting on the back of the black jet-ski that earlier I saw towing my boat.*"

"*On the trip to my boat we weaved our way under overhanging sterns of derelict freighters that had completely rusted out on the water line but whose super structures were sound enough to be occupied by swampers.*

"They had become part of the environment with verdant mangroves and other vegetation growing from the mud in their bilges.

"When we finally came to my boat she had morphed from a sixteen feet long open sailing boat into a sleek forty footer. Her two masts where unharmed and her clean white sails were neatly stowed on her booms. Except for the fact that she was stuck in the mud, she looked ready to sail.

"The man who took me to her told me that I would probably become a swamper because he could not see how my vessel could come afloat again. While pointing at a rather narrow channel into the mangroves he told me that if I could refloat my boat that channel would lead me to the open sea."

"The dream left me with a feeling of dread and gloom."

After a pause Abdullah replied, "The emotions you experienced during the dream are probably more important than the visuals. If you ask me I would say that our experiences in the river delta where we delivered those two castaways played an important role in setting the scene for this dream and the worries about getting out of there provided the paranoia."

Just then Samu came from the direction of the healer's hut. Kal noticed that the man now wore the amulets that had adorned the skeleton's neck. He sat down and Kal perceived that Samu was awe struck as he quietly conversed with Brutus cum Abdullah.

In the end Abdullah told Kal, "Samu slept in the Healer's hut and the ancestors came to him and told him to carry on the Healer's work. He says that when he woke this morning he suddenly knew the powers of the herbs that he could not identify yesterday."

"I don't know if I would be prepared to subject myself to his ministrations. Would you?"

After a short pause Abdullah replied uncertainly, *"Yes I think I would; after all he believes he has the power to heal and all healing begins with patient and healer both believing in the power of the medicines used."*

"Yeah well, that could get you dead as well!"

Abdullah laughed, *"At least that way you could have a chance, your way you're dead for sure."*

"You might have a point there. Anyway, let's leave the lady healer to her ancestors and let us be gone from here."

"Where to next?"

"I have a feeling that Samu as the new healer has a pre-ordained place in the Balon Island community and besides that I have a premonition that Jordie and Harry may be coming back soon."

Samu was decidedly excited about the prospect of going home. With his new found station in life the prospect of matrimonial harassment was reduced significantly as nobody in their right mind would dare to point an accusing finger at a man in such close contact with the ancestors unless the accusation was true.

CHAPTER 34

WSA INVOLVEMENT

THREE WEEKS WENT by during which Dr Franklin was working inside the containers to well into the night. His daily schedule included six hours work in the university lab followed by at least another six hours inside the containers. Concerned lab assistants (suspected WSA informers) were curious about the dark shadows under the good doctor's eyes but he blamed them on sleepless nights and the rooster residing next door.

The WSA was able to verify the existence of the rooster next door and seeing how they had not been able to insert one of their spies into the doctor's bed, they had to accept his sleepless nights in good faith. They kept a close watch on the doctor's Skoda but that never left his drive way until he drove it to the university in the mornings and back late in the afternoon. The 'Russian' employing a number of devious tricks organised transport to and from the wharf for the doctor and quite a few times for Sandra as well.

Right under the nose of the WSA operative watching the Franklin home, a non-descript vehicle would pull up in the doctor's driveway, right behind the Skoda. The area was fairly dark but not dark enough for the observer not to see one person, the driver, leaving the car and entering the house. A few minutes later just one person would leave the house and drive away. That person was Dr Franklin while the driver of the car would show his silhouette a few times in front of one of the curtained windows.

Sometime after midnight the same or a different car would pull up in the drive and again one person would exit the car, go inside for five minutes and then leave.

Finally the day came when the doctor announced he was ready to start the experiments. He decided it would be safer to operate the equipment remotely from outside the containers until he figured out a vibrational level of sound that would not blow any eardrums.

The 'Russian' provided them with an old van in which they could set up their remote control equipment and which could be parked inconspicuously anywhere among the shipping containers on the wharf as it had the Shipping Container Maintenance slogan painted on the sides. Anybody curious about the array of antennae sticking out of the roof would be told the maintenance people were using supersonic sound waves to check the integrity of the steel containers, hence the aerials and sound dish.

The first time the good doctor tried his experiments he started off with a low vibrational frequency that produced a low, growling sound. When he turned up the volume to see what effect it would have, all the steel containers on the docks started to vibrate which produced quite a racket and bits started to fall off some of the older ones. After that he brought in a trusted friend who was a renowned sound engineer and equipment was modified to allow for a much faster transition through the lower sound bands and into the supersonic bands where the vibrational frequencies could be accelerated.

It was this acceleration that had the Doctor worried, the subject, in this case Harry, would have to be in the middle of a sonic boom for the time it took the sound frequencies to reach critical mass. How long could the boom last before it would blow apart Harry's eardrums and whatever other organs that might be impaired by sound frequencies or vibrations? That was the million dollar question.

It was the WSA that, unwittingly, provided part of the answer.

The day had been particularly hectic for Dr Franklin. Things in the university lab had gone wrong all day and just as he had been closing down for the night one of the lab assistants got the power run-down on one of the sound particle accelerators wrong and the machine would have exploded had Dr Franklin not noticed it. Very gently he had to reverse the process and bring the accelerator back up to full speed before he could shut it down in the right sequence. As a result he was late in coming home and his ride to the wharf had left. Perhaps he should have phoned for a cab but he felt that was too obvious so he drove his Skoda to a pub near to the harbour and walked from there.

It so happened that by this time Buster, the WSA agent living in SSgt Harry Knott's house, was becoming suspicious of the frequent visits of all kind of Harbour Authority vehicles to the doctor's house. There always was only one person exiting the vehicle and the visits were never long enough for him to sneak up to a window to see who it was that came calling.

—Later Dr Franklin would boast that during this time he learned to drive all types of vehicles from his house to the harbour and back—.

Anyway, on this occasion there had been no visit and the doctor came home much later than normal. When he left sometime later in his Skoda, Buster felt compelled to follow. When Franklin slowed down looking for a parking spot near the harbour pub, Buster had been lucky enough to find a parking spot back a bit where one of the street lights was out and left a nice dark spot where his black SUV would not stand out too much. Not that Buster thought the doctor had the nous to know he was being shadowed by a pro.

It had not been hard to follow Franklin and he had watched him as the dopey academic had punched in a numeric code to open a non-descript shipping container. Buster having been a Boy Scout, came prepared and as soon as the doctor had entered the container, Buster rushed over and with his little scanner—secret WSA technology—could read the Last set of numbers entered and in the order in which they had been entered. Together with his new-found knowledge Buster withdrew into a dark corner and waited patiently.

He had been waiting for about fifteen minutes when suddenly the flood lights in that part of the container yard went out. He assumed a fuse had blown somewhere and all that meant was that the doctor might come out running a bit sooner because without light he could do nothing. Anyhow, what was he doing inside the container and why did the container have an electronic lock? All things he had to work out so he decided to stay and see what would develop.

Up to a point Buster was a patient man but after waiting for just over two and a half hours he decided that enough was enough. He stepped out from behind the corner from where he had been watching. He took one step and all the flood lights started to glow and crackle, they were coming back on line and he only had just enough time to jump back into the shadows. He watched the container with renewed interest. Another fifteen minutes later Dr Franklin exited the container and closed the door. Buster heard the click when the lock engaged. He followed the good doctor back to the Skoda and watched as he drove away.

After a moment's hesitation Buster decided to try the code he had scanned and to have a look at what was so interesting inside the shipping container.

At first when he typed in the scanned code nothing happened but when he tilted his scanner so some of the light from the nearest flood light could shine on it he realised that where he had typed in the figure

3 as the last number, the number actually was a 9. He typed the code in again and this time he heard the click of the electronic lock as it released the tumblers. Slowly he pulled the door just far enough to squeeze through only to find his path blocked by the door of the inner shipping container. Luck was with him, there was no lock on that one and a small door gave access to the inner container. With his flash light at the ready he slowly pushed open the inner door. He ducked through it and let the beam of his torch play over the array of computer towers, loud speakers, a microphone, a couple of computer screens and a whole bunch of gear that he could not recognise except that it was all electronic gismos.

One of the computer screens was still on and files were scrolling down but much too fast for him to read. He stood for a while fascinated by the scrolling screen and wondered what it was all about. Did the doctor forget to turn off the computer or was it updating something? But what? Perhaps, if he could freeze or slow down the screen he could discover what was going on. He played his flash light beam over the consoles but could not get the overall picture. It was two or three hours after midnight and the outside container door was only open a little way so he felt secure enough to look for a light switch. He saw a normal light switch but when he toggled it nothing happened, there must be a main switch or something like that.

A closer inspection led him to the other side of the chamber where a large dome shaped dish with a cone in the centre, like one of those long distance microphones, hung from the ceiling. It was made of a shiny black material that looked like onyx and the cone looked like sun-bleached coral. Just behind it on the wall there was a large, open bladed lever switch, like the ones used for high voltage circuits. That had to be the main switch.

Buster smiled, it seemed all a bit melodramatic but that was not going to stop him. He was here to find out what was going on and by

Jove, nobody was going to stop him now. Resolutely he walked over to where he could reach the switch. He was vaguely aware that where he was standing, right underneath the onyx dish thing, was a thick mat of black rubber. After a moment's hesitation he reached out and placed his hand on the insulated bar handle of the switch. Slowly he pulled it down to the halfway mark and stopped. Some sixth sense made him stop and for long moments he stood there motionless but with his hand still clasping the bar.

He had a little talk to himself about being a 'sissy' and 'scaredy-cat'. He did not realise that although he only whispered the words, super sensitive microphones picked up every one of them and they were recorded for posterity.

The onyx dome above his head was making a vibrating sound and the white cone became red hot in a matter of seconds. A mild electric shock ran through the hand that held the switch bar and he jerked the affected limb away. As soon as he removed his hand from the bar switch, the handle drooped down and the connection was established. A split-second later there was an explosion of sound, a sonic boom that only lasted one-tenth of a second but that had great consequences. The flood lights on the wharf went out again and the gulf of sound blew open the half closed container doors. Fine, dust like particles suddenly filled the air and every window in a half mile radius as well as every light bulb in that same radius, shattered.

The only person within that radius was of course Buster but he never heard it, he heard the start of the sonic boom but not its end. The effect of the sound heightened vibrational frequency on his body instantly increased his natural frequency to that of the sound wave. As a result Buster shrunk to one third of his size and body mass because all of the fluids contained in the cells of his body evaporated leaving only the insoluble particles of him. Of course he was quite dead and what was left looked like one of those shrunken heads produced by some jungle tribes.

The 'Russian' who at the time was, for reasons of his own, camped in his office heard what sounded like a truck back-firing in his outer office and when he got showered in slivers of glass he knew that not all was 'roses and moonshine' at the sound lab and that he had better spread a few rumours before he would have the news hounds baying at his door.

His first call was to the electricity providers. Except for a sudden fluctuation in the power consumption of the wharf precinct they had not noticed anything untoward and wanted to know why he was calling them. The 'Russian' had to do some fast foot work and explained he was going to have his crew changing flood lights first thing in the morning and had turned the lights off so they could cool down.

Next he rushed over to inspect the shipping container. He found the door of the outer container wide open. Not wanting to go in there out of fear of being exposed to things like radioactive fallout or whatever, he pulled out his cell phone and rang Sgt Jeffrey Tomkins to tell him to get Dr Franklin and to come and check out the sound lab.

Jeffrey was on night shift but Sandra promised to go and fetch the doctor and that they would be there as soon as possible. Meanwhile, she told him to close the shipping container. Just in case.

CHAPTER 35

THE HEALER

SOME DAYS AFTER leaving the atoll of the dead healer, Kal came down with a malaria attack—a reminder of his time as a captive in an Asian jungle camp—it was a bad attack and by evening he was delirious and burning up with fever. One moment he was shivering uncontrollably while a few moments later sweat poured out of every pore of his body.

In his delirium he was fighting the war again and had it not been for Brutus standing in his way, Kal would have surely fallen overboard.

Samu, realizing Kal needed watching decided to lay the 'Bintang Balon' hove-to so he could nurse Kal. Getting his first patient to go to bed was no great problem, he just picked him up and carted him off into the deckhouse and stuffed him in a bunk.

While he was on deck to get a bucket of seawater with which to cool off Kal, he heard a ruckus in the deckhouse. He heard Kal swearing and shouting but he knew that was the delirium speaking; however the other sounds he heard concerned him greatly because it was Brutus growling menacingly. When he raced back into the deckhouse to do battle with the dog if need be, he nearly burst out laughing after the first shock wore off. Kal was flat on his back on the floor while Brutus stood over him with legs spread to either side of Kal's body. Her nose was touching Kal's who looked cross-eyed in his attempt to see her properly. The most fearsome growls came from Brutus' throat and a trace of spittle threatened to fall on Kal's chin—why must there always be some drool involved?—. Two things tickled Samu's funny bone, Brutus was wagging her tail as if to tell Samu not to fret because it was all a put on show. The second source of amusement was the fact that Kal was trying frantically to push Brutus away but his hands could, of course, not find any purchase on the spirit dog. Brutus knew it and Samu knew it but Kal in his current state could not figure it out. Abdullah remained abnormally quiet.

Ever since the night on the healer's atoll, Samu had been wearing the quite plentiful amulets of the dearly departed. In his idle times he could be seen walking the deck and mumbling recitations while fingering one or another of the amulets as though he was reading their meaning.

During the twilight of the evening, Kal and Abdullah—with Brutus attached—had been watching Samu. Kal posed the question as to what Samu was doing. After a while Abdullah replied, "*He belongs to an old race and their connections with the ancestors or the universe or whatever you want to call it go very deep.*"

"So, do you believe that he can learn how to heal people by just wearing a dead healer's amulets?"

"*It's all to do with faith. In our world, if a man dressed in a pair of shorts walks up to you and tells you he is a doctor, you may or may not believe him. Now had that man come up to you dressed in a white coat and with a stethoscope hanging around his neck, he would not have had to tell you his profession and in fact you would have credited him with an aura of knowledge based on your pre-conceived notion of the capabilities of a doctor of medicines…*"

"Hang on a second! My doctor studied for seven years, or something like that! This fellow got his degree from a skeleton."

"*No, not his degree, just his stethoscope. His knowledge comes from his faith in his ancestors. We may know and agree that we are the product of our ancestors but do we believe it? In most cases we believe in the here and now and that we are what we are through our own endeavours. That mindset labels all 'intuitive' knowledge as unproven therefore false and of no consequence. The people here believe in the super-natural, the ancestors and their collective knowledge and that the ancestors will pass on specific knowledge to specific people. You'll probably find that Samu has had a life-long interest in herbs and their healing powers. Had he not, he would not have taken the skeleton's healer-amulets. Now that he has obtained his 'stethoscope' he will try to recall all he ever learned from all sources plus he also believes that the ancestors will inspire him and that at times when he does not have the answers they may work through him while he is in a trance. The faith of the patient in the healer's capabilities is also a significant factor.*"[14]

"What? Like faith healings? Like putting suction cups on your body to suck the pain out? Yeah right!"

"*Yes, right. It might not work for you but why scoff at it if it works for someone else? It's the final result that counts, isn't it?*"

In a reluctant tone Kal said, "Yes I suppose so but, I don't know, there seems a large margin for duplicity."

"*Like I said before, it all comes down to faith and intuition; faith that the doctor did not get his degree out of a Corn Flakes packet, and, intuition that tells you that the doctor isn't a quack.*"

After Brutus had pulled her stand-over tactics on Kal, the latter decided to play nice and stay in his bunk. Meanwhile Samu concocted a

---

[14] For a more in depth report on the Balon Islanders' beliefs see the Adjunct.

mixture of herbs procured from some of the many pots he had salvaged from the healer's hut. The mixture was as bitter as gall and later Kal would claim he got over his malaria in a hurry just so that he did not have to take any more of the medicine, in short, he claimed the cure was worse than the ailment. In private circles Samu did admit that he might have slightly overdosed his first patient, but hey, he didn't die! And as a spin-off Kal developed a healthy respect for Samu as a healer who could not name the ailment but who knew the cure!

Kal recovered from the attack in record time and two weeks later they arrived back at Balon Island. It was amazing to see the change in attitude toward Samu when the local population became aware of his new status.

Of the two young women who had laid claim on him as the father of their yet to be born child, one withdrew her claim and herself to a relative living outside the village and the second young lady although no longer actively campaigning for his commitment as a parent, did still insists on his complicity in her circumstance.

Both Abdullah and Kal agreed that the second young woman might have found the pathway to Samu's heart and might eventually be the one to make him a good partner.

Over the next few weeks Kal was interested to see the relationship between the tribe's shaman, Paolo who buried Serah, and Samu. The old shaman did not view Samu as an opponent but treated him like her apprentice and the pair could be seen walking along the beach in deep conversation. Paolo took Samu on day long treks to gather this or that herb or some mineral they would then grind up for poultices and salves. Paolo was shaman to the court of Mailiku's mother, Mailiku who would succeed her mother as the tribe's matriarch would have Samu as her shaman; a state of affairs that seemed to suit all those concerned.

The moment the 'Bintang Balon' dropped anchor in the lagoon, A'anu, the boat builder, came on board with a hundred and one questions concerning the trip. Apparently he had some vivid dreams in which he saw the 'Bintang Balon' rolled over on the muddy flood plains of some river surrounded by savages throwing spears. In the end Kal agreed to let him haul the junk out for a close, below the water line inspection.

A busy time began in preparation for the haul-out. Every man, woman and child had to make preparations well in advance because once the haul-out began there would be no time for planting and/or harvesting. Home and garden maintenance would have to wait in favour of preparations to be made for the festivities.

Any excuse for a party. Right?

Oh yes, somewhere amongst all that, time had to be found to haul the 'Bintang Balon' on to the beach as well. To make things even more complicated, the old gentleman who helped with his leftover anti-gravity powers to launch the 'Bintang Balon' had died in the meantime.

Two weeks later the time for the haul out had come.

This far out in the Pacific a spring tide was only three inches higher than the normal high tide of six inches but every inch counted. The trunks of coconut trees were laid out and greased and a stout rope was attached to a hole in the forward edge of the keel—there for this exact purpose. Both ends of the rope were split into three thinner lines each long enough for up to ten people to take hold of. Other lines were attached to anything strong enough to withstand the pull. Lines attached to the top of the main mast, allowed two groups of men to keep the junk in an upright position until wooden chocks could be placed under the bilges.

Like every other communal activity the haul-out was treated as a game. The master of ceremony, in this case A'anu, sat on the foredeck where everybody could hear and see him. He was dressed up 'in feathers and bows' and held a small drum on which he accompanied a rhythmic haul-out chant. A'anu would chant a short line and everybody would join in the one syllable chorus 'Huh' while at the same time throwing their weight into the pull.

Kids and dogs were everywhere. The kids were smart enough to stay out of the way and organised their own haul-out by dragging someone's fishing canoe out of the water using his coconut fibre fishing lines as haul-out lines. The lucky owner would have some fun untangling his lines!

The actual pulling of the junk onto the beach only took about an hour but that was enough to declare the day a national holiday. Kal, wise to the ways of the island, made sure there was plenty of kava and he had organised the slaughter of some pigs and together with fish and vegetables they were cooked in the traditional island way, the style referred to by the Polynesians as 'luau', or 'hangi' by the Maori, or 'lovo' by the Fijians.

A large pit was dug that morning. In the bottom of this hole a fire was lit and rocks were placed on top of the fire to be heated until they were red-hot some even hotter still, to white-hot. Once the rocks were deemed hot enough any still flaming wood was pulled out of the hole. Using long poles the rocks were spread to make an even platform on which a thick layer of green leaves was spread. Next the meat requiring the most heat, in this case the whole pigs encased in plaited coconut leave baskets, was lowered. The meat was covered with a thin layer of green leaves, around the edges taro was imbedded whole. Last the fish and fowl were placed on top. The gutted fish with the head left on was placed in coconut leave trays specially woven for each individual fish and woven in the shape of the fish. Fowls were wrapped in banana leaves. Over the top of all this was placed another thick layer of banana leaves and split banana tree trunks. Finally the whole lot was buried with the soil that came out of the hole. For the next half hour or so the apprentice cooks, the kids, were employed to watch the mount for any escaping steam. Once the steam escaping from the soil top was stopped by plugging each vent with more soil, the waiting began.

For the next three to four hours the men engaged in some serious kava drinking while the women had their hands full with the preparation of the table setting and keeping the kids from plundering the side dishes.

It being a festive occasion the guitars and ukuleles were brought out and the singing started. The dancing would not start until later well after the meal even though a number of kids were practising various dance moves much to the amusement of their elders.

Kal was amused by the islander's approach to the setting of the banquet. The table consisted of a long strip of mats laid end to end on the village common. Once the mats were down any kid coming within spitting distance was chased off by some irate lady with a hand broom made from the spines of the coconut leaves—the dreaded 'sa-sa'. The 'sa-sa' is to an island kid what a folded newspaper is to a dog; a wack from it is more scary than painful because of the swishing sound it makes.

In the centre of the strip of mats, lay a strip of banana leaves that had their spines removed, this then was the serving platter. The main ingredients of the meal would be placed on the strip of leaves and everybody would sit down on the mats and help themselves. Half coconut shells that had been highly polished were placed at strategic places filled with raw chillies and other accruements to the meal. Most of the food would be so well done, succulent and tender that no knife was necessary. The foods, like taro, that would need cutting, would be divided into manageable portions before being placed on the table.

The men would have the first sitting followed by the women and kids. The village elders had their own spread and received the best portions as many had no teeth to speak off. The heads of the largest pig and largest fish—considered delicacies—were presented to the chief.

All eating was done with the fingers and washing up was done by dumping scraps and leaves into the smouldering cooking pit. The only washing-up done was that of the polished coconut shells and a few wooden bowls.

By order of the chief their alcoholic drink, a concoction of fermented coconut juice, palm sugar and the sap of the coconut tree was not to be consumed before the meal. The drink 'blood of the coconut tree' is collected by incising the unopened young leave at the top of the tree and feeding the tip of the leave back through itself. This causes the leave to 'bleed' and that sap is collected, then mixed with the other ingredients before the concoction is allowed to ferment and mature in large pottery jars that are buried for a notional three months.

The first cup is murder but after that it becomes quite pleasant and intoxicating. Over indulgence carries its own reward, a smashing headache that may last for a day or two.

During times of serious conflict it is drunk in large quantities because while under the influence—and before the headache starts—the warrior knows no fear.

A'anu told Kal that in earlier times the drinking of Kava was solely the prerogative of the higher echelon of chiefs and priests. The commoners were not allowed to drink it so they developed their 'blood of the coconut tree' drink. Priests and other dignitaries soon developed a taste for it as well and in return relaxed some of the rules surrounding the drinking of Kava. Still the drinking of Kava carries many traditional customs and taboos observed by all to the present day, both in the Dimension and the Core.

Once again Kal felt like a fringe-dweller and after the official part, the Kava drinking and the meal, were over he withdrew to a somewhat quieter spot away from the throng of dancers and drinkers. This did not prevent Samu and A'anu armed with a jug of 'blood of the coconut tree' from finding him. Later Kal had a sneaking suspicion that Brutus gave away his location because she, with Abdullah in tow, arrived on the scene just before Samu and A'anu announced their presence.

With a big sigh Brutus dropped herself at Kal's feet and gently lowered her head on her front paws. Somehow this gesture conveyed the message, "I ain't going nowhere and neither are you."

Kal gave in gracefully and accepted a bowl of the heady drink knowing already that the morning would bring a smashing head ache. Ah well, you only live once! Jordie never was far from Kal's thoughts but he did not want to burden his companions with the moanings of a love-struck soul, but, once the alcohol mellowed him he could not help himself. He voiced his concerns by asking, "I wonder how we are going to find out where and when Jordie and Harry are getting back?"

It was Abdullah who came up with an answer, *"I suppose Tjitjira the elder, will let us know."*

"Perhaps it would be better if we were in the location here in the Dimension that corresponds with the location of where they are in the Core."

"How do you mean?"

"Well, if we are in that location it might be easier to establish a connection along which they can be transferred from the Core to the Dimension. Don't you think?"

"You might be right but how do we know where they are in the Core?"

"I assume they were transported to where Harry came from?"

"Yes, but where did he have to go in order to regain his physical shape?"

Having no answer to the problem they sat down to some serious drinking. For them the night ended some three hours later when Kal addressed the stars with a line remembered from his youth, "'Sterren stralen overal'[15]. Good-night Jordie. Hell I miss you! Jordie that is! Ahg you know what I mean!"

He closed his eyes, slowly toppled onto his side and began to snore.

---

[15] "Sterren stralen overal." Dutch: "Stars shine everywhere."

349

CHAPTER 36

WILL IT OR WON'T IT?

THE DOCTOR HAD only just arrived home from the shipping container yard when the 'Russian' rang to say that the sound lab might have been broken into. The 'Russian' was not a coward but he was a cautious man and decided that he did not want to be a witness to whatever was hidden inside the containers. The doctor on the other hand wanted to have a witness so that he could not be accused of having a leaky memory if it came to a police investigation. As a result the two men stood in the dark twiddling their thumbs until Sandra arrived. Sandra on her part had brought along Jordie for moral support and Harry Knott had tagged along because he was invisible anyhow.

Right on the last minute the doctor became aware of Harry's presence and told him to wait outside. A bit of an argument developed over that but in the end Dr Franklin won and Harry stayed outside the container to keep the 'Russian' company.

It had been the 'sound bomb' that had shattered the light bulbs but the electricity supply had not been affected. As a consequence the electric locks worked fine and the container opened up. The doctor followed by

Sandra and Jordie trooped into the lab proper. The doctor had brought a couple of light bulbs and it did not take him long to install them. When he turned on the light the first thing they saw was a pile of clothes on the floor under the 'onyx' dome. It took a moment for them to realise that among the pile of clothes there was the shrunken corpse of what looked like a kid but turned out to be a man. It was Jordie who recognised the leathery body as that of Buster, the WSA operative.

Dr Franklin stood there with his left arm across his stomach and his left hand supporting his right elbow while his right hand stroked his chin. Sandra watched him and thought that the doctor was thinking of a way to hide the evidence. Quietly she said, "Don't worry Dr Franklin, I'm sure that the 'Russian' and my husband can come up with a plausible explanation, after all, the man was a trespasser."

"Oh I have no doubt about that!"

"So why the glum look then?"

"Glum look? Oh I see. No I was just thinking that the experiment was a part success."

"How do you mean, sir?"

"Well, the vibration and the frequency reached the level where the solidification took place but the sound duration although of the right level took too long. That's why the lamps and glass shattered. The sound impulse was set for one tenth of a second but probably should only have lasted one hundredth of a second."

All this was of little interest to Jordie who did not have the foggiest of what the discussion was about, instead she worried about discovery, "What be the reaction of this WSA when their man nay returns?"

Sandra shook her shoulders, "What can they say or do? Both Harry and Kal found out that the official policy is that they do not exist so how can they be missing an operative?"

Dr Franklin now showed some interest in the non-science aspect of the situation by saying, "Yes, what are we going to do with him? Interesting though, the body is so desiccated that no taxidermist could have done a better job to preserve it. It is as hard as stone and possibly as brittle so I suggest we handle it with care."

Sandra piped up, "What is with the 'we' business? I'm not touching it! It's giving me the creeps!"

"If it needs to be moved, I can do that." Jordie offered.

The 'Russian' who meanwhile had found the courage to enter the lab now said, "Is he gonna be 'on de nose'? Dah?"

"No more than a stuffed animal I suppose."

"In dat case we'll keep him until we send dis container oversees and he can be de surprise package. Dah?"

With the immediate problem solved Dr Franklin returned to the autopsy of his sound experiment, "We'll have to shorten the sound-bomb explosion time but by how much?"

The 'Russian' again, "Why?"

"Well, we achieved solidification but we also caused a fair bit of damage."

Harry now butted in, *"Hey, it's my molecules you're playing with! What if you hit me with a—what? Slower, lower—or smaller thingy-me-jig, might that be too whatever and leave me only half cooked?"*

Dr Franklin slowly nodded his head and from his tone it was evident that by now he had removed the human element from the equation and the whole problem had become an academic one. Without any direct connection to Harry's question he said, "Judging by what we found, the sound vibrational frequency appears to be right. What we do have to establish is how much we can shorten the duration of the sound pulse. Ideally we should run a series of sound bombs each a fraction of a second shorter. Eventually we would find a level where no more glass shatters…"

"How would we know that the resultant sound bomb is still strong enough to solidify my molecules?"

Suddenly somewhat agitated the good doctor snapped, "How can I predict what has never been tried before?"

"You want another subject to try it on? Dah? You tell me, I know a lowlife or two dat nobody would miss." The 'Russian' stated so matter-of-factly as to leave nobody in doubt.

"That would be great... Eh, I mean, that may not be necessary the instruments will tell us when we have reached the absolute smallest sound duration and still retain the required frequency and vibrational output."

"Yeah well, let me know if you need anything. Dah?" With that the 'Russian' departed.

The others decided they too had enough excitement for one night and after locking up they all went home. As they left the wharf Sandra spotted Buster's black SUV and wondered how long the vehicle would remain there un-noticed. She did not have to worry, it was gone by midday. The WSA must have kept a close watch on their operatives in the field.

Two days later Dr Franklin came over to Sgt Tomkins' and Sandra's house, he did not look happy. Once they got him to sit down and to stop rattling off streams of scientific jargon, Jeffrey finally got the doctor's attention, "I am sure that what you are saying is most exact and accurate but it makes no sense to any of us. Just give it to us in common language, short-comings and all."

The doctor took a hasty sip of his coffee and promptly burned his lips. After a hiss and splutter he finally did settle down. "Well, what do you want in layman's terms? The good news or the bad?"

Harry now got into the act, *"Aw common doc! You can't see me but I'm hanging on by a thread! What's the good news?"*

"Oh yes of course this is not purely academic in your case…"

"Oh! I'm going to hurt you if you're not going to get to the point this minute!"

"OK, Ok! The good news is that I have been able to establish the exact duration of the sound bomb to effect your transformation from vapour to solid!"

"Good on you doc! Now what is with the bad news?"

"Well, hmm, the transformation will only last for twenty-four hours after which you will revert to your present state. That regression will take approximately twelve hours."

"Are you telling me that I have to listen to one of your sound bombs after every twenty four hours?"

"No, it's worse much worse! After every time you undergo the procedure the time to regression will become shorter as more and more of your system's molecules are destroyed!"

"So what is the solution? There is a solution right?"

"To be quite honest, I don't know. When the WSA blasted you into the other dimension they must have used a method that probably was cheaper or they might not have been aware of the irreversible damage they did to your system…"

Jeffrey Tomkins snarled, "Or they couldn't care less, after all their only interest was to get rid of him."

"Quite possibly so. We are now faced with a problem where we have to find an environment that has the same lower vibe/freq. that allows Harry to be solid again. The higher vibe/freqs of *this* environment would eventually shrink and solidify him like, what's his name? The WSA guy."

"Great! I had to come here to get zapped with a dose of high vibe frequencies so as to become normal again but now I have to regress to a place where the vibes are lower and in sync with mine. Where do I find such a place?"

It was Jordie who now spoke up, "May haps those invisible conditions ye speak of and that appear to control so much, may be present in my world?"

Dr Franklin mused, "That may well be so! Alas we have no control over when a spontaneous transfer will take place and where."

"There be a strong pull betwixt Kal and I and my most sincere wish be that that be the connection betwixt this world and mine along which we may return."

Sandra now asked, "Can you feel that pull as a physical experience?"

"Aye, to me it feels as though it be in waiting until Harry has his shape change."

"Ok, say that I revert back to being solid and say that somehow I get transferred back into the dimension, does that mean I'll be a Wraith again?"

"Nay, I dost nay think so. Kal, who entered the Dimension, as ye calls it, by spontaneous transfer didst keep his shape and didst nay transed later to become a Wraith, nor didst yer friend Morgan, by the way Kal tells the tale."

Dr Franklin had to pour water on that little spark of hope, "I am afraid I cannot with any certainty support or deny that supposition."

"Well let me have a restless night of hope and despair and by morning I will let you know what is what. I tell you what young Jeffrey, when all this is over and I am solid again you better have a bottle of whisky handy because you and I have some serious catching up to do! That brings me to another point. Can you see your way clear to go over to my place to get me some clothes? You still have the key to the back door I hope?"

"Yes, sure."

The next day was Jeffrey's day off so the four of them decided to go for a drive to show Jordie some more of the sights. It was interesting to observe Jordie's reaction to anything she had not seen before. She was fascinated by the tar-sealed roads and the size of the average suburban house. She still cringed every time a 'road monster'—car—met them while driving along. As the trip progressed Jordie seemed to become depressed. So much so that Harry felt compelled to ask her, "*What is the matter Jordie, you seem unhappy why?*"

The girl shrugged her shoulders and said sombrely, "Would we but have this kind of wealth in the dimension!"

"*Why do you think that would make you happy?*"

"Well, we nay longer would have to go fishing or hunting and we would nay have to go planting and harvesting."

"*All those things still happen here but on a much larger scale. And what is more, for you to be able to put it on the table you would have to pay for it. In your society if you do not have money you will not starve because you can go fishing, hunting or harvesting what you planted earlier. Here you need money for everything, you need money to buy food because you no longer are allowed to go anywhere to hunt and fish, on top of that, if you still would want to fish or hunt you would have to buy permits or licences. In this society to get all the things you need and want you need to work for somebody, to earn the money to get it and you would not have the time to do anything else.*"

After some thought Jordie and with a frown asked, "What be a licence?"

Jeffrey now got involved and said, "A licence is a piece of paper that you buy to be allowed to fish, or hunt, in certain places."

"Surely ye say that in jest?"

"No way! That is true!"

"Ye tells me that ye pay coin to be allowed to fish? Who then claims the coin? The fish?"

"Of course not! The government does."

"Who be the government?"

"Not 'WHO' but 'WHAT' is the government. You know what a council is?"

"Aye."

"Well the government is all the different councils put together."

"But why must ye pay them so ye can catch a fish for the table? Do they own the fish or the water the fish swim in?"

"At times one would think that they think they do."

"A bit like the WSA, huh? Sticking in thei... its nose where it nay belongs."

The tone of Jordie's voice indicated that she had lost interest in the subject and they drove on in silence while she was enraptured by suburbia.

As they drove through a fairly new subdivision the girl remarked, "The people I see working in the gardens around their homes all look so young! How didst they amass the wealth enabling them to purchase their houses?"

"They didn't, they borrowed money from the bank to buy their houses."

"What, a bank will give money so they can buy a house? Why would a bank do such a thing?"

"The bank does not give them the money, the bank gives them a loan that has to be paid back over, say, thirty years. On top of that you must pay the bank what they call, interest, on the loan. By the end of the thirty years you will have paid the bank a hell of a lot more than what you borrowed and you would not have time to do things like travelling, fishing, hunting or any of the other things you would love to do but for which you just do not have the time or the money."

A short while later they arrived at Harry's house and they all piled out of the car. The garden, Harry's pride and joy, had been neglected and the weeds were starting to show their dominance, much to Harry's displeasure. They followed the path around to the back door. Apparently Buster had not been a proud tenant even though he probably would have claimed to be the new owner had he still been there, yet the back landing was littered with empty and half empty pizza boxes and a wide variety of beer cans—all empty though.

After stepping over and through the garbage they entered the house. The place was a pig-sty in urgent need of a decontamination crew. Harry was aghast and all he could say was, *"I want Buster re-zapped so I can kill him myself!! Just look what he has done to my place! He ruined it!"*

What they did not know was that Buster had a live-in buddy. This worthy had come from the bed room when he heard them entering the house. Realising that there was more than one person approaching through the kitchen and being well aware of his status of unlawful tenant, he waited until they all trooped into the living room to marvel at the chaos in there.

Jordie was the last to enter the living room and whirled around when she heard him stepping on something that made a noise. He snarled at her and adopted an aggressive stance. Jordie was well acquainted with the aggressive demeanour of those with a limited vocabulary. She at once recognised his mall-intent, faced him and stood ready to await further developments. Slowly he approached making the un-intelligible sounds produced by his kind indicating he was going to question their right of entry, after giving somebody a good trashing first to establish his status.

Jordie stood, legs spread and bent at the knees. Her body leaned forward and she had her hands on her knees and her elbows spread. With the light behind her she was no more than a dark silhouette and her auburn her was a dark mass but with an orange outline. It is doubtful that the WSA agent saw anything angelic or beautiful in the scene, he growled like a rabid dog and suddenly rushed her. Jordie had been waiting for that move and burst forward herself. She came in so low that her shoulder bashed into him at the height of his groin. On the moment of contact she wrapped her arms around the top of his legs and stood up. Using the man's own weight and momentum she flipped him over her shoulder. With his arms flailing in an attempt to keep his balance—a doomed exercise to begin with—he did a complete somersault and head and shoulders landed on the rubbish strewn floor before the rest of his body followed. Meanwhile Jordie spun around and dropped her full weight on her right knee. Too bad that the man's head was between her knee and the floor. The impact resulted in the crack of breaking bone heard by all those present. The bone was not one of Jordie's and in fact was her assailant's bottom jaw—and possibly his skull or one of his cheek bones. Jodie did a kind of bunny hop and once more landed on her right knee. This time her knee backed up by her full weight, impacted the man's solar plexus. The air escaping from his lungs through his mashed up mouth made a slobbering sound but that was nothing compared to the scream that passed those same quivering lips when Jordie cow kicked him and her slender and shapely heel drove his testicles up into his throat. Mister—suspected—WSA agent moaned once more and decided that it all was just too much.

As cool and merciless as Jordie had been while on the job, that had only been a façade for the onlookers. Now that the attention shifted to another section of the drama as it was unfolding, Jordie suddenly began to shake and angry tears rolled down her cheeks. With a lump in her throat and a croaky voice she demanded, "Why nay can we be left alone? We didst nay take anything from them and all I want's to return to my world. If they be so keen to be rid of us, why nay help us!"

"*Whoa there! Steady on girl. Those they have helped so far all seem to end up as Wraiths or jabbering idiots. I for one do not want or need their help.*"

Jeffrey was kneeling next to the fallen gladiator when they all heard a soft moan-like whimper near the kitchen door. Sandra looked up and exclaimed, "Well, I'll be! Harry! That is Skipper! We have been looking all over for him ever since you were gone. Come here boy!"

"*Who, me or the dog?*"

"The dog of course! I can cuddle him, you are just an arm full of hot air!"

Harry muttered something unflattering and floated over to Skipper. The dog, a Labrador, was uncertain, he knew Harry was there but he could not see him. Even so, dogs being what they are, he soon got used to the idea that Harry was there 'in-spirit' and from then on Skipper was never far from Harry. At one point Harry chided him by saying, "*Listen dog, your constant adherence to me is blowing my cover big time.*"

Skipper wagged his tail and looked in the direction of Harry as if to say, "Yeah, so what? If I can sniff you out others can too."

At this point Jeffrey looked up from the fallen combatant and said, "This here perp has defaulted on his WSA contract. What are we going to do with him?"

"*What's with the 'perp' business? You watch too many detective sitcoms on TV; the word is 'per-per-trator'. I got no idea what to do with him but I'm open to suggestions. We got to solve the problem before he 'gets on de nose' as the 'Russian' would say.*"

"That's an idea! Can't we ask the 'Russian' to send him off with his mate to a faraway place?"

"*Nope. In the first place this one will become odorous and in the second place how are we going to get him to the harbour?*"

"In the car I suppose."

"*Yes and with the whole neighbourhood watching the strange goings-on?*"

"Well, *you* come up with an idea! After all I'm only a temporary sergeant, you are the officer commanding being a staff sergeant and all."

"*Hmm, hiding behind your rank, you'll make an officer yet!*"

Even though the conversation was a kind of banter, both men knew they had a problem on their hands. Neither was prepared to let the circumstances slip out of their control with the danger of causing some innocent bystander the trauma of the discovery of a dead person most likely in an advanced state of decomposition.

With a soft, shaky voice Jordie said, "I didst kill that man and for that I be deeply sorrowed. Ye, Jeffrey, being a member of the constabulary and all that, surely, must place me in the stockades? What be the punishment I may expect?"

Jeffrey scratched his head, "It clearly is a case of self-defence and we all are witness to that."

He paced the floor and eventually spoke to Harry, "Harry, what is the best solution here? I can just imagine it! How is Jordie even going to prove who she is? No drivers licence, no address, no birth certificate or passport, no Medicare card, no job, and no Centrelink record! She just does not exist, yet there she is and she stands accused of murder! How is the law going to prosecute a person that the computers claim is not real?"

Harry refused to take the situation too serious because he did not want Jeffrey, or Jordie, to go into panic mode, *"Just tell'em I done it because of the mess him and his mate, Buster, made here and that as horrified as I was over the dastardly deed I had done, I snug outa backdoor."*

Jeffrey shook his head, "Won't work."

"Why not?"

"Still does not explain who or what Jordie is and besides that they would soon know where you are."

"How so?"

"Skipper would give away your exact whereabouts!"

At this point Sandra spoke, "Can't we drop a hint somewhere?"

"Like where? WSA HQ, wherever that is?—"Hey you lot one of your chosen ones is laying deceased in the house of our missing friend staff-sergeant

Harry Knot. We don't know how he got there because our friend has been missing for so long that we no longer have any reason to visit the place. Anyhow that's where you'll find him. And, oh yeah by the way, we got no idea where your man, Buster, is either. Now you all have a nice day'."

With a voice that brooked no disagreement, Harry laid out his plan, *"You lot leave the house, hop in your car and drive away in the direction of Townsville. Follow the Bruce until you reach Ayr. Act like tourists and have lunch somewhere where people will remember you when questioned. When you enter Bowen on your way home be on the lookout for Skipper, I'll be with him and we'll be looking for a ride."*

"OK but what are you going to do in the mean time?"

"Don't worry about that, just make sure a couple of those mosquito coils are burning in the most recently used bedroom."

With a suspicious look on her face Jordie asked, "Be ye that much worn out that ye need to retire to the, no doubt, vermin invested bedstead of this wretch?"

"Yeah, something like that! Now off you go!"

While the two women, under the direction of Harry, brought out the mosquito coils and lit a couple in the flame of the gas stove, they tried to change Harry's mind but to no avail. Once Harry made up a plan there was no changing it, Jeffrey knew that from bitter experience but he thought it better for the girls to find out for themselves.

He had a sneaking suspicion as to what Harry was planning to do and even though he saw it as a rather drastic course of action, he had to admit that it would be effective.

After placing the corps in a position where a casual observer coming into the yard and peering through a window would not be able to see it, Jeffrey and the women left the house. The last one out made sure that the outward opening back door looked closed but was not because Harry would have to rely on Skipper to push the door open.

Sandra waved at some neighbours as they drove past on their way to Ayr. At a service station just out of town they stopped for fuel—another unknown for Jordie—and some take away food.

Harry estimated that his friends would be at least three hours before they would be back in Bowen so he spend a couple of hours looking at the mementoes of his life. It made him feel angry and sad to see his home ruined by thugs. Photo albums lay wrecked in front of his book case and most of his books had been torn apart. Apparently Buster and his mate had been looking for something but Harry had no idea what that could have been. Then again, they might have been practicing the intimidation techniques recommended in the latest WSA training bulletin.

Like Brutus, Skipper too could hear Harry's voice inside his head and Harry was pleased to see that the dog had not forgotten the things he had been taught. When the time came for Harry to carry out his plan Skipper was ready too.

Together they checked that the mosquito coils—two of them at opposite ends of the bedroom—were burning happily.

Before they left Harry made sure that Jeffrey had placed a small pot filled with water on the gas stove. He also instructed Jeffrey to send the women out to the car before lighting the stove.

At first Jeffrey wanted to light the burner under the pot of water but Harry wanted the one next to the pot lit.

Now Harry instructed Skipper to push over the pot on the stove. At first the canine was not too keen on the idea thinking he might get a paw scalded and it took Harry a while to convince the dog that pushing a pot of cold water towards the flames was not going to get his tootsies parboiled. In the end Skipper took his word for it and gave the pot a shove. The intended outcome was achieved on the second try, the pot sloshed water over the lit burner and doused the flames. Harry could hear the gas escaping and guided Skipper to the outside kitchen door.

Skipper nosed the door open and once they were outside Harry ordered him to close the door by jumping up against it. With his tail wagging Skipper was proud to show he had not forgotten this trick of closing a door behind him. After that they headed to their rendezvous on the edge of town.

To the unwary bystander it just looked like a somewhat skinny—true—Labrador dog walking along the side of the road.

About ten minutes before the others arrived at the spot where Harry was waiting for them, the gas reached the burning mozzie coils. The old Queensland home blew up with a bang reminiscent of a wartime exploding bomb.

Being an old timber place the cause of the explosion later was determined to have been *'a combination of a leaking gas appliance'*—the word 'stove' was too hard to spell in the official report—*'and an electrical short in the old place's ancient wiring. The resultant explosion was devastating and the fire was fierce but no-one was hurt. Although there were unofficial—therefore unsubstantiated—rumours that what looked like some skeletal remains were found in the ruins, they were denied because the owner, Harry Knot, was overseas and the relative who had been looking after the place during his absence left town two days earlier. The few badly burned bone fragments found in the ruins may have been of some animal that had died in the breeze space underneath the floor of the old home.'* So the newspaper said.

The mood at the Tomkins' house was a mixed kettle of fish. On the one side Harry was glad that he had 'socked it' to the WSA, two of their agents within a week and no known lead for the WSA to follow, but on the other hand he was sad over losing his old home and more so the mementos of his previous life that had gone up in smoke. He tried to console himself with the knowledge that he could not have taken any of them with him into the Dimension anyway but that thought let to the realisation that he had had no choice in the matter. Thanks to the WSA he had to return to the Dimension in order to stay in a physical form—that is of course if the conversion would work—or remain in the Core as a Shimmerer in which case his mementos were of not much use to him in any case.

Jeffrey suddenly realised that the burning of Harry's house had broken out Harry's anchor to the area and whatever happened from then on would only result in one outcome, he was going to lose a good friend and mentor.

Should Harry remain a Shimmerer in the Core, he had very little reason now to hang around. Jeffrey knew his friend well enough to realise that the latter would not want to impose on Jeffrey and Sandra and would just quietly float away. Should Harry's solidification be successful he still would disappear because he would have to go back to the Dimension to retain his shape or die a slow death in the Core.

Sandra was aware of the anguish in her husband and felt for him, making her less than chirpy. Jordie was homesick and missed Kal, the subdued mood of the others did not help. Skipper was the only one with something to smile about, half a Kentucky fried chicken in fact.

CHAPTER 37

HARRY'S LOT

THE MORE KAL thought about it the more he became worried that Jordie and Harry would materialise in the Dimensional equivalent of Bowen in the Core, and how was he going to find out when they would arrive, if they had not already. In the end Abdullah suggested he try and contact Tjitjira for an update. Kal looked at Brutus, "How about it B.? Gonna call him for me?"

Brutus who was laying at his feet with her head on her front paws opened one eye, heaved a big sigh—her way of saying "Nah, not interested"—and went back to sleep.

Meanwhile in downtown Bowen, Sgt Tomkins made himself unpopular by handing out a few infringement notices to some trawlers caught fishing in the wrong place using illegal nets and, to top it off, some of their safety equipment was either missing or defective.

Sandra went back to the university to teach and to pretend that Dr Franklin was no more than a passing acquaintance. They still collaborated in the secret sound lab on the wharf and were making headway in the fine tuning of the equipment.

While everybody was at work, Jordie often took Skipper, on a lead, window shopping while Harry explained all the wonders she saw.

At first Harry was hesitant about taking her to the shops because he worried that when she got back to the Dimension she would pine for the things she had seen in the Core. After a while, however, Harry discovered that anything the girl saw that was there as a result of technology not know in the Dimension, such as electronics or materials such as plastics and synthetics, were of only passing interest. For instance, she could not understand why such things as food blenders were of any use. What was wrong with a good sharp knife with which to cut up fruit and vegetables? The one tool for most any job. Looking at all the kitchen gadgets, she told Harry that she would have to spend more time on cleaning them than on preparing, cooking and eating the meal.

During this period of limited activity Skipper, the true Labrador he was, saw the opportunity to put on a few pounds of extra weight. Sandra who was rather weight-conscious and who was envious of the complete lack of restraint with which Skipper approached any food he could legally or illegally obtain, tended to criticise the dog but Harry would come to the rescue by saying Skipper needed the extra weight in order to prevent Harry from floating away in a stiff breeze. Rather sarcastically Sandra asked, "You pair expecting a cyclone?"

Harry left it at that and so did Skipper who, at the time, had a mouthful of McDonald's best.

The WSA either was running low on expendable operatives or might have been otherwise occupied. Whatever the reason on the surface at least that organisation appeared to have lost their focus on the Tomkins and their guest. The fact that Harry's dog Skipper now was part of the Tomkins household and was often seen being taken for long walks by their guest the young women with the flaming hair, did not seem to arouse their interest.

However there was an undertow of concern, how could they orchestrate Harry's solidification and a spontaneous Dimensional transfer within a twenty-four hour window?

KAL SAT BOLD upright, sweat plastered his hair against his forehead and in his mind's eye he watched his nightmare slowly dissolve.

Once again he was a prisoner in the extremist camp where he had received most of the injuries that scarred him both mentally and physically. Only this time he had not been the victim but a bystander witnessing Jordie being tortured the way he had been. Her naked body was stretched out and suspended horizontally by her tied ankles and wrists, like he had been, above a pig pen where hungry wild swine were jumping trying to get at her. She was facing down so she could see the pigs. Every time one would jump, Jordie involuntarily would jerk upwards. This placed tremendous strain on all her joints and Kal could feel the remembered pain.

He grabbed his klewang and was about to start swinging it when the last of the nightmare dissolved and he realised that it had been just that; a nightmare.

In an attempt to reduce his anxiety over her he brought to mind memories of better times. With a faint smile on his face he remembered the cute dimples in her cheeks as she smiled. Her large, expressive green eyes would twinkle when she was happy or could spark darkly when she was angry.

In his memory he could feel her small hands on his chest and the smell of her clean, auburn hair. Her hair intrigued him and he could well understand that it was her pride and joy. It had a deep auburn colour bordering on dark red-brown in the shade while, when light hit it, it often looked bright orange. Her untamed tresses were straight and reached well past her waist. She would often gather them in a pony-tail but he liked it best when she would gather the hair on the sides of her head into a pony tail that sat on top of loose hair from the back of her head, or, as she would say, "Side boards up, tail board down."

Her body was something else! Even though she was quite athletic, there were plenty of awesome curves and all in the right places. Her skin was tanned to a honey colour and as smooth as the proverbial. She had a few scars on her lower legs due to childhood mishaps.

The triangular branding mark, hers with the compliments of the erstwhile 'Earl' of Brine, although covered by the bird tattoo still had the power to upset her but her hair usually covered it. There were some whip marks on her back but Kal did not even notice them. Anyway, he decided quite a while ago that no matter what she looked like her character and soft nature were such that he wanted to spend the rest of his life with her. The fact that he was crazy over her small, slim stature as well, was a bonus.

Longingly he looked at Jordie's belt that still sported 'Reggie' her poniard. It was there waiting for her.

He was still mooning about the 'Bintang Balon's' cabin when Brutus sauntered in. She flopped herself down in a rather abrupt manner and Kal asked her, "Did you bring Abdullah with you?"

"Of course she did but why ask the dog but not me?"

"Oh, hi. Now wouldn't I look silly if I had asked you if you are there and you were not?"

"And you don't look silly talking to a dog?"

"You better watch what you are saying! You might hurt her feelings."

Brutus put her head on her paws and gave Kal the 'Yeah whatever' look and dozed off.

"OK Abdullah, what is the sudden interest in me?"

"Huh? Oh nothing, just a friendly visit. However now that you have opened up the conversation, I do have something I would like to run by you."

"And that is?"

"Well, you remember when Tjitjira brought Harry and Brutus to Shimmerville?"

"Yeah?"

"Well, I thought that perhaps it would be easier for whatever powers that are involved with bringing Jordie and Harry back into the Dimension, if we were at a place where Tjitjira brought somebody before?"

"So you're suggesting we move the 'Bintang Balon' around the head land to Shimmerville?"

"Yep"

"Have you spoken to Samu about this?"

"No, it was just a thought and I was not going to mention it to anybody unless you feel that the plan has merit."

"Yes, well I'm ready to try anything. We'll have to get the boat back into the water first and I'll have to trade for some supplies from the village. What about the anchorage there?"

"There used to be a channel in the mouth of the river that lead to a basin near the resort but during that last cyclone it was silted up. Perhaps the river has washed the silt out by now. We won't know until we get there. Anyway the anchorage in the bay is as good as it is here."

Later that day Kal together with Abdullah and Samu told the chief about what was happening and although the old man and his daughter, Mailiku, were sad to see him go, he promised the village would put the 'Bintang Balon' back in the water on the next spring tide.

Through Abdullah, Kal asked Samu what his plans were for the future. Samu had a note of sadness in his voice when he told Kal that his place as the village healer and prospective father was by the side of his brand new wife and in the village where the building of his hut was about to start.

I T WAS JUST after seven at night and the storm that had been threatening the harbour all afternoon finally broke. Sheets of lightning and torrential rain alternatively lit up the wetly gleaming shipping containers only to lose them in an inky pouring blackness. During the brief moments of blinding light a furtive shadow could be seen darting from one container to another.

The 'Russian' stood in the driver's cab of the gantries crane high above the shipping containers next to him stood one of his men. Actually it had been that associate who had made the 'Russian' aware of the strange goings-on.

"I told you that bloke seems to be looking for one container in particular and I think it's the one your mates are using."

The 'Russian's' deep voice rumbled when he said, "Perhaps we shall ask him, dah?"

"Sure! How do you want him? Dead or alive?"

"Use noodle, dah? How he is going to answer my questions if he is dead, dah?"

"Ok. Boss! It just would make it a bit easier if we can bang him up a bit."

"Banged up is good, dead is no good, dah?"

After a fierce look at his underling the 'Russian' continued, "Ok. You go to office, get boys ready. Close off passage ways around west end of container yard. Dah? When boys in position turn flood lights on and catch him. Dah?"

"Ok. Boss. Where are you going to be?"

"I watch from here so I can see if he gets away. You bring him to office and let me know, dah?"

The man nodded his head and disappeared down the ladder of the gantry.

The rain was still sheeting down but the lightning and thunder were moving away. Just as the rain was easing up some, the flood lights came on. The scene was like that out of a silent movie. In between the dark silhouettes of two rows of shipping containers light reflected from wet pavement while the rain passing through the beams of the spot lights looked like silver curtains.

Against a background of light reflected from the wet pavement in the passage three back-lit silhouettes were visible. Like in the silent movies two of the shadows were hoeing into the third shadow and like in those same movies the one that got the beating wore a wide brimmed fedora and a belted raincoat.

Ten minutes later the 'Russian' did have some trouble convincing the wet and battered spy that to answer the questions honestly and quickly would reduce his suffering dramatically. It turned out that he, the spy that is, from time to time received a phone call asking him to do a bit of 'industrial espionage'. Later, at some pre-arranged time the same voice would ring him again and he would make his report. If the report was to the satisfaction of the voice on the telephone, payment would be made to his bank account.

He was unable to confirm or deny that the voice belonged to a WSA operative.

On this occasion he was instructed to find a specific shipping container and to attempt entry to ascertain its contents. It was no surprise to find out that the container in question was Dr Franklin's sound lab. It took two broken toes, one busted knee cap and one broken thumb to gather this information but, hey, Felix the spy was neither sent to another dimension nor was he sent home in a body bag; so he had very little to complain about.

The upshot of all this was that Dr Franklin realised that it was time for him to stop procrastinating and to take some definitive action: implement the procedure, or, make the laboratory go away. The WSA was closing in and heaven only knew what they could do to him just to shut him up. He had a fair idea of what the WSA would consider the 'final solution' in his case. Furthermore there was a distinct possibility that Sandra Tomkins might suffer the same fate for her involvement. Unwittingly she had awakened a protective urge in him plus a few others but those are not under discussion here.

KAL STOOD AT the helm of the 'Bintang Balon' as she ghosted over the quiet waters of the lagoon. Here and there coral heads, or 'bommies', reached for the surface of the crystal clear water. As the shadow of the 'Bintang Balon' slid over the white sandy bottom like a cloud, fish of all sizes would streak away to find a hiding place in the shade of the bommies. Brutus stood on the edge of the deck jumping up and down in her excitement. Every now and then she gave the impression she was about to launch herself overboard in pursuit of some fish or other much to the alarm of Abdullah who could see himself drowning in the peaceful lagoon. Keeping in mind that until he came to the Pacific Island resort 'Trade Winds', the only ships Abdullah had any dealings with were the 'ships of the desert', the one or two hump variety and he had kept well away from them because of their mean temperament and their habit of spitting at you. So, Abdullah was not sorry when they rounded the headland and Shimmerville, or what was left of it, came into view.

The first time Kal had seen it the place had been far more intriguing with its variety of shimmering oblongs and rectangles of different hues. All the shimmering oblongs and squares were transparent and would change colours as other coloured oblongs, all imprints of erstwhile buildings, could be seen behind them. For instance the shimmer imprint nearest to the observer could be red in colour while behind it there were yellow and blue ones; where the red overlapped the yellow shimmering the resulting colour was orange while where the red overlapped the blue one a purple colour resulted. Of course when the position of the observer changed so too did the colour play of the transparent residues of what had been luxurious buildings, covered swimming pools and outside gardens.

Before the cyclone went through it there were some hundred and fifty guests left, all shimmerers of course, who called the 'Trade Winds' resort home but only Abdullah was left now. The others? Who knows? That question made Abdullah sad and both Kal and Brutus were quiet while Abdullah silently paid his respects.

The channel at the mouth of the river had washed out but not enough for Kal to sail the 'Bintang Balon' up to the resort. Anyway there was nothing to be gained by it as the anchorage in the lagoon was good enough.

Then the waiting began. At times it was still hard for Kal to realise that Brutus was a spirit dog and not one of the flesh-and-blood variety. Like one afternoon when Kal sat on deck and Brutus was lying near him. Abdullah was reminiscing about something that happened at the resort before it became Shimmerville and drew Kal's attention to a particular spot on the beach. When Kal looked over to where the occurrence had taken place he was surprised to see a dog similar to Brutus, sauntering along the tide line, sniffing here and sniffing there.

"Hey Abdullah, see that? That just looks like Brutus!"

"Have a look at where Brutus is supposed to be and you'll find it is Brutus. The hound has ditched me for an interesting seagull dropping!"

To Kal's surprise it was true, it was Brutus who—bored with sitting on deck—had willed herself over to the beach. An hour later she was back on board.

JORDIE, SANDRA, JEFFREY and Dr Franklin were sitting at the kitchen table in the Tomkins's house. Harry was shimmering somewhere near the ceiling. Dr Franklin told the others about the latest WSA attempt stopped by the 'Russian'.

"I think that the 'Russian' is getting a bit worried about the whole set-up and so am I just quietly."

"So what is our next step?" Harry asked.

"I think we should no longer delay."

"So what? You're going to sound-blast Harry in the hope that during the next twenty-four hours a spontaneous transfer is going to take place? And what about Jordie, she cannot be in the sound chamber with Harry while he is being zapped or she'll finish up like Buster! She is small enough as it is!"

"Ha-ha, funny one."

Dr Franklin chipped in, "Not a very sensitive remark but a correct observation however. None of us can be in the sound chamber with Harry for that exact reason. Jordie will have to be in close proximity however she must be outside the sound-blast radius."

"So, where is that?"

"Just outside the container should be close enough I hope."

"And what if that is not close enough? Assuming that a spontaneous transfer is available at that moment."

"In that case you will go but she will stay until the next time a spontaneous transfer occurs."

"That's a lot of 'ifs and may-bees'. Don't take it personal Doc I know it is your first time too."

"Thank you. Believe me I too would like to be more certain of the outcome…"

"Nothing like a straight answer full of confidence and re-assurance, is there?"

"Uhum, let's prepare for tomorrow night shall we?"

"Ok. Are you OK with that Jordie?"

"Aye. If only we could inform Kal of our pending arrival."

"That would be nice but I would prefer to let Tjitjira know we're going to have a bash at it! However, I have got no idea on how to reach him."

"There be nay alternative so let us proceed."

Soon after Dr Franklin went home and an electric but at the same time gloomy atmosphere descended on the Tomkins household.

Sandra shed a tear as she held Jordie's hand and her gesture was more to give herself confidence rather than Jordie.

What could any of them say, they could not exchange addresses or phone numbers, nor could they promise any future visits.

It was as if Jeffrey and Sandra could see Jordie standing between themselves and the black wall of the unknown. It towered over the slight form of Jordie and even though Jeffrey and Sandra were aware that Harry was there too, they could not see him so Jordie looked very alone and fragile.

Harry too felt the anxiety of the unknown and remained very quiet. At last he muttered something about Jeffrey better having some clothes ready for when he, Harry, became visible again.

It was just after six pm the following day when they congregated at the 'Russian's' wharf office. All piled into the harbour maintenance vehicle they had been using and the 'Russian' drove them to the containers. When the van pulled up in front of the sound lab, Jeffrey asked, "Since you sorted out that last WSA character, has there been any more activity from them?"

"Nyet! My boys watch container 'round clock." After a moment's silence he continued, "When job is finish we move container to different part of wharf, and plant empty one here wiz door welded close. Dey have much pleasure opening empty container, dah?"

From somewhere Harry chuckled, *"Dah!"*

A heavy mist was rolling in from across the bay and by the time the van pulled up near the container, the flood-lights were no more than woolly balls of white in the otherwise grey and swirling mass. It was a silent group of people standing in front of the sound lab container. They were waiting for the 'Russian' to come back after parking the van when Jeffrey remarked, "All we need now is a few scary bats and a creaking door!"

It broke the tension a little bit but not much.

Dr Franklin's fingers danced over the keyboard of the container's lock and the door opened. Sandra and the good doctor entered leaving the rest standing outside. A few minutes later the flood lights went out and a soft hum could be heard from inside the inner container. Harry, who was hanging onto Jordie was fidgeting causing Jordie to admonish him, "Harry cease yer squirmin'! Ye be worse than a maiden on her first un-chaperoned outing!"

"Yeah well, I'm about to get zapped by Dr Frankenstein!"

"Frankenstein? Who that be? Our friend be called Dr *Franklin*."

Before Harry could explain himself, Sandra walked out of the container and burst out laughing when she saw Jeffrey. Even though Jeffrey knew that the laugh was more to hide her nerves than anything else he had to ask his wife, "What's so funny?"

"You are! Look at you standing there like a butler waiting for the master to step from the shower."

"What on earth are you talking about?"

"You! Silly! The way you stand there with a change of clothes for Harry over your arm!" and another peal of laughter sounded eerily through the mist cloaking the wharf.

Before Jeffrey could retaliate his wife turned to Jordie, "I assume Harry is hanging on to you? Can you let him go so I can take him inside?" In a graveyard voice she added, "The *doctor* will see him now."

Jordie could feel Harry's feather touch releasing itself and Sandra took over.

A few moments later inside the lab Franklin spoke, "Harry, are you here?"

"Wouldn't want to be anywhere else Doc! OK, do your thing!"

"Everything is in readiness for you. You see the black dome, the heavy rubber mat on the floor below it and the blade switch on the wall?"

"Couldn't help but notice them when I came in."

"Yes well, after Sandra and I have left, wait until a green light comes on, here on the console. It will come on when the outer doors are sealed. Once the light is on you must stand on the rubber mat under the dome. An electronic force field will give you the necessary mass for the next phase. Make sure you stand in the middle and all your body parts are within the column between the floor mat and the dome. Once you are satisfied that the experiment can continue, you place one hand on the handle bar of the blade switch and pull it down halfway, to the first stop. This will allow the charge to build up. Once the red light, next to the green light, comes on the required charge is ready to be unleashed. Pull the handle bar all the way down and bring your hand to your side. There will be a five second delay after contact has been made. The rest will take care of itself and five minutes later we will welcome you back."

"Or so you hope!"

As Sandra patted his invisible hand she muttered, "Ye of little faith!"

Some minutes later Sandra followed by Dr Franklin came out closing the container doors behind them.

The mist was swirling lazily over and between the shipping containers and even though the flood lights on that part of the wharf were out, it was not completely dark. The swirling of the mist created the impression that mysterious, shadowy figures were moving about.

The 'Russian' looked intently at Dr Franklin for so long that the latter asked irritably, "What?!"

The big man balled his fists and Sandra, being aware that everybody was on edge, put a placating hand on his arm. The 'Russian' got the message and asked, "We better stand not so close to container. Dah?"

Nobody answered his question but all decided to move some distance away. The group had only just arrived at their new location when the flood lights came back on. This meant that the process in the lab was completed.

Was Harry back to normal or was he too, a shrink-dink like poor Buster?

No one appeared eager to find out and in the end they more or less had to shame Dr Franklin into opening the sound lab. Just as he was about to punch in the locking code, the heavy container door slowly swung open and Harry in all his—visibly—glory stepped out.

It was interesting to see the different reactions his appearance provoked.

Sandra who was the closest to him wanted to rush forward to give him a hug until she noticed that he was quite naked and that brought her up short.

Jordie who knew his voice so well had never seen him before and she stood there with a shy smile on her face not knowing whether she should go and hug him or that that was too forward and that she should wait to be introduced.

Jeffrey stood there with an ear to ear smile on his face, completely forgetting that he held Harry's decency drapes over his arm.

Dr Franklin embarrassed by Harry's nudity had turned his back and was tinkering with the shipping container's electronic lock.

The 'Russian' was the only one who proposed any positive action, "We all go to office and drink Vodka! Dah?"

There were several happy 'Dah's and then everybody stood there and watched Harry as he struggled to get into a pair of tight shorts—Buster's actually—and a singlet.

The others had drifted over to the van and were waiting for him while Harry was still struggling with his much too tight shorts, when suddenly there was a tearing sound and a flash of bright orange light. The mist seemed to turn into steam and for a short time all visibility was gone. The 'Russian' must have thought himself back in one of the Bolshevik conflicts of his youth because he made a dive under the van. When everything returned to how it was before, the 'Russian' was half under the van and Harry was gone.

It took a while for the penny to drop but Jordie said it all when she whispered, "Harry be home now."

Those four words spoke volumes of the sudden desolation the poor girl felt. She could not cry but neither could she talk. It was the 'Russian' who was most in tune with what she was going through. After he had extracted himself from under the van with as much dignity as he could muster, he wrapped one of his huge arms around her shoulders and said, "We find solution but first we drink Vodka to lose sadness and den to loosen brain! Dah?"

She let him guide her to the van while the others followed in a subdued mood.

Slowly Harry became aware of his surroundings even though he was dizzy and nauseated he knew he was on a beach somewhere because he was down on all fours and he could feel sand between his fingers and his toes. One of his knees was resting on something sharp like a small rock or broken shell and he was just about to shift his knee away from the offending object when he heard a voice behind him, "About time you got back!"

His surprise was genuine when he turned around so fast that he fell on his butt in the sand. Of course the voice belonged to Kal but his ear to ear grin disappeared when he cried out. "Where is Jordie?"

Harry slowly looked about and in a low voice said, "Looks like she did not make it as yet. Probably she was not close enough to me when the transfer took place!"

"Was it a spontaneous transfer?"

"Yes it was. Kal, she'll be right! Jeffrey and Sandra will take care of her."

"Who is Sandra?"

"You remember my off-sider Jeffrey Tomkins?"

"Yes."

"Sandra is his wife and we have been staying at their place all…"

Just then Brutus came bounding up, she had been half a mile down the beach with Abdullah in tow of course. Her arrival was punctuated by some fierce and critical language threatening both her past and future but Brutus took no notice and danced a fast, one-dog hop-scotch dance in a tight circle around Harry and Kal. At the right moment Abdullah let go of Brutus and clamped on to Harry.

"Welcome back my friend, next time though let us know in advance so we can either hog-tie that dog or be present at the exact spot of your landing. By the way where is the fair maiden?"

"She hasn't come yet but hopefully she won't make Romeo, here, wait too long 'cause he'll drive us bonkers otherwise."

Kal realised that his friends meant well and the fact that Harry told him Jordie was in good hands was a relief but he still would have liked her to arrive with Harry. In the end they boarded the 'Bintang Balon' for a meal.

JORDIE SAT ON the edge of the bed nursing one considerable hangover. After Harry was transferred the 'Russian' had poured at least three quarters of a bottle of Vodka into her. At the time it felt pretty good and she accepted the fact that the transfer was 'fully booked' and that she would be on the next available flight.

By the end of the night she even managed a smile just before she drew the curtains and passed out. Somehow Jeffrey and Sandra must have gotten her home because she was sitting on the edge of her bed in the Tomkins's guest room. The Vodka might have been a lifeline the night before but in her present view of the world everything seemed to be in a slow spin, not to mention the crackling head ache, and her stomach wanted out!

She only just made it to the bathroom and poured out what she estimated at being at least two full bottles of Vodka in amongst some other but unidentifiable goodies. Head still spinning she got under the shower and let the cold water pelt her skin. It made her feel healthier but not happier. She wanted to go home to Kal.

As if she was walking on egg-shells she approached the breakfast table but even though there was a platter of fried eggs and bacon, she could only do justice to a large mug of black coffee. She took it out on the back deck and sat down. From where the Tomkins house was placed, anybody sitting on the back terrace had a pleasant view over some dunes leading down to the water of the bay. Further across to the left she could see the wharfs with at least half a dozen container ships either tied up along-side or out on the bay at anchor.

CHAPTER 38

AND THE WAIT GOES ON

WEEKS PASSED, THE tropical sun blazed in the near white sky and the heat reflecting off the sea and strand would have made life a torture had it not been for the trade winds blowing steadily day in day out.

Harry was concerned about Kal's state of mind, his friend, never much of a talker, became more withdrawn with every passing day. There just was no sign of Jordie or any indication as to when or if she would come back into the Dimension.

For a while they kept themselves busy with the building of a substantial sun roof where they could sit in the shade while they did their cooking and rope repair work and other house-keeping tasks. Then came the day when neither Harry nor Brutus could motivate Kal to come ashore and have a meal of freshly caught and fried fish. In the end Harry with Brutus and Abdullah went on shore and it was Abdullah who broached the subject of Kal's mood, *"Kal is taking this waiting for Jordie very hard."*

"Yes, I wish that Jordie had come through first!"

"Is there nothing we can do about it?"

"No, as I understand it, Tjitjira and his crowd can orchestrate transfers from here to the Core, to a certain extent, but not the other way around. I would like it though if Tjitjira could come and visit to let Kal know Jordie has not been forgotten! That would help a lot."

"Can't we somehow get in contact with him?"

"How? I lost the phone number for 'dial a saint', or in this case, 'dial a wizard."

"Ha! Funny! Leave it to me, I'll have a talk to Brutus."

"That's been tried before."

"Brutus, Kal is unhappy can you help him?"

Brutus slowly lifted her head and looked toward the 'Bintang Balon' where she knew Kal to be, next she let out a mournful howl and dropped her head back on her paws.

"You say you can feel his pain but you don't know what to do about it? Well, I can tell you what to do, go and fetch Tjitjira!"

Much to their surprise Brutus looked at Harry, stood up, looked at the 'Bintang Balon' and faded away.

"You still there Abdullah?"

"Yeah, only just! One of those days that dog is going to lose me! Here let me get hold of you, this bamboo upright has splinters."

"Stop complaining! You told her to go and *fetch* Tjitjira. Let's hope she does not drag him over here like she would a fetched stick!"

"Oops, that could become a problem especially if he was having breakfast or something!"

"He doesn't have breakfast."

"Yes well, I said 'or something'!"

The hours passed slowly and later in the day the wind dropped away. The air became still but all along the horizon clouds were building into towering thunder heads.

Late in the afternoon Kal came on deck of the 'Bintang Balon', saw that their borrowed canoe was on shore with Harry and Abdullah and dived overboard into the crystal clear water for the short swim ashore. As he walked from the surf, what little there was, he looked at the cloud-castles with their brilliantly white heads that faded into near black curtains near the surface of the silver sea. Overhead the sky was still an unblemished expanse of brilliant blue. Kal flopped down next to Harry in the shade and asked quite conversationally, "Where is the hound?"

Before Harry could answer Abdullah remarked, "*The mutt ain't here but ah is masa.*"

"What? She finally realised she was better off on her own?" after a moment he added bitterly, "Just like Jordie?"

Abdullah did not reply but Harry did, "Stop feeling sorry for yourself, Kal! I'm sorry I came back first but that is how things turned out. There is nothing to indicate that Jordie won't come back. If there was an insurmountable problem Tjitjira would have told us. As a matter of fact Brutus has gone to get him!"

For long moments Kal sat there with his head bowed. Finally he looked up at Harry and in a whisper he replied, "I apologise for the mood I've been in but I finally realise that a scarred battle-horse 'has-been' like me cannot expect to be of interest to a young woman like Jordie!"

"What a load of bovine manure that is! What has she got to do to make you understand that, warped as her thinking may be, you are the one for her!"

"Yes, well, she still isn't here!"

"Go for a long run along the beach to pound some patience into that head of yours and if you see Brutus by any chance tell her to come back, Abdullah is starting to crowd my space."

Kal grinned as he heard the good-natured spluttering from Abdullah and he suddenly realised that he was a lot better off than Abdullah. He took up Harry's suggestion and went for a run.

He nearly ran halfway around the island and back, a distance of some fifteen kilometres mostly through loose sand and he was well and truly exhausted. As usually happened when Kal was in a mental stew, the run gave him time to take out his frustrations on himself without actually causing anybody else pain. It also allowed him to think through his problems and to come up with some solutions. At last, panting heavily he staggered into the lagoon for a dip.

As he climbed out of the water he looked at the sky-show put on by the setting sun and the cloud banks all-round the horizon. The sun had sunk behind the towering cloud bank. Spears of orange light radiated from the silver lined cloud to stab at the still blue sky. Towards the east the cloud banks took on a brooding dark demeanour while the sea still tried to keep a comforting blue tone although towards the west the sea and the lower part of the cloud banks there took on a deep purple colouring.

Sunsets and sunrises always filled Kal with awe and he was only sorry that in the tropics they never lasted long.

In a totally different mood he sat down next to Harry and accepted a plate of food. By the time the meal was finished it was totally dark except for eerie sheet lightning all-round the horizon. It was kind of unnatural, the air was still and not a sound could be heard except for the occasional splash of a fish in the lagoon. The lightning on the horizon was too far away for the associated thunder to be heard.

Their cooking fire had burned down to glowing coals and the dark surrounded them. Suddenly Harry pointed at the water's edge, "Look at the phosphorus in the water."

Spell bound they looked at the display of flecks of light in the water. Both Harry and Kal said at the same time, "Like flying over a city."

They had been standing at the water's edge every now and then stirring the water with a foot to re-energies the light giving plankton when they became aware of two larger concentrations of phosphorescence a short distance from the shore. In awe they watched as a four-legged, glowing apparition bounded towards them. Not far behind a human shaped denizen rose like a golden statue from the water. By this time the hell hound had reached them and they were more than relieved to discover the apparition was no other than Brutus. The dog was so boisterous that she took their full attention and somewhere in the back of their consciousness they expected Tjitjira to announce himself. Brutus was instantly forgotten when the golden statue cried, "Kal! It's me, Jordie! I'm back!"

The End

ADJUNCT–GLOSSARY OF TERMS USED

Jordie
(THE DIMENSION OF WIND, WOOD, AND WATER)
GLOSSARY OF TERMS AND DEFINITIONS

Belief system of the Balon Islanders.

Theirs is a 3 or 4 tier system, depending how one wants to look at it.

Tier 1

The four elements (Earth, Water, Fire and Air) combined create matter from the most basic cell to the highest evolved creature. Each such expression of life has as foundation the four elements of which Earth and Water create the physical or material aspect while Air and Fire create the spiritual aspect of each life form. The animation spark—both on a physical as well as an esoteric level—is provided by the One. The material aspect of a life form is subject to decay and therefore to time—time being a measurement of decay. When the material form eventually fails there is the residue of the elements Air and Fire. Together they retain much of the life forms identity and it—the soul or spirit—moves onto the next Tier.

Tier 2

The life form's material expression has degenerated through time to such an extent that the elements of earth and fire have returned to other forms of energy. Of the original being only the elementals water and air remain. Together they are a mirror of the original without the encumbrance of a physical body although the memory of that body is still there.

This is the realm of recognisable ancestor spirits—they may make themselves present in the minds of the 'living' through the projection of a voice in the head, a sudden or profound insight or a recognisable apparition, ghost, etc. At this stage they still have an interest in the daily affairs of those they left behind and are quite willing to impart the knowledge they gained during their 'physical stage'. The problem is that most often the paranoia of the physical self—as present in Tier 1—is unwilling to listen to that what has no physical presence and usually can only communicate in a one-way direction so cannot be questioned.

As time goes on and this can be many years or many generations, the water element will evaporate and eventually only the Air element is left. With the demise of the water element the Air element loses its last connection with the original life-form and with it its identity.

At this point it rises to the third Tier.

Tier 3

The Air aspect arrives with knowledge gained mainly in the first Tier and scrubbed of all emotional value in the second Tier. By now it has no longer an identity that would be recognisable by any life form in the first Tier. However on occasion it can still influence the living by means of causing instinctive knowledge, a gut feeling, Deja-vu or any form of—seemingly—unaccountable knowledge.

Tier 4

Above Tier 3 lays another realm where the purified Air element from Tier 3 comes to reside and this realm is simply known as The **One** or The **All.** Its works and manifestations are such that they are not dwelt on by humans and enough is to know that eventually its residue returns to make up the Air element in Tier 1, so completing the eternal cycle of birth and rebirth.

Tier 4

The **ONE**, the **ALL**

Tier 3

Air

Tier 2

Water and Air

Tier 1

Earth, Fire, Water, Air

BRUTUS: A spirit dog

SHORT DICTIONARY OF LANGUAGE USED BY BRUTUS

+ A full fletched growl with a show of white gnashers and bristle: *Promise of impending doom and a promise of severe pain.*

+ Big sigh: *Nah! Not interested.*

+ On guard but not really perturbed or interested: *growl and flash of pearly whites while hackles are raised to give a fair imitation of a scrubbing brush. The whole display will lack somewhat in sincerity because Brutus will not get up off her fat tail.*

+ Head tipped to side of floppy ear while uppermost ear stands and accusing look in eyes could mean: *"Well, you could have reminded me!"* Or *"Why should it be my fault/responsibility?"* Or *"Like hell you will!"*

+ Accusing look, head slightly tilted and tongue hanging out of side of mouth: *"That better not be true Sunshine!"*

+ Scratch behind either ear: *"Relax man, let me get rid of this (imaginary) flea."*

+ Head thrown back and long mournful howl: *"I feel your pain as though it is mine but what can I do?"*

+ Ruff: *"Good to see ya but whatever tall tale they tell you about me, don't believe a word of it!"*

+ Wuf: *"What? That pair of moaners. I'll show you whom looks after whom! Hang on boys!"*

- Grrumf: *"Go away and let me sleep."*
- Woof: *"Take some notice, already!"*
- woof: *"What the hell!"*
- WOOF!: *"Well, if you're not going to do something about it I WILL!"*
- A bounding or bouncy approach, tongue flapping in the breeze: *"Hey! Life is a gas, aren't you happy/lucky to know me?"*
- A lopsided look: *"Trust me! I may have a plan."*
- To stop suddenly and growl: *"Let go of me boys! I have a job to do"*
- A loose swagger in her gait: *"I know I've done it again and some praise will be gracefully accepted."*

Brutus yelp? Or whine? Never happened.

CORE

The Core is the spine along which human endeavour develops. In itself it is the product of the earth's vibrations; keeping in mind that *all matter is energy at specific rates of vibration.* When the frequency of matter-vibrations speeds up enough, there is a shape change from solid to energy.

Symbolically the Core is represented as a narrow cone. At its base is the solid matter energy of Mother Earth. As energy travels further up the Core its frequency of vibration increases. The Core vibrations inspire man to 'invent' new technologies, as well as new philosophies but that is a different subject than the one dealt with in this writing. People 'inspired' to 'invent' new technologies are people most in tune with the Core vibrations of their time. At its base the frequency of vibrations within the Core are not much higher than those of the solid matter from which it sprang but as the Core's tip moves ever further away from its base the vibrations increase.

The ever-increasing frequencies of the Core vibrations inspire ever more complex and new technologies.

For people finely tuned in on a specific vibration it is hard, quite often impossible, to tune in on the new vibration that is 'inspiring' a new technology, which is replacing the one to which they are attuned.

DIMENSION

When the Core vibrations have increased to such extend that they inspire a new technology the slower vibrations, which gave rise to the technology being superseded, do not cease to exist. The slower vibrations cannot coexist with the faster vibrations within the Core, so they move outwards from the Core. This then creates the vibration platform called the Dimension.

Within the Dimension the rates of vibrations remain the same therefore there is no further *upward* development as that is dependent on an increased speed in the Core vibrations resulting in *new* technologies. In the Dimension where there is no further increase in the frequencies of energy vibrations, only a *lateral* expansion is present that explores and enhances the known technologies.

Both Core and dimensions exist in time, as does the earth. They all exist in the same time frame therefore what is today's date in one, is the same in the others. The Core and the Dimensions are separated in vibration frequencies but not in time and place.

Q. If there is no further *upward* development within a dimension, what effect does time have on the dimension's technology?

A. It inspires people within that dimension to *laterally* expand the technology to which the dimension is dedicated. (Lateral expansion means the enhancement of known technology without inventing new technology with which to replace the known.)

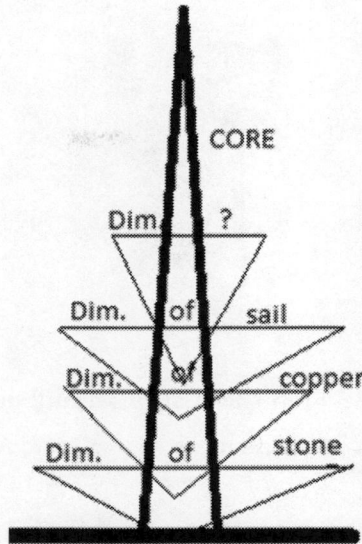

VIBRATION

Q. <u>Why do the Core vibrations increase while those in dimensions remain static?</u>

A. The Core grows *perpendicular* to the earth's gravity therefore, the closer to the tip the lesser the slowing down effect of gravity on Core vibrations. On the other hand, the Dimension grows *parallel* to the earth's gravity and as a result the gravitational pull on the dimensional vibrations is the same everywhere in that dimension.

WRAITH

The Wraith is a being in the shape of a human; he/she is of solid shape during the night but is no more than a gas during the day.

Q. Where does the Wraith come from?

A. According to the Wise (see Wise) the Wraith can be divided into two groups. Both groups originate from the Core. The longest known group consists of Core people who, it is suspected, were engaged in dabbling with the occult. They are those who seek knowledge or excitement through the media of *forced* or *deliberate* out-of-body experimentation. It is suspected that through their rituals they accidentally succeed in activating the Core side of a corridor but not the Dimensional side. As a result, their transfer 'hangs-up' and they become caught half way. The second group is of a more recent occurrence. The Wise suspect certain Core agencies such as certain government agencies have mastered the art of partially opening a corridor—the Core side. Those agencies are engaged in the transfer of undesirable characters from the Core to the Dimension. Again, they have not been able to open the Dimensional side of the corridor and their victims also are 'hung-up'.

Q. <u>What are the characteristics of a Wraith?</u>

A. Visual characteristics of a Wraith are that both male and female are of un-kept appearance and go naked. In those who have been a Wraith for any length of time, the expression in the eyes is vacant even though their eyes may be bright. Very often, the Wraith has an extremely bad breath. This is due to the fact that during their very first shape change they lose from their body *all that is not naturally part of their body.* Among those lost parts are such things as tooth's fillings and dentures, steel pins in bones, artificial implants, artificial limbs and very importantly, tattoos. Where an artificial implant is required to keep a body alive, like in the case of a pacemaker, the Wraith is fortunate and will be dead or dying when next he changes to his physical form.

Q. <u>What happens during a Shape Change?</u>

A. Every morning at dusk, the Wraith changes from a solid entity of flesh and blood into an entity of no visible substance. The experienced Wraith will seek a draft free niche in which to hole up for the day.

While in his non-physical state, the Wraith is at the mercy of any airflow. Consequently, the Wraith's existence is disjointed. The Wraith has no guarantee of still being anywhere near the place where the last shape change took place when next he becomes a physical being. During his non-physical state the Wraith has an awareness of self but none whatsoever of his surroundings.

When at dusk the next shape change takes place the Wraith becomes a physical being once more. If, during the day, he has been blown about his essence may be spread over a large area and has to contract during the shape changing process. This apparently goes accompanied with tremendous physical pain. It is not unusual for the quiet of dusk to be shattered by cries of agony of a shape changing Wraith.

With every shape change the Wraith loses a bit more of his *learned, or acquired, knowledge* until eventually he becomes a being in whom only the most basic of instincts are present. An all-consuming urge to procreate coupled with an equally urgent need to feed. While still capable of some form of coherent thought, the Wraith believes the act of procreation will liberate him from the everlasting cycle of the shape change. Some believe they will become normal, physical beings again, others believe the act of procreation will result in blissful oblivion.

Q. In what manner are the Wraiths a threat to society?

A. The urge to procreate in both male and female Wraiths results in a real danger of rape. The rape by a Wraith results in the terror riddled death of the victim. Something in the Wraith's psyche is transferred into the victim, causing death through fear. The end will come but it may be preceded by hours of hallucinating fear. In the first stages, the victim hallucinates and sees demons. This stage is followed by one during which the victim loses all contact with reality and becomes quite insane. Next comes a period during which the unfortunate tries to kill him or herself through self-mutilation. During the last stage the raped sees, feels and experiences horrors of which the normal person has no idea. The person in this stage of mental torture is too far gone to give even an indication of what they are going through. Death is the inevitable end.

Q. Are there any exceptions to this fact?

A. Yes. Where a Wraith rapes a Levitator (see Levitator), the roles are reversed. The Wraith dies an agonising death by internal combustion.

This combustion takes until his next shape change to consume him. It is not known whether the Wraith ceases to exist or whether he will reappear as a physical being during the next night. However, it is a fact that all Wraiths are instinctively aware of the consequences of raping a Levitator. The Wise believe a burning Wraith sends out fear patterns that affect the instinct for survival in other Wraiths.

For a normal male raped by a female Wraith there is no escape and he will burn instead of the Wraith female.

Q. How do the people protect themselves against the raping Wraith?

A. The women achieve some protection by pretending they are Levitators. There is no such protection for the males who became involved with a female Wraith some of whom can be extremely beguiling.

Q. What about the males?

A. They cannot use any disguise and have to rely on their judgement. The only safeguard they have is to make sure any woman who approaches them has a tattoo. Wraiths lose their tattoos during their shape changes. All men and women display elaborate tattoos for this reason. Where a woman without tattoos approaches a man, he has the automatic right to kill her. No court would convict him if, at a later stage, the woman was found to be normal or that her tattoo was not easily visible.

Q. Are there many female Wraiths?

A. Their numbers seem to fluctuate but it would be safe to say some thirty percent of Wraiths are female.

Q. <u>How common is their appearance?</u>

A. Because of their 'liquidity', it is very hard to make an estimate of their actual numbers. There may be a period of months during which no Wraith is sighted in a particular area. This can change overnight and suddenly twenty or thirty may hang about for just one night or for weeks. However they appear to be more prevalent near the more populated areas but that could also be because there are more observers to notice them.

Q. <u>Do the people try in any way to control or get rid of the Wraiths?</u>

A. Once he is physical, the Wraith has the cunning of a beast and the strength of desperation. Killing him will lay him low until dawn, when his physical shape once more becomes gas. Not enough is known to establish whether he will once more rise at dusk. When, during the day, people find places where a Wraith might be present in his gaseous state they will ventilate it.

Q. <u>Wouldn't a Wraith be at his/her most vulnerable during the dusk shape change?</u>

A. Probably, but nobody in their right mind would go anywhere near a Wraith at that time. The reason being his lust and his hunger are so strong during the changeover that some of the emotion is transferred to anybody near. In the person so affected, it becomes a battle between his/her knowledge and his/her own basic instincts. Regardless as to whether his/her head or heart wins he or she would be in no fit state of mind to do battle with the Wraith.

Q. <u>You mean to say a person would be inclined to succumb to those emotions even though aware of their consequences?</u>

A. Yes, that happens quite a few times.

Q. <u>How would you recognise a daytime hiding place?</u>

A. New Wraiths often still cling to the Core notion of having to be dressed. Even though they lost their Core clothing during their first shape change, they will steal whatever clothing they can lay their hands on. If one finds discarded clothing, especially if several garments are still within each other, like a shirt within a vest, there is a good chance a Wraith had a shape change there. They soon realise their best protection against daytime discovery is to go naked.

Q. <u>Can a Wraith find enough to eat to maintain his physical shape?</u>

A. It seems impossible in view of the fact they cannot do any planting or husbandry, neither is there a guarantee they will take form night after night in populated areas where they can steal their needs. The Wise have concluded they must absorb the greater part of their sustenance from the air while in their non-physical state.

Q. <u>What is known of their ultimate fate?</u>

A. Their bodies must eventually wear out, like ours do. They must die a physical death at some stage but whether their non-physical existence ceases at the same time is not known.

LEVITATOR

It is not only the science of Sail and Wood that comes under the influence of the *sideways expansion vibrations* characteristic to the Dimension.

All other sciences and technologies, present at the time of the final separation from Core into Dimension, are subject to the same Dimensional Law. As a result, some rather startling expansions have come about. In the field of 'man manipulated energies', for instance, we see the emergence of the Levitator.

The Levitator is a person, always a woman, who has the ability to channel and modify the energy required to nullify gravitational forces. To do this she must absorb through every pore of her body the natural forces around her as well as those present in the object she is to move.

The mental process involved is a learned art which heightens a natural ability found only in women and then only in about ten percent of them.

The Levitator's whole body is an 'antenna' collecting surrounding energies. The covering of any part of her body reduces her powers proportional to the total area covered. Like a drape over a loudspeaker will distort sound vibrations, so would clothing distort both input and output of the Levitator's energies.

The Levitator's body behaves like a battery on a trickle charge. It has to be recharged constantly through unrestricted contact with the nature forces around her.

As soon as a Levitator gives birth to a child, she loses her powers forever.

Levitators are very much sought after in any area where heavy objects have to be moved. She does not require any clumsy but expensive machinery and does not take up any usable space when her services are not presently required as in the case of cranes and the like. She simply positions herself in the most appropriate spot, goes into deep concentration for some minutes, and then touches the object to be moved. As long as she touches the object, and *both* her feet are in contact with the ground, the object will float and others can steer the object to its new location.

NUDITY

During the late 1600s and early 1700s in Australia and the Pacific, it was only a minority group that went about clothed. The majority went about nude, or nearly so. When Antipodia came into being, the position had not changed. Rather than imposing minority rule, majority rule prevailed.

This was further strengthened by the advent of the Wraiths.

In the minority group, the Europeans, the superiority complex based on a more advanced technology only had some influence for a short time, as there was no further *upward* development.

The *lateral expansion* of knowledge took place not only in the technology of Sail and Wood, but also in all other aspects of science compatible with the Dimension's environmental vibrations. In many fields the people of the Pacific and Asia were more advanced than the Europeans who really only excelled in some material aspects of technology. Consequently, the Europeans, in Antipodia, were more prepared, or indeed were forced, to more readily accept other people's norms.

The prudery of the Victorian era, still affecting even today's Core society, never hit Europe until the early 1800s, therefore its influence on Antipodia was negligible.

Other factors affecting the swing to nudity were the worldwide realisation that man's most powerful source of personal energy is the instinct to procreate the species. Once it became understood, that that energy is available to achieve 'supernatural' results, beneficial to man as an individual and society as a whole, the whole approach to nudity changed.

Another factor was the swing from the age-old preoccupation with 'honour' to a preoccupation with 'honesty' and 'no pretence'. *This resulted in the belief that a person in the nude is 'honest' about him, or herself, while those feeling the need to hide inside clothes do so because they want to pretend to be something they are not.*

To be called a 'peacock' or a 'dandy' has become a fairly serious insult. This label is only used to refer to a certain group of males who still go about done up to the nines.

TATTOOS

Although tattoos were far more acceptable in the 1700s than what they are today in the Core, in the Dimension they became even more acceptable because of the Wraith presence. The wearing of tattoos became a protective measure for both men and women. The female's need to be individual could no longer find expression in clothing but tattoos provided the alternative. The custom to come into widespread use was to tattoo a simple 'bracelet' around the wrist or ankle of newborn babies. After that, the parents will not allow any further tattoos until the child has come 'of age', usually at the age of fifteen or sixteen.

At that age, it is deemed both boys and girls have enough insight into their spiritual personality to be able to come up with a design that will not become an embarrassment in later years. Especially among the Europeans, this is important. The Polynesian, Micronesians, and Melanesian all have their well-established tribal patterns of tattoos and will only seek a small amount of individuality or 'uniqueness'. Among the Europeans the trend seems to be to either have one tattoo encircling the body, like around the waist or the shoulders, or to have two tattoos, one on the back and another somewhere on the front of the body. The Europeans do not seem to go in much for facial tattoos. Expert artisans apply all tattoos and badly drawn tattoos are a rarity indeed.

THE WISE

The Wise, of both sexes, are the Spiritual Leaders, Philosophers, Scientists, Moral leaders and Politicos of society. *Very early in the independent existence of the Dimension the public realised the only true guidance a society can get is that which the old who, without the prospect of financial gain, feel called upon to offer.* As a result, the community would ensure their Wise would not go short in their daily needs provided they did their bit.

The 'grandparent generation' is held in high esteem. This seems to be so for two main reasons. The slower rate of live allows the young to take the time to profit from the experienced advice of the older generation. The second reason is based on a motivation now quite absent in the Core. By respecting the old, the young feel they allow a dignified old age for those who nurtured them when they were helpless in childhood.

In no small measure due to the influence of the Australasian and Pacific people, the Antipodean Wise have developed occult and supernatural powers quite unknown in the Core. The Masters of Science amongst them have expanded the natural sciences, laterally, to reach horizons never dreamt of in the Core.